KENO • RUNNER

Keno Runner: A Romance by David Kranes was originally published by the University of Utah Press in 1989. The 1995 University of Nevada Press edition reproduces the original except for the front matter, which has been modified to reflect the new publisher, the deletion of the subtitle, and a new cover design.

The paper used in this book meets the requirements of American National Standard for Information Sciences—Permanence of Paper for Printed Library Materials, ANSI Z39.48-1984. Binding materials were selected for strength and durability.

LIBRARY OF CONGRESS CATALOGING-IN-PUBLICATION DATA

Kranes, David.
Keno runner   /   David Kranes.
p.   cm.   —   (Western Literature Series)
ISBN 0-87417-276-4 (pbk. : alk. paper)
1. Man-woman relationships—Nevada—Las Vegas—Fiction.
2. City and town life—Nevada—Las Vegas—Fiction.
3. Journalists—Nevada—Las Vegas—Fiction.
4. Las Vegas (Nev.)—Fiction.   I. Title.   II. Series.
PS3561.R26K4   1995
813'.54—dc20   95–11041
CIP

University of Nevada Press, Reno, Nevada 89557 USA
Copyright © 1989 by the University of Utah Press
All rights reserved
Cover design by Heather Goulding. Cover art by Edward Martinez.
Manufactured in the United States of America
2 4 6 8 9 7 5 3 1

This book
in thanks for their
Spirits

is for four friends

Bud Church
Paul Messer, S.J.
Ethan John Phillips
Dr. Len Schmidt

"You cannot love what shocks you!"
—Nathaniel Hawthorne,
The Birthmark

*E*verything was blood. Operatic. Blood and relentless. Lives dispatched. That was Clark Henderson's logic. In the heat and darkness: relentless blood; blood relentless. Henderson would simulate—in cruel script—the black logic of untamed blood. Let loose. Spilled out. Unstopped. Here was violence uncontained at its own carnival. And the world would see. And the media report: "Such are our times." Because these were Henderson's times. Filled with broken needs. Filled with rage and license. So Clark would stage nothing more than a headline—what we wash down with our coffee, taste in the daily glaze of croissants: the public, broken logic of unbracketed passion.

    After all—Clark knew as we all know—ours is a world of the random and the unchecked. Ours is a lost world, a world fallen from past restraining codes. "Things fall apart." Here, shattered, spills what we once called Love. There, torn, hang the rags of, formerly, Truth. Dis-Order! It was present. It was common. It was daily. People did these things. People walked hourly into the houses of strangers with strop razors and firearms and garden tools. The phrase "senseless massacre" had fallen into cliche. There were Gold Records about children firing into schoolyards. "Senseless massacres." "Senseless violence." Homicide bureaus and night desks all had phrases handy. "The Henderson family massacre appears to be just another in a growing national epidemic of senseless violent crimes."

    The Theatre of Senselessness!

    And the Princeton graduate, Henderson, loved theatre! Dramatic gesture! Irony! How irony played!

· · · · ·

So Clark Henderson crossed the carpet to the bodies of his wife and mother. Perhaps, in the ormolu-framed mirror, he saw himself. Unclothed. So that blood traces on garments would be impossible. Then, likely, seeing himself, he stopped. "He was in love with his own fucking body!" His brother's claim had found echo, less bluntly, in the reports of surgeons and nurses who'd seen Clark Henderson scrub. "He can be a bit self-enamored," Wolk, the Chief of Surgery, had said. So Clark may have taken the moment: to admire what he'd carved through regimen. Hard, conditioned frame. Wide shoulders, athletic waist tapered by relentless daily swimming laps. The thick neck. The polished pectorals. "The Decathlon Doctor." He was gorgeous! He often watched himself!

So—let's say Clark Henderson stopped, caught by his own body and image. Did he see? What he'd really done? What had really happened? Did he absorb? Take in the blood splayed across his rippled and stark flesh? Or did the blood register only in commonplace: A Doctor smeared—of course!—from his daily heroism! The Miracle Surgeon! The God Covered With Blood!

So perhaps, when he moved again, made adjustments and walked now into his children's bedrooms, it was with a deliberate cause, not unlike the "blessed" "healing" mission with which he operated any day . . . And while the headlines would cry: "Senseless Intrusion" and "Violence in Respected House," and though there would be more blood, perhaps, in his own tripped mind, Clark Henderson would be only more Miraculous! More a God! What was blood?! From his first high-school biology through his residency, his hands had been forever-now-it-seemed aswim in it. How was any of this different?

· · · · ·

Kohlman looked up from where the small, morning west-side Manhattan light made the page of the bestseller in his hands slick with haze. He breathed, closed the book. GOD COVERED WITH BLOOD. By Randall Keller. Good author's name. Sounded literate. Also sounded like *killer*. GOD COVERED WITH BLOOD. Not bad. As title. Serviceable. *Old Testament*ish. Which never hurt. Kohlman made a note for the naming of his own project: "Use something with *destiny* . . that sense . . better, *deliverance*." Perhaps FIRE. HOUSE OF FIRE, or, he thought, SET THIS HOUSE . . except, no; that had already been used . . though, in the trade, stealing played. Kohlman's last editor had wrapped the "writing trick" in three words: "*Lie*, *cheat*, and *steal*." So, maybe, an old forgotten title . . . He'd advised Kohlman: "Fallen world, Man!" then laughed: "Rough–but it's what we got! It's what they gave us!" And though Kohlman felt disturbed by the ways in which such ideas, somewhere, hurt; still, they made that agreeable buzz: like . . what? . . perhaps work songs across a river in a foreign country or . . throaty blues down a broken tenement flight, baleful, painful only in some vague connection, the kind of sounds savage truths make far enough away and yoked to serve. Prospero and Caliban.

So Kohlman had taken the words. Filed them. Passed them off. Told himself: *Writers wrote*. Told himself: *It's a fallen world* and *it's what they gave us*. The phrases made sense. Had . . whatever: neatness. Served.

Also, an ABC Morning News director, when Kohlman had worked *there*, had said: "Stories turn corners. They bump into you: You take them!"

So he had. That had happened. There had been an opportunity. A person: a wild woman apparently . . or essentially, named *Janice Stewart*–a long-term headline accused of a bizarre arson/murder: her wealthy father-in- law in his Essex, Connecticut, estate . . any number of weird, who knew, probably *kinky* implications–had fallen into his lap . . *in a way* . . in a way: he'd called her . . and she had said: *write my story* . . *write my life*. And of course his friend had been right: you *don't* turn down opportunities; you *don't* pan for gold and then throw the nugget back into the stream. It turns up . . it presents itself: if you're a writer . . if you aspire: then that's what you need to be alert to. Gift horses are . . *whatever* . . *that* business . . *that*.

Kohlman felt anxious.

So . . .

GOD COVERED WITH BLOOD! Whatever. It was a foothold. It was *more* than a foothold. Capote had done *his* book; Mailer had done his. America was an outlaw camp: it was an accepted rap; it was a standard take on the culture and its myth. Great actors, any number, had begun doing daytime television. Mugging shamelessly. Slapping booze-riddled, clutching women. It wasn't *art* . . but it was . . *craft*, certainly . . *some*thing.

Kohlman touched the book jacket's slick cover like braille. It wasn't *bad*. It was a *title*. The book wasn't bad. It read . . maybe a little "pumped," but it read. So . . . It worked; it drove. Certainly it had the requisite "hook." More advice: from an agent: "You want bottom line? With these books? This is free: For *nothing* you get to think about the sound of a word: so you can *say* the word . . to yourself . . forever . . until it means something. 'Primal.' That's all. That's all I'm passing out. 'Primal.' One word."

So he was reading . . what the hell! . . a *primal* book. If someone needed a term. To prepare. As homework. One writer studies another. It couldn't hurt. Strategy and style. Exercise. Preparation. It was a way to get into the requisite genre: GOD COVERED WITH BLOOD. The title stood out in red, wide letters, thick and palpable and filled with microphotographed blood cells.

. . . . .

Kohlman set the book down on a glass table. He lifted the phone. He needed to call Janice Stewart, the woman, his subject, in Las Vegas and remind her of his arrival. She always seemed so . . *scattered* wasn't the word but it was all that came . . . *Elusive?* . . *ephemeral?* . . *some*thing over the phone. *Disoriented? Different* . . *singular . . hard to pin down?* She'd gone to Las Vegas after she'd been acquitted and served her "observation" time in Danbury Psychiatric Center. And she was working there, in Vegas, as a . . whatever-it-was . . *keno runner* . . at the Golden Nugget Hotel/Casino.

He dialed her. His wrist vaguely electric with a tremor. He tried gripping the receiver less tightly to stop the buzz. The line rang three times. A woman answered. "Yes," she said.

"Miss Stewart?"

"Interesting: 'Miss Stewart,' " the woman said. She seemed amused.

"Is this Miss Stewart?" Kohlman said. "This is Benjamin Kohlman . . calling from New York."

"Part of you sounds different," she said.

"What do you mean?"

"Every time you call," the woman said. Her voice began to confirm itself. He'd spoken only a half dozen times with her. It had always been curiously brief, oblique, unbusinesslike.

"I just wanted to remind you: I'm flying in," Kohlman said.

"I'll be watching," she said.

"Tomorrow, probably, sometime," Kohlman said.

"I'll be watching," Janice Stewart repeated.

"I'll call you."

"I'll be watching."

"We still . . ?" Something slipped, somewhere, in his sentence.

"Mr. Kohlman?"

"We still . . have our agreement? You never sent the papers back."

"No; I don't do that," she said. "I don't send papers back. I *bring* them back." Her voice had a lift.

"But we're still . . . ."

"Still . . ?"

"I mean: together on this," Kohlman said. "We're still on."

"You stress your prepositions," she said. "That's interesting. I've never heard that . . in quite that way before. Is there a reason?"

"You haven't given the rights to anyone else," Kohlman said, worried.

"I've given myself the rights," Janice Stewart said.

"Okay."

"I've given myself the rights—and it feels good. But we need to meet."

"But you haven't given the rights to someone *else*," Kohlman said.

"No; but that's an idea," Janice Stewart said. "Come. I'll be watching. We can see. I'm optimistic."

"I'll call," Kohlman said.

"No. Don't call. *Come.*"

"Right. I meant that," Kohlman said.

"Good," Janice Stewart said. Her voice wasn't unkind. She hung up.

. . . . .

Kohlman hung up. His hand had trouble leaving the phone. Was it Janice Stewart? The difficulty? Or . . he hesitated to wonder . . *women?* All women. Recently he had felt vulnerable. Kohlman stood in a room almost emptied of breeze, breathing, taking great sweeps of the impoverished air into himself, holding it, a habit which his . . did you use *ex* for *non*-husband/wife lovers? . . anyway, a habit Sharon had hated. "Kohlman: Christ!" she'd say: "I have serious questions about my space, to *begin* with, living with you! Then you *vacuum* it! You worried you'll *deflate*? Should I bring in, say, a portable *oxygen unit*?" And then she'd wait, and he would sense her smile and pull away into some blanketed lull, and she'd start in with a new glee: "Hey, Christ: good: be sensitive! But could you make it something *important*—okay? There's a contender: in there: I moved in with a contender. Let him out!"

Hopefully, Janice Stewart would demand less.

Though dimly Kohlman knew: Sharon wasn't without cause. He was private. He was stiff. He threw protection up in patched, makeshift gates against her weather, strung out windbreaks. Hid.

Still, that wasn't the whole picture. Was it? Because good things, too, chased and wanted at his pulse—far things, fragile things—and along the soft, cup-shaped hollows of his skin: old things; things familiar, though . . okay: perhaps mute in shape. Things he saw but sometimes couldn't name. Image kinds of intimations he might watch at forty feet but then not reach for. Like the sweep of corn silk or the sense of . . yes, all right: *women* . . once his mother behind him on their Iowa farm, present, Kohlman pressing his face sweetly into the long neck of a fevered horse. Kohlman had been embarrassed.

Maybe it was all embarrassment, somehow. Women. Sharon. Not wanting to have another person, like that, slip up or come behind you and find you open, find you caring.

He loved Sharon. Something . . *like* . . love: did one have to name? Her storms. He would crouch low, cover, feel her, raw and wresting, near, her swirl. He'd admire the power, want it, feel pride, wait. She demanded *for* him. She unleashed, insisted *for* him, refused to forgive, held every light accountable. She was who he—grown, moved East and launched—now, maybe, couldn't be. Or, say . . admit to. She was an unabandoned purpose. She was him without compromise. She was crazy Righteousness. He could wake up to her, and she'd be like good, loud music.

Yet, even beside her, *in*side her sometimes though not always, he could still be *away* and on his own, shut down in part. He could be tight against himself, some personal wall, and still watch her toss the furniture. She was something. She was the *Kohlman* he could live with and not remember at the same time. She was the first minister he had ever heard in church. She was the air turned yellow-green and wildly dangerous in Templeton, Iowa. She was his father, except she spoke. She was his mother, unreined and angry. She was something forbidden in his house. She was the one who said *no* and then said *yes* and there would be no revisions.

And he loved having her . . on his skin sometimes, at his ear, pressed against his eyes. He loved her impatience. He loved her demands. She was the exaggerated Adult. And child. And she'd left. Gone. She hadn't been with him for two weeks. Well, but then of course *it had had to happen*—right? Kohlman said that now—*it had had to happen*—alone, in the room, though he had no real idea who the audience was or even, really, what he was saying.

So: that was Sharon. That had been Sharon. And now he was going to write the book about Janice Stewart.

Though, Kohlman thought, he should see her. Before he caught his flight West to start the book: he really should stop by briefly at her loft. "I just stopped briefly by . .": would he put it that way? She got angry when anyone interrupted her painting. Or maybe . . . Could he pose a bargain? If he posed something like: "Look: I'll be gone three weeks. Maybe getting the book behind me will allow us to . . . What if we plan, when I get back, to try this whole thing . . ." *Whole thing*: She'd savage that; she'd tear him apart! How should he begin? What approach? "I'm just leaving for the interviews with Janice Stewart . . in Las Vegas." Good! Great setup! That he had even *thought* such a book had been their major issue. "Neat idea, Kohlman! Write pathology. Write about some poor *other* lost soul's pain. Write about a *fucked-up* person. Don't put your*self* at risk. —I'm sorry. You'll do that later: right? After . . how does it go? . . after you've gotten a 'foothold'? After you've gotten 'established'? Is that the . . . ? When you have more—help me, prompt me with this—'credibility'? . . is that the word I'm looking for? . . 'leverage'? How'm I doing? Am I close?"

It didn't matter—that he kept repeating to her that he felt on the "edge of something" . . something different, something important . . if she'd just be patient. Each time, she'd throw the phrase back at him mercilessly. Once he'd said, trying to simplify, perhaps taking the cue from elsewhere: "Sharon: Look . . hey: it's an opportunity."

And how she'd leapt! "An opportunity! An opportunity! How dense, really, of me not to have *seen* that! Kohlman? This is just a question, but: what do you suppose people did . . you know, like, *Pre-Opportunity?*" Then she'd snapped her fingers: "No; that's right! I remember! I remember reading about it: *they named things!* Right? They stood in this garden and they named things! Pre-Opportunity. Back then. But that was so long ago."

.   .   .   .   .

Kohlman twisted. He did isometrics in place then moved, toured his three rooms—past the Nagra recorder, past the Compaq computer and luggage, all standing, ready, near the door. His plane left in four hours. Had Sharon overlooked anything, left herself behind? His tour said *no*. It would have been more heartening had Kohlman been a more disorderly person, such that litter might have snared one of her earrings. Or a cheese knife. Or a contact lens. A powder-blue emptied pill box. A scarf. An Emmy Lou Harris tape. A button. A #5 camel-hair brush. Broken heel of a shoe. Stem of a wine glass. Dried eyeliner tube. But Kohlman's care, his placement of all things his . . his daily vacuumings ("Oh, yeah! And it's not enough that you in*hale* like a possessed person— you have to *vacuum* three-times-at-least a day!") . . . None of his habits had left any space to trap Sharon, some part of her, in an overlooked prize.

The only vague disarray was Kohlman's corkboard: postcards spilling crazily, hundreds in overlapped scales, out beyond their block. All from his parents. From across the continent. Kohlman's parents had sold their Iowa farm and had bought an Airstream, which they drove from American place to American place, sending postcards. No messages. Often the cards were even unsigned. Sometimes they said simply, "Mother & Dad." Sometimes they just bore initials. Kohlman had imagined that, to his brother, Adam, the Ph.D. university professor in Michigan, they sent more traditional letters: describing, say, a rainstorm driven through in North Carolina or some scarlet long-legged birds seen at dusk across a pasture in Missouri or perhaps a roadside reptile museum. With Adam, they might inquire after his health or ask about the welfare of their son's children. But with Kohlman: no; no letters. He was their *other* son; prefigured to stay, yet who hadn't. He was the son for whom Iowa hadn't been enough. "You wouldn't trust our pleasures," his father had said once, on a brief visit, "so you'll forgive us if, being with you, we fail at conversation."

So . . ? What? What was his father's logic? Postcards were like truck stops? Or motel lights? They "didn't stay." But were . . *media*? And so Kohlman, being away and in New York and in the *media*, got postcards . . ?

He untacked a card. It pictured a man on Myrtle Beach, South Carolina, head crimson with sunburn, and was captioned: "Having a wonderful time. Wish you were hair!"

Kohlman hadn't seen his parents in four years. "You're a great guy, Kohlman!" Sharon had said: "The Continent of North America has eaten your parents—and you don't even wonder on it!" "I wonder on it," Kohlman had said; "I wonder on it all the time. Don't be so smug. Don't be so sure you understand."

Sharon overstated; still, she took your legs out. Kohlman's version, most times, to himself, was: his parents were different people. They'd been final inheritors of a passed life-style, a previous continent; they'd worked a three-generation family farm—and Kohlman loved that; he admired it; he did not deride it. He loved the way it had felt around him in the tall stalks, growing up, and he'd loved the dark magic of an earth basement, which had smelled always like the underbellies of large stones . . and the mason jars. There had been a sweetness often. Closed certainly: that, but a safe electric kind of sweetness that tasted, when he remembered it, like the charged hour after a lightning storm.

But it had seemed bound, too. Too bound. Closed. Choked. Wasted. Used up. Departing. Each year more. Until all he could see, all Kohlman could imagine, nearly, was his parents getting beat up by an economy whose machinery and ruthlessness only laughed at them.

And so he'd tried to imagine . . *other places*, places, for himself, *beyond*. Reach there. Stretch his hand. So that his acceptance to Princeton had seemed immense, a miracle—though it had made little difference to them. They'd seemed to treat it like a bad crop or a short drought. And so some kind of . . *separation* had begun. Some kind of change. Some kind of *shift* in whatever had been their Kohlman-family geology. That was all. That was it, only. He wasn't *opposed* to them. He wasn't their *enemy*. He wasn't in combat. Still, Sharon had made him feel, at times, as though that was the perception.

They were dedicated. Very dedicated people. And that was good. But . . perhaps "uninformed." That was the way he, in words once, had marked the difference. "You mean, *dumb*?" Sharon had said. *No*; he hadn't meant *dumb*, not dumb; "dumb" was an ugly word. "I don't think I have those feelings," he'd said. "Right!" she'd said: "I understand. What you *meant* was '*ignorant*'–right? After all, they're your parents." "Give me a break!" he'd said. But she'd gone on: "More along the lines of . . like you were talking 'strong simplicity' . . right? *Sturdy* 'folk.' Beasts of burden. Lovable plow horses."

"Why do you always have to give me such a hard time?" Kohlman had said.

"Oh . . darlin' . . Oh, darlin': because you're *there*, you know? Because you're such a target. You're so set up!"

. . . . .

Kohlman tacked the Myrtle Beach card back and looked at the board of his parents' cards, unsure why he'd ever kept or displayed them. Huge potatoes, filling entire truckbeds. Nineteen different postcards of the "Famous Jackalope!" Cartoons of outhouses. A card from Amarillo, Texas, made to order: his parents riding on the back of a giant diamondback; the caption, "Fangs for Everything!" The cards were, in part, embarrassing. Had Kohlman and his parents ever shared a language? They must have. But what had that language been? They were both silent people. *Taciturn*. *Reserved*. Weren't those the words people used? "Do you think I don't *love* my parents?" Kohlman had asked Sharon. Kohlman couldn't explain his feelings. "Right! Don't do *that*," Sharon had said: "Don't explain your feelings: hard to imagine the disaster!"

Okay: His parents had different sensibilities! Their *bodies* seemed more their antennae . . while *he* . . they had different . . he . . *fuck*! . . tended . . he took things more through his head! So . . ! *Anyway*: he had kept the board of postcards. So, obviously, wherever his parents were–Kohlman hadn't trashed them. He'd kept their presence. However his mounting and displaying the postcards *did* that. He was not dismissing them.

. . . . .

He would see Sharon and say good-bye. He'd go there. They'd been close, more, and it was right. She'd rail; she'd complain, but he needed to not just slip away. He needed to say . . whatever his visit would say. He needed to make the gesture.

He checked his message machine: that it was on and ready for calls in. He checked his five windows: that they were locked. He stood in front of the board of postcards, wondering if there might be anything he'd overlooked. Then he gathered his baggage and left, triple-locking the apartment behind.

. . . . .

Sharon's studio loft was nearby, just down West 67th, then up not-quite-two blocks on Ninth Avenue. He'd walk. Awkward with baggage, Kohlman, nevertheless, felt a need to move, sense some weight and strain, mark his own graceless reality. Somewhere the stubborn child liked that: the sweat, the dry fire in his hair, the sense of stumbling into what he carried. It had no logic, but it gave pleasure. A few blocks. He could manage himself that far, see Sharon, get a cab.

What he'd forgotten, though, this June Saturday, was the Ninth Avenue Food Fair, which tumbled nonstop, washed in swells and backcurrents around him, caught him in small eddy pools. Any margin of safety Kohlman had hoped for—between the setting down of GOD COVERED WITH BLOOD and his flight, between his departing inventories and his arrival at Las Vegas to meet Janice Stewart and record her, between the familiar and the unmapped—such a margin was quickly swept away in the street. And Kohlman fell into another world: the broth of sausage and teriyaki; shrimp creole, souvlaki, metal drums and street mimes, spring rolls and stuffed mushroom caps, break dancers, baklava, and jugglers. The street was thick for as far uptown as he could see, clotted and rife with human tastes that made Kohlman wonder.

Would Las Vegas be like this? Would it be a carnival? He had never been. It was in the desert, right? So . . desert hot? He felt the dim recall of some moment lived once as a child, when he'd been borne by something not-quite-sleep and turbulent, after a day enflamed on him by a terrible sun. He'd thrashed in images. And he felt the same tossing now, somehow, of unsorted, unpredictable memory. His bags were heavy. The Nagra, particularly, with all its wires and miking equipment, regardless of padded case, cut against him. Kohlman was not a heavy man, so he could feel his belongings and all his equipment thud and slap onto his bones.

Perhaps he shouldn't visit Sharon. Ninth Avenue was closed off from traffic and there were no cabs. Still, Kohlman, once committed, found it difficult to not at least take steps. "Dolmathes?" someone asked. Kohlman heard the cry, "Cold Corona beer!"

Where he had not previously been, he was, suddenly, tired: too much being demanded of an instant. Kohlman saw a tanned, heavy man in a red-and-white tank top tease a child with a soft ice-cream cone, holding the cone, pushing the soft creamy white into the child's face frontally, while the child cried and, blinded by the ice cream, groped outward, hungry. Kohlman dropped his computer case and slapped the cone out of the man's hand. "Jesus: don't *do* that!" Kohlman ordered. "Don't do that. He's just a child."

"So: what? You wanna die, mister?" the tanktop said.

Kohlman regripped his computer and moved on . . through the crowd.

"So: mind your own fucking business!" the tanktop yelled. "He's *my* kid!" The threat staggered over the heads of a hundred people behind.

Kohlman had no idea why he'd done what he'd done. It was unlike him. It was all the tide and undertow of the street and crowd. It had to be. Because, though such acts, on a level of instinct, outraged him, he nevertheless understood the rules of interference and distance. How many unforgivable scenes had he crossed the street from? He remembered his father, once, confronting a bully in the parking lot at a Grange dance. The man, Parkins, had held a thresher against a girl's breast, the girl backed against a hay wagon, and Kohlman's father had disarmed the man, getting his hand cut to the bone and beyond in the process. Once at Princeton, Kohlman, a bit edgy at a semester's end and perhaps thinking he was his father, had spoken out against a distinguished, chaired professor who'd humiliated another student for his question in an Economics class. "Are you taking me on, Mr. Kohlman?" the professor had asked. "Are we in combat here?" "Don't ridicule people," Kohlman had said. "Just . . don't ridicule people – that's all." And, the next day, he'd dropped the class. Such moments were inexplicable and rare. Usually, Kohlman was a careful reader of reality and fact.

He arrived at Sharon's building in a sweat – which was not the way he wanted to fly and begin his book. She had a bathroom; perhaps she'd let him shower. He rang her loft.

"Yes?" her no-nonsense voice cracked through the speaker.

"It's Benjamin," Kohlman said.

"Who?" the voice grated.

"Benjamin. I'm just dropping by—briefly," he said.

"I'm painting," Sharon said.

"I won't take long," Kohlman said.

"That's true."

The door lock buzzed. Kohlman let himself in, awkwardly stuffing and pushing his bags in front, then stuffing and pushing them into the ancient lift-elevator, which, with the sound of cables and gears, wound itself up toward the seventh floor. Riding up, Kohlman remembered when they'd met. He'd been having coffee at D'Angelino's in Soho. She'd been at a nearby table. "Who are you?" she'd asked. "Are you a particular person? You look like somebody."

"Al Pacino," Kohlman had said.

"I don't think so," Sharon had said. "Al Pacino's vulnerable."

"You don't think I'm vulnerable?"

"The point is: You don't look vulnerable—where Al Pacino does."

Kohlman had found the nerve—not sure where from—to say: "Actually, I'm his brother, *Studs* Pacino. Younger and tougher."

"I'm Sharon Elsworth," Sharon had announced. "The Painter."

"Right. Sharon Elsworth, the Painter."

"Exactly."

"Have I heard of you?"

"No, but you will. In a minimum of seventeen months."

And she'd been right. And that had been the start of their relationship.

·   ·   ·   ·   ·

Sharon's loft door was open. Kohlman moved all his baggage in.

"No way!" Sharon said. "You're not checking in! No! Our act closed."

"I wasn't . . ."

"I'm painting," she said. "Focus is important. But you can watch."

"Well, I . . ." Kohlman caught himself, stopped talking, closed the heavy fire door. He stood aside. He always liked to watch Sharon paint. She was dressed in her spattered work clothes, ripped brown cords, blue work shirt. Her whole frame seemed both more intent and more relaxed than usual. On the north wall of the loft was a canvas, roughly four by six, a portrait of a middle-aged woman, eating by herself at a formal dining table. All the details in the painting seemed, to Kohlman, muscular. Nothing seemed delicate. Even the knots in the lace on the tablecloth seemed fat. And yet, Kohlman would be the first to admit, the work intrigued him, the bloated colors and shapes worked. The whole image had a tough, blunt loneliness.

"I like it," Kohlman said.

"It isn't finished," Sharon said. She worked an area around a brass candlestick. "You *will* like it, though. It's going to be good."

"No false humility!"

"I'll be another forty-five minutes," Sharon said. "There's some beer. I got the new Fuentes novel—if you're up to books that make demands."

"Why are you so relentless?" Kohlman said.

"What: You think only the bad guys should get to be relentless?"

"You don't pull back."

"What would be the profit?"

"None. I'm sorry: paint. I just came by to say I was going. To do the book. Start at least. And I don't know for how long. So . . ."

"The famous book about the Wild Woman!" Sharon turned away from her painting and head-on.

"Well, we'll see," Kohlman said. "I mean, whether she's in fact . . . Who knows? Yeah: about the wild woman. Janice Stewart—*whoever*. At least, I'm going to try."

" 'At least try,' " Sharon grinned.

"Don't bear down," Kohlman said. "I'm just here. I'm being sociable. I'm saying good-bye and hello."

"Hello, Benjamin!" Her voice sprang demonic. "Good-bye."

"Hi."

"So . . what if she cuts your head off? This woman. What if she lights your bed on fire in the middle of the night?"

"I've lived with you. It won't be new," Kohlman said.

"Good!" Sharon smiled. She liked his fighting. "A little fire there—*good*."

"I've missed you," Kohlman said.

"I'd miss me too—if I were gone," Sharon said. "I'm a great lay—and I'm exciting company!"

"I guess. . ."

"What?"

"Well, just . . I guess one thing I needed to ask you . . before leaving . . was . . I mean, whether you . . *fuck* . . *this*: how unequivocally you saw us as being . . you know: an item of the past."

"Pretty unequivocally," Sharon said. "Unequivocally un-equivocally." She stared hard, grinned, shook her head, threw her head back sending her dark-blond hair up like a fine spray, shook it again.

"Well, because . . I mean, I, for one, would, I think, be will-ing to . . ."

"Kohlman: you had your chance," Sharon said. "Okay?" There was no game now, in her statement. "You've got great potential—as they told us all in secondary school. And God knows we talked about that. I beat your brains out. But you don't, finally, really, let anybody in. And you have all these, like, *abandoned mine shafts* . . in your head. Am I communicating? Because, I mean: I love dan-ger . . but I'm not interested in the ground giving way. I don't like sudden falls."

"You're being oblique."

"I'm not being oblique. You know *exactly* what I'm saying. Exactly!" She lit a cigarette. He watched, knowing the absolute curtain speech was headed home. "I try," she began. "You *know*. You know: no one gives more of a try. I go nonstop: the limit. I don't try just a little, run away, come back, try some more. Like sex: you know: With me, it's never any good unless I can barely breathe. But I remember . . that the first time that happened for us . . *you*, on the other hand, got fucking *terrified*. I think you were falling down one of those abandoned mine shafts in your own head and didn't know where you were going to land and got really freaked out about it." She came over, put her face up, kissed him on the lips. "Benjamin . . I'm not one of those "why-don't-you-come-back-and-we-can-give-it-another-try types. I *give* it a try . . the first time. When I'm there. And the reality is, I think—here and now—that you don't *want* me to say 'yes.' If I said: 'Let's not play tag anymore; *marry* me, you'd be on the next plane to *Tibet*. So: . . no. Your answer is *no*. Is that unequivocal enough?

Should I say something now like: 'But I really want for us to be friends'?"

"I just thought I'd ask," Kohlman said.

"And I appreciate it," Sharon said. "And I don't mean to be the ball-breaker that I suppose I am. *Am* I a ball-breaker? Kohlman? Benjamin? Benjamin Kohlman?" she asked. "Am I? Do you think that? Do you feel that way? Am I doomed to a solitary life, in my hardness, of disparate coupling?"

"No. —No." Kohlman had to repeat the word twice to be sure he'd said it—then tried another tack: "But you know," he said, "you know, there are times . . I don't exactly know—if I'm honest with myself—why I hooked up with you."

"Kohlman . . ." She threw her head back and laughed. A ferocious laugh. "Kohlman: You know *exactly* why you hooked up with me. You just didn't have the *stamina* is the point. You just didn't have the *follow-through*."

. . . . .

Kohlman caught a cab to LaGuardia on Tenth Avenue, just down from Sharon's. The Ninth Avenue festival still held sway, but felt quieter. And when he caught glimpses, from the cab, banked by his apparatus and bags, of the east-west crossblocks, of the fair, the crush looked small enough to be televised, that tame.

. . . . .

He took one of his breaths. Enough air in to implode the cab. He looked through the tinted cab window, up and into the sky he would be in in another hour. It looked without margin and pale. It looked unpredictable.

– TWO –

Kohlman stood in the LaGuardia Delta lobby, flanked by bags and his equipment. He'd had a thought . . more a notion, in the cab; still, the notion had edged in as he'd scanned the development housing and expressway traffic. It was that: since he had no confirmed schedule, no set lead meeting with Janice Stewart, he might fly, instead, first to *Iowa*, rent a car, drive to Templeton. He was curious about where he'd been raised, where he'd been young, curious, in ways, to see his landscape and sense how it felt—now, today—wrapped around him . . in the way the smoked tenements and streets, the hundred languages and drifts of cooking wound him daily in Manhattan, in what had become, here, his life. He'd been thinking home. Where he'd grown up. It had been eight years. Perhaps the postcards; perhaps the questions of his parents, where they might *be*, this hour, as he stood considering; perhaps he wondered whether any reluctant set of nerves or capillaries in him still felt connected—it was hard to sense where the notion had been born or what its prompt was. But it was there; he had felt it.

He found the breath he held feeling light; his chest cavity aflap with wide, airy distances. He rewrote his nonstop to Las Vegas. The new schedule had him landing first in Des Moines, then, the next afternoon, catching a late plane from Omaha to Nevada. Kohlman would have a lead article in the next day's *New York Times Sunday Magazine*: "American Pastorals and the Stranger." Perhaps he wanted to see if any store in Templeton, Iowa, *carried* it. The article took a half dozen sleepy towns from Virginia to Oregon torn open by "the reverberative violence of an outsider." It was about: "the rooted and the unrooted," about "codes and those who can't conceive of them." *And, so . . this is what you call . . "prose style"—right? Am I getting the term correct, here, hotshot?*, Sharon, reading the second draft, had said. Kohlman had written it all from a month of telephone interviews.

· · · · ·

He flew to Des Moines, replaying an earlier conversation he'd had, long distance, with Janice Stewart. He'd tried to tell her his proposed date of arrival. He'd hoped for guarantees of his exclusive rights to her unusual story and had requested an address—other than the Golden Nugget, Fremont Street—so that he might send his "simple letter of agreement" more personally, more confidentially. She'd begun laughing. The laugh had gathered and had had trouble coming to a stop. "But I *love* not knowing," she'd said. "I love not knowing *anything*. I'm devoted. I try to practice . . Not Knowing. And I wouldn't think of violating my own principles. When you come—call. When you call—I'll be so happy!" It had been like the conversation they'd just had . . curious, strange, and yet. . . Her story balanced so many elements or *possible* elements: madness; a strange, dark, New England family history; acute though different, decidedly different, intelligence; accused revenge and arson. Her voice, floating the transmitted waves, always came so weightless, so unburdened. Was that a pose, Kohlman wondered, *persona* or . . ?

· · · · ·

At Des Moines Municipal Airport, Kohlman rented a Plymouth Sundance. Iowa-5 took him to the north-south leg of I-80 before it headed West again. It was dusk. Iowa had looked on fire, from his aircraft heading down; the sense had been startling. Kohlman had never seen agricultural Iowa roil with such unstable light. It seemed capable of *making up*, almost, like wildfire or a sea. As he drove, then, would it swell around him, cut him off? Would it trap in new ways the land had learned? Lift, swallow, engulf him? But no. No. Of course, no. In his car, now, *within*, it all quilted and grew soft. The dusk turned, with familiar pre-image, to twilight; all the flame and fruit colors cooled to leafy green. The state seemed again the state Kohlman had always known: the earth, its quiet and rotated self; the swallows in silhouette against a low and constant, ice-dark light. His own. His own place, own landscape . . in the same position he'd last noticed . . whenever: Kohlman, age nine; Kohlman, age fourteen; Kohlman, age twenty-two: here, this land, this place, rural Iowa.

So, then: relief—right? *Familiarity*. What was the word? If he were writing a piece about it: what would it be called. *Ease? Integration? Reintegration?* Had he been *reintegrated* with his landscape? But, then, what was that sadness somewhere—what felt like a lazy snake along his spine? And chill? Was it something *there*: in the images? Something on the outside coming in? Or just the rental car's air conditioner?

. . . . .

At Brayton, Kohlman hooked up with U.S. 71, which took him, in the new dark, through space made unhomogeneous, it seemed, only by gravity. He played his radio. Conway Twitty sang about wanting to know a woman before making love to her. Small lights marked farmhouses and surprised Kohlman, in the even dark, the way lights of farmhouses might surprise in a dream. He passed through Exira and Hamlin. He had run the 220 low hurdles twice in Hamlin: once—alfalfa caked, dry, on his lungs—setting a regional record, pushing himself hard as he could sometimes do. *Pushed to craziness*. That had been his phrase . . he'd never told anyone: *Pushed to craziness*. It felt, those times, like a part of his brain—above his left eye somewhere and midway back, near the roof—would let go its magnets and simply "float." He'd *pushed to craziness*, sometimes, growing up here, just to break the monotony.

. . . . .

He stopped in Audubon at eleven-thirty New York time. He'd not changed his watch. He'd eaten one of Delta's vegetarian meals only, and so the lights in the Audubon Cafe looked flatly welcoming. There were a pair of farmers and a young married couple and a trucker on a long haul. Bits of conversation, words like "backhoe," phrases like "the baby" and "baling wire" floated up into the quiet flies on the pest strips and all the banked flat fluorescence and went nowhere. The waitress wore a uniform striped with gold, and Kohlman studied her, feeling he might even recognize her, that she'd been, maybe, his second-grade teacher once, or, if that weren't right, that she'd been in some monthly-meeting club with his mother. He ordered a T-bone but couldn't ask whether she'd known a family named Kohlman. Or if she'd had a friend, once, in Templeton, named Natalie.

Kohlman ate his steak and felt uncomfortable and, to a degree, in error. Perhaps his impulse had been wrong. Perhaps he didn't want a day in Templeton, didn't want to see his farm, drive past and see its acres, watch its relentless irrigation wheels, wonder what large-boned family now—his parents having scraped what they could from the place—were trying to make failure pay. He felt seventeen. He felt undirected. He didn't like his feelings; they were nonsense. He felt a crust of alfalfa dust again dry on his lungs, stinging his eyes, the price for trying to *win* something in a place so arid. He'd gone to Princeton for Chrissakes! He'd had features on the ABC Evening News at the age of twenty-five! He'd been a senior editor at Random three years later! *No* one even took the Sunday *New York Times* in Templeton: It was absurd! Who was he kidding?! He knew that! What was he here for?

He took a room in the Bluebird Motel, which he remembered for its colors, not painted blue for the bird but rust-orange for the bird's breast; the roof, only, a curious mottled, dark lazuli. It was *Templeton's finest*; that was how his father had expressed it. Comfortable enough, certainly. It had been subsumed by Best Western, always a careful franchise. His room had cable and a working desk; both drink containers were glass; his queen-sized bed swelled with four down pillows.

Kohlman paced his room, crazy adrenalin blindsiding him. He'd turn to the door. He'd pull a drape from the window. He undressed. The cable played a 1966 movie, *The Chase*, which Kohlman let gather in its white noise—voices, familiar, all impossible, it seemed, in the same film: Robert Redford, E. G. Marshall, Marlon Brando, Jane Fonda, Angie Dickinson. There was a party; people were acting badly; Marlon Brando seemed disgusted; someone named *Bubba* had escaped from prison. Kohlman switched to MTV, then to FM easy-listening, which surprised him in its clarity. He let it play, trying to remember each store on Templeton's main street in its sequence. He read a first chapter, another *true-life* study, "The Dark-Corridor History of a Family Need," MINE ENE-

MIES, ASHAMED, which began: *The house cost $750,000 in the 1940s and left no child's needs in want—unless, of course, the child were unnaturally wanting.* Kohlman thought about what it might be like to be stretched out in Templeton's Bluebird Motel, there with a drink, in the town where he'd never once tasted liquor. The book in his hands had brought its writer a half million, including a miniseries. Kohlman set it on the floor. People bought houses in Vermont for such money. He pressed the light and, in sleep, conjured a dream of Janice Stewart, the woman he'd never met. The dream came as a loop, interview after interview. In it, though never seeming in the least uncooperative, Janice Stewart, increasingly, bore the teeth of a savage animal.

·   ·   ·   ·   ·

In the morning he walked Main Street for its feel, but none came distinctly. He liked the adult weight of himself, on the concrete . . in this light which was like varnish: Benjamin Kohlman: the writer . . from New York . . in a coat and tie! There was a new insurance office. The Mercantile had expanded. There was a Burger King at the north end of town, a new Stop-'n-Go gas station and market. Eighty percent of the faces nearly had names, but then the names pulled back. Not one citizen passing recognized Kohlman. So much for small-town America, he thought. So much for *Pastoral*. So much for *Heartland*!

Still, as he unlocked his car, a voice broke through and into his isolation: "Benjamin," it said; "Young Kohlman . . ."

Kohlman turned and saw the man who'd employed him—evenings, weekends, summers—when he'd lived here, the pharmacist. ". . Mr. Silento!" Kohlman said.

Silento nodded. Kohlman offered his hand. "Hello," he tried.

"You're not here," Silento said.

Kohlman felt confused. ". . No," he tried. He trapped a smile and thought: no; *not here*; no; I'm invisible.

"Your parents left." Silento lived north of town; he'd raised golden retrievers. Kohlman remembered him coming in to the store sheathed in a canine smell, caught certainly in his clothes. He'd arrive, disappear, reappear in pharmacist's coat, now harsh soap his envelope. He'd never spoken of dogs. Kohlman had always hoped that, once, he might offer, say, the runt of some litter.

"My parents left," Kohlman repeated. "Yes. It's good to see you, Mr. Silento. How've you been?"

Silento looked at Kohlman; his eyes said *How've you been* was the silliest question he'd been asked. "You're wearing a tie," Silento said.

"I am," Kohlman said. He remembered a night, at the pharmacy: a very ragged, pale young man had come in, his stock Camaro running, spitting unmuffled smoke into the blue night in front of the store, and demanded drugs: how Kohlman had said *no* and how the young man had produced a small pistol and fired into Kohlman's protesting hand. Silento had never thanked him for . . whatever it was it seemed Kohlman had done, though Kohlman's father had said, "What you did for Mr. Silento was right. It was proper."

"I suppose you're married—with the tie and everything," Silento said.

"Not yet," Kohlman said. "Though I'm sure . . obviously . . someday."

"It's not a law," Silento said. "Well . . ." He renodded; "Certainly I didn't mean to stop you."

"Hey: no stopping *me*, Mr. Silento!" Kohlman smiled.

"They're stopping everybody," Silento said, no humor; he tipped his hat and moved off.

·   ·   ·   ·   ·

Kohlman drove the seven miles to what had been the acreage of his farm; the passing land, harsh in Kohlman's memory, all flat and muscular: island houses; windbreaks of trees; grids of gold and lemon, ochres; cultivators with their dust trails. He took a detour—out of some memory but not really knowing why—out to the East Fork of the Nishnabotna River. He got out of his car and stood in the dry brakes on the shore. He remembered how he'd watched the river, seasons, rising to flood, spilling its limits sometimes and making marshes. Every Spring, when he'd begun again to walk or fish it, it had seemed different, a different river, frightening in a way . . but thrilling. It had always seemed like a new place—at least for a stretch of years. He'd had a reverence for it; he'd lain on his back in the brakes and watched circling hawks and been amazed at a kind of *authority* he'd found in them. But now it just seemed like the old East Fork, the same.

Jesus: how *young* Kohlman felt, now, remembering—how use-less; how ineffective and inoperative. He got back in his car and drove until he was in farmland, *dry* land: *this* was what felt true. And he could see his father, in bold-relief memory, loading some-thing onto or tossing something from the flatbed of his truck: stoic, struggling, humorless, undisplaceable. "I'm a poor man," he'd heard his father say: "I've not added to the world. I've not taken away. I've churned my own butter, fought my country's war, and wouldn't take a Cadillac if I won one in a raffle." Kohlman shook his head. On the AM, Crystal Gayle sang about someone making her brown eyes blue, and Kohlman had the memory of a small girl: all smile and blue eyes, with bony shoulders. She came in a picture . . then went. Who was she? Kohlman tried a name: she . . whoever, whatever her name was, was who he had watched the hawks with by the East Fork. Then he tried to remember what time his Las Vegas flight left Omaha.

He drove the small farm's perimeter twice—to the north and west, having to take the graded but unpaved roads. He felt out of breath. *Someone* was working the land. The high rooster tails of irri-gation etched fading and refading lines on a lucid midmorning light. *Someone* had taken the job—"bless their souls!" his mother would have said. Near one fence, Kohlman saw a child, a girl no more than seven, in a "Sunday dress," standing on the saddle seat of a tractor, arms out like a magpie. Once *he* had invented a world straddling farm machinery—while his brother had practiced hand-writing sitting always by the heat register in the small parlor. Who was the girl? What did she want? She seemed so young. Kohlman remembered the girl, his friend, growing up: the one with the blue eyes and smile and bony shoulders. *Pamela. Pamela Arnold.*

Kohlman circled a third time. A junked Cadillac lay tipped on its trunk against a brake of poplar, innocent, like a useless rake set against barn siding. In an unplanned move, Kohlman undid the swinging drive-gate. He stood, hands tentatively hinged over the flat, gray, splintered planking. What did he have in his mind? He put his nose to the weathered wood and inhaled it, fragrance red-olent half of itself and half of the soil which lay turned and planted, beyond it, soil which Kohlman knew for a fact had a life on the planet that was now limited.

He moved awkwardly, waywardly, in, leaving the gate, as if his stride had forgotten itself. He moved to a place where the long, choked and maverick grass broke and gave way to the turned earth. And he stood there, dry and sweating, as he had done sometimes as a young man, when he ran: breathing heavily. And then did a crazy thing! He bent and swept dusty nuggets of earth up with a slap of his hand and stuffed them into his mouth and swallowed them. It was an act too late to reverse. It was done and over, lunatic and inexplicable, before he could spit them out. And so he stood in the place and cried for no reason, before he drove up to the house, shook the leather strap of cowbells, and introduced himself. "My parents were the Kohlmans who used to live here," he said to a fully unfamiliar red-headed woman when she met the door.

"Is there something I can do for you?" the woman asked.

"I don't . . . Probably," Kohlman said. He tried to laugh; he tried to smile. *Pamela Arnold*, he thought; *who the small girl was!* "But I don't know what it would be—what you could do," he said. In New York, the comment would have been a joke. Here, the woman's mouth only dropped; she sucked her lips close to her teeth. *Pamela Arnold had been the girl's name!* "I thought I'd introduce myself," Kohlman said.

"You don't look like your parents, but . . how do you do," the woman said. Kohlman could see her place her foot hard against the doorframe should he be dangerous and try forcing an entry. He *didn't look like his parents*: *What did she mean?* Kohlman wondered. *What was that comment?* It had never, for Kohlman, been a question. She was probably right. "My husband's sharpening his knives," she said.

"Certainly," Kohlman said; "I remember that's what you do here Sundays." He smiled again, this time more theatrically, more broadly. If the woman had been Sharon, she would have said, *Jesus: I love living with a New York intellectual and his flippant ironies. I feel so lucky.* But she wasn't Sharon, clearly, and she simply bore the look of a deeper concern. So Kohlman thanked her and excused himself and drove back to the town, checked the Mercantile and the 7-Eleven for the Sunday *Times*, paid his bill at the Bluebird, and moved West.

·   ·   ·   ·   ·

Kohlman slept his entire Omaha-to-Las-Vegas leg; not aware, even, he'd left the ground. He looked quiet, had anyone noticed him in his sleep. All the cinder and metal-filing particulate of urban air hadn't scarred him; he still had the skin of something well grown. His eyes, closed, hardly made a seam. They bore no evidence of themselves. His mouth, slack and at rest, looked decorative. Only his brow worked. He slept with a copy of the *New York Times* folded on his lap, his Compaq cased, beneath the forward seat, at his feet.

When the TransWorld flight touched down at McCarran, the landing jarred Kohlman to a memory or pod of memory—perhaps what had been in his dream—of how, with the young girl he'd grown up with, Pamela Arnold, their friendship had been so effortless, or seemed so: how they had just been friends and just talked. And yet she'd been girl; she'd been woman, the *other* gender; he'd known that; it hadn't been unnoticed or invisible. Pamela Arnold, in fact, had been the person, when there had been another person, he'd gone out to the East Fork with. And lain in the brake. And watched hawks. And . . sometimes talked . . others, not. Just lain; just been together. What had allowed that then? And why not now? Age? Place?

The present closed world he'd slept in idled, with its expectant sound, and Kohlman heard it and opened his eyes. He felt movement. He could still taste the Templeton dirt in his mouth. They were at the gate. Women ran brushes through their hair; men checked their billfolds; heads turned in to the scratched Lucite portholes to pick out landmark casino towers. Kohlman had never *been* here; he had never been in this city; it was a *location* at best for him, a background in generic films on television, not on any map. Were there schools? Obviously. And as obviously one could buy the *Times*. But what about, say . . *greengrocers*: could you buy a kiwi or a nectarine?

He was staying at a place downtown Janice Stewart had recommended, the Ogden House. She'd said it was cheap and comfortable. What time? Would he be able to reach her now? Would he be able to see her, possibly tonight: begin? Kohlman walked the concourse. It was a tube banked with slot machines and resort glitter, a computer voice looping a twenty-second greeting, *WelcometoLasVegas*. It seemed very unlike either Kennedy or LaGuardia; neither so assaulted their travelers. Kohlman yanked his bags from the carrousel. The air outside felt choked and phantom, not a place to feel particularly at home; probably the faster the woman gave him her story the better.

"What's the temperature?" Kohlman spoke to the ungroomed head of his cabdriver.

"Hundred and four," the cab driver said. "Cool spell."

"Right," Kohlman said. It was just after eight; the day, slipped into a light the color of rose neon. "You *live* here?" Kohlman asked.

"No; I commute from Denver," the driver said.

"*Always* lived here?" Kohlman asked, disregarding the joke.

"*No* one's always lived here," the driver said.

"Pretty unreal," Kohlman said. He sat back. "I live in New York," he remarked. He added: "City." It seemed hotel billboards leapt up like *papier-mache*, like the cutouts in books he'd read, once upon a time, as a child. One, he remembered, with a pony: the pony spiriting up from the bookbinding every time he'd turn a page. It had been the color of amethyst, the pony: dark. Such a *confident* pony. With parents? And had it seemed to him, then, that his landscape, there, could serve up, could *deliver* such animation so spontaneously? Had it ever held that kind of hope and force for him? At what point, then, had life become a matter of getting out? Of things *beyond*? Kohlman remembered the book; he remembered the pony—how real had it seemed?—entirely unafraid, standing up in cutout after cutout. Magic. "Unreal," Kohlman said again.

"That's the idea," the cabdriver said.

The north tower of Caesar's reflected the tower of the Flamingo Hilton which reflected the immense cement screen of Bally's Grand.

"Pleasure palaces," Kohlman said.

"Absolutely," the driver said.

"Hard to feel natural," Kohlman tried.

"Where?" the driver said.

"Here."

"It creeps up."

Kohlman nodded.

"You here on business?"

"Yes."

"They all say that." The driver looked back and smiled.

"What do you mean?" Kohlman said.

"It's just what they all say," the driver said and whistled.

．　　．　　．　　．　　．

The television in Kohlman's room at the Ogden House had too much color. His room had no phone. He unpacked and set up his word processor, then stopped at the front office. There was what Kohlman imagined to be a bulletproof shield between himself and the desk clerk. Where the shield left off, a little space, a till, allowed money or credit cards and receipts to be exchanged. The desk clerk, to the bone, looked secondhand.

"How do I get a phone in my room?" Kohlman said.

"You don't," the desk clerk said. His teeth were jammed, stacked, holding each other in.

"What do you mean?" Kohlman said.

"None of the rooms have phones," the desk clerk said.

"Then I'd like to *pay* for a phone."

"You mean have one *installed*?" the desk clerk said.

"Yes; I suppose."

"For how long?"

"I'm not sure."

"For how long are you staying?"

"I'm not sure," Kohlman repeated.

"An hour?"

"Okay—a week. Two weeks, probably. At least."

"Well . . if you want to call the phone company . . pay your deposit . . etcetera, etcetera: be our guest. If not . . we'll take your messages—best we can. You can use the pay phone *there*." The man nodded to a back corner.

"Thanks," Kohlman said. "I'll let you know."

.   .   .   .   .

Outside, dry heat rose from the pavement; Kohlman could feel it on his legs. And it had a taste—like talc, or tarter, different from crop-prepared earth; he stood at Ogden and Fremont trying to name what was on his tongue. He tried to name the way the air felt *weighted* as well, thick and beaten and set up like . . *pudding*. He took a spiral notebook from his blue linen jacket and jotted the phrase "air like pudding," but knew, as soon as it was on the page, it was wrong.

He called Janice Stewart at the number she'd given. He didn't expect her to be there and she wasn't. First things first—he had to try.

.   .   .   .   .

The story he would have to flesh out was this: She had killed her father-in-law. Or . . that had been the trial; that had been the accusation. At night, two Julys previous; she'd . . *allegedly* . . burned his Southport, Connecticut, home to the ground. The defense at her trial had read a catalogue of the man's cruelties. Janice Stewart, herself, had taken an "oath of stillness." She had said nothing when she was arrested. She had said nothing during the trial—to her attorneys, to either side's examining psychiatrists. Her lawyers had taken various routes: self-defense, provocation of a crime of passion, insanity. The jury had finally found her *not guilty*, and the judge had ordered more intensive psychiatric study *inside* a facility. She'd begun to speak again. She'd been found competent and released. She'd flown to Las Vegas and had begun work, imme-diately, as a keno runner. That was the story—obviously, just in its outline, what had become the popular and known newscopy-surface. Which, now, Kohlman had to bring to life. He'd fill it out, give it everything it needed to be compelling, make it real.

He'd clipped some pictures in making his preparations, and Janice was not unattractive: a little ghostly in her face and eyes, perhaps. "But what women weren't?" he'd joked, sharing the wirephotos, with Sharon. "Funny, Kohlman," Sharon had said: "*Funny. 'Women as ghosts.' That's . . . I think there's a lot of humor in that.*" Why had Sharon always seen her mission as undercutting him? Pamela Arnold had never been like that.

Regardless . . Janice Stewart would be his book. She *was* his book. She was here; she'd seemed open for him to write . . *what-ever* it was he would write; from all indications, glad he'd wanted to; pleased—though she could be a little evanescent at times—pleased that he was coming. She was here: her ordeal behind her; she was a free citizen, working as a keno runner—and Kohlman had her exclusive rights.

.   .   .   .   .

At nine-thirty, Kohlman tried her phone again. She answered.
"This is Benjamin Kohlman," Kohlman said.
"I can't talk," she said.
"I'm here," he said.
She made no reply.

". . Is someone there?" he tried.

"I can't talk," she repeated.

"Are you working tonight? Can we meet later?"

"I can't talk," Janice Stewart said a third time and hung up.

. . . . .

Kohlman was at the Fremont. The place was like some exposition arena or airplane hangar—endless, vaulted, overlit . . *under*lit, noisy, hollow, dark, filled with color. The phones lined a back corridor, all with Comcheck stickers above them, reminding anyone that they could wire for money.

Kohlman wandered the casino. He had no urge to enter the games. And perhaps because Sharon had made it as emphatic as she had that they had no future—Kohlman found himself noticing women. The women milling, playing, all looked like secretaries on vacation; the drink girls looked, generally, like whores. And though he'd never done it, even considered—the whole prospect seeming distorted and pathetic in his mind, such a patent owning of need— Kohlman thought that maybe, since he was here, since he was in this place, for the experience if nothing else, he might give it a whirl, try: pay, buy a woman. Still the whole AIDS thing seemed like such a dreadful risk.

He watched a dice table. Dice rolled. Dice rolled again. Dice rolled with the dull regularity of tidal water down a table: What in it was exciting? The one woman playing wore too many jewels. She looked like an editor Kohlman knew at Harper's, the same hungry, female, intentional look.

He bought the *Review Journal* at a street vending box and read it through, at the Union Plaza, over a late dinner. He knew the national and international news; he'd read the *Times*. So he studied Las Vegas. A group of teachers felt their new contract wasn't being honored. A clothing store at one of the malls had had a break-in. A casino called *The Marina* might be forced to close at midnight because they hadn't fully complied with the new fire-code standards. Three executives had left the Dunes and were being hired by Circus Circus. Japanese moguls now owned three major hotels in the city. None of the local news seemed very compelling. Kohlman did a crossword that went too quickly, was too simple; he checked the movie page, and there were no foreign films. His veal picatta was okay—small blessings.

Before Kohlman went to bed, he tried Janice Stewart again. He let her phone ring seven times then abandoned it. His bed at the Ogden House seemed too soft; the mattress, too thin. He hoped Janice was not—with him here and ensconced and ready—going to back out now or withdraw her willingness. "What's her address?" Sharon had asked the week before she'd left Kohlman and they had argued about what Sharon had questioned as being the "underlying *purpose*" of his plan: "I want to write her and warn her! I want to tell her: *Give this sonofabitch the worst possible time!*"

And when he'd sent his brief "letter/agreement," she'd replied on a postcard ("What *is* it about you that draws the fifteen-cent stamp!" Sharon had laughed), the postcard picturing the Holy Eventuality Wedding Chapel: "No signatures! Just signs! Come! This city is a city of signs. Everything is ordained. If you want me . . come. If you come . . I'm here. //J.S."

Kohlman had set aside four thousand dollars to get him through whatever interview period and substantially into his writing. He didn't have a great deal of margin; it would not work were she to be too unpredictable or elusive.

The next morning, after checking his morning stools for "topsoil," Kohlman created a second "simple" exclusive-rights document and called Janice Stewart. She answered and seemed happy. "When can I see you?" he said.

"You have a very formal voice," she said.

"It's the way I am," Kohlman said. "I just . . sometimes come off that way over the phone. It's not intentional. People get over it."

"It makes me laugh a little," she said.

Kohlman hadn't a response. Blood rose quietly to his neck, his cheeks and forehead.

"I didn't mean that to sound . . however that sounded if it didn't sound welcoming," Janice Stewart said. She paused. Kohlman thought he could feel an amusement in the gap. "I always just tell the truth," she said.

"That's admirable," Kohlman said; "That's fine. That's good. I like that. We'll do straight business."

Janice Stewart laughed.

"So . . when? *Are* you free? *When* are you free?" Kohlman asked.

"I'm free now."

"Have . . you had . . ? Might we have breakfast?"

"I don't eat breakfast."

"Do you have coffee?"

"A great deal."

"Is there a place you could, then . . recommend . . where we could . . ?" Kohlman could feel impatience creeping into his voice; there were other people, he knew, after this book. He understood he needed to be careful. ". . Place you could recommend where you could have coffee . . and I could have some breakfast . . and we could . . begin to talk?" he finished.

They agreed to meet at nine o'clock at the coffee shop in the El Cortez. "The women waiting there look like women in scenes by Caravaggio," Janice Stewart said.

". . Fine," Kohlman said. "Good." Sharon would love this woman's dialogue! "The El Cortez, then. At nine."

.　.　.　.　.

How did people dress in Las Vegas? Should he care? Mr. Silento had scored him for wearing a tie. That had annoyed Kohlman. Kohlman put on a tie, took it off, put it back on again. He ran a brush through his hair. He washed his face, dried it, caught his image in the mirror. He looked younger than himself: Did other people think that? He slipped a light sport coat on and left.

.　.　.　.　.

The El Cortez smelled like abuse, abuse crowded in on itself. The ventilation was too cold. The surfaces baffled none of the sound. There were noticeable numbers of Orientals and Hispanics. Kohlman's eyes began to smart. He had just brushed his teeth, still he wanted some freshener. He found the shop. A line of thirty or forty people waited for a table. He looked for Janice Stewart.

"Mr. Kohlman?" She took his arm, from behind.

"How did you know me?"

"I know people." She smiled. She looked fragile and apparitional: a ghost, but not the ghost he had meant when he'd offered the phrase to Sharon, joking, half-joking, in New York. "That's my strength," Janice Stewart said. "I find and know people."

Kohlman gently shook off the hand she had laid on his elbow. He put his own hand out. "Pleased to meet you," he said.

Janice Stewart took his hand, smiling. "So you *are* formal," she said.

"People greet people when they meet," Kohlman said. "I don't . . know that it has to be considered as a formality." He surprised himself. Why was such a frail woman making him feel so defensive?

"But it *is* a formality," Janice Stewart said. "Some people kill other people with no introduction whatsoever. Other people have breathtaking sex." She laughed. "Not that I'm suggesting a course of action."

"Certainly," Kohlman said. Curiously, the woman reminded him of his memory. Janice Stewart reminded him of Pamela Arnold.

"But you are stiff. You're a very guarded person. Aren't you? That's accurate. Have you just had an unhappy love affair? Was your father a man whose language was in his back? You *are* very formal."

Kohlman drew in as much badly ventilated air as he could bear and held it. ". . Whatever," he finally said. "Is there some other place? To do this? Where we don't have to wait in such a bloody line? Where it might be just a little quieter?"

"There is . . but we're not going there," Janice Stewart said and smiled.

"Okay," Kohlman said.

"This line moves fast."

"Okay. Good." He tried his first smile. "I'll take your word."

"Good."

"Listen . . ." Kohlman reached into his inside jacket pocket. "While we're waiting . . I drew up this document."

"Do you like the light in here?" Janice Stewart asked.

"Do you want to look this over?"

"I like the way it comes *out* of the machines. Don't you? And then moves—have you noticed?—it moves in a series of planes and angles to the corners."

"Do you want to check this . . and make sure . . ?"

"Would you like me to call you *Mr. Kohlman*? . . or *Benjamin*?" she asked. "Don't answer; I know. You'd like me to call you *Mr. Kohlman*. But I'm not. I'm going to call you *Benjamin*. When I use your name. That's a nice name. It has a sense of *history* about it. Tradition. Do you have a lot of traditional history, 'Benjamin,' in your family?"

Bones seemed very close to the surface in her face. When she talked, there was a strange play, a rippling. Kohlman found himself not concentrating on her words, but watching instead the rippling, watching her bones. She had cheekbones like Pamela Arnold's shoulder blades.

"You're studying me," she said. "I think you do that. I think you must; it's apparent immediately: you watch and study. *With* people. Has it gotten you, generally, where you've wanted? Has it served the 'greater purpose'—whatever your greater purpose might be—well? I don't mean to intrude; I don't mean to be personal. You just strike me as a person who's, perhaps, *thought* too much about . . too much. Do you *add* things? Is that what you work to do? Numbers, I think, are just . . after all—aren't they?—numbers. They're just patterns."

The line moved forward a half dozen steps. They moved with it.

"Put the 'document' away," Janice Stewart said. "I would never read a private document . . standing in a public line."

.   .   .   .   .   .

She ordered three cups of coffee. Kohlman ordered the "Dealer's Special," ham, hash browns, and eggs.

"Why don't you just order one cup and then have them refill?" he asked. "Are they not good about that?"

"I like to watch three different cups," Janice Stewart said. "I like to see them lined up. Steaming."

"I see," Kohlman said.

"No, you don't," she said.

Kohlman didn't like all of her veers and turns; he didn't like being contradicted. Certainly she was *canny*; still, he'd bet that, whatever the final truth was in her father-in-law's death, she'd done sleight of hand. And probably managed more than a few psychiatrists! She had that "gift"—words, inviting half-perceptions—like light playing off a fountain. So, then—trying to be alert, himself, and open to the distinct possibilities—how many would-be chroniclers was she stringing along, keeping herself amused by? "You're studying me again," Janice said. She held her first cup of coffee out in front of her. Her mouth was hidden behind it.

Kohlman felt it was time to draw hard lines. "Look," he said: "Maybe I didn't make this crystal clear when we set this up . . or *tried* to, anyway, long distance, but . . ." He watched Janice Stewart set down one coffee cup and pick up another. "I don't have some big conglomerate behind me. Okay. I'm a single person. This is just something I want. This is just something I've had to scramble for—not that I don't appreciate your saying 'yes,' given that there are . . I mean, I know there are other people—but the fact is . . when all's said and done . . this is speculation for me—okay?—this is all on my . . own initiative and personal expense. I don't have a lot of slack—if you understand what I'm saying—that someone else is gathering in."

"Those are interesting words: 'slack' and 'gathering in.' "

"Fine, but . . did you understand them?"

"Yes."

"Good." Kohlman drained his coffee; he spun the salt shaker so that it danced on the flecked formica. He stared past Janice Stewart at the lit keno board.

". . Are you feeling hurt in some way?" Janice asked.

"No. . . No. I'm sorry—no. No; I'm nervous."

"That's wonderful."

"No; I mean . . what I mean is: I feel I have a lot invested in this. Of myself. Of my future."

"I feel that way too."

What was she talking about?! "I'm a person, I guess, who's always . . who likes to do things on his own. I like to look back—do you know what I'm saying?—and say *I* did what was done . . take my own measurement. I *want* this."

"Yes."

"Right. I want *you* and I want your book . . for myself. But I also realize—and if I'm nervous, that's why I'm nervous—I also realize that I have absolutely nothing to stand on. I have no guarantees—someone else can just come along and pull this whole . . project out from under me—I mean, that is . . unless you sign an exclusive agreement. . . So if I've been pushing or whatever—I'm sorry. But as straightforwardly as I can put it: I need this; I need you; I want it; and that's why."

"You want *me*."

"Yes. —I'm very . . drawn in. I *have* been. Since I first began to read about you." Again, Janice Stewart traded coffees. "What I mean is: . . I'm hooked. Okay? I'm taken. I'm . . obsessed. I'm fascinated."

"Why?"

"Well . . ."

"Why?" She picked up a coffee, set it down, picked up another.

"Well, obviously: because of what's happened. To you. I mean: What your whole story is. Your involvement. The death. The fire. Your part."

"So . . you're . . taken by . . the whole story about why I became a keno runner and what it means to me?"

"Well, no . . . Well; *yeah* . . right. I suppose. Yes. Of course. Roundabout. In that sense. That's exactly it. That's exactly what I meant. Yes."

"That's very dear."

Kohlman looked hard at Janice. She moved her hands, like a pianist's, back and forth again across her coffees; then she moved the coffees, each to the other's place, like a shell game. She looked at him. His breakfast came, the waitress asking if he wanted steak sauce or ketchup. He waved her away. "So where does that put us?" Kohlman asked. "You have an agreement?" Janice said.

"Exclusive agreement. Yes. Right here. I showed it to you. In very simple terms."

"Which means . . ."

"Which means . . principally: No one else. That's very important in the business of . . . No one else gets to tell your story."

"Not even me?"

"No: of course. I mean . . *besides*."

"So then: I will give—I just want to get this straight—I will give . . *whatever* . . to you and to you only."

"Exactly."

"Like a marriage."

"Well . . in a way. Sure. Perfect. That's a good analogy." Kohlman was shaking. He pushed his document forward toward the woman. It felt like anything in the area, within their circle, could burst suddenly into flame.

Janice Stewart took the document in her hand, leaned forward, studied it.

"It's straightforward but covers everything," Kohlman said in her reading silence.

"I like this word," Janice said, pointing to the print. "And this one here."

"Which words are those?" Kohlman said. "Let me see."

" '*Party*' and '*with*,' " Janice Stewart said. "My favorite word, though, is the word 'binding.' "

Kohlman felt it better if he said nothing. He had stumbled on his own language and intentions. Janice was pretty; soft and mildly unconventional but with a beauty, still, sitting there, studying the page and nodding. Kohlman thought of what had failed to happen with Sharon. *"Am I too . . ?"* *"Too what?"* one night, she'd teased. *". . conventional?"* he'd asked.

She'd laughed, kissing him. *"Oh, dear!"* she'd said: *"Dear, dear!"* Then: *"Dear, dear, dear!"* Sharon had such an original, such a *struck* beauty: each feature marked so perfectly, and placed, beauty that *hurt*, it seemed so born of itself in stone.

"What's the problem?" Kohlman had asked. *"Just tell me: For you. With me."*

"Just all that mannered passion," she'd said.

"What do you mean?" he'd asked her.

"I mean: That passion . . watching itself . . and being so aware! I mean: all that wild Indian corn . . in all those acres of geometry."

Kohlman had told her that, if she could, perhaps, just exercise a bit more tolerance, accept difference, allow him his work, its pursuit, just that area—he allowed her *hers!*—if she could grant his work, so that he might go about it as *he* saw it and its necessities, be patient in those ways and also explain herself just a bit less obliquely, then he could, maybe, *do* something about what she saw as mismatched. He *wanted* to. He'd *told* her; he'd *said* that. He could change. In ways. He could be the right kind of person for her. If she could just not bear down on him the way she did about his *work*.

·　·　·　·　·

Janice Stewart began to fold Kohlman's document and put it away in her shoulder bag.

"So . . ?" he said.

"So . . ?" she said, gently mocking him.

"Right. So: what's the verdict?" he said. "Where do we stand?"

She flashed both hands suddenly to her head. Her fingertips hooked above and below her eyes with the concentration of a rock-climber's.

"Are . . ? Are you okay?" Kohlman asked.

She didn't respond. Twenty, thirty seconds—Kohlman waited; Kohlman watched. He wanted to do something; he couldn't bear his own helplessness. Blood began a thick seeping from one of Janice's nostrils. She clenched her eyes. Her brow and upper cheek bones seemed to wring some sort of unspeakable vision. Then she lifted her fingertips. She took a napkin and brushed away the blood. The absolute caution of her stillness and then her movements had Kohlman staring at the curious balance of her head: Would it stay? Would it topple? Kohlman held his breath. Janice Stewart seemed satisfied; she moved her coffees, looked at her hands, bit one of them as if to restore circulation, moved her coffees again . . chose and lifted a cup.

"Was there a . . ? Are you all right?" Kohlman asked.

"Fine. I'm fine. It's just a thing that happens," Janice Stewart said.

"I see; but . . ?"

"Once. It just happens once." She tried to smile. It seemed less effortless. "If you talked with my brother, he probably said . . I was *possessed*. Or *afflicted*. Or something. Those both are words my family used . . when I had these there. At home. In *their* home. Well, it's not *my* home any more, really, is it? In Connecticut. In Essex. But now I just get one. A day. One a day. And I've learned how to . . *accept* them, I suppose is the best way to put it. *Accept them*. I accept most things."

Kohlman nodded.

"You were asking?" Janice Stewart said.

Kohlman tried to clear his focus.

"Something about this paper?"

"Oh . . !" Kohlman remembered medical testimony from her trial: that growing up she had suffered repeated "cerebral episodes."

"Mr. Kohlman . . ?"

"Yeah. Right. I was asking: Is it all right? The document. Does it seem all right, does it seem reasonable to you."

". . I like it," Janice Stewart said.

"Good. Terrific. Wonderful. Sign it."

"I'm sure I will," she said.

"So . . ?"

She made a face at him and teased him again: "*So* . . . ? You like that word; don't you?"

"Come on. I'm serious. So . . what I meant was: sign it."

"I have to show it to my advisor," she said.

"Your . . ?"

"I have to show it to my advisor."

"Financial advisor?"

"He's my advisor," she said. "He advises me. I show him everything."

– THREE –

Kohlman couldn't shake her impression. He imagined her picture on the cover of his book, called her seven times during the day, but she would say only, "Benjamin–be patient." He walked down Ogden, then up Fremont Street, hiked the grid of numbered streets that crossed, went into places with "Silver" and "Gold" and "Lucky" in their names: the Lucky Silver Gold. They all looked and smelled and sounded alike. It was like lower Broadway. In New York, such places would have wiry black men outside saying: "Check it out!" Why was he so loaded with hurried and nervous energy? What might happen: with her? . . in his absence? . . why the need to be *close*? His brain felt like an open window; the sky, making up: dangerous and blown with long cloud-sashes of uncertain imminence. What was this drive? What was this necessity triggered by his being once briefly *with* the woman?

He called again. "Have you seen your advisor?" he asked. "Did you get together yet?"

"Benjamin . . !"

"I'm anxious."

"He's in Aruba. He gets in at two this morning."

"Is he a *lawyer*? Is he an *attorney*? 'Advisor': is that what he is?"

"He's my advisor."

"Did you leave a *message*?" Kohlman felt himself accelerating, but he couldn't stop the release. "Does he know it's important?"

"I have to be at work in an hour and a half," she said. "I always meditate first. When he gets in from Aruba, he'll come and

– 39 –

see me at the Nugget. He knows to always check in. I'll see him then."

"So when can we get together?"

"Come by the Nugget at four—when I get off my graveyard shift. Make it four-thirty."

.   .   .   .   .

The logic was: to sleep, and Kohlman tried but he couldn't. There was too much electrical light in the world outside, even with the hotel's curtains drawn. He felt that, within just two days, he'd begun to breathe differently. Why would . . ? Were there *forces*, given that . . he meant: particular sorts of . . larger . . *things* which so much electricity in a given place might . . set up? What . . were there effects of . . movement of *ions* or . . *whatever* . . bombardments of . . *waves*, in a city with so much unleashed . . rampant . . *flagrant*, really, electricity . . were there charges or particles which might alter sleep patterns or the way a person . . ? Or: what about electromagnetic *fields*?

He turned on his light. He pulled his dated clipping files—a thick chronology of manila folders, tabbed and indexed, starting with the night of the fire. He reviewed them. What had he expected . . from any of this as he'd begun to gather it? From his research? It was just before one a.m. Kohlman, not knowing really why, chose, as a starting point, the specific details of Janice Stewart's former husband, Kenneth Levinworth.

They had divorced six months before the fire. Levinworth was a stockbroker for Dean Witter. His father, Salem Levinworth, "the victim," had graced the boards of both Monsanto and Union Carbide. Kenneth Levinworth had been reasonably tight-lipped about his wife. His testimony had been spare and careful; he'd said they'd been divorced due simply to "different life-objectives." She'd stopped "supporting him in his ambitions." It had been "clear to him" (and this was the harshest tone struck anywhere by his testimony) that her primary reasons had come through "a growing interest, unfortunately, in Feminism." Asked whether his ex-wife, he felt, were a person capable of arson or murder, he'd said: "Her hands shook when she lit her goddamn cigarette." *What had he meant?* he'd been asked. And he'd said: "I mean, she's not capable of that. Of arson. I wouldn't *marry* a woman capable of setting fire to my family home."

In his pictures, Kenneth Levinworth looked like men Kohlman had made conversation with at too many parties. He wore dark suits and looked, in all shots, slightly impatient to move on. Again: asked once to "describe the quality of your marriage – during the five years it lasted – to Janice Stewart," Kenneth Levinworth said, "Uncomplicated" and then added, "Traditional." What he'd meant by either of those words, what he was trying to say . . or *not* to say, was less clear to Kohlman.

. . . . .

Kohlman put a disk in his Compaq and began a journal of his day, a review of his notes. He wrote: "She has the face of a fever victim," then deleted the entire sentence, then wanted it back but couldn't remember it precisely as he'd written it. He wrote: "Compared to Sharon, she's a mirage." What did he mean? "Mirage": what was that supposed to capture? *So, then, am I too* real *for you?* he could hear Sharon ask. And it would make no sense, anyway, to any reader, let alone editor, to draw such comparisons.

He tried to describe Janice Stewart's *episode*: "I was afraid she might . . ." he began. He deleted *afraid* and inserted *concerned*. He couldn't finish the thought. He tried "afraid" again: "I was afraid she might . . ." He deleted it and substituted, "I was afraid I was going to . . ." He erased the entire start and went back to "I was afraid she might . . be in pieces like fine bone china, suddenly, at my feet." He hated *at my feet* but couldn't think of anything else. And did Kohlman even mean that? That he saw her thus? That she was so fragile? Had that been his emotion? Without cutting the first sentence he began another, "I was afraid, as well . . ." What was all this "afraid" business? Jesus! And all his attempt to build a case for her impermanence? In part, she seemed in absolute command. Had he seen Janice Stewart's hands shake? No! Not once! Rather, he'd seen them almost float, light as origami creations, over the steam of her three coffees. So . . was Kenneth Levinworth to be trusted? Why was he doubting Kenneth Levinworth? What had Kenneth Levinworth said? Was *Kohlman* to be trusted? Christ! He'd been on the whole thing only a day – without even the benefit of contract – and he was already throwing nets out and trapping . . what? . . *himself*! He shut his computer down, dressed, and left the Ogden House.

On an impulse, he took a cab to the Strip. *The Sands* sounded exotic and so he asked to be let out there. "Bad place," his cabby warned; "Too much heat."

"What do you mean?" Kohlman asked.

"Pressure. From the pit."

"I see," Kohlman said—though, of course, he didn't.

The casino, inside, stood nearly empty. The male dealers all looked like aging prizefighters: their necks were thick; their faces looked to have been ripped open; they bore those scars. Maintenance men in gold and brown jumpsuits ran hand vacuums down the felts of inactive dice tables, and even the vacuums seemed in need of replacement; they drew the air with death rattles.

Kohlman left and strolled Las Vegas Boulevard. Directly facing the Sands stood the darkened *Castaways*. Chain link roped the casino front and wound back past the resort pool and guest units; a demolition ball hung like a dead black moon from the cable of a huge crane, squat among the closed buildings. Kohlman walked west. Every fifty feet, by the traffic, stood dispensers of cheap brochures for escorts, models, dancers—*Flashdance* . . *Ingenue* . . *Elite Escorts*. The free brochures promised large-breasted and open-legged girls "just a phone call away." The bad ink on the bad paper came off on Kohlman's hands, and he tossed it—then stopped, angry, walked back, picked it up, picked up the trash of others, and dropped it all in a mesh refuse basket. Tin Dixieland piano from the Holiday Casino made his bending and reaching and tossing away into a kind of dance.

Beyond the Holiday and in front of the Imperial Palace, Kohlman passed a quadruple amputee, stationed, in a motorized chair. The man had a red stubble beard and wore a New York Yankees baseball cap, with a T-shirt, a globe imprinted, which read: "WORLD HUNGER." What struck Kohlman about the man were his eyes. They took up half his face. They seemed like flashcubes, firing again and again, socketed deep in the bronze stubble. Kohlman dropped three ones into the open cigar box in the man's lap. The man said nothing. He may have nodded. As Kohlman passed, all he could hold in memory and feel, burning then into his back, were the man's eyes and an awful, dreadful sense of judgement.

.   .   .   .   .

He crossed the Boulevard and rode the aerial moving sidewalk into Caesar's Palace. It was two-thirty, and he felt much more at home in Caesar's luxury than in the Sands or in the downtown squalor. Although that wasn't entirely fair; he needed to stop dismissing; Sharon caught him in it; it was too easy: places like the Fremont and the Horseshoe weren't without their own kind of class.

He had a drink. It helped. A large-breasted black girl tried to pick him up: "You have somebody to go home with, honey?" she said.

"Home's New York City." He winked at her.

"I travel," she smiled. She touched her tongue to her nose.

"How many jobs do you take a night?" Kohlman asked. He thought: *I'm awake—have some fun with it. Be a researcher.*

"Is this an interview?" she said

Kohlman finished his Cabernet.

"So what's the answer?" she asked.

"I have an appointment," Kohlman said.

"Oh. Really. 'An appointment'!"

"Maybe another time."

" 'An appointment'! I'm impressed. I'm disappointed."

"Sure."

"Clean and mean!" the black girl said as Kohlman walked away. "Clean and mean! I've got you scoped, honey. I've had you before—on many occasions—clean and mean! I *know* you." Kohlman moved as directly as possible without it seeming a retreat. He thought of the small girl he'd seen, flapping her arms, birdlike, from the tractor seat in her Sunday dress, on his Iowa farm property, the day before. She'd seemed so . . what? . . *contained*, really, so framed by the still, local landscape and by its dusted sky. He thought of Pamela Arnold: where would *she* be? where living now? still in Templeton at age thirty-five? So were there Pamela Arnolds *here*? Did such children—so accepting, so uncomplicated (was that *true*?)—ever leave and move . . from place and then to place . . and then arrive and work at lounges in such places as this? At a *Caesar's Palace*?

· · · · ·

He watched some blackjack. A fat man in expensive resort clothes bet stacks of black chips. Kohlman at first read their denomination as $1.00 before rereading them at $*100*. It seemed incredible. Four, five, six hundred dollars would disappear in front of the man with each hand. Suddenly, he won a hand, doubled his stack, won again, doubled, won again. Was he ahead or behind? A Japanese girl bumped into Kohlman as he wound an aisle. "You fine?" she asked him. She seemed high. "You win any big jackpots?" she said. "Not tonight," he told her. She took the arm of a man just beyond Kohlman: "My husband," she said.

The Japanese man nodded at Kohlman.

"Come with us for oysters?" the girl asked.

"No more shellfish," her husband said.

"Pizza?" the girl asked. "Manicotti?"

"Nice to talk with you," Kohlman said and walked away.

. . . . .

A mechanic was wheeling a dollar slot on a dolly toward a gap in a dollar carrousel. His shoe caught on a ripple in the carpet. The slot machine toppled forward. Kohlman saw it. *"Watch out!"* he yelled. One hand, instinctively, went out against a powerfully built black man who wore an open silver shirt and a gold medallion. The black man wheeled on Kohlman but danced backward. The slot machine fell at his feet. The slot mechanic began sobbing in Spanish. The black man moved past the mechanic, up to Kohlman, put his enormous hand out. A crowd had gathered. Kohlman reached and felt his own hand disappear as if into an unlit cave. "I owe you," the extraordinary black man said. He eyed Kohlman as though photographing him. "I owe you, Man," he repeated, turned, and moved away.

"You just saved the Challenger!" someone in the crowd said to Kohlman. "He just saved the Challenger!" the person announced to any of the gathered who might listen.

. . . . .

Kohlman left Caesar's and took a cab downtown to the Golden Nugget. It seemed almost impossible that it was four a.m. Everywhere held a lusterless and homogenous noon light.

Kohlman liked the Nugget—the etched mirrors, the dealers' vests, the orange- and lipstick-colored carpets with their floral poppies, the white marble, the brass and frontier paintings on the walls. He marveled at the numbers of people: there were women in gowns; there was a lit—downtown!—tropical pool area; there were two crap tables busy, a dozen blackjack games. Did most of these people know it was the middle of the night? Were there some who, in four, five, six hours would walk through the door of some local office, brokerage, law firm and begin conventional work? Or were all of these other people *travelers* like himself, people who set down at McCarran Airport on one day and flew out on another?

He looked for Janice. They should have set a place to meet. He went to the keno lounge. It seemed enormous—part waiting room in some not-quite-familiar station, part theatre. He looked at the large keno boards, numbers appearing, flashing, on them, lit, on the wall. Kohlman looked at the long wooden counter with its clerks and alcoves. He sat down in a chair to study, more carefully, the place he was in. He took a keno card. It made no sense to him, no more than any grid of eighty numbers. He picked up a pamphlet. Thumbing through the pamphlet, he could see a person might wager in what weren't always clear combinations, on certain clusters of numbers. Kohlman stuffed the pamphlet and the card inside a jacket pocket. If keno-running was what Janice Stewart did, he had better understand it. He approached the counter.

"Do you know a Janice Stewart?" he asked a man whose hair twined like a small bird's nest, yellow and white on his head, and who wore wire-rim glasses.

"Who?" the man said.

"Janice Stewart."

"I don't think so."

"He means 'Angel,' " a girl moving behind the man, working the marking area, said over her shoulder.

"Do you mean *Angel*?" the man asked Kohlman.

Kohlman produced a picture. "Her," he said.

"*Angel*."

"Okay. Fine. 'Angel.' That's who I want. Exactly. Sure."

"Yeah."

"So then: Could you tell me . . ?"

"Are you getting in this next game?" the man said. "Do you have a ticket?"

"No. But I was just . . . ."

"Then could you step aside for a moment, please? While I get the two people behind you?"

Kohlman checked behind himself. There was a woman with a walker and a man with an Italian bicycle under his arm who wore dark glasses.

Kohlman stepped out of the way. "Well, if you could just . . ."

"*Mr. Benjamin Kohlman?!*" a broadcast page inquired: "*Mr. Benjamin Kohlman—please pick up one of the gold courtesy phones? Mr. Benjamin Kohlman, please.*"

Kohlman found a gold courtesy phone and answered it.

"Hi . . ."

The voice was Janice's.

"I was looking for you," Kohlman said.

"Say 'hi' first. Then we can talk."

". . Hi," Kohlman said. He felt stupid.

"Does this seem mysterious to you?"

"No. Where *are* you? Does *what* seem mysterious to me?"

"Being in the same place, the same 'room'. . but talking over a telephone?"

"I don't think so. Not really. . . Possibly."

"Only 'possibly'?"

"Well, I don't know that I . . ."

"It does to me."

"Can we get together?"

"I'm at the fourth table . . from the end . . on the upper level . . of Lily Langtry's.

"What is 'Lily Langtry's?"

"Where are *you*?"

"I'm at a phone. Along the wall. There's a bar to my left . . as I face the wall. And some tall potted plants just down to my right. And a lot of goddamn noise and screaming bullshit—I'm sorry; I'm tired; I'm feeling impatient—*stuff*, 'noise' going on behind me."

"Walk up to the plants. Introduce yourself. Turn left. Walk down the hallway there. About a sixteenth of a mile. Look on your left. You'll see a sign: Lily Langtry's."

"Is your 'advisor' with you?"

"He'll be here."

"He's *there*?"

"No."

"What do you mean?"

"He called. He'll be joining us."

. . . . .

Lily Langtry's was long and narrow, like a diner. Janice was in a booth. She had a tall drink that had been served in something that looked carved from wood. She smiled at Kohlman.

"You found me," she said.

"Interesting place," Kohlman said, observing.

"Sit down," Janice said.

Kohlman did. He looked around nervously, adjusting to the naugahyde of the booth cushion, expecting something, somehow, immediately to happen, one of the potted plants to flare up in light.

"Hello, there," Janice Stewart said.

"Right," Kohlman said. "It's good to see you again. Hello."

"It's nice to see *you* again."

"Thank you."

"Hello. Here I am. Look at me."

Kohlman looked. Something during the intervening hours had softened her. She looked less pale, more spirited. Something had happened to make her appear more . . *brushed* in her skin texture. And there was more *air* in her face, roundness, color, *something*. "You look nice," Kohlman said.

"Thank you."

"I mean it."

"I didn't think you didn't."

She wore pearl earrings and a light peach cashmere sweater with an open V neck.

"How did work go?" Kohlman asked.

"I'm having a Kon Tiki. Would you like one?"

"Sure," Kohlman said. "Whatever. Anything."

Janice signaled a waiter. "I love my work," she said. "I view my work as essential."

"Right," Kohlman said. He tried to remember the card in his pocket, its block of numbers, and imagine what she might do. He began looking around again.

. . . . .

They made small talk. Kohlman tried. She kept asking him things like: "Did you ever see Charlie Chaplin in *City Lights*?

Chaplin had the eyebrows of Christ." Kohlman changed the subject: "Tell me about your ex-husband." She wouldn't. He kept watching for her to have one of her "attacks" again, whatever they were . . *episodes, encounters* . . headaches. Kohlman held his Kon Tiki in both hands. He liked the feel of his fingertips on the carving of the wooden . . what did you call it? not *glass*; *what* then?

"Why do they call you 'Angel'?" he asked.

She smiled. Then her eyes seemed to tear up for just a moment. He saw her turn hard toward the entrance and turned with her, checked over his shoulder.

Approaching their table was a male—about five foot eight or nine, styled hair, three-piece suit, Piaget watch, expensive shoes. The figure carried a soft-leather briefcase. By all appearances, the approaching person was extremely young, barely out of college.

The young man arrived, stood by the seated Kohlman and waited.

"This is C.E.O.," Janice said. "My advisor: C.E.O. Barnett. C.E.O., this is Benjamin."

Kohlman managed to get out of the booth. He could see he was expected to stand. He did, unsteadily, feet nearly atop one another, too close; then he regained a base, and extended his hand. It was clear that Kohlman stood a half foot above the young man. "Glad to meet you," Kohlman said.

The newcomer took Kohlman's hand. His grip was bone-crushing. "Nice tie," he said.

"Thank you," Kohlman said.

"I'm glad to meet another person in this city—casino personnel aside—who wears a tie."

Kohlman nodded.

Barnett nodded. "So you're the writer," Barnett said. His voice had the most profound bass resonance Kohlman had ever heard.

"Yes," Kohlman said: "Well . . that's why I'm here. That's what I'm here *for*, I suppose. Yes."

"You don't look like a writer."

"C.E.O.—come on; sit down," Janice urged. She scooted over in her booth, and the young man sat down beside her. His eyes never, for an instant, detached themselves from Kohlman.

"How was Aruba?" Janice asked.

"Aruba was an island," C.E.O. said.

"Was it pretty? Was it nice?"

"Nothing's nice . . nothing's pretty when what I'm dealing with are particular objectives," Barnett said. His voice made Kohlman's water glass vibrate; Kohlman thought he could hear the tines of his place-set fork humming. "*You*'re pretty, and *you*'re nice," C.E.O. said, reaching, placing a hand, Kohlman presumed, on Janice's knee.

"Behave yourself," Janice said.

A Chinaman in coattails brought a blood-colored phone to the table and set it beside C.E.O. Barnett. Barnett gave him a twenty-dollar bill. "Cellular," he said of the phone to Kohlman.

Kohlman nodded.

A numbered light on a side-panel of the phone was lit and Barnett pushed it, lifting the receiver: "Yeah," he said, then listened, his face drawing tighter and tighter with the count of time. "Unforgivable," he said to whoever was calling. Janice and Kohlman watched his tension and conversation. "*Unforgivable,*" he said again, hitting the word harder and then: "Absolutely un-for-fucking-givable! Take out his windpipe: we can't have that!" He hung up. He smiled at Janice Stewart.

She smiled back. He winked; she winked.

"So you're going to get the Big Crime Story of the Decade— hmm?" C.E.O. Barnett asked Kohlman.

Kohlman took a breath. "Well . . ."

"This going to make you the envy of all your peers and . . what do you call them, 'colleagues'? Do you *have* peers and colleagues? This going to make you a *fat cat*? Right? This going to make you . . *rich*?"

"Hey . . ." Kohlman held out his hand in mild protest.

"How about . . *famous*?" Barnett asked.

"That's not the point," Kohlman said.

The young man, C.E.O., laughed. He tossed his head back and threw his voice up into the spackled rafters of the Chinese Victorian restaurant. Kohlman swore he could see a tapestry on the sidewall shaking. " 'That's not the point,' " the young man repeated. He roared again.

Kohlman didn't like being ridiculed by an adolescent.

C.E.O. brought his face level. He put a hand over his mouth, grabbed the smile away. "So, then: what *is* the 'point'?" he asked.

"I want to be appropriately serious about the 'point' here. Whatever it is."

"Don't try to make a joke out of me," Kohlman said.

"Be good," Janice said.

"Why do you think I'm not appropriately serious?" the young C.E.O. Barnett said. "Why do you think I don't want to know what the 'point' *really* is? The true and deep and serious, meaningful . .'point'?!"

"Tell him what the point is," Janice said.

Kohlman took a long tug of his Kon Tiki.

"Who's paying for these drinks?" C.E.O. asked.

"He is," Janice said.

"I'll take one of these," C.E.O. boomed three tables down to a cocktail waitress. "Another for the lady. Do you want another?" he asked Kohlman

Kohlman felt anger, not a public emotion ever, really, at play, often, in him. Perhaps *some*times; maybe occasionally. He felt heat. "I'm fine," he said.

"So, okay: so let's have it: I'm ready: The Point! Capital *T*– capital *P*! What's The Point of your writing the fascinating story of this beautiful woman into a book?"

"He's taken by me." Janice blew a kiss from her fingertips to Kohlman.

"Let *him* say."

"He wants me." Her face took light.

"Shhhh."

"He wants me *exclusively*."

The young man cleared his throat hard to end the banter. Kohlman saw the pepper grinder on the table move.

There was a silence.

"The point . . ." Kohlman thought he might as well try. "The point of my writing this sort of thing . . sort of book . . her story *into* a book . . is . . very personal."

C.E.O. was pinning him to the needlepoint back of his chair with eyes like lasers.

Kohlman struggled on. "When it happened . . I remember . . I remember reading about it in all the papers. And I remember . . thinking: 'There is something very amazing here. There is something very remarkable. This is no simple Crime of Passion.' "

Kohlman paused.

"And . . . ?"

"And . . I got *obsessed* with it. Don't *play* with me. That's all you need to know! I got *obsessed* with it, and I decided I was going to do it: I was going to write the book!"

C.E.O. looked at Janice. She was staring at Kohlman.

Something reminiscent of a smile played at the edges of C.E.O Barnett's lips. "Janice said something about a contract," he said.

"A letter agreement—yes."

"Show it to me."

Kohlman produced the paper. Barnett took it. He drew some reading bifocals from his jacket pocket and studied the print.

"You don't have a major publishing house behind you on this?" he asked.

"No," Kohlman said.

Barnett drew a deep breath. He read on.

"I'm doing this very much at my own expense," Kohlman inserted.

Barnett lifted his head; he pulled his bifocals down, looked at Kohlman, went back to reading.

Kohlman looked at Janice Stewart. She smiled at him.

What the hell was going on?! He was sitting there with butterflies in his stomach while a *goddamn kid* checked over the contract he'd prepared! Jesus Christ: he'd worked as a paralegal at Levitz-Steiner in New York for eighteen months, just out of Princeton, helping to prepare documents of *infinitely* greater complexity.

A mustached man in tails—silk handkerchiefs draped over his arm, a small black suitcase of magic effects in his hands—approached the table and set his tricks on a tray stand. He began to pull a chair up.

"Not tonight, Collosso," Barnett said, eyes still on the document. "Thanks anyway, but we're doing business."

"That's fine," the magician said; "I understand. . . Evening, Angel," he said to Janice.

"This is Benjamin," Janice introduced Kohlman.

The magician extended his hand; Kohlman took it. The hand dematerialized, and in its place Kohlman found himself clutching a live, tiny kitten.

"Be careful," Janice said: "Don't squeeze it. It's very young."

"Tomorrow's chow yuke," the magician joked.

"He's kidding," Janice said.

"Here." Kohlman handed the small, mustard-colored kitten back.

"Nice to meet you," the magician said. He picked up his case of effects and moved away.

Barnett, who had been waiting, drumming his fingers, slid the paper back. "You want to do this?" he asked Janice.

She nodded.

Barnett pulled the paper from under Kohlman's fingertips. He moved it to the woman, but didn't take his own hand from its surface. "I read: that this is binding," he said to Kohlman.

Kohlman almost said *Yes, sir*; instead, he nodded.

"You have certain binding obligations to respect the person of Ms. Stewart."

"I understand that," Kohlman said. "I respect that."

"My reading is: You are contractually *tied* . . to a considerate handling of my client . . in every aspect of her life. Her life is your responsibility. And you are responsible – in a deep and committed and important sense – for a fair and respectful treatment. No unforgivable behavior."

Kohlman nodded.

C.E.O. Barnett turned to Janice Stewart. He lifted his hand. "Sign it – if that's what you want," he said. She smiled. He produced a pen. Barnett turned back to Kohlman: "This woman took my sister and myself *in* thirteen months ago," he said. "We were on the streets. We were two kids from God-knows-where-exactly in Pennsylvania on the edge of deep trouble here. Deep – if I weren't as refined as I am, I would say . . but of course I won't – shit. This woman is amazing. This woman is heroic. This woman almost *died* one night because of us: we thought we'd lost her. In just over a year, remarkable things have happened. My world now's incredible. My sister's studying to be a concert pianist. And so I am very protective – you need to understand – of this woman. I will watch over her. I will protect her. Because I see you as a very thin, badly frightened, unreflective, very humorless person. Someone who could walk past himself bleeding to death on a street corner. Someone who could hit and run himself and not understand what the fuck had happened. . . You're so 'eager.' How do you know this woman isn't capable of setting fire to *your* house? What about that? Have you thought about that? Have you considered that possibility as well . . with all your 'need' and 'want' and 'obsession'? That she could burn your fucking eyeballs out—and it would be a moral act?!"

Janice had finished signing and had lifted the paper—like a jewel, a tiny bird—toward Kohlman. "Here," she said.

Kohlman took it. He felt relief. He felt fear. He felt anger and self-preservation and confusion and strange, unfamiliar insecurity. "Can I ask one question?" he said to C.E.O. "Ask," Barnett said.

"How old are you?"

"Eighteen," Barnett said. "My sister, Alyce, is twelve."

"Thank you," Kohlman said. He felt stunned. He felt dazed. He felt himself in a craft on a sea neither of which he understood the dimensions of. "If you'll excuse me," he said to both C.E.O. and Janice. "I don't think I've slept really since I got here. I'd better do that."

C.E.O. struck his fist, hard, on the center of Kohlman's contract paper. He left it there. "Where's our copy?" he said.

"I just have . . . I'll make another and give it to you tomorrow." Kohlman felt bone weary. Iowa 71 and its gold roadside stubble flashed before him—redwinged blackbirds on telephone wires.

C.E.O. took the paper in his hand. "*We*'ll make another. We'll give it to *you*," he said.

"Really. Please. I promise I'll . . ." Kohlman began to feel unattached, crazy.

"But don't we begin now?" Janice Stewart said.

"Soon," Kohlman said. "Let me make a copy. It will only be a matter of hours, really—I'll get some sleep; I'll get a copy back to you; then . . ."

"But I thought, *now*, we'd begin," Janice said.

"Just give me six hours."

"Are you backing out on your agreement and your obligations already?" C.E.O. Barnett asked.

"*No!*" Kohlman said. Again: the anger flash; again, the impatient fulmination; bursts, for Kohlman, so uncharacteristic.

"It's all right, C.E.O.," Janice said. She looked sympathetic, concerned; her eyes locked on Kohlman. "It's fine," she went on, stopping her advisor. "Give him back the agreement. He's a good person. I can understand. It's a different place for him. It's a different light. Let him go."

"Thank you," Kohlman said. He was standing. He had the contract in his hand and was slipping it, unsteadily, into his coat pocket. "Now which way's out?" he asked.

"There," both advisor and advisee said—and pointed.

.   .   .   .   .

In his march to the exit, Kohlman didn't see a black hand reach out and take him hard by the elbow.

"You okay, Man?"

It was the Challenger.

"You okay? I'm just checkin'; I need to check; I'm obliged. Listen: if that slot machine would've messed wi' my form, Man: hey, it woulda been over—womp!—no challenge—right?—no title. —So I be doin' this, you see—time to time—keepin' my eye out—because I owe you. Be my person!"

"I'm fine," Kohlman said. "I'm okay. I'm fine. Don't worry. I can take care of myself."

"You're in good hands," the Challenger said. "Call me 'All-State'!" He laughed. He lifted his hands high into the light. "You got the World's best hands watching you! 'Shed a tear . . Challenger's here.' Rest your heart. I'm watchin'. I owe you."

Kohlman backed away. The man was grinning. Kohlman turned. In seconds only, he was on the street.

– FOUR –

Kohlman hated his room.

What kind of place had no telephone or television?

Why couldn't he sleep? It was seven in the morning on a Wednesday! Kohlman hung his bedspread over the existing window drapes to block the morning light. *Assholes!* Who was he calling 'assholes'? Christ! the goddamn *light* in this city was going to drive him crazy! His brain felt perforated and barraged. His breath, against the thin sheeting of his bed, smelled like Iowa.

Now Kohlman slept for an hour, woke up, felt refreshed. Was that possible? Had he slept *thirteen* hours? No: the printout on his digital watch said *one hour*.

He sat up on his bed. Was it possible there had been amphetamines in his Kon Tiki? The Kahlua? Did Kahlua have caffeine? He'd have to get a phone installed . . *whatever*. It was necessary. He was going to need to talk constantly with Janice Stewart. A standard phone would be reasonable. Perhaps he'd rent a TV. Kohlman liked to relax, sometimes, watching baseball. All sorts of baseball facts rattled in his head. He liked keeping averages.

He showered and dressed: light grey slacks, blue oxford-cloth shirt, gold and maroon striped tie. He spent five minutes tying the tie, then took it off. He looked like a bloody tourist! Or he *didn't* look like a tourist. Had he noticed the tourists: which *were* they? what did they look like? Anyway, he didn't always have to wear a tie. Maybe he'd buy different clothes today. More casual. Cooler. Fit in. Why would he want to fit in to a place like Las Vegas? Goddamn that Barnett! *Was* Kohlman the sort of person who might walk past himself bleeding on a street corner? What would *Sharon* say? Funny how he summoned her, and their conversations, at moments when he felt accused. He'd accused *her* as well, sometimes—once of too many cigarettes: "You'll kill yourself with those," he'd said.

"I'll kill myself with other things," she'd smiled, "way . . *way* before."

He'd accused her of having no sense of humor.

"I have a sense of humor," she'd said.

"What do you laugh at?"

"You."

"What else?"

"Funny paintings."

"What's a funny painting?"

"One with too much yellow."

Half the time, when Sharon wasn't accusing him, she was giving instructions, especially in their lovemaking: "Use this!" "Get on your side!" "Hurry— goddamn; where are you?!"

"All I do is, half the time, ask you to back off and leave me alone . . and the other half, follow your instructions!" he'd complained.

"What's wrong with that?" she'd said. "They're good instructions."

"Possibly."

"So: shut up, and go out and get us some nova scotia!"

He was *not* a person who would walk by himself bleeding on the street! That was absurd. He was not a person who would walk by *anyone* bleeding on the street!

So the hotshot little prick advisor could go fuck himself!

Once he'd walked by someone doubled over in a doorway. Once; all right! But what about the time he'd tackled the Hispanic guy wielding the screwdriver so that the guy's wife, or whoever the woman was, could run away? All right: that was four years ago, but . . ! Actually, when he'd met Sharon, she'd noticed him because he'd grabbed the hand of a kid who was going to lift a waitress's tip from a table. The kid had called him *asshole*; Sharon had said, "Nice move. Nice to see someone with a moral sensibility." Three weeks ago, in an argument about his taking on the Janice Stewart book, she'd accused him: "Benjamin, you're *losing* your moral sensibility."

Jesus: why did he even *stay* with a woman who accused him half the time?! And gave him instructions the rest! And even if she were right, partly, in the various things she said, *which she wasn't* . . wasn't a person supposed to be allowed to be who they were? What was the problem? It took all kinds! And where did Barnett come off? Kohlman had graduated from Princeton and the Columbia School of Journalism! Barnett was eighteen fucking years old . . and wore a Piaget watch and Italian three-piece suits. Kohlman felt unhappy.

He went out to the Strip. He liked it better there. He went to the Riviera; he liked the sound of the casino's name. Never mind! He could be different! He could be a freer person! More alert! More aware! More imaginative! More spontaneous! More . . what was the word? . . at *peace* with himself! More integrated! If he were determined to do *any* of those things and set his mind to them: no problem; they'd *be* there. He'd be them. They'd be him. Kohlman wasn't ready to concede they *weren't* him, anyway! Fuck the twerp! Fuck a snotnose telling him about himself. C.E.O. Barnett was a *minor*. C.E.O. Barnett was a *juvenile*. Was that true – age eighteen – in Nevada? Kohlman was none of C.E.O. Barnett's business anyway! . . Well – perhaps in *one* sense.

Kohlman stopped a cocktail waitress traveling the casino aisles and ordered a bloody mary. *That* was out of character, *was*n't it?! What about that?! The girl brought Kohlman his drink. He tipped her a dollar. He roamed, taking far longer steps than usual, through the gaming area. He sang to himself, a Willie Nelson song he remembered that seemed appropriate. "It's a bloody mary morning . . !"

He sat down at an empty blackjack table. The dealer nodded. A smiling man in a pewter-colored suit moved forward from the pit to the table. He stuck his hand out to Kohlman. "Mr. B!" he said. "Finally back! How's the war?"

Kohlman shook the man's hand. *Mr. B?* ". . Fine," he said.

"We haven't seen you!" the pit boss said.

"No," Kohlman said.

"You've been away."

"Yes."

The pit boss put a hand on the dealer's shoulder. "Start Mr. B with a mark of two, Lonnie." Then he looked up at Kohlman: "Two – Mr. B? Am I on target? Did I remember?"

"Fine," Kohlman said. He had no idea what was being transacted.

"Standard fare," the pit boss said to Lonnie, the dealer. "Whenever you see Mr. B—start him off with a mark of two."

Things were happening; Kohlman was watching. Something was being filled out on a voucher pad. The dealer was gathering stacks of chips from his tray, lining them up, counting them, restacking them, lining them up again, counting. The pit boss pushed the voucher pad to Kohlman, handed over his pen. Kohlman hesitated, then scratched a signature where the man had indicated on the pad. The pit boss took the pad back, smiled at Kohlman, touched his own vest: "Jerry Lessac, Mr. B. I know you're scrambling. Jerry Lessac. I'm sorry. I know I should've reminded you."

"Jerry Lessac," Kohlman repeated.

"It's good to see you," the pit boss, Jerry Lessac, said.

Kohlman nodded and smiled.

"They been keeping you busy? —Give him the chips," Lessac instructed the dealer. The dealer complied.

"Busy. Yes," Kohlman replied.

"No rest for the weary!" Jerry Lessac said and laughed.

"You need any show tickets? You had breakfast? Are you all set as far as women are concerned?"

"I'm fine," Kohlman said. "For now—no problem."

"Sensational!" Jerry Lessac said. He pointed to the chips, now in front of Kohlman. "You gonna ruin us again?"

Kohlman began to feel himself getting *into* something, whatever it was that was happening at the table. "Actually . ." he started . . and a kind of momentum began: "Actually . . I'm feeling sort of 'what the hell' this morning. I'm in a sort of . .'what-the-hell' mood and attitude."

"Hey! Right! Go for it!" Jerry Lessac laughed.

"What the hell—why not?" Kohlman said and laughed.

"Absolutely!" Jerry Lessac said. He laughed as well.

"Blow a little bit—right?" Kohlman said. "Why not?"

"Well, you don't want to *blow* it, Mr. B."

"Why not?!"

"Well: if you say so! The important thing is—right, though?—is to have fun!"

"Absolutely!"

"Do what feels good!"

"Sit here. Drink my bloody mary . . !" Kohlman felt on a roll of some kind. It was weird. But . . what the hell! . . he had gotten Janice Stewart to sign the binding and exclusive agreement. She was in his pocket. He could write the book. Let C.E.O. Barnett make whatever bad jokes he needed to make about Janice setting fire to his bed . . or whatever Barnett had said. Kohlman flashed his best, brightest smile at Jerry Lessac: "Sit here . . drink my bloody mary . . and if I blow a little bit–that's life! What the hell!" Kohlman laughed at his own vocalized abandon and flair.

"Man after my own heart!" Jerry Lessac said.

"Do you want to bet, sir?" the dealer, Lonnie, asked.

Kohlman slid two chips into the box.

"When you're ready to take a break," Jerry Lessac said, "give a wave; we'll see how we can set you up."

"You got it!" Kohlman said. The dealer had dealt him two cards. He picked them up. They were two queens. He noticed a person at the next table sliding cards under their chips. He did the same. The dealer opened his cards–nineteen, losing to Kohlman's twenty.

Kohlman had seen the man at Caesar's letting his bet ride. If he was going to loosen up, try to make himself just a bit more reckless–then he could do that.

He won again. "Well, if I'm here to blow a little bit, I'm not doing a very good job of it," he said to Lonnie, the dealer.

"Mr. B–if you're here to blow a little bit, I'm sure–like everyone else who comes for that–you will. I don't especially recommend it, though." He dealt again. Again Kohlman won. Again Kohlman let the chips–this time *sixteen chips*–ride. Lonnie took a deep breath and redealt. He dealt Kohlman an ace and a ten.

In fifteen minutes, Kohlman had more than tripled his original chips. "How much do I have here?" he asked Lonnie. He was feeling *up* for the first time in days. He was on his second bloody mary. He was feeling expansive.

Lonnie eyeballed the stacks. "I count eighty-six hundred– give or take," Lonnie said.

Kohlman felt his mind go to white turbulence. His brain felt atomized. He lost orientation. Then pieces and gravity and light began, all, to slide back together. He had made the same error that he'd made when he'd watched the heavy man at Caesar's. His chips were *hundreds*, not, as he had assumed, *dollars*. "I . . I . ." he began. "I think I'll take a break," he said to Lonnie. His heart was like a loose marble in his rib cage.

"Would you like to cash in your mark, sir—Mr. B?" Lonnie said.

"Sure," Kohlman said. "Right. That's a good idea. Cash in my mark."

Lonnie gathered all the chips and rearranged them. He drew off four stacks of five, separated them back toward his tray. He produced the voucher that Kohlman had signed. "Do you want to rip this up yourself? Or should I?" he said.

"Oh . . go ahead," Kohlman said. "Rip. Fine."

Lonnie ripped the voucher. He set the chips he'd separated back into the tray. "Should I change these up for you?" he asked.

"Sure," Kohlman said. He felt lunatic. He felt buoyant, absolutely outside any laws of logic.

Lonnie gave Kohlman thirteen gold chips and a black one. "Sixty-six," he said.

Kohlman handed the black chip back. "Thank you," he said.

"Thank *you*, Mr. B."

Jerry Lessac was on the scene as Kohlman rose. "God, you did it to us *again*, Mr. B," he said to Kohlman.

"Well . . . "

"What can we get you? What can we do? How can we be there for you? It's ten minutes past nine: Breakfast?"

.   .   .   .   .

On his way to breakfast, Kohlman visited a men's room. Within seconds, C.E.O. Barnett was at the urinal beside him, the splash of Barnett's urine, its force, sounding like the stream of a horse. "We meet again," C.E.O. Barnett said.

"What are you doing here?" Kohlman asked.

"Is that a serious question?"

"Have you been following me?"

"I'm *pissing*," Barnett said. "When you take your dick out of your pants and aim it into a urinal and relax certain muscles, it's called *pissing*." He shook himself, hefted his member, and rezipped.

Kohlman was a long urinator: more duration than force. "I have *business*," Barnett said. "This is a very small town. You'll find that. You bump into people. Sometimes you bump into five or six people at the same time. I have *business* here—as I do at *all* the casinos. If it makes you feel any better—if you're one of those jackoffs that has to *explain* things always to themselves—file it in your mind as *coincidence*."

"I would *not* walk past myself, bleeding, on the street," Kohlman said. "You said that last night. You made that judgement—it's not true."

"Glad to hear it," Barnett said. He moved away from the wall and crossed to the sinks. He ran some water. He opened his brief-case, took a gold razor out and some gel. He inspected his face, spread some gel just below his sideburns, above his lips and on his chin. He worked the gel in. Kohlman was just finishing. "Do you just piss once a week? Is that why it takes you so long?" Barnett asked.

Kohlman's intent was not to answer, to just move on behind him and exit.

"I'll take that copy—which you said you'd make—of the agreement, now," Barnett said.

A large man in shorts and a terry-cloth top stormed into the lavatory. He bit an enormous cigar and marched directly into one of the stalls, slamming its door hard behind him. He started pounding the stall from the inside, making growling noises. Barnett nodded in his direction. "Man just lost . . more than he can afford," Barnett said. Then he turned directly to Kohlman: his gold razor, poised in his hand; the gel, worked into a lather where it had been applied. He raised his voice to be heard over the stall-battering. "So . . just lay it on my briefcase—right? okay?—we'll be fine. The copy of the agreement. Like you promised."

"So . . what do you *do*?" Kohlman asked Barnett.

"What are you asking?" Barnett said.

"I'm asking what you do: what you do for, I suppose, I imagine . . *work* . . employment, your job; I'm asking how you earn your money."

"Nothing illegal," Barnett said. "Where's the agreement copy?"

"I don't have it."

"I didn't think you could be trusted."

"I'll have it later today!" Kohlman shouted. He felt angry again and moved closer, so that he stood his full height above Barnett. "Look: I realize that Janice Stewart *relies* on you," Kohlman said. "I realize you're indebted and that you have her best interests at heart. But I want you to stop looking down and shrugging me off and treating me like some idiot flunky. I was polite last night for a long time. I always try to be polite. If I can be. And patient."

"That's your first mistake."

"Right. And my second is, probably, to refrain from punching your fucking nose."

"I love it; I love this! This is great!" Barnett roared. "Promises!"

"I'll have your copy of the contract in your hands by dinner!"

"Promises, promises."

Kohlman and Barnett had both shouted. The pounding on the metal stall had stopped; nothing had replaced it. There was a kind of silence, glittering off all the tile and stainless steel, that Kohlman had never heard. Barnett waited for Kohlman to shout again. He seemed delighted and fueled and in lifted spirits.

"So, okay," Kohlman finally said: "So, okay. So you don't do anything illegal: So then . . what *do* you do?"

"A lot," Barnett smiled.

"Such *as?*"

"Such as *what?*"

"Exactly: Such as *what?*! I'm asking *you.*"

"No single product."

Kohlman saw the amusement Barnett felt in the sparring. He could see Barnett watching him, hoping for him to go up, combust, lose focus. "I'm sorry," Kohlman finally said. "I'm sorry. I've been on edge. I'm not sure I understand why. I'm usually really not quite so . . well, it doesn't make any difference, really, *what* I am . . or am not . . but I'm better usually at managing myself. Better than this at least. I'm sorry. It's none of my business, really, *what* you do . . or why you do it. I just won some money; maybe *that* has something to do with it. Why I'm acting so . . . Or perhaps it's because you're so young."

"It's a youth culture," Barnett said.

"Right. Anyway: I'll get you the contract . . that's a guarantee . . later today. I apologize." Kohlman started out.

"Mr. Kohlman . . !"

Kohlman stopped.

"What I do is . . *eclectic*—okay? Do you like that word? I'm taking a vocabulary course. Janice's suggestion. *Eclectic.* I love language! Also squash: I love squash: You play squash?"

"I've played."

"Good. I'll take you to my club. Whip your ass. My work's eclectic. No *single* product . . no *single* commodity that I'm tied to. – I'm into . . a lot. Escorts. I'm into imported liquors. Amphetamines. But I'm open. I keep my eye out. Whatever's legal . . and has a good turnover . . and has markup. Those are the items I try to stay up on. Those are my criteria. Opportunities. Opportunities create opportunities . . create opportunities. Do you know what I'm saying? That's, basically, the way I work. Basically, the way I've found life, here, in this city, for the most part, to be. –And of course I spend a great deal of my time on the career of my sister Alyce." Barnett stopped and looked hard at Kohlman; it was a look that said: *I've tried to be as straight and to answer your question with as little bullshit as possible.*

"So you mean . . as in . . I mean, in terms of your . . various . . *lines*, your . . *eclecticism* . . you're talking, then, *women*? Is that the gist of what you're saying? *Female* escorts?" Kohlman asked.

"Female. Yeah; right. Female . . male . . switchovers. Opportunities."

"Right," Kohlman said.

"Opportunities create opportunities."

"Right; I heard you. So, then, does . . ?"

"What?"

"Nothing. Just a thought. Never mind."

"No: ask. I'm a book. I'm open."

"Does Janice . . ?"

"Wait a minute: wait a minute; wait a minute, Mr. Kohlman: Does Janice what?"

"Well, I mean . . well, I'm sure that isn't the case."

"What?"

"Work . . ?"

"For me?"

"Yes. I mean: *No*: I can't imagine . . . ."

"Don't get me angry, Mr. Kohlman. Do we understand? I'm getting angry. I don't want to get angry. Don't get me angry– please."

Kohlman nodded and, again, started out.

"You don't wash your hands? You don't clean up? What kind of personal habits do you have? Maybe we need to talk."

Kohlman felt pinned in Barnett's face, fixing him, in the mirror. He needed breakfast.

·   ·   ·   ·   ·

The waitress brought a telephone to Kohlman's booth; she plugged it in to a wall jack. "It's not cellular?" Kohlman asked.

"No, sir," the waitress said.

"Appreciate it," Kohlman said. "Anyway. I didn't mean to seem ungrateful. Thank you."

"You like that nova scotia and eggs?" she asked. "Excellent," Kohlman said. "Thank Mr. Lessac. And thank him for the Dom Perignon. Excellent."

He called Janice Stewart. She'd been to his room twice. She felt *abandoned*. Where *was* he? He told her about running into Barnett, also told her about his good fortune. "They thought I was another person," he said. He laughed. "It was amazing!"

"Maybe you were," she said. "When do we start? I signed a paper. I gave myself away. I feel very insecure."

Kohlman said *noon*: there was time; she'd be fine; it wasn't as critical, or at least *immediate*, as she seemed to think. He wanted to talk to the phone company first.

"But noon seems so far away," she said.

"It's less than two and a half hours."

They settled on eleven-thirty.

"Can we meet where there's water?" Janice asked.

"Sure," Kohlman said.

"Where?"

"*You* tell *me*."

She named the pool at the Flamingo.

·   ·   ·   ·   ·

On his way, walking to the Flamingo, Kohlman suddenly felt eyes pinned on him, almost *photographing*: eyes taking every bit of him in. A block later, he passed the curious quadruple amputee—unchanged: same cap, same T-shirt: WORLD HUNGER—and knew whose eyes they'd been. Kohlman shivered in the passing: what was going on? He turned back and dropped a twenty into the man's cigar box. It was fine; he felt wealthy in his recent good fortune. Was the man nodding? Was he acknowledging something? Something in Kohlman felt he should stay and *talk* . . but say *what*? He tried to move but, at first, couldn't, felt rooted, then forced himself. Behind him, the man, perhaps, said something, but Kohlman wasn't sure.

. . . . .

Across the boulevard, Kohlman saw an enormous billboard. The billboard read: "THE FIGHT TO END ALL FIGHTS! THE CHALLENGE TO END ALL CHALLENGES!" and almost exploding through the edges of the billboard was the Challenger. In the lower left-hand corner of the billboard appeared: "*Training Camp Southwest Sector Lot, Caesar's Palace*."

Curiosity got him. Kohlman had nearly half an hour, so he routed himself behind Caesar's to find the camp.

There was a roped-off area, flanked by bleachers. There were perhaps three or four hundred people sitting in the various bleachers, in the sun, intent, quietly waiting. Kohlman climbed up the platform seating of a bleacher until he felt he might be able to see something and looked out. The Challenger was in the center of the roped-off lot area. There was no ring set up: no bags, no apparatus, no sparring partners. Instead the Challenger squatted, coiled in upon himself, head lowered prayerfully, fists raised and tight against his shoulder blades. Kohlman turned to a woman on the bleacher nearby.

"Is he all right?" Kohlman asked.

"He's fine," the woman said. She kept her eyes hard on the asphalt where the Challenger knelt.

Kohlman looked back. Nothing was going on; nothing was happening. There was the cab of a Peterbilt semi truck in the roped-off area with the Challenger.

Kohlman turned, again, to his neighbor. "What's he . . ? What's going on?" he asked. "What's the thing people are waiting for?"

"Just watch," the woman said. "It sometimes takes him only ten minutes. Sometimes it takes him three hours. It's been two hours and seventeen minutes this last time."

Kohlman looked again. The Challenger wore only trunks and ankle-high sporting shoes. The huge black man's *breathing* was not even visible. "He looks like he's . . in a *trance*," Kohlman said.

"He *is*," the woman said. "He calls it 'The Africa of His Mind.' He calls it 'The Original Continent.' It's an exercise. When he *gets* there . . when he gets his *mind* there . . then . . ."

Kohlman looked back. He checked his watch. It was eleven-thirty; he would have to run. He left the bleachers and started across the lot toward the Flamingo. He heard the assembled crowd all draw their breath in unison. He rushed back. Between two spectators, he could see the Challenger holding the cab of the Peterbilt truck, arms extended, out, at a 45-degree angle, to his body. It was an impossible feat. The mechanics, the laws of leverage, the physics of the human anatomy didn't allow it. Once, when Kohlman had been eight, he had stood by with ice water while his father had dug postholes in the sun for twelve consecutive hours—but that had been an entirely different thing. There was an amazing silence. It was the second and *different* amazing silence Kohlman had experienced in three hours. The Challenger lowered the cab. The crowd started to buzz. The Challenger squatted into his position again. Kohlman ran for the Flamingo. As he waited on the sidewalk to cross Las Vegas Boulevard, he heard the crowd buzz again. He looked at his watch. It had been only six minutes.

· · · · ·

It was obvious, when he arrived, that Janice had been crying. Her face was streaked. There was blood just below one nostril, and Kohlman believed he could almost see her finger imprints, still dug in, where she'd pressed above and below her eyes. She'd had one of her headaches. "I just saw an amazing thing!" Kohlman tried, hoping to lift, hoping to shift whatever might have been her pain into something easier.

She said nothing.

Kohlman took a white handkerchief from his jacket pocket. He wiped the blood from below her nose. "Is this the sort of thing Barnett was talking about when he said you almost died one time?" he asked.

"I can't talk about it," Janice Stewart said. "I'm fine now. You're here. Don't ask me. I always get places first. I mean: before the people I want to have be there with me. But that's me. I can't expect other people to . . . I mean, it's who *I* am. I'm just glad you're here now."

She asked that he rent an inflatable mat. They sat on it on the grass, beside a garden planted with gold and red and blue flowers, all with *tongues*. Kohlman thought: *I should learn their names . . these flowers, get them in: Verisimilitude.* "Can we accept that a woman who would sit so vulnerably on resort grass, in the sun, beside florid banks of . . braggiolas (or whatever they were) . . might be capable of brutal and wanton arson?" Janice Stewart kept reordering grapefruit juices.

"Are those good?" Kohlman asked.

"It's what I need," she said.

He nodded. He wanted to tell her about the Challenger. "Tell me anything you want about yourself," he said, instead. "We'll start there." He'd bought a portable Quasar, much smaller than his Nagra for when they might be places like this—public, outside, between one thing . . and another.

She asked where he'd been born. She asked how old he was. She asked: did he have feelings about trains, traveling on them? She asked what colors made him feel uneasy, what colors he wore, whether he watched certain objects change color in different lights. She asked whether he *liked* light. If he had to name it: what would be his favorite light source. "*Favorite* isn't exactly what I mean," she said, "but I can't think of what I'm trying to think of." What religion? So, then: Had it rejected it? Why? Did he think rejecting a religion made him superior? Was it a pose? How sure was he? Did he ever waver, ever doubt? Did it make him afraid? Was he being smug; was it just an attitude? Had he read Camus? Had he read Camus *closely*? Quote a passage! "I'm sorry," she said; "I get carried away. That wasn't fair."

"Who's giving this interview?" Kohlman asked.

"Oh—I'm sorry," she said.

"No problem."

"This is an interview, then?" she said.

"Well, it's the *beginning* of an interview. It's the beginning of our talking—which we have a lot of to do. So, in that sense . . ."

" 'Which . . we . . have . . a . . lot . . of . . to . . do'?" she said. "Is that correct, grammatically?"

"*I* don't know. 'Which . . we . . have . . .' What difference . . ?! I write differently than I talk. I write . . ! My writing style— most people feel—is . . really quite *crisp*. It's clear . . it's lively. It's vivid. I have—and I don't mean to blow my own horn, but, I think—an eye for, I suppose, 'telling' detail; do you know what I mean by that?—'telling' images. I have an ear for speech. You're welcome to read the manuscript . . before it goes to print, but . . . We can't . . ! I mean if we dissect every word spoken . . we won't get *any*where. Did you know your 'advisor' was dealing in call girls and amphetamines?! I'm sorry. I don't mean to get excited. *Did* you know that?"

"Of course."

"It doesn't bother you?"

"Why should it bother me?"

"Well, I mean, I suppose, because . . he's dealing in whores and drugs—to put it bluntly. . . I'm sorry again. It's been . . an unusual day. I still haven't slept."

"Benjamin: Everything C.E.O. does is legal."

"Yes; I understand that. I understand, given where we are—this state; this city—that that's true. So . . all right; fine! I don't mean to be a prig about human activity."

"Why are you upset?"

"I don't know!"

"Think!"

"He's eighteen!"

"Yes. What's your point?"

"I don't . . ! —Look: I've done things, during the last six hours, that aren't exactly my image of myself. Not that I mind . . not that it's bad. Maybe that's *your* point."

"I haven't *made* a point."

"But it's just . . . Let's—can we?—get *off* this—might we do that? Just pack it up for just a little bit. I'm tired; I'm, actually, *very* tired. I'm very much on edge. I'm a person who needs his own . . *some*thing."

"Privacy?"

"Well, certainly something *like* privacy."

"What's *like* privacy that *isn't* privacy?"

"Perhaps I'm just . . temperamental. Okay? Or more temperamental than I thought . . I was temperamental. That's probably not grammatical either: I'm very grammatical when I write. You've made me feel self-conscious. That's not a feeling I particularly . . ! Why do they call you *Angel?*"

"I can't answer that question . . when you ask it in that tone," Janice said.

"I understand," Kohlman said, though he didn't. "I can appreciate that. I'm sorry. I'm worked up." And he began nodding.

Janice leaned forward and kissed him on the cheek. Once, when they had been children at the river, Pamela Arnold had kissed him like that: as the person beside her whom she felt happy about: as a friend. Janice smiled. "You talk very fast when you get excited. It's nice," she said. "It's nice to not see you planning every word." She reached a hand out and touched his jacket. Behind. Below his left shoulder. Affectionately. She rumpled it. "I mean it," she said. "Some people—when they're planning words—they talk very slowly. Almost as if the next word may never come. Those are people to watch. Those are the dangerous people. Let's have lunch!" she said. "Here! Now! Let's share fruit!"

. . . . .

When Kohlman replayed the tape later, downtown, at the Ogden House, after he'd made two copies of the letter-agreement, and after his room telephone had been installed, and after he'd studied the forwarded postcard from his parents—no message; a picture of the open-pit copper mine in *Ruth, Nevada* (God: they were *in* the state! Where was *Ruth*?!), he was amazed to hear *himself*. He found things out. He didn't know he believed some of the things he'd said he believed. She'd asked whether he believed in *vengeance*. He'd said, "No—*codes*." "Name one," she'd said. He'd said he meant, more, "codes in general." She'd asked whether he thought that was how people should act: "in general? . . or should they act, more, do you think . . *in specific*?" Kohlman was surprised, too, by some of his choices, statements, definitions, preferences. Perhaps not so much that he was *surprised*: he was the one talking, after all. But he was startled, caught off guard. And perhaps he'd just been making noise with her, anyway: rattling on, not thinking, saying whatever. To get her relaxed. Loosen things. You had to do that. You had to clear the air, sweep away barriers, relax tensions. It was important to build trust. He rewound the tape, listened to it again. Why had he said his favorite light source was a *desk lamp*?

. . . . .

He called her and gave her his new number.

"I knew!" she said. "I called! 734-5109! I called the phone company. Have you missed me?"

Kohlman struggled for an answer.

"Keep a week from Thursday open," she said. "Alyce is giving her first concert performance in the college civic and cultural auditorium in St. George, Utah."

"*Alyce?*" Kohlman asked.

"Alyce Barnett. C.E.O.'s sister."

"Oh," Kohlman said. It was almost too much to imagine: what the sister of C.E.O. Barnett would be like.

"I told C.E.O. we'd be there."

Kohlman said nothing. *Concert.* His mind repeated the word: *concert.* He thought of his once playing the oboe in the Crawford County Youth Orchestra. On warm nights, sometimes, he'd sit, out in a field somewhere on his family's property, caged by corn-stalks, and play . . just *play* . . improvising, imagining himself a person whose *life* was what he was playing: was music. And it would all be, *he* would be . . in another place; in . . *the South of France*! He'd heard a person use that phrase once, had no idea where *the South of France* was, but the sound was perfect. And in the fantasy—in the South of France where his life was music—he'd built a house for his parents . . "on the coast," because he was successful, and because he could afford to: he could free them from work, of all they did that they *had* to do because, to quote his father, "a working farm is a *working* farm," free them of all those things and from all their *civic* activities as well, and, because he was successful, give them their own . . "cottage"—he had liked *that* word too—"cottage" "on the coast." And . . was that right? . . *had* she? . . had *she* been there, in that *south of France* fantasy too? . . with him? . . Pamela?

. . But then, once, one evening, when Kohlman had been in the corn inventing on his oboe, his brother, Adam, had fired their father's shotgun into the stalks, rushes falling all around, and then said: "I thought there were *wolves* eating the crops." Jesus. Come on! *There were no wolves in Iowa!* His brother, Adam, had known that! Wolves! So, then, when Adam had been unable to kill Kohlman "by mistake" in the cornfield,—where were all these memories coming from?—he, *Adam*, had developed a "passion" for classical music, and played the FM from Ames all the time, as loud as he could, when Kohlman was practicing–until Kohlman gave the oboe back to the leader of the Crawford County Youth Orchestra. And Adam had said, when that had happened: "Anyway . . I know more about J. S. Bach than *you* do!"

.　　.　　.　　.　　.

"Do you have a Day Book?" Janice's voice landed like a startling bird on the thin wire of Kohlman's reverie.

Kohlman's thoughts couldn't keep pace.

"Write it in your Day Book. Alyce's concert. Appointment calendar. Whatever. Whatever you use. *October eighteenth*. He wants us the whole day. Because we have to drive over. Make sure everything is okay. The auditorium. Check the piano. Check the sound. Check the acoustics–it's supposed to be very good. Make sure the ticket sales are on schedule. It'll be a full day. C.E.O.'s very excited. Alyce is terrified. Well–not 'terrified.' She'll be fine. She's a determined person. And she's been working incredibly hard. She's amazing."

"I'm going to try and get some sleep finally," Kohlman told her.

"Benjamin: It's dinnertime."

"I know. But . . ."

"I cooked something."

"Listen, Janice: That's very nice, but . . really . . not tonight. I'm sorry. I'm unraveling. My brain feels like it's been in a crockpot. I can't."

There was a mournful silence.

"Come up to my room," Kohlman offered. "Tomorrow. Eight o'clock. Morning. I'll take you somewhere special for breakfast. Then we'll do interviews."

"You're not mad . . are you?" Janice asked.

"No. No; of course not. No; not at all. Why?"

"I just thought . . . You haven't–this sounds stupid, I know, but . . . You haven't found somebody else?"

"No! What do you mean? Who? I don't understand what you're . . . Why would I do that? *Who* else? What would be the point?"

"I'm relieved!" she said. "Benjamin, Benjamin, Benjamin! You don't know how relieved I am."

They agreed upon eight the following morning.

Kohlman lay on his bed. He didn't even take his shoes off. He fell asleep and dreamed of black casino chips, shuttling like rush-hour traffic. There were no people. Only hands. One pair, black, immense. With jewelry. Rings with enormous stones looped by smaller stones. Rings stacked on rings. And though he couldn't see them, he could hear the music of bracelets.

– FIVE –

They had had interviews for four days, and Kohlman had grown more and more unsure about the *center* of the book. *You mean: your "project"?* he could hear Sharon–half a continent away, yet over his shoulder–jeering. He had flown in with such *intent*; it had seemed a possible knock-off, even, but now, when Kohlman would play back a segment of any *one* of the fourteen cassettes, it would baffle him. He'd hear:

. . . . .

I don't mind giving you my life. It's fine. It pleases me . . it's like pure pleasure. Do you know what I'm saying: "Pure"? . . in the sense of "pure"? "Pleasure"? It's very thrilling. Very spiritual. It makes me cry sometimes–when it's happening. What's between us. This giving. This life. It seems very sacred and holy. I once went to church. I once believed very deeply. I suppose I still do. But I'd forgotten. Do you like the word "nimbus"? That was a word I always liked . . when I read it. Yesterday, by the MGM pool . . you had a "nimbus." Did you know that? Did you feel it on you? Say the word for me. . . Really. . . Go ahead, Benjamin. Don't be afraid–don't ever be afraid–of feeling foolish. For me: please: say the word . . "nim . . nimbus." (Himself: "Nimbus.") . . I love it! Did you see the light shift when you said that? It did!

. . . . .

Janice Stewart saw their agreement as a marriage contract. She *said* that. "I gave my life to you," she said. "I gave you my life *exclusively*. It's a beautiful contract. You have me. It's on paper. We both signed. With witnesses! We both have copies! I can't give myself to anyone else!" Their roles reversed. She pumped *him* with questions, wanted more and more of his time. He couldn't get to her crime. Her marriage. Her husband. Her father-in-law. The trial. The night of the fire.

.   .   .   .   .

No, Benjamin, really, I love this. I love giving: my life away. Lives are meant—I believe this; I've thought about it and I believe it— lives are meant to be disseminated. St. Francis broke his life up and fed it to the grackles.

.   .   .   .   .

What the hell was she saying? Hour after hour, she would chatter—animated, no seeming restraint. And it would sound, while the two of them sat with the recorder on beside a flower bank at the Sands, at times even remarkable. Like the most remarkable stuff. Like stuff that sets pages ablaze. But then Kohlman would replay some tape, when he could squeeze time in his room alone at the Ogden House, and it would be . . *crazy*: St. Francis! Gibberish. Four days! With an average taping of ten hours a day! And there had been two more unsigned postcards from his parents: one from Sparks, Nevada, the picture of a trout standing tail-upright in the Truckee River, waving at tourists; the other from Carson City, the state capitol building. Jesus: they were circling him! Kohlman grabbed another "Extraordinary True Story of Violent Crime" book he'd brought as a possible model for his own, a million-seller, soon-to-be-a-major-motion-picture paperback, INSIDE OUT. He cracked its pages to a chapter titled "Holocaust at Home" and read a section of personal testimony:

I mean, like you see all these assholes with their pictures in the paper. White politicians. White models in white dresses. White movie stars. White musicians. Almost the only black folk with their pictures in the morning paper are guys like Jabbar or Patrick Ewing or Tony Dorsett, the Refrigerator—guys the colleges and universities have all fucked over and who've busted their butts to get to the top and who are gonna be over the edge in five years with a coke habit so they got no place to go but to rob liquor stores. And I kept thinking: I wanta get my picture in the morning paper, Man! How about me, Baby! How about

*this boy?! Where's my picture? Where's my money?! Where's my
fame?! I'm gonna cut me up enough pretty white dudes on a spree and
get my picture there!*

.　　.　　.　　.　　.

Janice's testimony was *nothing* like that.

.　　.　　.　　.　　.

She pressed the marriage notion. "It's so wonderful," she said;
"The *first* time . . when I was married the first time . . I never *felt*
like a bride."

Kohlman reasoned. "Janice: this is a *book contract*."

"I know. Exactly. It's so wonderful."

"A business agreement!" he'd say.

"Yes! You're so sweet!"

"Why can't you *see* that?"

"Because it *isn't* that way." And she'd run her fingers, like two
huge combs, back through her hair. "I love you . . ." she'd say. "I
love that this has happened. I love that I've been offered the chance
to *give*, to give myself again. Away! Because . . it's my *life*, and it
should be given—every day . . *more*: every day I have the chance for
more, and not many get that. It's the gift of my *life*."

"Yes, but, Kiddo, really . . !" Kohlman would protest.

"Put my hair in your mouth."

"Excuse me?"

"Put my hair in your mouth. Just for a second. Between your
lips. It will make me feel so wonderful. Please—just for a second.
It's very clean. I washed it this morning."

And Kohlman would, not wanting to disrupt or alienate her—
put her hair softly between his lips, and, it resting there, light as
wind, try to go on, explaining their connection, explaining his distinction between an "exclusive agreement" and a "marriage contract":
"Janice . . No: it's not . . well, of course, no question about it, it is
your *life*, but it's not . . . It's just—I mean, *my* connection with
you, is . . it's . . more *limited* than I think you're seeing it; it's your
story. I'm sorry. It's only your *story*." But while he would try to
explain such things, the light and herbal-scented lashes of her hair
would wrap around his tongue, and only half his words would
have any distinction.

"Benjamin: it's all right," Janice would say. "I'm fine. Don't worry. I can be very good about this—because I know. I can be extremely patient." And she would kiss him.

.　.　.　.　.

He *did*, though, get the facts of her early years. Very established family, established stock. Essex, Connecticut. Father: Head of Immunology at Grace New Haven Hospital. Mother: on innumerable councils and boards—serving: Grace New Haven, the Long Island Sound Chamber Society, the Long Wharf Theatre, the Guild of Connecticut Seascape Painters. And her brother, Philip, had been a New England Perfect Older Brother: Andover, Yale, Rhodes Scholar, two years pitching for the Philadelphia Athletics, a term as State Senator. He'd studied at Wharton, had begun at Goldman Sachs before, at first on a lark, he'd tried film acting. He was due out momentarily in *Dick Tracy III: Flattop*. Interesting. Fascinating. But where had *she* fit?

.　.　.　.　.

I was always there, Benjamin. I was always on the grounds. I tried to find wherever there were patches of sunlight. I loved it under the weeping beech. I could hear the Sound—always—even though it was seven miles away. The Sound was in my head. I was like a tanager there. On the property. Under the trees. Around the clapboarding. I was forced, sometimes, to spend a good deal of time in bed. Starting when I was about fifteen. I was the family tanager. Always trying to find available sunlight. Uncertain of my coloring . . whether it was an advantage or disadvantage. I loved the wind. I was intrigued by insects . . but didn't understand at that time, really, "nourishment." The concept of "nourishment." My father nourished my brother. My mother fed vast populations: she was a global feeder—although she never saw a soul she fed. Nor they her. Because, of course, they were unfed. My brother nourished himself. He's always fed off himself. He's "An Extraordinary Cannibal." I was a weather vane; I was a tachometer . . although my family never read me, really; that's interesting. My brother once said that he would call me "Sleeping Beauty" (because of the time I had to be in bed) . . he would call me "Sleeping Beauty"—if I would just become beautiful. I think that it was a comment he thought funny. I was the daughter in the house.

.   .   .   .   .

"Janice: . . ." Kohlman cleared his throat and said her name, pausing again: "Janice. . . Are you aware you speak, often, elliptically?"

"Oh, yes," Janice said. "Yes. Certainly. Of course. It's a choice. I used to speak very directly. For many, many years. I still do. At times. Sometimes, frequently. I have—spoken directly, that is—often, with you. But it's a choice. You knew that! Didn't you know that? You *must*; you're a writer! As a writer, don't you have to understand . . that people have that choice . . always: . . language?"

Kohlman, in his mind, ran through seven possible responses to what it seemed she'd said. He grew aware of himself doing nothing, simply moving his jaw, rotating it slightly and looking at her. . . "So you felt—to a certain extent—an *outsider* in your family," he said finally. "Is that fair? To a degree? *Unnoticed*?"

Janice smiled. "Is that what people sometimes call: 'capsuling'?" she said.

.   .   .   .   .

Kohlman lost any sense of outline or direction. There was a logic, certainly, that told him he shouldn't predetermine: that the book would be *itself*, its own book, take its own form and be the better, if he just—God, Kohlman hated that phrase!—"went," "found the flow," "let the *book* write *him*." Still, he kept trying to find denominators, handles, foci, loci. What if he spent two weeks with this woman, got a hundred hours of tape, took his plane back to New York, and found that all he had was *metaphors*?

Maybe that . . . METAPHOR WOMAN! No! Terrible! No one would even crack the cover of a book called METAPHOR WOMAN.

.   .   .   .   .

Kohlman went and watched the Challenger train one afternoon. He loved the rotunda entranceway into the grounds of Caesar's Palace: the tanned men in white suits always polishing the brass, the gladiator with his spear standing there to welcome visitors; then the walking sidewalk, tunneling first through the diorama of ancient Rome with its holograms, the looped basso voice: "Enter Caesar's World," the strange and futuristic approaching dome of the Omnimax Theatre. It was like being in a landscape, surrounded by an architecture which was (the landscape and the architecture) imagining, as you were right there *in* it, things it might, on impulse, decide to *be*.

He watched from the parking-lot/training-camp grandstand for an hour and a half and nothing happened; the Challenger simply stayed in his crouch. Two days before, Kohlman had been having a late-afternoon fifty-cent shrimp cocktail at the Golden Gate and the Challenger had been there, suddenly, behind him, pulling his head back in a playful lock. "So everything's okay?" the Challenger had said. "Fine," Kohlman had said, and the Challenger had literally almost vanished.

. . . . .

On the evening of the day Kohlman again watched the Challenger, he explored the Frontier. He wanted to move inside different motifs. If he was going to write the virtual *world* of Las Vegas, he needed images. There were always the issues—and having learned what he had about the marketplace, he knew their importance—issues of verisimilitude and of texture. So, in line with that understanding, he was going to the Frontier—walking past the Castaways, which was beginning to be torn down, and past the Fashion Mall.

From the inside, the Frontier felt casual. It was massive. Or there was the *sense* of the massive. And of space. It was busy— rough, congenial, milling. All the security personnel wore stars as badges. The dealers wore bandannas. There was more noise than at Caesar's. But the crowd seemed happy, enjoying it, all pleasantly boisterous. *Whoops* went up from the dice tables, but they didn't grate on Kohlman. It seemed like the kind of place where noise could flourish. Walking through the crowd, and just because he thought it would be uncharacteristic and momentarily amuse him, he let out a "Yeah! All right!!"

Other cheerful voices answered, joined him as a friend, made a spread community . . fun: *Yeah all right! . . Yeah all right . . Yeahallright!*

But then, suddenly, the din turned. An impression, muted, at the edge, grew to a dim panic . . somewhere, rumbling and spreading. Kohlman couldn't place it, but he knew that something-people-were-finding-frightening was stirring the air. Had he caused it? Had he stopped the fun just by letting a little craziness out?

Abruptly, two doors, at the east end of the casino, flanked by signs reading SIGFRIED & ROY and BEYOND BELIEF, burst apart. Space cleared. And in it, suddenly—as sudden as the instant, amethyst pony in his child's book—was a huge, white Bengal tiger. The tiger charged. Players screamed. The white tiger leapt to a dice table, stood frozen, confused. It had such life force in it! Even its eyes shone white . . then shone red; it seemed to be gauging a thousand measurements; it roared. Kohlman felt his whole throat go soft, go liquid. The immense white tiger rose from the table and bounded again, racing across the casino space, scattering crowds, scattering cocktail waitresses, strollers. A shrieking wave followed the cat. It chased the remarkable cat—beyond the casino pit, beyond visibility. At the casino entrance, Kohlman could see the tops of two glass, electronic doors divide, then could hear, echoing back into where he stood, *"He's out! . . He's out! . . He's out!"*

For maybe twenty seconds, the terror inside held and measured itself. It was a spent, brain-dead, exhausted quiet. But then the bells on the slot machines started to ring again; the dealers' voices again called their games. The pleasant, random noise of the Frontier—in a blink and as if by some built-in homeostatic law or circuit breaker thrown again to its *off* position—was reestablished.

· · · · ·

Out on Las Vegas Boulevard squad cars converged: one, two, three, four, five, six—their lights slicing, blinding the huge, the titanic white cat, circling, locking him, officers bringing him down, keeping him down, with tranquilizer darts.

· · · · ·

It troubled Kohlman that every time they met an aquaintance Janice introduced him as: "My betrothed: Benjamin." He'd tried, once, to explain. But it had only gotten complicated, more confused. So he'd just taken to letting it go by. He tried to argue in his own head that it meant nothing. It was harmless. He would finish his interviews; time would run its course; everything would fall into some sort of proper place and be fine.

· · · · ·

"So are you saying about your family, then . . ." Kohlman felt the need to bear down: "Are you saying . . about your growing up in your home in Essex—that you felt they took no . . substantial *note*? Of you? That you weren't validated? That you felt little or no sense of being *integrated* into any sort of *family structure*?"

"That's an interesting question, Benjamin."

"No, but, is that—I mean when you talk about being a *tanager*, being a *tachometer,* your brother calling you 'Sleeping Beauty'—are you essentially saying that you were made to feel that you were just some extraneous *object* in that house?"

"I was an extraneous object. I was the daughter. I was the daughter in a New England family with a firstborn Perfect Son."

"No, but:—well, I see what you're saying—but what I'm trying to ask is . . ."

"Benjamin: I was a tanager. That's very precise. If you think about it, you'll realize that there isn't really a much better way I could put it. I came to the feeder occasionally . . and they looked *at me."*

"Of course, but . . . But okay, but then: *that* . . that state . . made you feel . . *how*? Angry? Did that sort of . . exclusion—is "exclusion" a fair word?"

"Is it important to writers that words be *fair*? That seems ridiculous! Camus would never think that! Or the Apostle Mark! Mark! Mark says: 'If any man have ears to hear, let him hear.' Let him hear the *truth*—never mind 'fair'! Did you think language was a democracy?!"

"Well, no; of course not. But I . . ."

"You never felt like an object in *your* house?"

"Well . . actually, that's an interesting question."

"You felt, then, 'totally integrated into your family structure'?"

"Well, my family was . . I guess still *is* . . quite . . they're *different* than I was, *am* . . constitutionally."

"Constitutionally. I see. So, then, language *is* a democracy for you."

"I wasn't saying . . ."

"But still, you felt 'totally integrated'—even though you were different."

"Well, I didn't feel that I didn't *belong* in my family: if that's what you mean." Kohlman, suddenly—although, these days, *sudden* was more common a thing—found himself angry.

"Tell me the ways in which you *belonged* in your family, then. I'd be interested. Maybe it was because you were a male. Males tend to *belong* more. But I suppose that's *to the World*, really. Not restricted to American Families."

"What are you getting at?" Kohlman said.

"What am *I* getting at?" she asked.

"Yes."

"Benjamin, my darling, my love, my dearest and my betrothed: I'm not getting at *any*thing. You're interviewing me, and I'm just trying to answer you."

"Right," Kohlman said. He was sweating, *waves* of sweat, breaking in a clear rhythm with his heartbeat, not the slow dripping kind. "Right," he said. "I'm interviewing you . . and you're . . simply responding. Thanks for reminding me."

There was a pause. Kohlman thought he could hear his sweat *forming* . . inside his brow.

Janice nudged him. "Let's finish," she said. "You were asking . . how my being excluded *felt*. *Is* that what you were asking? Is that what you want me to respond to?"

"Right. Did that . . right: it *was* the exclusion. Did that make you feel . . ? Well, what I wanted to ask, of course is: . . ." Kohlman's breath felt like a medicine ball. "How *did* it make you feel?" He felt as if he'd just been playing pickup basketball with much stronger men. "I don't mean: what did it make you feel *like*?: you've answered that; you've spoken about that. But . . how would you characterize . . ?" His mind was swimming. Thoughts unlocked their parts and fell in pieces. Kohlman felt years of agility with language abandon him absolutely, capriciously. He wanted to punch something. "How would you characterize . . is what I mean . . the *long-term* emotional response? What *built up in you* . . as a result of feeling you were a tanager?" He thought he might scream.

She smiled. She brushed his cheek with her fingertips. "*What built up was*," she said, ". . *an incredible appreciation for season and climate. For wind. For light. I suppose: for any of the basic conditions of nurturing environment.*"

Kohlman felt he couldn't go on. But such a feeling was crazy. He needed to go on; he went on. "So . . . ." Had the word come out? His throat was so dry; his vocal cords seemed so detached. Had he made any sound? He started again: "So . . why were you forced, sometimes, to stay in bed?"

"I wasn't forced—no—did I say 'forced'? I was *told*."

"Okay. Okay." His tiredness began to feel unrelieved. "Okay.
. . Thanks. . . But *why*?"

"*Eve.*"

"Excuse me?"

"*Eve.*"

"I'm sorry . . but I guess I'm not getting, precisely, what you
mean by . . . 'Eve': What is that referring to: What is that trying to
describe: 'Eve'?"

"*Eve* is what my mother said."

"I see. About . . ? . . about what?"

" '*Eve's disease.*' "

"So . . ?"

"She said that it was fine. That many had it. Many women.
That it had happened before. Not infrequently. In history. She said
I had 'Eve's Disease.' "

"So . . then . . what *is* 'Eve's disease'?" Kohlman was trying to
slow his breathing—as best he could.

"What I had."

"Jesus, *Janice*!" Kohlman exploded yet again. He heard violence firing his voice and wanted to be another person, not the
person speaking, not someone who had raised his voice to such an
open and undefended woman. He wanted to be by himself, alone.
"I'm sorry," he said. "It's inappropriate. I was just . . ."

Janice touched either side of her head. "These," she said.
"These are what I'm talking about. My headaches."

"Of course," Kohlman said. Now his voice sounded ashamed.
He hated his emotional veering; maybe he should just *send* her
tapes with his questions . . let her answer them on other tapes,
send them back.

"Mother said they had to do with the 'sin of Eve,' " she said.
"And with menstruating. It started them. *They* started. It. Is it 'it'
or 'they'?"

"I'm not sure."

"I had blood tests. I had a lot of things: hypnosis . . mercury,
arsenic . . other poisons: laudanum. Some days I couldn't stand
up. And so I stayed in bed, was told to stay. My father knew. He
paid all the specialist bills. Still, my mother said I was never to
mention it . . them. She said: 'It's a woman's matter.' " Janice drew
a deep breath, and it startled Kohlman: that a woman would have
the same respiratory habit he had, seizures, almost, of intake. She

threw her head back, looked up at the sky, and seemed to want to take all of *it* in as well, draw in as much ethereal distance and light as would come to her. She rotated her neck. She smiled.

"Did you . . ?" Kohlman felt curiously guilty for interrupting what appeared to be a new luxury now in her breathing. He wasn't aware that, with himself, the intake reflex completed its course in any pleasure.

"Did I what?" Janice asked.

"Never mind," Kohlman said.

"No: what? Did I *what?*"

"Get the nosebleeds too? Then. Back then," he said.

"Oh, yes. Yes. And sometimes in my mouth. Blood there. On my tongue. On the walls of my cheeks."

Kohlman tasted blood in *his* mouth. He tasted, too, somewhere, the dirt that he had eaten some days before. He nodded. "Hard," he said. "Painful."

"There isn't a word," Janice smiled. "Anywhere." She smiled again; she seemed to be working on it. "For what it was. For what it felt like. I've looked for one . . for almost twenty years, but . . nothing. 'Hard.' 'Painful.' I say both those words, and they make me laugh." She laughed. " 'Eve's disease.' " She laughed again. Her eyes had tears.

.   .   .   .   .

Later that same day, a call came to Kohlman, in his room alone, at the Ogden House, while he was trying to piece together his tapes and notes, trying to do something with the blood imagery, trying to write something with a center, with coherence. The voice sounded fractured and muffled, threatening and dangerous. Its sound triggered images: torn strips of aluminum siding, razored glass: "Mr. Kohlman . . ." it began.

Kohlman wasn't sure. He waited, the ragged images breaking in his head. He thought the voice intended to go on. It didn't. ". . Yes?" Kohlman finally said.

"Mr. Kohlman . . ." the voice said again.

"Yes?" Kohlman could taste an enzyme coating on his tongue.

"Hello?" the voice said.

"Hello," Kohlman said. "Who . . ? To whom am I speaking, please?"

"I understand you're in town," the voice said.

"Obviously," Kohlman said. Again, his control threshold wavered and an anger loomed, began slowly to seep in.

"I understand you're in town asking questions," the grated voice said.

Kohlman paused. He saw the words on his computer monitor arrange and rearrange themselves, shift their density and their light. He focused a sentence he'd written: *Certainly to be close to her—is to be close to blood.* What was that attempting? What had he meant? Why had he written the word *close* twice? Symmetry? Balance? Was balance an important element in his kind of style? What had he meant to say?

"I understand you're in town"—the voice started up again—". . asking questions about the hotel fires."

"No," Kohlman said. "No. No; that's wrong. *Not* the hotel fires."

"Take a trip," the voice said.

"What are you talking about?" Kohlman said.

"Take a trip, any trip . . away. Don't stay here. This isn't where you want to be," the voice said.

"Hey, look . . !" Kohlman began. Some riveting gunned across the street, high above, on the El Cortez Hotel expansion.

"Take a trip," the voice drove on: "Take a trip, any trip; don't let me see the trip; put the trip back in the deck, shuffle the deck, forget you were ever here—or someone's going to find the trip and find you . . and that is not the card you want. This is not a place to ask questions about hotel fires."

"*I am not* . . !" Kohlman had had *enough* of elusive and cryptic bullshit! He had had enough of run-on sentences! "*I am not asking questions about any hotel fires!*" he shouted.

"Are you here?"

"Yes!" Kohlman said.

"Are you in Las Vegas?"

"Stick it in your nose!" Kohlman shouted again. What was happening? Sharon would laugh: *Is this the same Benjamin Kohlman I've known and fucked?* "Am I in Las Vegas?!" Kohlman let his shouting reach the limit of his lungs. "Am I in Las Vegas: Is that what you're asking?!"

"Are you in Las Vegas?"

"Yes! Of course! *Obviously* I'm in Las Vegas! What are you talking about?!"

"Are you asking questions?"

"About . . ?"

"Fires?"

"Yes, but . . !"

"*But* . . !" The voice shot the contraction like a magnum. "*But* people heard you *ask* those questions. *But* people heard you use the word 'fire.' So, I'm saying . . ."

"*But* . . !" Kohlman shot the contraction back. "*But* I am *not* asking questions about *those* fires, the *hotel* fires!" Kohlman said. "I am writing a *book*! The person I'm interviewing . . . Yes: there *is* a fire that figures in the book, *but* . . ."

"*But* . . !"

"Jesus Christ! *But* it is not a fire anywhere near Las Vegas. It's a fire all the way on the other side of the goddamn country! In a *residence*. You know what a *residence* is? It's *not* a hotel! Maybe people don't have *residences* out here in this crazy city: But it's a *house*. It's a *home*."

"All fires are connected."

"What the hell are you . . ?! Who the hell *is* . . ?!"

"Get out of town. *I*'m serious. That's all I'm saying. Get out now."

Kohlman heard the connection break. He was red-faced. It was insane: A figure from an espionage movie calling up and threatening. It was a *wax museum*! The city was a back alley for *side shows*! What did it mean? He wasn't giving up his book. Some scumbag creephole eavesdrops and misunderstands!? Get serious! People saying things like: "Get out of town," "Take a trip"?! How could you take people like that seriously?! If you did–here, any-where–you'd live under your bed. "*Take your own trip, Man!*" Kohlman shouted to his walls; the back of his shirt was weighted with sweat.

His phone rang again. He grabbed it. "*What!*" Kohlman barked.

"I think you should send me flowers," Janice said. "It would be nice. It would be sweet. It would be appropriate. Couples should do things like that for one another. Would you like *me* to send *you* flowers? I'd be happy to."

"I can't talk right now," Kohlman said.

"Have you lost your voice?"

"No. Please. This is a bad time." He hung up.

. . . . .

A rap on his Ogden House room door, fifteen minutes later, startled Kohlman's shaving. He had taken a shower, which he did often when he was upset or anxious. *Did you get it all off?* Sharon, when they lived together, would ask, her grin wicked as only the grin of a woman like Sharon might be: *Anything left for me to scrape down . . or did you get it all?* she'd say. Kohlman had begun the shower habit when he was a boy. It was his father's habit, had always been. Kohlman could almost hear the shower running, his father in it, the curious dampness in the air, and his mother saying: "If you're looking for your father, he's in the shower." It had always seemed like such an illogical statement: *If you're looking for your father, he's* . . . But his father's showers were a regular thing. In the dark house in the morning before he'd go out, in coveralls, and down, into the waking land . . and in the dark house nights, after having said grace and, most nights only grace during the eating of his evening meal . . they would occur. Kohlman remembered himself: playing basketball at church and being the smallest player on either team, then standing in the shower, feeling as he supposed his father must daily feel, tired, standing, a boy trying to feel the skin of a man, for sometimes half an hour.

Kohlman moved to his room door hesitantly. "Yes?" he said. A cartoon fantasy – born in the reading of too many "true-crime-of-passion" stories and watching too many miniseries *based* on such "truth" – half-expected a hail of gunshots to rip jagged holes in the hollow-frame door.

The voice on the other side was unmistakable. It was C.E.O. Barnett's, shaking anything not sunk in concrete like a viola string. "Open this," it said.

Kohlman opened the door.

Barnett stood there in a brown three-piece herringbone. "Get your things together," he said.

Kohlman stared. ". . Was it you?" he asked.

"Was it me – *what?*" Barnett strode into the room and looked around. "Send Janice flowers," he said. "It's only right. Would you like me to send them for you? She likes calla lillies, lavender, and larkspur. She can take or leave the long-stem roses."

"Did she talk to you about . . ?"

"Come on . . come on!" Barnett rolled his hand in a gesture to move Kohlman along.

"Are you the person who just called me? A few minutes ago? And told me to get out of town? And shouted *but*?" Kohlman said.

"No; but I was listening," Barnett said. He accelerated his gesture. "Don't . . would you move it along, please? And not dawdle?" he said; "I heard a woman in a supermarket say that once to her kid: *Would you not dawdle*?! It means: move your ass and don't fuck around."

Kohlman was staring.

"I have a tap on your phone," Barnett explained. "It's connected to a pagette. I listen in. I'm concerned about Janice. I'm concerned that you treat her the way she needs to be treated. – When people make calls . . like what you just got, in this city, they're very serious. It means *shit* that they may have jumped to a conclusion. These kinds of people: they're just trying to *get* to a conclusion *however*–jump, run, take a cab, windsurf!–it doesn't matter! They're just trying to *be* at a conclusion . . before someone beats them *to* it! Get your things. I've made arrangements. There'll be a cab outside. Everything else–once you get in the cab–will take care of itself." C.E.O. Barnett cleared his throat. The window glass ballooned out with his final words: "Mr. Kohlman: Please! I'm serious here! I know the world I live in! Move!"

Kohlman pulled the soft luggage cases from under his bed and began to fold and hang items.

"Just throw things in," C.E.O. said. "Toss them. You'll be taking them out again in just a few minutes."

Kohlman resented Barnett. Still, he complied. The phone rang. Barnett took the call. "Yes?" he said. Kohlman could see him listening with a special scrutiny. "Did it even occur to you . . ?" he heard Barnett finally saying, ". . to ask whether this was the person you assumed it was? –Just a minute." Barnett held the phone out to Kohlman. Kohlman gestured to know, but Barnett was unresponsive.

"Hello . . ?" Kohlman said.

It was Kohlman's brother, Adam, the Distinguished Professor of American History, calling from Ann Arbor. He was arriving in Las Vegas in the morning to deliver a paper at the Meeting of American Colonial Historians. "When I didn't get any response at your apartment in New York, I called Sharon's studio," he said. "I found she'd disconnected herself from whatever your common-law bond might have been more than three weeks ago."

What did she say? What did she say about it? How was she feeling?! Kohlman wanted to asked. But he said nothing.

"It's remarkable," his professor-brother lectured on, ". . what Caprice and Venality and Lack of Obligation can engender, given the opportunity. I think you must, really, be some sort of paradigm: the Emblematic Post–Civil War, Post-Industrial American."

What in the world was his brother, Adam, saying?

"Perhaps," his brother went on: "I should do some sort of comparative study–given the fraternal access–but I'm not sure I could bring myself to it, Benjamin."

Kohlman opened his mouth to respond.

"Sharon was very amusing–given Sharon, of course. She said you'd gone off to work on some sort of tabloid, prurient, underbelly-of-the-culture potboiler in Las Vegas."

Barnett was hurling all of Kohlman's clothes into the luggage *for* Kohlman. He was shaking his head, like a father of a son who dismays him in his inability to take care of himself.

". . Am I supposed to . . ." Kohlman imagined his brother, Adam, pacing and gesturing as he talked. "Am I supposed to see your life-style as Faustian in some way, Benjamin? See you appended to some sort of Postmodern tradition of Romanticism? Well, I don't. You're a Carny. You're a tent-man. Midways, trumped-up ecstasy and snake oil: You're a Rainmaker. Why do you have this need? Why not attempt a little maturity in your life: you might enjoy it."

Barnett was giving Kohlman more *move it along!* hand signals in the background.

"At any rate," his brother, Adam, went on, "I have a day before I give my paper, and I thought maybe we might spend it together. It's a gesture. I tell people we're 'alienated,' but I know that's not really true. I can't imagine you have more important things to do, but if you do, I'll certainly accept your saying that you do if you need to do that . . and respect it and understand."

"What time's your plane get in?" Kohlman asked. He was surprised by the flatness and lack of body in his own voice.

"Nine-forty-five. Western," his brother said.

"I'll be there," Kohlman said and hung up.

.   .   .   .   .

He carried his two bags, his Nagra recorder, and his Compaq computer into the lobby. He paid his bill. He still had the money he'd won at the Riviera, over eight thousand, in his wallet. When he dragged his luggage out onto the street there was, indeed, a cab waiting, and he entered it.

On the way to McCarran, the cabbie said: "There's a cabbie hat and jacket in the back there. . . Put them on. . . Throw your sportcoat over into the front. . . Don't worry; it'll get sent back. Keep your wallet; don't forget that. . . When we get to the airport, I'll be grabbing some other luggage out of the trunk. Leave yours where it is. . . I'll pay you for the ride. . . Then you take this cab to the Maxim Casino. . . There's a reservation for you there under the name of . .'Jack Napoleon.' 'Jack . . Napoleon.' . . Mr. Barnett's made all the arrangements. Register and check in."

Kohlman complied – the whole scenario: switch at the airport, drive down Las Vegas Boulevard, turning onto Flamingo for Maxim's, registering under the Jack Napoleon reservation. When he opened the door to his room, it was a suite. And there was champagne and fresh fruit there for him in a pewter bowl. He called room service. "I'd like to send some flowers to somebody," he said.

.   .   .   .   .

He called Janice.

"Benjamin: I'm meditating," she said. "You know what time it is. You know it's just before I go to work. Why are you doing this?"

"Just answer one thing," Kohlman said.

"All right," she said. "But, please: not again. Respect me. Respect my quiet time. Reflection is the light we make out of light, and you know I believe that. What's the question?"

Reflection is the light we make out of light . . ?

"Were you in his house, your father-in-law's house . . the night of the fire . . the night your father-in-law died?"

"Yes," she said.

"Thank you," Kohlman said. "Thank you. I feel now . . that I have at least one piece of critical information. Or at least . . ."

"No. You're right," she said. "You're correct. It *is* critical."

"I thought . . . Oh, and listen: I can't see you tomorrow."

"You can't . . ?"

"My brother, for some reason, is going to be in town."

– SIX –

Kohlman drank half his champagne; he ate a peach, set up his word processor and his recorder. He showered. He stood at his south wall of glass and watched the lights and light reflections, a half block away, on Bally's Grand. His room was a corner room on the eleventh floor. He slid a glass door open and walked out onto his small balcony, high above the traffic of Flamingo Boulevard. He could see the pool at the Flamingo, glittering like a sapphire. He thought he heard a gunshot from the street. If someone should ever push him from this balcony, he would never survive. He went inside and showered again. Now, whatever postcards his parents sent him would not reach him.

He dressed; he drank more champagne; he ate a kiwi. He booted his files up on his computer; the sentence at the top of the screen read: "*All that is needed — in terms of strength — is to light a match.*" Had he seen Janice as strong? Had he seen Janice as frail but trying to make a point? Was he judging her? Which would he rather conclude, finally: that she had burned the Levinworth manse with absolute and clear intention . . or that she had not? He couldn't do anything with the sentence; he couldn't do anything with his questions, so he took the elevator down to the casino.

·   ·   ·   ·   ·

"Good evening, Mr. Napoleon!" several of the management immediately met him: "Good evening, Mr. Napoleon," "Good evening, Mr. Napoleon!" Kohlman responded: "Good evening." What had C.E.O. Barnett set up? Who did they think he was?

What sort of background? What sort of history? Under the name and inside the fiction: who were any of these people assuming him to be: who was the person?

"Nice to see you, Mr. Napoleon!"

"Right! Thank you! Nice to see *you*."

He strolled the casino. He sat down to play and lost a hundred dollars immediately. "Better luck," the dealer said.

"Thank you," Kohlman said.

He was terrified. That was the simple truth of what he felt: Somebody had threatened his life; here in this city where any convention he'd known didn't apply—where to be amused, where to be ironic, where to be detached, where to be *informed*, even, would serve, it seemed, nothing. Someone had called and made it clear that, unless Kohlman left town, he would die. It made him angry: *Voices* walking into his life! Presuming! Ordering! Being flippant! Talking in codes! Trying to position him . . or remove him! Was he being melodramatic? Barnett, in so many words, had said *no*, and Kohlman now believed that Barnett, in such essential ways, could be trusted.

He went to walk outside, but a man in a sharkskin suit stopped him. "What can I get for you, Mr. Napoleon?"

"I'm fine," Kohlman said. "Everything's good."

"Where were you thinking of going?"

"I was just going for a walk."

"There's a wind outside like you wouldn't believe."

Kohlman got the message. He strolled the casino a bit longer, had a brandy, and caught the Maxim management watching. He said goodnight to people, took an elevator to the eleventh floor, took a staircase back down again to the arcade below the casino. He used a back exit. Outside, there was no wind.

Passing every open lot, he felt accelerated terror and, perhaps more than terror, an irritation that the ignorance of others should so confine him! And eyes! From somewhere he felt the hot rivet of eyes. Well: he would *not* give up this book. Whoever! Whatever! He had planned the project; he had set it up for nearly eighteen months, and he would not simply get on a plane now and walk away. The metallic taste, nevertheless, in his mouth, was no small thing; Barnett's last words had been: "This shit's no fun. I know; I live here. Transactions!"

Kohlman walked to Caesar's. "Do you have the Challenger staying here?" he asked at the desk.

"Do you mean . . as in 'The Challenger'?" the desk clerk said.

"Yes."

"He is: yes."

"Could you tell me his room number, please?"

"No, sir. We can't do that." The clerk smiled at him—as if the smile might send him away. But Kohlman stayed. "If you would like . . you can get on one of the house telephones." She pointed to a row of white wall phones. "And we can put you through to his room."

Kohlman thanked her.

. . . . .

The Challenger answered on the fourth ring. "Say what?" he said.

Kohlman froze. He had rehearsed an introduction but it swept away.

"Is this my man?" the Challenger asked. "Don't be afraid. Is this my Savior? . . I know that my Redeemer liveth," the Challenger laughed. "My man; my man!" he chided: "Don't be afraid: Say who."

"This is . . ." Kohlman's throat was dry. He cleared it. He knew the Challenger knew who he was—but he needed to say. "This is the person . . from the slot machine," he said.

"The Phantom of the Opera! The Ghost in the Slot Machine!" The Challenger laughed. "I know! I got it! I knew! My man!"

"Yes," Kohlman said. "Can I see you?"

. . . . .

Kohlman rode the North Tower elevator to the top floor, where the corridors were disconcertingly still. He could see a bank of surveillance cameras, a field of electronic eyes on either corridor side of the Challenger's door. He moved toward the room. Twenty-five feet away, he triggered an electronic voice: "Think twice!" it said: "Think twice. You are on screen. You are being observed. Think twice."

The Challenger's broadcast voice upstaged the electronic. "It's all right, my man," his voice said. "Keep walkin'. Keep on comin'.

It's fine. Walk slow. The Spirit from the Slot Machine! Leave your hand on the doorknob for twenty seconds. Turn it. Open it. Come in. Just move cool. Just move slowly."

Kohlman followed the instructions. The Challenger's door swung in easily. "Come in!" he heard the Challenger call.

The Challenger was immersed in an immense jacuzzi centered in his suite.

"Close the door," he told Kohlman.

Kohlman did.

"Come in!" the Challenger said. "Drop your silks! Get yo'self nekked; plenty 'a room in here; join me!"

"I'd rather . . ."

"Git *in* here." The Challenger bellowed the command good-naturedly.

"Not tonight," Kohlman said.

"Some *other* time," the Challenger smiled.

"Possibly."

"When you *up* to it. When you *up* to bein' in the *soup* with the Challenger. Right?"

Kohlman stepped closer.

"So what's the line, here?" the Challenger asked. "What's happening? What's the concern? You're in trouble, my friend: and I can see that: and I want to help you!"

Kohlman told his story: his interviews, the phone call, the warning, C.E.O. Barnett's intervention. He paced the suite, talking, speaking, mostly, to the north wall of glass. Motion—when he was trying to say something difficult or complex or important—was another habit Sharon teased him about. *Jesus, Benjamin, stand still! You afraid I'm going to grab you in mid-thought or something? And what if I do?*

It's a habit.

Right. Good. That's what the rapist said.

I need to move to think.

How American!

The Challenger focused his eyes on the spackled ceiling all the while Kohlman paced and recounted, and when Kohlman finally finished, the Challenger lowered his head. "I tried to pretend it was just bullshit," Kohlman said. "I tried to pretend I didn't take it seriously. To myself. But I do. I take it seriously. I'm scared."

"You're wise." The Challenger nodded.

"And my brother's coming into town tomorrow, " Kohlman went on. "We don't, actually, get along. But he called. And he wanted to see me. He made the gesture. I *take* it as a gesture; what else should I think? I said I'd pick him up at the airport. I don't want to just *hide out* in my room."

"You're *right*—to do that. You're right to feel that way. You're wise." The Challenger stood in his jacuzzi. All of him was immense. His body was a body cut and polished from marble. And why hadn't Kohlman seen it before? He had no hair. He was a sculpture. He glistened. He stepped from the jacuzzi, reached for a gold, initialed towel. ". . So I came here," Kohlman said, finally, after a silence.

"Wise. You're wise. You knew the rules. You're extremely wise," the Challenger kept repeating. "Wise."

"So then, but . . what do I do?" Kohlman asked.

The Challenger toweled. "Close your eyes," he said.

"What?"

"Close your eyes."

Kohlman closed his eyes. This was a man with whom obedience seemed an uncomplicated act.

"Your eyes closed?"

"My eyes are closed."

"Stand very still."

Kohlman stood still.

"Good. Good. Now: image. You know what I'm saying?"

"I'm not . . ?"

"Image. Imagine. See. Image a volcano."

"I'm sorry . . ?"

"Image a volcano. Image the rim of a volcano. Get the picture: Image of the rim of a volcano—*see* it—*get* it—you're lookin' down *into* it—get that in your mind."

Kohlman tried. He saw some color, some reds. But it all kept turning back into the image, when he'd stood moments before, of the Challenger. Suddenly Kohlman felt the Challenger's thumbs hard behind his ears.

"Keep your eyes closed!" the huge man instructed.

Kohlman clamped his eyes shut again. He felt the Challenger's other fingers playing his temples like a cathedral organ.

"Now go for it . . go for that image again: the rim . . the *rimtherimtherim*," his voice beat: "the volcano. Go. Work . . work for it."

Then suddenly it came! Molten rock seething, terrifying. Kohlman felt his skin prick then go waxy.

"Good! I can tell you got it!" the Challenger said. "Good. Excellent." The giant took *Kohlman*'s hands—releasing his own, canceling the volcano—and set them against the sides of Kohlman's head, placing them in the bone depressions where his own had been. "Now play . . play with the pressure . . play around with the different pressures until it comes again."

Kohlman did. The volcano, rim and lava, came. And then a . . flower of sorts, an adrenalin surge—blooming, contained, delicate, huge—came with it.

"Good!" the Challenger moved Kohlman's hands away. "Now try again." He returned Kohlman's hands to the proper places.

Kohlman tried. The image happened. The sweet infusion came.

"Good." Again, the Challenger lowered Kohlman's hands. "Now try it yourself."

Kohlman tried. He groped his skull, his temples. He found the depressions. The images came.

"They're there—aren't they?! *It*'s there."

"Yes!"

"Good. —Again."

Kohlman repeated. He found the pattern more easily.

"Good. Again."

Kohlman repeated.

"Excellent. Good. Now open your eyes."

Kohlman opened his eyes. The Challenger handed him a smooth rock about the size of his fist.

"Squeeze that," the Challenger said.

"What?"

"Squeeze that. Slowly. Focus. Hard as you can."

Kohlman squeezed. The rock turned to talc in his hand. He felt his heart surge. The Challenger nodded . . then smiled.

"Exactly," he said. "So—if I'm not around—do that."

"But how . . ?

"If . . I'm . . not . . around . . do . . that." The Challenger slowed his voice so that it was like the *memory* of a voice.

"But so . . how does it work?" Kohlman couldn't help himself; he asked.

"Just remember. Remember it. You get in a tough situation— I'm not there—remember what you just did; remember how to do that . . I'll probably usually *be* there . . but you should be okay."

Kohlman nodded. He closed his eyes. He set his fingers to the side of his head. He found the image. He dropped his hands and opened his eyes again. "Do you have another rock?" he asked. The Challenger handed it to him. A second time he reduced the rock to powder. Kohlman nodded to himself again. He felt drugged. He felt wonderful. He felt no need to pace . . or to take a shower . . or to draw in air.

"Get some sleep," the Challenger said and clapped him on one shoulder.

Kohlman couldn't stop nodding.

The Challenger walked him to his door, opened it. "Main thing," the Challenger said in parting, "is . . only use that when you have to. Don't get eager. Don't get hungry. You'll get yourself in trouble."

"Right," Kohlman said. "This is amazing. This is really . . ."

"Be well."

"I have friends who meditate . . but I never actually . . . Thank you."

"Be fine," the Challenger said.

"I appreciate it," Kohlman said.

"Be the person in charge," the Challenger said. "That's all you need to think about. That's all you need to work for."

Kohlman smiled at the Challenger. It was a shy smile. The door shut.

. . . . .

When Kohlman walked back into the Maxim, one of the floor managers greeted him. "Mr. Napoleon," the man said. "We were concerned! We were worried about you."

"I'm fine," Kohlman said. "I was just getting some air."

. . . . .

C.E.O. Barnett and a child in an evening gown were in Kohlman's room. "Wear this," Barnett told Kohlman and produced a blond Afro wig and a blond beard. When Kohlman balked, Barnett helped Kohlman, moved him to the mirror. "This is good quality stuff," Barnett said: "Excellent hair. Looks good. —This is my sister, Alyce—the concert pianist . . whose first concert you're going with us to see in two days."

"How do you do," Kohlman said to the image in his mirror. *Twelve?* Had Barnett said she was just . . ?

"Very pleased," Alyce said.

"Wear this," C.E.O. insisted, of the hairpieces. "Whenever you go out—wear this: Nothing will happen. You'll look totally like somebody else. —How do you like Alyce's gown?"

Kohlman turned from the mirror and looked directly at C.E.O. Barnett's sister. She looked displaced: as if someone had slipped the child-that-she-was into the dress of a torch singer and had said: "Wait." As if, had she been a boy, she'd worn full football pads. The gown was expensive. "It's . . good," Kohlman said. "It's . . nice." What was he telling her?

"I hate the straps!" Barnett said. "The straps'll cut into her every time she runs arpeggios. We've got an appointment right now to get the straps changed." He moved with Alyce toward the door. "Remember—if you go out—put that on."

Kohlman nodded. "What do I owe for this room?" he asked.

"We'll worry about that when the time comes," C.E.O. said.

"Very pleased to have met you," Alyce Barnett said again from the threshold.

"Catch you tomorrow, Jan!" Barnett barked in toward the bath.

"Night, C.E.O.!" Janice's voice came. Then Kohlman heard the water run.

Barnett and his sister vanished.

•   •   •   •

Kohlman listened to Janice's toothbrushing; he listened to her humming under it. His mind felt empty. He had no idea what he would do.

When she appeared at the threshold, finally, she wore a robe of blue satin, her body shadowing under it. There were pearls at her ears and a cross of pearls on a gold chain around her neck. "It seemed the right time," she said. Her voice had a body which, though soft, was almost palpable. "It was my free night. And I had been thinking about it. And it seemed time," she repeated.

"Janice . . ." Kohlman said.

"It's been eight days," she said.

Kohlman tried but couldn't talk. She moved to him. She set her arms on his neck, drew herself in, set her lips to him; her mouth, softer than any woman's he had ever kissed, lips that seemed so unresistantly to wrap his lips, fit around them, hold them. Her mouth was sweet. Kohlman felt a dizzying, a weightlessness, a drift. He vaguely, in the first moment, thought to voice resistance. But the impulse went. With other women, he had always seen the moment in advance, worked its arrival, moved along a known anatomy. But this was different. Where were they? On the bed? The floor? Whose hands . . his? . . Janice's? He saw the volcano at one point: *Jesus: What would happen? Would he crush her? Would her bones turn to chalk? No!* Who had initiated . . ? Where were . . ? What . . ? Suddenly, in a wrapped union Kohlman had never foreseen, he found himself, pleasurably, wondering whether he would make his next breath, be able to draw it. His bloodstream felt absolutely conductive: a question gloriously coursing there—whether he would be able to withstand it all and remain alive.

But of course he did. They did. All with incredible softness. A gliding ease.

After, Janice only made sounds: hummings, nuzzlings. There was none of her song of metaphors, her aria of rambling. Kohlman found himself, curiously, missing the question-and-answer pattern he couldn't quite figure or manage. He wanted more bright sounds and unknown references.

"You're very quiet," he said.

"Mmm," she said.

"I don't know you this way."

She wrapped her legs on him tight, squeezed.

"I felt in jeopardy during all of that," he said, trying to joke, knowing in the small of his back the joke's limits, the joke's truths. "For my life."

"You were fine," she said.

"Pretty amazing aerobics," he said.

"It was time," she said. "It was more than time. It was feeling unnatural—giving you all of myself that I was . . and—well, you know what I'm trying to say—*not* that."

Kohlman felt his spine arc and shiver.

"I feel better now," Janice said. "I feel less . .'bound up' . . less crazy."

"Do you think you've been crazy?"

"I *am* crazy," she said; "at least some people would measure me that way. . . But I know who they are. And I know how they measure. I haven't had a headache in two days—because, I think, of you. —I may never have one again."

She was looking at the ceiling. And she was crying. Kohlman kissed her tears. He didn't understand them. "You're very different," he said.

She laughed. She was trying to be offhand, it seemed, but still it was a scornful laugh, the kind of sound and attitude that Kohlman had never heard in her voice. "Do you love me?" she asked.

"Janice . . ." Kohlman kissed the lines from her tears. They were lying on pillows on the floor. "I'm a man writing a book. I'm a man doing a job. We've spent time together. We've gotten . . okay, close. And this happened. This occurred. Somehow. You wanted it to. It was fine. It was lovely. It was *very* lovely . . if the truth be told. But—really—we have got to stop talking about things— I'm serious about this: *you* have, you have got to stop—carrying on about things like 'love' and 'marriage.' I'm not in any position to . . ."

Janice sat up. He kissed her back: one shoulder blade, then the other, then between. She stood. She moved to the television, turned it on. "You'll see," she said. A late movie with Robert Stack shone and fluttered. She lowered the audio so there was no sound. "I think a lot about Jesus lately," she said. "Do you mind my talking about this?"

Kohlman shook his head. He wasn't sure where she might go. He wasn't sure he wouldn't, in fact, mind . . were attention the issue and were he to analyze it. Still, it was familiar. It was what had been happening between them, and as such, as a way they talked, being that—the lilt, the wind chime of upward inflections free of words—of course, in *that* sense: he didn't mind at all. He welcomed it.

". . Jesus and Camus. I get in states," Janice said. "I suppose they're really ungravitational. Where I just drift up . . or seem to. Lift up into the sun . . or, actually, that light. I believe that there is a light, an energy source, a solar cell, in a way, inside you, *us*, any of us . . somewhere . . and if you can find it—I'm speaking gener-

ally—if you can find it . . then . . a great deal is possible. Or not
*im*possible. Actually, I think I mean *possible* more. I believe that
Nevada's an existential state, ultimately. Jesus lives here. In his way.
And the ghost of Camus."

Kohlman saw his hand, combing gently through her hair. It
seemed separate, and in its separateness, its own course free of
instruction, free of any restraining history, it touched him. He
wished all of his body parts might live that way, as separately,
might have such lives of their own. "How did you almost die?" he
asked. "I mean: . . What C.E.O. mentioned: How did that happen? What *was* that?"

"Would you be sad had I died?"

"I know, certainly, I would have missed something."

"Me?"

"*Some*thing."

"What?"

"I'm not . . I can't say yet."

She filled out with air, with a breath infiltrating her whole
body. "I think we all 'almost die' every day—don't we?" she asked.
"Is life that sure?"

"Well, no, but . . ."

" 'How I Almost Died'—is that the story you want?"

"Yes . . please."

"I'll tell you."

"Thank you. Good." And he *meant* "good." Beyond "that
will pass the time" or "I'd appreciate it."

She began. "It was Eve," she said. "It was Eve's disease again.
It had gotten . . so much better—since the fire . . since the trial.
And, after the trial, when I'd been 'evaluated,' the doctors had
given me a medication which cut things out almost entirely. But . .
taking the medication . . I guess, it seems, *depressed* me. I'd stopped
feeling that the headaches were *sick*. But then, when I had to take
pills for them, even though they weren't coming, I felt I was *sick*
again. Am I talking *elliptically*—or can you follow?"

"I can follow."

"Good. So . . I stopped taking the medication. And they
began to build. Up again. The headaches. And then, one night at
work—I was carrying more numbers that night than I had ever carried—I could feel the blood coming into my mouth and my nose.
It was like . . a very strong man—Paul Bunyan: remember him?—

had hit my head with an axe. I felt electrocuted inside. All the lines of communication . . all the tubes and wires of me stopped. I fell against a Texas Hold 'Em table and slid to the floor. I could see and hear everything–*in a way*. It was 'in a way' and not the usual. People were rushing over. Other people were saying, 'Give her space!' Some people were screaming. One man, crouching beside me, holding my wrist, started saying, 'No count. No count: she's dead.' I wanted to say: 'Don't say that! People will get the wrong idea!' But I couldn't *form* anything. Words. I could only take things in. I could just *receive* things. *Into* me. I could just *accept*. I could just *absorb*."

In a reflex of current chasing through him and not, really, with a grip on his control, Kohlman held Janice's hand and squeezed, hoping he had not hurt her. His throat felt dry.

"Then I saw–kneeling there on the ground too . . with the man who was holding my wrist–C.E.O. and Alyce. I had taken them in just a month before. And they were crying. And they looked *so young*! They looked so dear and close and young that I wanted them not to hurt, not to be alone again. I was thirty-six! '36.' I saw the number . . as a number . . in my head. *I* was young. I was not *too* young: they could have been my children–but I *was* young. Thirty-six only! I had stopped one existence and was at the start of another! And so I did a thing with my brain. Or something *in* my brain. Or something *in* me . . *some*where . . that sent a call out to my brain. And I unstuck. I unfroze. I came together again. And something must have moved. Because someone in the crowd said as much, and someone else said: 'She's alive again!' and the man kneeling, holding my wrist, said: 'It's back! I've got a count!' And that was that. That's the night everyone started calling me 'Angel.' Because I'd 'gone and come back' is what one person said. I think it happened because I'd stopped taking the medication and had begun storing the pain, fighting it, letting it build up. Since then, I've learned different kinds of meditation. I have one episode a day–quick really; it just comes and passes. And now, being in love again, with you, I'm not having any."

Kohlman wished it weren't the case–but he knew he was shaking.

"Do you see these burns?" She turned to him, frontally, touched certain islands on her skin. "These are from that night," she said. "These are from the fire."

. . . . .

She slept so quietly. Kohlman had never been with a woman so still in her sleep. He kept thinking about her—her voice, hearing her words, feeling her skin—the whole night. *Angel, Angel, Angel* . . he said to himself at one point. He said her name aloud. Then he said to her sleeping eyes: "Janice, I'm saying your name aloud in my room. Why do I want to do that? Will you know?" In the morning she fit into him, and they made love again. "I can't keep doing this," he said.

"Why not?" She smiled.

He began to dress, and she watched.

"Your ribs are very balanced," she said.

"I've got to meet my brother," Kohlman said. "I'm sorry: Had I . . ? I thought I told you that last night. I have to meet his plane. In two hours. An hour and forty minutes. If I'm not prompt, he'll construct a *thesis*. The *airport* will get a bloody *dissertation* on the psychosexual implications of my repeated lateness."

"Are you close?" Janice asked.

"To the airport?" Kohlman smiled.

"To your brother."

"Well . . ." Kohlman felt a spinal surge of . . what? *regret? fury?* "Oh . . ." He shook his head. Finally *bitterness*, the jury out, stepped in. " 'Close'?" he said. A lip peeled; he mouthed the word like a raw oyster. "I don't know. I can't say. It's not a word I use a lot: 'close.' " Who was he talking to? Where were the listeners? He sounded as though he were in an East Side bar at rush hour: waiting for a table . . or in a network editorial office, or . . . It was a voice he hadn't used in a week. Kohlman wished himself back in Manhattan . . not really . . but why not? . . actually, *yes* . . where his words, their tone, their pressure all sprang from some acknowledged language. But, no. No; he didn't; not at all; he liked this place.

"Wear what C.E.O. brought," Janice advised.

Kohlman moved to his vanity, lifted the hairpiece and beard, tried them. "These are bizarre," he said. "I put these on . . who am I?"

"Please," Janice said. "For me. It doesn't matter. I just don't want anything terrible to happen to . . . Oh—and oh . . !" She hopped from the bed. Kohlman noticed, for the first time, that her skin bore a geography: discrete countries, raised areas, lines, rivers, like a map. He remembered her confession about the fire. "Here!" she said. She slid open his closet. "C.E.O. brought these too. Left these. He thought they should be about the right size."

Kohlman could see clothes he had never seen hanging—leisure clothes, bright shirts, silk shirts with patterns. And there were cotton slacks in colors he had never imagined. And white leather shoes!

"Wear these," Janice said. "They'll be perfect. They'll help."

She looked both thinner and more fleshed than herself by the closet. She looked bruised and scarred and beautiful. Kohlman wanted her back in bed. He felt his breath growing tidal. He turned away.

"What's the matter?" she asked.

"Nothing," he said. "I need some breakfast. I need coffee. I need . . ."

He disguised himself. They ate in the casino Tree Room where Janice held his hand the entire breakfast. What would a day be like with his brother? Kohlman couldn't think.

．　　．　　．　　．　　．

He arrived at McCarran early and rented his brother, Adam, a Skylark.

Deplaning, Adam looked in the throes of some insoluble thought, his wide brow tortured and lined. His mind seemed anywhere but on the moving crowd and his arrival. Kohlman waved. Adam offered no recognition, walked past. "Adam!" Kohlman said.

Kohlman's brother stopped and turned. He clenched his brow more furiously; he bit the pipestem in his mouth.

"It's me," Kohlman said. He extended his hand. "It's Ben. Benjamin."

His brother moved cautiously. "Blond?" he said.

"Don't worry," Kohlman said. "I'll explain it. How was the trip? You shaved your beard."

"Academic beards are tiresome," Adam said. "Lord in Heaven, Benjamin: You look imbecilic. Like some burlesque of yourself!"

"I rented you a car," Kohlman said.

"I have no use for a car," Adam said.

"Well . . I rented it. And so we'll use it." Kohlman tried to smile. "I won some money—I blew some . . on a car for my brother." Kohlman touched Adam below one of his corduroy shoulders.

"Don't use me as an excuse," Adam said. "So, then, you've actually been here . . *wagering?*"

"Gambling," Kohlman said. "Yes."

"The fast buck!" Adam Kohlman's lip curled.

"So—this is a conference—hmm?" Kohlman began, working for an exchange. But his mind riffled pages of a scrapbook, fat with moments of his brother's disdain. He tried to make memorabilia only, from them, incurious history. Once, for a month only, fall of high school senior year, Kohlman had been filled, trembling, with "mission" and had thought, *in* that, he'd been called of God and into the ministry. It was an awkward, febrile memory most times: Kohlman kneeling as a flat backlit figure against the Iowa sky, with both hands clenching the freshly rotated soil—his feeling penetrated both by Voice and Spirit. "*You're* going to serve God?" he remembered Adam mocking—at fifteen, judgement already a knack. In the air, Adam had drawn a headline: "Benjamin Kohlman Serves God—Run for Cover!" Kohlman refocused: "So . . you're delivering a paper?" he asked. "How's Beth? How're the girls?"

"Everybody's taking care of himself," Adam said. ". . As intended. Or *her*self, as they're requiring these days." He seemed to sweep half the airport population away and stare across miles. ". . We're all busy; we're productive; we're engaged; we're dutiful; we're fine." Adam swung his eyes through the concourse. "Lord: this is even more dreadful than I thought," he said. "Satanic!" He stopped moving. He paused, then turned full front to his brother, legs apart, hands clasped behind him, brow narrowed: It was, Kohlman knew, his lecture stance. "Satanic," he said again.

Kohlman wanted to defend Las Vegas.

Adam began: "You walk out on a dedicated if not entirely respectable woman; you come to a corrupt city . . ."

"Ad: Wait a minute . . ." Kohlman began. He'd vowed: *just spend the time; make the gesture.* But . . "Ad, really: come on: I mean, if we want to count heads . . *you* are *also* present in this city for whatever . . ."

"Don't try to catch me!" Adam said. "I'm not interested in fallacies of misplaced concreteness!" *Fallacies of . . ?* "My point is merely: It's clear your values need to be recuperated. . . Is that *real* hair? Is that beard *actual?*"

". . Where are you staying?" Kohlman tried to reroute the conversation.

"It's called . . is there a . . *Desert Inn?*" Adam shifted his carry-on to his attache-case hand, reached inside his jacket. "I have a confirmation slip. The Conference booked . . ."

"I know where the Desert Inn is," Kohlman said.

"Yes: you would. Having *soaked in* all the local . . ."

"Do you have luggage?" Kohlman made his voice level to not argue.

"I never check luggage," Adam said. "It's a waste of time."

.   .   .   .   .

They registered Adam at the Desert Inn twenty minutes later. The lobby and check-in lines spilled with registrants clutching dog halters and white canes: "The Western Sagebrush Vendors' Association," Kohlman and his brother were told. "Hideous!" Adam snarled. "Grotesque! I can't believe that a professional organization to which I belong . . would be so misguided as to schedule meetings here!" He looked around at the waiting blind. "Don't they have *colonies* somewhere for these people?!" he said in a voice too loud. Kohlman knelt and scratched the ears of a German shepherd.

.   .   .   .   .

"Nice room," Kohlman said, when they were upstairs.

"You're, of course, being ironic," Adam said.

"Well, I meant . . spacious."

"Ah," Adam sneered. "Yes! The West!" And he waved his hand as if it were a handkerchief.

"Yeah; well . . but it does have a separate sitting area. With a desk. So, I mean, *that* will be good . . to work in."

"Where the sky isn't cloudy all day! Is that what I've flown into? Is that where we are? Except, of course, the mushroom configurations over the desert . . right? . . and those enticing billowy clouds of Greed . . and Lust."

"It's got a nice view," Kohlman said. He was determined to stay neutral, make his gesture, spend the time.

"Look at the wallpaper," Adam said. "Who would *buy* wallpaper like that?"

. . . . .

They drove to Lake Mead. It was Kohlman's idea: a drive, offhand talk, time at a historic landmark. Adam, reluctantly, concurred. He said, given what he supposed to be the alternatives, they might as well. Kohlman tried to make conversation; his brother read a book about Governor John Winthrop of Massachusetts the entire drive. When they stood, finally, on Hoover Dam, the air giddy with vertical space and Adam still reading, Kohlman felt his neutrality begin to slip and fought anger. "Quite a structure!" Kohlman tried, having to shout his words over the dynamos and wind.

Adam looked up. "What?" he said.

"I said this is quite a structure! . . Here! . . This place! Quite a phenomenon! I'd never seen it before!"

Adam looked to either side.

"I think it's jejune," he said and swept his hand, his small white flesh looking like a blown candy wrapper. "It degrades monumentality," he said. "Though I suppose it's just what Las Vegas deserves: a power source as hideously misconceived as the city. 'Misdirected moral otherness!' " Adam pronounced, as if quoting, then laughed, his laugh like the far sounds, on campus, of a vivarium. "I mean: look at it!" he went on. "It's inescapable."

Kohlman nodded.

Adam barked a single last note of laughter—*Ha!*—into the edged wind whipping them where they stood. Its sound sped away, fled, nearly, and left them to silence.

Kohlman continued nodding. It became, more, a bobbing, a light rhythmic motion that seemed an attempt, perhaps, to measure or stay something. He grew aware of his brother watching him.

". . So you're writing a *book* here?" Adam finally asked.

Kohlman paused. "I'm . . Yes; writing a book; trying to," he said.

A father, ten feet from them, held his shrieking four-year-old high over his head: "I'm going to throw you over!" he teased, making his voice do something: half animal, half maniacal. "*Pleasedaddypleasedaddypleasedaddy: No!*" the child screamed.

"*Jesus! Don't do that!*" Kohlman lashed out at the father. The father looked at Kohlman. Kohlman's brother looked at Kohlman, shocked. "The child is frightened." Kohlman hoped to make his voice even and reasonable, not the voice he'd unfurled seconds earlier. "The child, when you held him up like that, was very, very frightened," Kohlman said—again: the struggle for reason and moderation, the attempt to make it work. He tried for closure. "You shouldn't do that," he managed; "It's very frightening. It's not good."

The father was still. He held the child in a bear grip to his chest. The child studied his father. The father looked from the child to Kohlman, from Kohlman to the child. He looked past the guardrail of the dam and out into the chasm . . wide, so wide, so deep it consumed all texture in the light and ate the brain's consideration of it whole. There was the sense that whoever might own the next word, in the box between Kohlman, Kohlman's brother, the man, and his child, might own considerably more.

In the gap, in the silence, Kohlman's brother, Adam, led a retreat from the overlook. He stopped by stairs that led up from the paved thoroughfare above the dam, turned back, and saw Kohlman mouth something to the father and son before leaving them, words lost to the roar. "A potboiler?" Adam said, when Kohlman arrived beside him: "This thing. Your book? It's a potboiler? Is that what you're writing? Something for the Philistines?"

"Well . . ." Kohlman began.

"And would you tell me, please . . what it was you thought you were doing back there?" Adam asked. "With that man?"

"What are you asking?" Kohlman said.

"I'm asking: what you thought you were doing by upbraiding that father. What made you think you had even the slightest right to intervene?"

"I don't know," Kohlman said. "I don't . . know what to tell you. Sometimes I . . do that. Sometimes I intervene."

"Just: don't intervene with *me*," Adam said. "All right?" He looked frightened. His face, for only an instant, was the face of a man turned down by a final bank.

"I never plan it," Kohlman tried. "It doesn't happen . . that often. It's just a thing. It's something left over . . I suppose . . from somewhere."

Adam right-angled his body to where Kohlman stood facing him. He seemed to be trying to find a certain breathing rhythm that would allow him to speak. He turned, not finding what he was looking for, and angled left.

"I think father . . may have done it . . on occasion. Or something like it," Kohlman tried.

" 'Father'?"

"Ad, come on. When we were kids, that's what we called him."

Adam said nothing. Some current had him. Kohlman watched, inside his brow, Adam search the bank for an exposed root to take hold of.

"*Isn't* that what we called him? It's what Mother called him too. She called him 'Father.' "

" 'Mother.' 'Father,' " Adam snorted.

"Mother . . Father," Kohlman repeated; "Mother . . Father": a primer lesson.

"Leave off," Adam said.

"Ad . . ."

"Leave off!" Adam snapped. " 'Father' is what *you* called him. All right?! Because you were the reverential son. He's a man who— when they open his skull after the last clarion call and in the name of medical science— they'll find a *walnut*."

"They'll . . what?"

"A *walnut*: Hard, dry, useless tissue . . with very little *meat*." Adam picked a trapped, downy feather from his jacket and flicked it off.

"Just because . . ." Kohlman didn't even know where he was *go*ing with his *just because*; they were words, only, in a direction.

"Why don't you just . . stop pretending—and write for the *tabloids*?" Adam said. "Why don't you stop backing into what the truth of your work is . . and write the pulp you crave . . write *headlines* for the *National Enquirer*: "ALIEN CLAIMS JFK ALIVE ON DISTANT PLANET." Or maybe I could get you to write the chapter headings for my next book: "PLYMOUTH ROCK A HOAX! . . WITCH CLAIMS: 'I HAD JOHN PROCTOR'S BABY!' " They were crossing the visitors' parking lot and heading toward the Skylark. Adam turned back to Kohlman and smiled. "That's, actually," he said, pleased, ". . don't you think?—sort of funny."

Kohlman tried to smile back.

·   ·   ·   ·   ·

"Have you *seen* the folks?" Kohlman asked, as they drove back along Henderson Highway. "Within . . ? Recently?"

"You mean: 'Mother' and 'Father,' " Adam said.

"Okay; but . . when, actually, *was* the last . . ?"

"Ask a serious question," Adam said.

"I've got a wall of postcards!" Kohlman said. "I have this jumbled construction of . . God-knows-what! I don't know what I'm supposed to piece out of it! I thought maybe you . . !"

"Maybe the better question," Adam began, ". . is: When—since you left Iowa—never looking back—for Princeton . . depleting resources such that *I* might only . . ."

"Ad: I went to Princeton on *scholarship*. What are you talking about?! And *worked*."

"Oh! Yes! And didn't I hear *that*!"

"But you can't blame *me* if . . !"

Adam set a mincing pose to telegraph his impression: " 'Did you know our oldest boy, Benjamin—he's so *capable*—won a scholarship to Princeton University? Adam—bless his soul!—will stay right here in Iowa!' "

Kohlman drew a breath—one which, were Sharon there, she might have marked: *Good! Deep! Possibly a record*. Kohlman clenched his jaw. Adam returned to reading. Kohlman punched the cool-air vent on in the Skylark, and thought about Janice. He played her voice . . words like "tanager," "electrocution," and "betrothed."

· · · · ·

They went to Caesar's Palace for late lunch at an umbrellaed table outside the Primavera by the pool. "This place is a Senecan comedy!" Adam said. "The performative hierarchy of our culture! Good God!" He laughed.

"Ad: straight question: . . What is a . .'performative . .'?"

"Don't be arch!" Adam barked. The two stared. There was the sense Adam might say a thing of genuine dread, his lower jaw moving forward and back, making small tic-like preparations. Then suddenly—and Kohlman could see it—Adam changed directions, snatching up a long iced-tea spoon to conduct the dry, chlorinated air in a grand gesture. "What the great Puritan American experiment hath finally wrought!" he said, then rolled a laugh, the guttural skim of which seemed to flake among light crescents on the pool. He had the curiosity, if not the attention, of all the lunching, drinking, swimming gamblers.

Kohlman felt an impasse. He was weary. He'd put in time; he'd tried; he'd been patient. He made a final attempt: "Ad, I'm sorry . . but you seem. . ."

His brother fixed him—eyes flared, teeth grinding.

Kohlman stepped off in another direction: "Is there some . . ?"

"Some *what*? Is there some *what*? Don't talk to me in incomplete sentences!"

"Is there some difficulty in your life?! . . To ask frankly."

"*You* ask that of *me*?"

"Yes."

"*You* ask that . . of . . ?!"

"No! I never said it! Never mind! I'm sorry."

"A person as *anal* as you?!"

"Oh, for . . !"

"Who wallows in *muck*?! Can't hold even a *mid-range* relationship with a woman?! You ask *me*—regarding *my* life— 'is there some difficulty?' "

"It was a question! Only a question!"

"Benjamin . . !"

"Don't instruct me! Jesus!"

"Your presumption is monumental!"

"Why did you call me?!" Kohlman shot his words, monosyllables—blunt and frontal.

"What do you mean?" His brother's voice turned, cut the stride it had gathered.

"Why did you call me? Why did you take the time? I don't get it. I don't understand. Again: I'm not being arch; these are serious questions. Why did you even contact me? When you're so . . bloody . . !"

"What?"

"Contemptuous!"

For the third time that day, Adam seemed panicked. His pupils ran for cover in his eyes. His jaw worked. Again, though, he would not take the moment offered. Reflexively, his lip peeled: ". . So," he said; "So . . . Then are we going to have a *deep* and transsubstantial conversation now? Something psycho-ideologically embedded?! Is this the Theodicy of Our Lives?"

Kohlman tried to remember if he had ever hit his brother. He had pushed, certainly, when they were younger. Adam liked to block the screen of their black-and-white Magnavox. Theirs had not been a house full of toys: building blocks and books, obligatory bikes, ill-inflated balls which always *thwunk*ed . . footballs when caught, basketballs when dribbled. Their father's idea of the perfect gift was a *tool*. And although the two brothers had certainly jostled to possess the same *any*thing, Kohlman could not recall ever hitting Adam. He'd held back. He'd felt strictures: "Never raise your hand against your brother." Something had always stayed him. But this was different: no longer the common roof, no longer covenants. Kohlman's head felt light with attempted reasoning; he gave himself up to being nonsensical. "Do you find *Civilization* an overrated idea, Ad?" Kohlman asked.

"That's certainly cryptic," his brother said.

Kohlman took a slice of avocado from a salad plate and spread it on his brother's light tattersall shirt. "Let's have a food fight," Kohlman said.

"What're you doing?" Adam said.

Kohlman lifted alfalfa sprouts into Adam's hair.

"Stop this," Adam said. "I mean it!"

Kohlman flicked egg salad at Adam's jacket.

"*You are not to fuck with me, Ben!*" Adam shouted.

Kohlman scooped up a handful of cottage cheese.

Adam slapped the cheese from Kohlman's hand and stood. He glared down. "You come out to this empty city . . with your empty values and your empty life: Who *are* you?!" Adam said. "You write trash about trash. Can't *find* anything of substance! Can't *do* anything of substance! Can't *live* with another decent human being, bring a family into the world, be productive. And as if that's not enough . . you *throw food*. You're incredible!"

Kohlman smiled. He was tired.

"You know, at one point, *really*, when we were younger . . ."

Kohlman shut his eyes to the flurry, the dislodged talus of truth and helplessness.

"I thought maybe *both of us*," Adam went on, "Benjamin: *listen* to me! — might be able to achieve something a little more than . . *running an auto body shop in Templeton, Iowa*. Take measurable steps beyond our pitifully agronomized parents! But . . I should take a *picture* of you here . . and *enlarge* it . . and send it to

'Mother' and 'Father' . . wher*ever* they are! 'Wages of a Princeton Education!' Let Ruth and old Tom Kohlman see how their soft-spoken but 'deep' Benjamin turned out! How he dresses! The *emporia* he frequents!"

Kohlman's brother wheeled and started away. In an instant, the Challenger had him by the shoulders and in the air.

"This the guy?" the Challenger said. Kohlman shook his head. The need had passed; the moment was over. The Challenger set Adam Kohlman down by the pool. Adam's eyes were white and enormous. "Sorry," the Challenger said.

"I hope your paper goes well," Kohlman said. "Truly. I appreciate that you called. I wish we might have talked. I sense something . . *in* you—but I can't . . . I'm sorry about the food. It was wrong. It was childish."

•   •   •   •

Kohlman spent the rest of the afternoon and early evening walking. At one point, he shuffled through concrete and plaster and I-beam debris to stand in the husk of the all-but-torn-down Castaways Casino, where, amid the scraped smells of metal and broken glass, and until a security guard approached to say he was trespassing, he cried. At several other points, he tried calling Adam: "Mr. Kohlman left instructions not to be disturbed," the desk clerk said. "Tell him . . his brother called . . and tried to reach him," Kohlman said.

Kohlman went from huge hotel to huge hotel, stood at the edges of tennis courts listening to the *pock* of balls shuttling. He sat alone in pool areas, stood by rough-barked trees in tended gardens, in a wash of tropical fragrances. He watched families. He watched men and women, especially those with children, thinking of his brother and, again, their parents, and wondering: Was there some unforgivable act he hadn't searched? Had one parent or the other *done* something . . beyond remission? Had a *closeness*, somewhere, thrust in too deep?

He felt helpless. He understood the amputee in front of the Imperial Palace . . with WORLD HUNGER on his T-shirt and the Yankee baseball cap . . *that* kind of deficit: as if nothing extended from him, except eyes: nothing reached, really. Or grappled. Had that been Sharon's meaning? Why she'd not stayed? That, emotionally, Kohlman was *like* that: at best a *trunk*?

What had happened? Where? Had *any*thing? Why was he so
. . ? His past seemed one born only in a constant landscape: clear,
pleasant, invariable, safe from jagged contour. True? Then, what
about the girl: Pamela Arnold . . who had seemed so . . weightless,
without burden of herself or gender? Or was that Kohlman's burden? So, then . . had Kohlman spent seventeen years in a house in
a small Iowa town with two kind, tacit, principled, undemonstra-
tive people he'd called *Mother* and *Father* . . but stored images
which felt no heavier in his heart, had no more valence than, say,
those of Mr. Silento, the druggist, or Mrs. Larsen, who'd taught
him junior English? Jesus Christ! True?! Possible?! Again Kohlman
cried. He was watching a family foursome tee off at the Dunes
Country Club. He shook. He couldn't stop his tears. Who *was* he?!
Was he *any*one?! He'd left home and never really thought to return.
Did he feel *different* from his family? Was he *less*?

He called his brother again. Again the clerk wouldn't put him
through. He called his brother's home in Ann Arbor. "Beth, this is
Ben," he said to his brother's wife. "Calling from Vegas. I spent the
day with Adam. Part of it. I acted badly. I lost control. When he
gets home, please say I called and understood I'd been wrong . .
and wished we could have spent more . . better time together,
somehow."

Adam's wife, Beth, made uncertain sounds at the end of the
line, then finally asked: "He didn't say?"

"Say what?" Kohlman could almost feel her voice trembling.

Beth's uncertain sounds took on the definition of crying. "I
can't talk," she said. "I can't talk really about it. The court asked
him to move out. He almost killed Lisa. His temper . . . He . . !
He has . . he can't control. . . I've tried. . . Really . . !" Beth's
gasped sentences slid to guttural keening. She tried to recover, say
something . . once . . twice . . but couldn't.

"I'm sorry," Kohlman said. "Jesus . . sorry . . really . . Beth
. . I didn't mean this."

"It's all right," she said. "It's all right." And they hung up.

It was dinnertime. Kohlman was hungry. In truth . . not. He
had a drink at the Stardust. A whore asked if he wanted cheering.
"What's your name?" she asked.

"I'm not sure," he said. "I'm not sure tonight."

"Come on."

"It's Mr. B!" he said. "It's Jack Napoleon!"

"Flako-flako!" the whore said and moved on.

He had, it seemed, only half-mechanisms for other people: Now, for the most part, close . . now, professional. Now, for all intents, direct . . now, essentially, ironic. Where had that started? Was that Princeton? "You're always scheming," Sharon had said. Inside his head, things weren't that way; it felt different. But . . . "I have ambitions," he'd say. "I never see you," she'd say. "And when I do, you're . . beside a phone, or . . writing something on your yellow legal pad . . and then, when I ask, you say: 'It's just notes. It's just notes for a possible project–don't worry.' " She'd asked him to explain the difference between a "possible project" and "the Future," and he'd been at a loss. *Christ*: he hadn't even been able to read his own brother's pain! Who *was* he?! A thirty-four-year-old man registered in a Las Vegas hotel under an alias . . wearing a blond beard and hairpiece and wearing clothes that belonged to some fat, hairy land developer!

He called Janice. She wasn't in. She was at work, of course. Running numbers. He considered calling the Nugget. Tomorrow they were supposed to drive with the Barnetts to Alyce's "debut" in St. George, Utah. Was he supposed to meet her? What time would they leave?

Kohlman walked to the Desert Inn. Again, he sensed eyes on him. It was ten at night. He saw his brother sitting in a cocktail lounge at the rim of the casino. He was alone at a table. He had set up a small Olivetti cordless travel typewriter and was drinking what looked like Manhattans. He was working. The image made Kohlman feel unbelievably sad. He couldn't approach. He couldn't break in. He couldn't interrupt what he saw his brother was doing . . however exiled it seemed.

He stood alone on the corner of Sahara. Why had he come?! He rolled sentences down his mind: *The glass door of the burn unit was wedged open. . . . Begin with a montage of tragic circumstances. . . . Salem Levinworth stared at the gulls picking carrion.* The words were . . not language; they were something else; they were *art deco* made into sentences! What kind of person crossed a continent to pick a woman's burns with such words . . then hold her close in love?! What was he attempting, finally?! Could he write Janice's life and feel his *own* skin slough away, his *own* head crack and bleed like tortured rock, his own heart command itself to beat and come alive again? Before some goon fired a slug into him because he'd asked about fires he had *not* asked about?

A blond scrolled down the window of her milk-white Caprice and asked if he wanted a blow job. All the lights made the night look like dusk.

He'd said *what* to Sharon? That he'd felt "on the edge of something"? That he "felt close"? He'd had no idea! . . What the shot might sound like. What it would feel like, entering. That it was only moments away.

- SEVEN -

The shot was percussive in its sound. It slammed and made that kind of bark—hard element against edge, metal against stone, alloy snapping. Sounds like it were everywhere: building cranes struck the I-beams of new hotel towers; steel-sheeted Chevron signs snapped like pennants in warm and cold air-current gusts; cabs broke for a clear space on Las Vegas Boulevard and high-centered on the median strip. Percussion was the talk of the city. You stopped hearing it. Specifically. You accommodated. Kohlman, in fact, was on the pavement, bleeding, before he heard the shot.

A couple rushed up. They looked down. They looked at each other. The woman was blond and elegant, beautiful, thin as a model in her black and gold cocktail dress and diamonds. The man wore a dark wool suit and bow tie. He held the gun.

"It's not him," the woman said.

"Oh, God," the man said.

"We're sorry," the woman said to Kohlman. She bent slightly forward. Her dress opened; he could see her small breasts.

"This is terrible," the man said. He flopped the gun back and forth, no idea, now, what to do with it.

"Walter," the woman said. "I thought you were sure."

"I thought I was too. I was *sure* I was sure."

"Well, you were wrong."

"This is awful."

"We thought you were someone else," the woman said to Kohlman.

"We're very sorry," the man said.

"We thought you were someone we recognized."

"Someone we knew."

"Help him up," the woman said.

The man knelt by Kohlman. "Where did it hit you?" he asked.

Kohlman, with a kind of removed, fractured curiosity, wondered whether he shouldn't be trying to find the image of the volcano, whether he shouldn't be moving his hands to the right declivities in his skull. Were these people to whom he should announce: *I'm not interested in the hotel fires?*

"Where did it hit?" the man said again. He smelled of cologne, his wool suit, and alcohol.

Kohlman felt a burning at his right shoulder. When he tried to rotate the joint, pain fired in to blur his vision and set up a raw electrical buzz inside the rim of his brow.

"Shoulder?" the man asked.

"Walter: this is unforgivable," the woman said above them.

"What time is it?" Kohlman said.

"We'll patch this up," the man said. "We're extremely sorry. I promise: We'll get it patched up." He slipped one arm skillfully behind Kohlman's back.

A man in disheveled dreadlocks and a beard spilling over his torn burlap robe approached, sandals scraping and shuffling the cinders and broken glass in the Flamingo lot. He carried an eight-foot wooden cross. The cross was pasted with reflecting stickers which bore quotes of Biblical scripture. The man was rank. "Can I help here?" he asked.

"No, we've got this," the man in the suit said.

"This is our affair." The woman turned her back.

"Does this man need ministering?" the ragged, cross-bearing man said.

"I'm a doctor," the man in the suit said and started to transport Kohlman.

"My husband's a doctor," the woman said.

"Forgive me," the burlapped man said and began to shuffle away.

Kohlman wondered: should he call the man back? Something in him hoped to be swaddled in the man's burlap. In his scrambled head he connected the shadowed ghost, light spilling around him from the casinos, with the WORLD HUNGER amputee.

"Careful," the woman said to her husband who had his hands on Kohlman.

"I know what I'm doing," the man said. He lifted and tipped Kohlman toward standing. "Okay – now, I'm going to support most of your weight," he said, "but I want you to see – while I'm doing that – if you can perambulate . . walk."

Kohlman looked for the burlapped man – but he was gone.

"We honestly thought you were another person," the woman said, leaning in again to Kohlman. Her scent was narcotic. All Kohlman could focus on were her extraordinary teeth and her tongue.

"Gloria," the man said, "Can we just take care of this first . . and deal with the details of the apology later?"

.   .   .   .   .

They moved Kohlman to a silver BMW, parked in the valet parking of the Hilton lot. The man took a doctor's bag from his trunk and stretched Kohlman on the back seat. Distantly, Kohlman saw his own passivity – himself watching himself placed and positioned – and was shocked. Was he being eliminated? Was he being removed? *Were* these people connected with the crackling voice on the phone that had said: *Get out of town*? "What if I don't *want* you to fix me?" Kohlman said finally. The man had Kohlman's shirt unbuttoned and off his shoulder. "The bullet went through!" the man said to the woman outside and behind him. ". . Gloria?!"

"I heard," the woman said. "Good. That's good."

"The bullet went through," the man said more assuringly to Kohlman. Kohlman nodded. The man was looking, it seemed, *into* his shoulder, into the entry opening, with a penlight. "Excellent . . !" he kept saying, then repeating: "Excellent . . excellent!" He took a small pill-bottle from his bag. "Can you swallow these?" he asked Kohlman, "without water?" Before Kohlman could answer, he called outside: "Glo? We have any more of that wine?"

"Here . . !" She handed in a small tooled-silver wine decanter.

Kohlman took two pills with . . it tasted like Chenin Blanc. The man poured something sticky and dark into the hole at Kohlman's shoulder blade. "You're very lucky," the man said. "No apparent fragments. No shattering." The dark viscous oil burned. The man taped some drainage gauze to Kohlman's shoulder. He rummaged in his medical bag, handed Kohlman a clear plastic container with capsules. "Antibiotics," he said. "Two every four hours. Do I need to write that down?"

"No," Kohlman said.

"We have to do something," the woman said, outside, behind. "This is terrible. We'll never forgive ourselves."

"We're taking you to dinner," the man said, rebuttoning Kohlman's shirt.

"You don't have to . . ."

"How about Tracy's?" he called to the woman.

"Will we need reservations?" the woman said.

"It's ten-thirty!" he said. "I don't think so!"

"Tracy's would be nice."

"Have you ever eaten at Tracy's?" the man said.

"No," Kohlman said.

"Good. You'll like it. Great atmosphere. We thought you were somebody else. Honestly. A friend. We feel terrible. It's the least we can do. —Is that hair real?"

•　•　•　•　•

Tracy's floated like a glass bowl above the casino at Bally's. Kohlman got drunk on fine wine. He told the man and woman, Walter and Gloria, nothing but lies. "I work with the CIA," he said. "My name is Bernard Bernard . . *Agent* Bernard." The woman, Gloria, kept laughing and leaning forward and touching him. "I'm the architect . . ." Kohlman felt crazy with bad words. He was like a rank and smoking landfill, all the trashed and fragmented sentences from true-stories-of-a-violent-crime books he'd been reading, and in some crazed and self-mocking way, he loved speaking the language: "I'm the architect . . of very intricate operations in Nicaragua—involving our country . . Australia . . and a military element from Kenya," he said.

"Oh, my goodness!" the woman, Gloria, said.

"I'm envious," the man, Walter, chimed in.

"I can't really talk about it," Kohlman said. He poured more of the expensive Medoc and grinned. "It's a bitch," he said. "It's a bitch . . secret operations. Bitch. Intelligence. Counterintelligence. Counterintelligence intelligence. Counter-counterintelligence." He laughed, then turned the page in his mind and roared right on again: "Plans within plans. Funds within funds. Intelligences within intelligences. Governments within governments. I'm a man of blood!" he announced. "I'm a man with blood on my hands."

"Good heavens!" the woman, Gloria, said.

"I'm a man with blood on my hands. Blood in my heart. Blood on my gums and in my word-processor. It's a messy life!"

Gloria giggled. She leaned forward and kissed him. "I'm so glad you let us do this," she said.

"You mean – shoot me?" Kohlman said and laughed again.

Walter and Gloria laughed.

"Well – we're all here to fuck each other over – right?!" Kohlman said. He didn't know what he was saying. "That's the call o' the wild!" he said. "That's the lay o' the land!" He spilled his wine. The thick linen tablecloth drew it up. Suddenly, Kohlman felt very sober. He looked at his companions. "This is a nice place," he said. "That was a nice meal."

Walter excused himself to go to the men's room.

Gloria put her hand on Kohlman's. "I see a sadness in you," she said.

He stared at her and couldn't say anything.

"I'm drawn to you."

Kohlman nodded.

"Take that as an invitation . . or disregard it," she said; "it's up to you."

Kohlman thought about his brother's nearly putting his daughter in the hospital. He thought of their parents: honest, unremarkable people. Were those qualities wrong? Were they dangerous? Did they engender violence?

"My brother's in town," Kohlman said to Gloria.

"I'm sorry to hear that," she said.

The image of his brother reading Colonial history on Hoover Dam swept through Kohlman on a wave, unexpected, sudden, like a wind. It shuddered then recomposed to become Adam sitting in the cocktail lounge at the Desert Inn with his Olivetti cordless typewriter. Were the two alike? Kohlman had never heard one person, in Templeton, refer to them as "the Kohlman Brothers." Why had Adam called? What debt had he been trying to redeem? And why . . *why* . . "in the name of God," as their father would say . . had he set himself up working *within* all that crazed public jangle? Was it some *test*? Was it some *feat*? Was it some *statement* of dedicated joylessness? An intent to *will*, to *determine* the lounge and casino *away*?

Gloria broke Kohlman again from his interior. Her hand went to his face, moved it toward her. "I see this night as being very arranged by fate," she said.

Kohlman took her hand and set it on the table. He righted his wineglass, poured himself more, poured for her. "I have a very incomplete sense of things," he said.

"That's what I mean," she said.

Walter returned. "Relief," he said.

Kohlman drained his wine. He poured another, drained that. He felt giddy again, off-balance, crazy. He felt outraged as well—at *some*thing, again at *some*thing, though it wouldn't announce any name, something loosed from where it had once belonged to live in the world now *too* freed and *too* unrestrained and *too* rampant. "I want to show you both something," Kohlman said. "Before the night's out. Before we . .'part.' " His laugh came, removed and strange, a laugh aware and incautious—a laugh he might invent as a gift for his brother.

"I wish you would," Gloria said of Kohlman's offer.

. . . . .

As the three stepped from the north entrance of Bally's Grand, what they saw, through the lit gold and lapis play of the exterior fountains, was what appeared to be a west-to-east ranging double pale of tribal torches. There were muted sirens of emergency trucks, coiling in, as well, from somewhere. Someone had set fire to all the "Flashdance" and Elite Escort call-girl vending machines up and down Las Vegas Boulevard. Each small post burned with a creosote flame, snaking black resinous smoke from an orange roil.

"It's for us!" Gloria said.

"Undoubtedly." Walter seemed amused and unsurprised.

"Do we have insurance?" Gloria asked.

"It discourages the mosquitoes," Walter said.

Crowds seemed to walk by the burning boxes without concern. The air smelled like a fruit orchard stayed, at night, against frost.

"Now that's what I call smut!" Walter said.

"Would it have been the man with the cross?" Kohlman wondered aloud.

"Show us what you were going to show us," Gloria said to Kohlman.

. . . . .

He walked them to their car. "Okay," he said. "Stand there. I just want to show you something. I just want to show you the sort of thing that can happen. . . I mean, if you can shoot me and take me to dinner . . then this is something that can happen, too."

Kohlman stood by the rear, rubberized bumper of the BMW. He shut his eyes. His head felt like warm bathwater. He groped around for the image. The volcano. Where was it? "What's he doing?" he heard Gloria ask. "Bernard: Are you okay?!" he heard Walter asking. *Volcano . . volcano . . !* "He looks like he's blacking out," he heard Gloria say, and then: "Walter: help him."

Kohlman shut down everything. He shut down the entire world beyond: closed gates, doors, window. He did not feel Walter's hand tentatively on his shoulder. The volcano came . . fierce . . active . . enormous! Kohlman could almost feel his interior expand. He opened his eyes. He squatted by the rear bumper, leaving Walter's hand suspended in the neon air. Kohlman took hold of the bumper—first left, then right hand. He drew a deep breath. He had no idea whether the intention in his mind would work. With one lifting motion and crossing over of hands, he hefted the couple's BMW in the air, flipped it, and set it down again in the Hilton valet parking lot . . on its roof.

Kohlman felt a heat and pressure on his chest. But he still stood. He turned to Walter and Gloria, who now clutched each other.

"Don't shoot people," Kohlman said. "Don't shoot people any more. It's wrong. . . Thank you for dinner." And he walked toward the Maxim.

. . . . .

Two new postcards had been set against the Compaq monitor in his room; the monitor itself glowed with a message. Janice, it seemed, had picked up Kohlman's mail at the Ogden House and had come back later in the day and written. Kohlman scrolled her words forward. They covered nearly three pages. He read.

Dearest Benjamin:

I take liberties. But that is who I am. That is who I've become and have to be.

I love you. I know: You say: "Don't say that. I don't want to hurt you. Etc, etc, etc.: I know; I've heard it all. But I'm saying: no, Benjamin; ha ha!—I don't care what you say: I'm saying it. Because I do and because we are and because we have—and you know that as well as I. You have my life. I've kept nothing. I'll keep nothing, and that's fine too; I don't want to: I love this, what's happening, this giving. But now you've loved me too and you know you have and you know you can't, really, say to me any more: "Angel—Angel, Angel, Angel (although you've not yet called me 'Angel'), Angel: Don't. Don't do that. Don't get carried away." You can't legitimately say that—because now you've gotten just as carried away. And I've felt it. And I know. I love that phrase, "carried away." When I was being observed in the psychiatric ward at the Bridgeport Hospital, I remember the doctors there asking me: "Do you see yourself as a person who can get carried away?" I mean, God: I was carried away! They carried me away to the hospital. And yes, of course; that's what's good about me: I get carried away. More people should. I'm very carried away with you right now— because I've given you my life and I love you. Of course I get carried away. What a stupid question!

I know that you've been wanting to find out about the night of the fire—that that's important to you. And I know that you think I keep talking around it, being . . what? . . "flighty" and "imprecise" (I've been trying to think here for the last three minutes what the word is that you would use . . to describe the thing that's been frustrating you . . "metaphoric"? Is that, if you were talking to someone else, is that what word you'd use to describe the way you think I've been? You've used that word a couple of times.

First: I am glad that Salem Levinworth is dead. I'm very glad. I'm very, very. I feel no sorrow. I feel no pain. I feel no remorse—or any of the other words I was asked in the hospital and at the trial. If he were to die once a week, I would only feel enormous relief.

. . . . .

Let me tell you some things. This will not be everything, but it will be some things and it will be, I suspect you'll think, closer to what you've been asking than what I've, 'til now, managed to say. What I'm trying to do here is to give you what you *want—though it will be less close to the truth* in me *than what I've already been and am still trying to say. But I want to give you what* you *want now because of what just has happened. You know what I mean: our love, our consummation—* "Don't say that word, Angel!" *Well, I don't care.*

First: My life with my own family changed when I brought Kenneth Levinworth home—during the time when we were what my mother called "courting." I suppose. In one sense. Anyway, for the first time in my occupation of that house, I became actual, visible, a member of the same family and species. My father and my brother came to life. They were delighted. Suddenly my father had someone to take flying lessons with, and my brother, Philip, had a partner to train with for the Boston Marathon. "Thank you for bringing Kenneth to us!" Both of them said that: at one point I was counting the number of times they said it . . but I stopped. "Janice: You have done the family proud!" I remember the first time my father said something like that to me (well, of course it wasn't like that; it was exactly that)—I started to shake. I couldn't stop myself. The reason was: I really didn't think he knew my name. It had always been "Dear" and "Young Lady" and, for a while when I was younger, "Pumpkin Seed." And so, what I'm trying to tell you here is: Of course it was wonderful: I brought Kenneth home and I was a physical reality—I had weight; I had mass; I took up space in my own house! Hooray! And the awful and sad thing was: I felt that way. "I'm here! I'm here! I have a specific gravity for my family in my family's house! Oh, thank you, Kenneth! Thank you! For being attracted to me and letting me bring you home: thank you for being a person who can make my family see me!"

But then I said to Kenneth: "Take me to your family." I thought my sphere of actuality could only increase. I had graduated. I had matured. I had broken from my tanager chrysalis out of my grub and larval condition and into the adult stage, into humanhood. And I couldn't wait to walk into another house and have it all confirmed: a person, a woman, recognized and addressed as such!

But Kenneth said: "You don't want that."

"Why don't I want it? Of course I want it! What are you talking about, Kenneth?"

"Take my word for it: You don't want that. Things are fine just the way they are. Don't rock boats."

But—doesn't it make sense?—I wanted to be celebrated in another house the way Kenneth was being so celebrated in mine.

So one day I went there. I drove to Southport on my very own. I was feeling immense. I was feeling powerful. I was feeling myself a person born into myself: luminous, powerful. There was light every-where—inside me especially. I would walk up to Salem Levinworth's front door and fulfill him with my brilliance, with his son's clearly radiant choice.

No house was visible from the road. Only a rock wall and mag-nolia and towering beech and a gate. I parked by the gate. It was locked. I climbed over the wall, walked up the drive. It was May and the tonic of bulbed early flowers, flowering trees, sea mist, new grass was thick as a tray of after-dinner drinks: liqueurs, cordials, brandies . . all open!

I knocked. A manservant came to the door. I said I had come to see the Levinworths. The manservant looked at me. He asked me to come in and directed me to a large room with bay windows that over-looked the extraordinary lawns that sloped to the sea. I could see a half dozen moored sailboats of various sizes. The manservant asked whether I would like anything to drink. I declined. He asked me to wait. I waited. While I waited I walked through the space of the room, know-ing I should smell the oiled wide floorboards under all the oriental rugs. One entire wall was bookshelves. Another wall was an art gallery: English landscape painters and French impressionists. There were two Albert Ryder paintings and several Winslow Homers. I felt "thrilled." It was the first time in my life that that word made any sense to me, thrilled. I felt the new light of me actually increasing. I felt myself as larger.

Then Salem Levinworth was there. I turned, and there he was . . watching me. I have no surety how long he had been doing that. "Good day, young lady," he said. "And what is it that I might do for you?"

I said that I was his son, Kenneth's, chosen. I said that I was Kenneth's betrothed. I said that I was to be his daughter-in-law. He looked at me with a sort of frightening penetration. I couldn't move. I was still, I thought, thrilled—but I felt frozen, immobile, paralyzed.

"Kenneth mentioned that he was seeing someone regularly," Salem Levinworth said.

"He is," I said. "Me." I tried smiling. I said: "We're planning marriage."

Salem Levinworth said nothing. He walked around me—two, then three complete circles. I couldn't move. I felt in danger of shrinking, being re-encapsulated in some new and lesser husk, losing my light,

*shrinking, becoming some other form of life again—other than a person
and woman. I admit to panic.*

"Where's Mrs. Levinworth?" I finally managed. "I would like to
meet her as well."

"Mrs. Levinworth is a drunk," Salem Levinworth said. "She is a
useless person. She is in her room—because she can't be anywhere else. I
despise her for her pathetic weakness. She will die in her room—and it
will be a great relief to anyone who has ever known her."

I learned later, from Kenneth, that his mother, yes, was alcoholic—but was in a sanatorium: she was confined, yes, to a room—but
her room was elsewhere.

I was frightened and excited. I was standing, locked in my
"introductory pose," waiting for a judgment. Waiting for Salem
Levinworth, my future father-in-law, to see me, recognize me, describe
me as an accepted woman and person in his eyes, see me not like his
pathetic, weak wife *but as a person with power, weight, mass, force,
all the things that I felt I'd now, because of Kenneth's loving and
wanting me, been born into.*

Salem Levinworth took a silver cigarette lighter from his pocket.
He looked hard into my eyes. "You appear to be a beautiful and substantial woman," he said to me. My heart cascaded! My heart raced
and leapt and burst—like the Atlantic, like the great falls of the Missouri River, like the white water of the Colorado! Not only in my own
house . . but in another's house: I was a living, visible force to be
reckoned with! *Salem Levinworth snapped on his lighter . . the flame,
white and blue, leaping up. He held the flame in front of him. I
waited. He waited. Neither of us said anything for two, maybe three
minutes. Then he said: "Hold your hand out." I complied. He moved
to me. His eyes never left my eyes. He extended the lighter flame until it
was under my hand . . until it was lapping at my palm . . until I
could feel my skin burn and even smell the burning of it. There was no
question but that the flame that he'd applied was consuming me. Still,
I did not dare to move. I did not dare to move . . and I did not dare to
move . . because I felt that . . should I do so . . he would withdraw his
recognition and approval, his validation of me in my new emerged and
adult self.*

Finally he snapped the lighter off. "You are a profound and
extraordinary woman," he said. "I could not be more pleased that my
son has chosen you." Then he took me by the wrist and led me over to
the bar, where he opened an ice bucket and set my hand into the

bucket, packing ice around it. "This will barely be noticeable in an hour," he said; "What would you like to drink? Scotch? Please say, 'scotch.' Were it to be scotch, I cannot tell you how much I would admire you."

"Scotch," I said.

"Incredible," he said. "Incredible. Finally."

We drank scotch together—one glass straight up . . two. I felt drunk and strangely cherished. Salem Levinworth threw open both bay windows on the sea side of the house and the entire room was thick, perfumed with ocean. Salem Levinworth began to laugh. I laughed with him. I had no idea why. Together, like lunatics, we laughed, braiding our laughter, for nearly five minutes. To this day, I do not fully understand what had happened—though I know that I will never never allow it to happen again.

And that was the start. That was the start that continued and only ended for me on the night of the fire.

I will tell you more later. But this is a good start.

Meet us—C.E.O., Alyce, and myself—in the circle in front of the Union Plaza tomorrow morning at 9:30. C.E.O. says: Please; you mustn't be late. Alyce's debut is of the greatest importance to him. He will not wait for you. I want you so to be there with us. I love you now with all my heart.

Your beloved,

"Angel"

Kohlman sweated. He was shaking. He moved from the monitor and crossed the room—forward, back; into the bathroom, out. He said, "Jesus Christ!" to himself: "Jesus fucking Christ!"; he picked a tangerine out of his fruit basket and threw it; punched the television. "Son of a bitch!" he said to himself: "Perverse fucking bastard!" He kept seeing Salem Levinworth's lighter flame in his mind, and Janice's sad, obedient hand over it . . waiting out whatever she hoped for, waiting out her . . what? . . "initiation." "*I'm glad you did it!*" Kohlman yelled with all the inhaled force of his lungs. He moved his hands to his head, spread his fingers, held his head like a medicine ball. He scrolled her message back, tried to read it a second time. He couldn't. He pounded the top of his veneer bureau and skinned his knuckles. "What is going *on*?!" he shouted. "What is *happening*?! What am I *doing* here?!"

He called the Nugget and got connected to the keno lounge. " 'Angel,' " he said.

"Angel's running," the lounge manager said.

"When's her break?" Kohlman asked.

"Angel doesn't break," the manager said. "Angel prefers not to break. She says the word troubles her."

Kohlman walked out onto his balcony. He slammed his fists into the wrought iron. *"I don't like who I am!"* he bellowed.

". . *We're not too crazy about you either!"* Two voices, a man's and a woman's, volleyed back from a balcony high up, across Flamingo, on Bally's. Kohlman lifted his hands over his eyes. He took them away. He tried to see beyond the lights into some other night, some other place where there might be a different kind of city. And though there was a moon—full, fat, and veined, north above the high desert and the Spring Mountains, it became just another globe, and Kohlman missed it. He tasted salt: his cheeks were stiff. A heat and tightness, like a barrel tie, strapped his neck and shoulders.

He went inside and placed a call to Sharon in New York, woke her. "Hi," he said.

"Benjamin?" Sharon asked. Her voice was hoarse and sleep-filled.

"Yes."

"Did I ask for a wake-up?"

"I'm sorry," Kohlman said.

"Are you . . back?" she said, her voice bringing itself to focus, stretching.

"No," he said. "I'm here."

"Oh . . right; you're 'here,' " she said.

"I'm in Las Vegas," Kohlman said. "Still."

"Well, that makes sense," Sharon said.

"I have to ask a question," Kohlman said.

"Try to make it easy," Sharon said. "I have some important work to do tomorrow. Today. Whenever."

"I need you to answer it," Kohlman said.

"I see."

"Why did you . . ?" Kohlman began, then stopped. He thought, tried repositioning what he'd asked: "Do you think that if I were to . . ?" He checked himself again.

"Somehow your voice is fading at the end of your sentences," Sharon said. "Is this a question that you're thinking of submitting, or something, for publication? Are you in the process of writing and revising this question *as we speak*?"

"How final do you feel about us?" Kohlman asked.

"Final," Sharon said. Her voice was level and without edge.

"I mean, if I were to come back a different person . . ." Kohlman began.

Sharon laughed.

"Don't do that," Kohlman told her.

She stopped . . and took a moment. "Which person were you thinking of coming back *as*?" she asked.

Kohlman had no answer.

"The answer's 'No,' " Sharon said. "Which I'm sure you knew . . before you placed the call. Accurate?"

"I suspected."

"Right."

"But, because of some things that have been happening, I . . suppose I needed to . . ."

"Benjamin: I'm not a 'reconsider' type. All right? I *do* hear something, actually, different in your voice. But, I can't . . . I *saw* you. I saw something: I saw heat; I saw a spark; I gave the spark fourteen—I think—pretty good months. . . But it didn't happen. We both know that. What I thought might happen . . what I thought might 'break through' in you . . or us . . but *you*, really, right now, are the issue . . didn't quite. Almost. *Close* a couple times. Nice. Hot a couple of times—exciting. And I did my best. I work at whatever I take on. I work hard. You know that. I hoped. I was rooting, for a long time, I think. But . . . time just ran out. If I have a failing . . it's that: I put things on a clock. I wasted my first nineteen years. . . Time gets critical. There's too little . . too much I want done. So . . your clock, I'm sorry, ran out. Blame me. Say: "She had no patience." Anyway, you were off to be a master of pulp . . or whatever . . composer of some sad lady's . . incidental music. And, so . . that became . . the end . . *it*.

"My work's first. Another flaw. But I can't have things that . . after a certain point . . bleed my concentration. I'm sorry. But you knew all of this when you called—I can't imagine that you didn't."

"I was . . right: pretty sure," Kohlman said. He was staring at the honeycomb of lights through his curtains.

"You need to lock yourself in a room with Cezanne for a week," Sharon said. "That might help. When I met you, I thought

you were almost a . . Cezanne person. Cezanne portrait. Something. That kind of . .'determined objectness'—excuse the art talk.
But . . . Sometimes your edges would get so hard. And tight. And
you would seem so . . formed! Modeled. But then there'd be these
other terrible moments when you'd melt into a bad Turner! I
mean, I love Turner—but I can't forgive him for what he did to this
century's *thought* and *purpose*—do you know?"

Sharon stopped talking. Nothing filled the gap. The two hung
on thick nightwires for an unnatural time. "You still there,
Benjamin?" Sharon asked.

"What about forgiveness?" Kohlman asked.

"What. . . What *about* forgiveness, Benjamin?" Sharon said.

"I'm not even sure what I'm asking," Kohlman said. "I thought
I was asking something about you—but I'm probably asking something about myself."

"Well, it's a better question than the *first* question you asked,
at least—about whether, when I said 'no,' I meant it. So there's
progress."

"Does it . . ?"

"Does what? Does *what* what?" Sharon asked.

"Oh . . shit!" Kohlman said. His voice choked and clotted.

"Benjamin: ask the question."

"Does it . . ?" Kohlman's chest was heaving. "Fuck . . !" he
said, angry at himself again. He was sucking air. His face was a
wash. Sharon, clearly, was determined to wait until he got the
question out. "Does . . ? . . Does it . . *hurt*?" he finally said;
"Does it at least *hurt* for you? I mean . . *this*? Us? That nothing . . ? That we weren't—that two good people—weren't able
to . . ?"

"Jesus: *Everything* hurts, Benjamin! Damn you: don't get
sloppy! You make me mad! *Everything* hurts! Every action that I
take . . *hurts* me. Every single thing that I move toward with my
heart or my mind *hurts* me to the bone and into my close muscles.
Every time I have a memory and reach out and say, "Yes! I will
claim this!" Every time I lift a brush. Every time when I would see
you! Sitting by your notes. Crossing a street. Drinking coffee. Any
time I imagine anyone in my family doing anything that I know,
by heart, they do, Benjamin: it hurts so bloody, bloody badly. It
seems so sweet! It seems so hard! It seems so sad! Or brutal! Or
dear! Or lost forever! So . . *fuck you and goddamn you for starting me*

Does going to bed at night hurt?! Does waking up every glorious, sad, possible, bloody, light-filled, corruptible morning hurt?! YES! *Yes, yes, yes! Does it hurt to make any . . ANY . . decision . . when you have given time to the other person involved in the decision?!* YES! . . YES! WHY DO YOU ASK ME SUCH A STUPID, TURNERESQUE QUESTION?!"
And now it was Sharon who was sobbing at the far end of the line.

Kohlman caught himself, caught his breath, caught his shaking. He felt strange. He felt calm. He felt steadied. He felt grateful. He felt as if, in some crazy way, in Sharon and in her determination to not allow him . . and in her refusal and in her breaking, she had shown him a future. "Listen . . ." he said.

"*What?!*" she barked at him.

"Thank you," he said.

"Yeah!" she said; "Right! Sure! 'Thank you!' My pleasure!"

"Be . . ."

"*What?!* Be *what?!*"

"Be well," Kohlman said.

"I will," she said. "Count on it! I see to that!"

"I know," he said. "It's what's so great about you."

"It's *one* of the things," she said; "It's just *one* of the things that's so great about me. And you know that!"

"I do," Kohlman said.

"Keep in touch," Sharon said.

" 'Night," Kohlman said.

" 'Night, Benjamin," Sharon said, then, "Oh . . and Benjamin?"

"Yes?" Kohlman said.

"So this is 'it'—right? You understand. You won't call . . try any more. The end of something is the end of it—you've got that—right?—you know."

"I know," Kohlman said. And they both hung up.

· · · · ·

Kohlman slept. In a dream, he woke and his room burned. It was a dream where Kohlman also stood watching the dream, thinking: *Of course*, but wondering: *Which is me? . . waking, scared? . . or watching?*

– EIGHT –

Kohlman's *actual* waking came after eight-thirty, the next morning. Janice had asked that he be downtown in less than an hour for the trip to Utah, to St. George—wherever that was. He dressed, chose his own clothes—blue shirt, madras tie, grey slacks, blue blazer. He left C.E.O.'s wardrobe on its racks, left the beard and hairpiece on the television. He would be himself. He would be himself and see what happened. At least today, out of town, he would be himself: he could do that. He took a cab.

Curbside by the Desert Inn, a woman in grey and dark brown burlap waved for a taxi. "Mind if I get this?" his cabbie asked. Kohlman shook his head. "Fine," he said. He wondered if the woman were related to the tall, dreadlocked *man*, the previous evening, who had carried the cross. The woman climbed in, swung an attache case onto her lap. "Thank you," she said to the cabbie. She turned to Kohlman: "Thank you. I have a breakfast coupon at the Lucky Strike Casino. Seventy-nine cents . . if I get there before ten o'clock. You take advantage of everything you can on an assistant professor's salary! —I teach," she said. "College. . . University."

Kohlman understood that she must be part of the Colonial American convention. "Do you know my brother?" he asked.

The woman looked quizzically at Kohlman. Her burlap filled the cab with a scent of vaguely rancid petroleum.

"His name is Adam," Kohlman said. "Adam Kohlman."

"Oh, Jesus!" the woman said.

They passed a billboard spread with an image of radiant sunlight. "DARE TO BE AMAZING!" the billboard said. They were past it before Kohlman could read any of the other words in smaller print.

"I'm sorry," the woman said. Her facial skin seemed suddenly attacked. "That's rude," she said. "It slipped out. He's brilliant. He's . . of course, his scholarship's . . immense. As we all know. He's formidable. And, of course . . of course, *discipline* . . to the bone." She looked out her window. "Anachronisms," she said.

Kohlman felt bad: even his brother's colleagues disliked him. The woman turned once more: "Please," she said; "that wasn't personal. He's your brother. You never think . . *one* never thinks . . that the person to whom one's speaking might be somebody's brother."

"We grew up," Kohlman said before realizing that, whatever his thought, it lay only half-delivered. He retried: "We grew up in Iowa," he said; then: "together in Iowa." His public words seemed so close that the woman tore the Velcro of her small woven purse and stared inside, shifting whatever its contents around for varying light. "We grew up on a farm," Kohlman went on, his voice speaking to . . what? . . his *eyes:* "Our parents . ." but then he had to back up and start again: "Our parents ran . . our parents farmed," he said.

The woman pulled out a gold coupon. "I thought I'd lost it," she said.

·   ·   ·   ·   ·

Kohlman stepped out at the Lucky Strike, paid for the woman's cab. The woman thanked him: "I spoke abruptly," she said. "I'm sorry. One doesn't think. Everybody respects Adam Kohlman. I wouldn't . . you shouldn't not think that." She tried to smile.

Kohlman nodded. She shrugged.

"But you're not like him," she said, her voice softer.

"I don't know," Kohlman said. He started off.

"No," she said. "No." He stopped. "One sees immediately."

". . Perhaps," Kohlman said.

"He has no warmth—you do." She smiled.

Kohlman thought about it. He set off again. "Have a nice breakfast," he said—one final turn back before he started jogging toward the Union Plaza.

. . . . .

It was nine-fifteen. Almost immediately, arms grabbed Kohlman from behind and forced him into an alleyway, pushing him forward along narrow spaces. Rags had been thrown and piled, and Kohlman stumbled over them into a space cleared at mid-alley, before more rags, in heaps and mounds, began stretching out again. There was a thick stench of oily hydrocarbon. The forcing hands let him go. He saw something lit being tossed into the alley from behind and in front of him. The rags in front blazed up. Kohlman turned back. The rags behind surged into flames. There were walls of fire before and behind. A voice called—was it from the alley? was it from one of the enclosing buildings?— "Last chance!" the voice said. "Last chance for a person curious about fire: *Out of town!*"

Kohlman checked his watch. It was nine-twenty-seven. He took a start at dashing into the burning alleyway. He felt the flames drift up his pantlegs, spun, and ran back. He tried the other direction. "Last chance!" the voice called again.

"*I'm not interested in the fucking hotel fires!*" Kohlman shouted. "*I have no interest in any hotel fires at all! . . I'm asking about a fire that took place in Connecticut!*" Kohlman waited, listened. Was his assailant there? Had he heard Kohlman's message? Would he reply? —But there was nothing—only the alley of rags burning on either side, flames climbing the abutting walls. He heard sirens. He heard approaching then arriving engines. He got caught in the crossfire of two pumptruck hoses.

. . . . .

They checked Kohlman for smoke and water inhalation. He fielded questions. "I have no idea," he said. "I really have no idea." They dried his clothes in a huge industrial dryer used for uniforms. The Challenger appeared at the station wearing workout clothes. It was nearly noon. "I'm here for assistance," the Challenger said.

"Mr. Kohlman's your friend?" the officer-in-charge asked.

"He's my Man!" the Challenger said and wrapped Kohlman with a massive arm. "Where're your clothes?" he asked.

"They're being dried," the officer-in-charge said.

"Release this man!" the Challenger said. "Let my people go!" He laughed.

"No problem," the officer said. He fixed the enormous black man with regard. "Ready for Thursday?" he asked. "We gonna have a good fight?"

"Is the Lord in Heaven black?!" the Challenger asked. He laughed again. "Be there!" he said.

"The Champ's soundin' pretty mean," the second officer said. "He's talkin' big; he's soundin' hungry! He's got the point-spread!"

"Well, there is a local . . and there is a *global* hunger," the Challenger said. "There is a local . . and there is a global . . point spread." He smiled. "So . . . Seventy-two hours . . ." He grinned more broadly, a flash of gold and ivory teeth. "We will know which is which."

The two officers beamed. Kohlman stood, watching.

"Monday night! Eight o'clock! Thas' all I can say." The Challenger spread his arms out in a mock helplessness. "Those are my only and most solitary words: Be there. For the miracle. The taste of the pudding!" he said.

"You got it!" both officers said.

"And that's how it be!" The Challenger grinned.

"And that's how it be!" the two, caught in his light, repeated.

. . . . .

When they walked out onto the granite precinct stairs, Kohlman asked: "How did you find me? How'd you know I was here?"

"I got a message," the Challenger said.

"You got a message?"

"I got a message. I got a call. On the WATS line wired in my brain—a call came. Call said: 'Your man's on fire!' 'Your man's in deep shit!' 'Your man's havin' trouble with the air!' An' I always answer my calls."

. . . . .

Kohlman told his friend he'd missed an appointment. "I was supposed to go with some people to a piano recital in . . is there a . . 'St. George'? . . Utah?"

"No problem," the Challenger said.

The Challenger found a phone. "We have this wired," he told Kohlman. He squatted where they stood on the sidewalk, put his hands on his hips, rotated left, then right. "Come on," he said. "Do this. Follow your Challenger. Be good."

Kohlman squatted. He followed. They did twists. They did sit-ups and stretching exercises. "I didn't know I had so many things to stretch," Kohlman joked. And then he asked: "So what's happening? What's 'wired'? What do I need to do, now, about my problem?" He felt good. He felt amazingly good though nearly breathless.

"What should I call you?" the Challenger asked.

"Pardon?"

"What . . should . . I . . call . . you . . if I want to call you a name?"

"Oh . . 'Benjamin,' " Kohlman said.

"*Benjamin*."

"Benjamin—yeah," Kohlman said. " 'Kohlman.' 'Benjamin Kohlman.' "

"*Benjamin Kohlman*."

"Benjamin Kohlman."

The Challenger sprang up. He started bouncing lightly in place. Kohlman followed. "Benjamin Kohlman: What size shoes you wear?" "Ten and a half *D*," Kohlman said.

The Challenger bounced on one foot; he removed the other sneaker as he sprang in balance.

"What are you doing?" Kohlman asked.

The Challenger changed feet. He unlaced the other sneaker. "Benjamin Kohlman: Take off those shoes," he said. He nodded down to Kohlman's black leather oxfords.

"What's going to happen?" Kohlman said.

"Take off those shoes," the Challenger said again.

Kohlman did.

"Benjamin Kohlman: Put on my running shoes."

Kohlman objected. What did the Challenger plan to wear? But the Challenger's authority was unassailable.

Once Kohlman had laced the fighter's shoes, his friend took off, running. Kohlman followed. "What are we doing?" Kohlman asked.

"You my *pacer*, Benjamin Kohlman. You my *sparrin' partner!*" The Challenger laughed. "Am I a black man? Do I talk like a black man?" He laughed again.

Kohlman didn't know how, precisely, to respond. "I jog sometimes around the reservoir in Central Park," he said. He felt breathless. "But . . . How far is St. George?"

Where the Challenger led him was down Las Vegas Boulevard, the four and a half miles back to Caesar's. Kohlman kept protesting: "I can't! I can't do this! When I was much . . when I was much, much younger . . I could have done it. I raced. I ran. But I'm a different . . I'm not that person . . I'm a different person now."

"I think not," the Challenger said.

"I have different lungs."

"Whose?"

"I've been living in different air. . . Don't make me answer so many questions."

"Which air you been living in?"

"Don't do this."

"I grew up on a farm. . . I've been living in New York City."

"What's your name?" the Challenger asked.

"You asked that!"

"What's your name?"

"Benjamin Kohlman," Kohlman said.

"Benjamin Kohlman!" the Challenger echoed.

"Right—Benjamin Kohlman."

"Benjamin Kohlman!"

"Yes."

"That the name you were born with?"

"Yes."

"So . . Benjamin Kohlman is Benjamin Kohlman is Benjamin Kohlman! Right?"

"I suppose."

"Now . . then . . an' forevermore—*always*!" the Challenger said.

"Well . . okay . . but *this* Benjamin Kohlman's not in the best condition!" Kohlman said.

"It's all mental," the Challenger said.

"Yeah—well . . ."

"It's all mental and *meta* and *para* physical."

Kohlman's rib cage burned like a banked woodstove. His thighs felt strung with piano wires. His knees sloshed like dishwater. "I'm not going to argue," he said.

"*Meta* and *para* . . and *para* and *meta* . . and *mental*!" the Challenger said and laughed and slipped behind, put his hands on Kohlman's ribs, thumbs to vertebrae, manipulated something. A spill like heat lightning rippled Kohlman's brainstem, spun his eyes, flashed out . . receptor into receptor: more wind came. "How's that?" the Challenger said.

"Amazing!" Kohlman said. "Good. Great. Better. What'd you do?" The envelope of his skin felt ionized and electrical.

"Not hard," the Challenger said.

"But what?" Kohlman asked.

"Try to breathe . . through the top of your head," the Challenger said. "Be better."

.   .   .   .   .

At times, what Kohlman took to be altitude – or exhaust fumes and dry heat – seemed to torch his entire respiratory system. But then the Challenger, once more, would slip behind and seem to reshape his spinal column . . until the hot pavement and reflected city clarified and freshened and cooled and slid past like spring water.

"How does that work?" Kohlman pursued.

The Challenger laughed. "Benjamin Kohlman," he said, "Don't question. Don't question everything. Just breathe through the top of your head. Don't think about it. Focus. Stay empty. Fullness comes. You be fine."

.   .   .   .   .

Back at his friend's suite, they took a whirlpool. The Challenger picked aluminum tab lids and fragments of bottle glass from where they had embedded themselves, from the boulevard pavement, in his feet. There seemed to have been no damage. They watched Phil Donahue on the huge wraparound video screen. Donahue seemed a more thoughtful man when he was concave.

Kohlman asked why so many police and security were in the lobby. "Is it for the fight?" he asked. "Are they gearing up?"

"It's for the President," his friend said.

"Of what?"

"Pres-i-*dent*!" the Challenger articulated. He sank below the surface of the water. Kohlman waited, counting, beginning to worry. Minutes later, the huge man resurfaced. "It's for my wind," he said.

"So . . were you saying . . . ?" Kohlman almost felt afraid to ask: "Like . . you said the *President*."

"Right."

"Of . . *here?*"

"Las Vegas?"

"No; I mean . . did you mean . . like . . the *President?*"

"You got it!"

"Why . . ?"

"Here making an MTV video!" the Challenger said.

Kohlman shook his head—he wasn't sure he'd heard what he'd heard. He nodded.

"He doesn't want—this is what my frien' on the *inside* tole me. The President's . . *concerned.* His popularity slipping. So he's makin' a video. We got a person here—called *Comus*—supposed to be the best special effects cat alive. Does, like, these earthquakes? You understan' what I'm saying? These waterfalls? And plane crashes? For all the big casino shows. President's got Comus doin' his video."

Kohlman nodded again. The Challenger resubmerged.

When the Challenger came up, Kohlman began talking about himself. He spilled, meandered. He described his project: the first thoughts when it had begun . . the sorts of feelings he had now. How different they were! How, now, he knew he'd never write the book he'd come to write. How he knew he'd have to at least *try* another. Same subject—Janice—but . . . A *right* book, he said. A *good* book. A *true* book.

The Challenger smiled at Kohlman's outpouring, as though he felt *washed* by it, sweetly carried. He nodded.

Kohlman confessed loving Janice. "I know absolutely *nothing* about her," he said. "I mean, it's *crazy.* I mean, on *one* level." He grew pensive, tried to follow the drift of his mind. "It's insane," he began again. "It makes no sense. We could go to bed . . and she could cut my throat . . and someone who'd been watching would just say: 'Right. Of course. It was obvious.' But she is so . . !'" Kohlman searched for an end to his sentence, but couldn't find one.

"I understand," the Challenger said.

"She is . . . I mean, she's so . . !" Kohlman shook his head. "I'm just, I guess, having trouble . . allowing myself—I'm sorry; I don't mean 'allowing myself'; I don't have to give myself permission; I know that. But . . I mean . . by responding . . by feeling as . . close or responsive or whatever as I do . . what I'm doing, on one level, I worry, is buying into—not 'buying into'; that's wrong;

it sounds . . *business*like or something—but more I suppose *consenting* to or submitting— 'submitting' isn't a bad word—to her version—you know what I'm saying?—of our arrangement. I mean: that it's a 'marriage.' Which it isn't . . yet. Or . . and probably couldn't ever . . . But by letting myself . . by being in love with her, it seems, in part, I'm *accepting*, in a way, the logic of the way *she* . . . Wouldn't you say? I mean, sometimes I think: *What am I doing? What is this all about?* But, then again, I think: what difference does it make? You know? Did I talk to you about my brother?"

All the time—Kohlman rambling—the Challenger stared hard, concentrating: his mouth below the surface of the water, his eyes steady.

Kohlman spoke about being threatened. "I couldn't care less about the hotels and their fires and whatever's behind them!" Kohlman said. "The whole thing is crazy! Someone overheard me say 'fire' to Janice somewhere—and now my life's not my own! What're you supposed to *do* when you're in this city?! Eliminate 'fire' from your vocabulary?!"

"Stay in touch," the Challenger said, finally, lifting his head.

"What do you mean? What are you talking about?" Kohlman said.

"I mean: Be cool, Benjamin Kohlman." Kohlman's friend held his gaze. "We deal with the fire-people when the time is the time. When the time is the time—we deal with the fire-people."

". . Okay," Kohlman said. He seemed to trust everything his friend said.

· · · · ·

An hour later, the two drove across the desert, east, in a white Caesar's Palace limo. Kohlman sat at the wheel; the Challenger read *The Koran*. "I shouldn't let you do this"—Kohlman had begun talking in the whirlpool and couldn't stop—"I shouldn't let you drive over there with me. You got me the car. That was great. But I mean I could easily do this alone. You've got a World Heavyweight Championship Title Match coming up in less than a week. God knows what you have to do, still, to get ready. The last thing you probably have time for is to drive over with me to some place in *Utah* to see a goddamn twelve-year-old skinny runaway sister of an eighteen-year-old pimp and drug dealer give a bloody *piano concert*! I'm sorry. I shouldn't do that. Barnett's been good; he's helped. I shouldn't . . I judge too quickly. Too easily. Something. I guess that's all right, though. We all judge. Have judgments. Feelings . . judgments—that's a very good thing . . something, in fact, I probably haven't really, in my more recent life, *honored* . . in the way I should have been honoring. But . . ."

"Benjamin Kohlman: please shut up," the Challenger said. And then: "You know I like you—but you use too many words . . to be who you are."

.   .   .   .   .

Between Las Vegas and St. George, the landscape was high mountain desert, like an Iowa without crops, an Iowa on the moon. Growing up, around Templeton, Kohlman had often stared into the winded shimmer of corn or soy or alfalfa and wondered what was beyond, under it: what were its *bones*. And here they were! Here was its bare anatomy: simple, stubbled, strewn with ephemerals, unrequesting, sure, ancient. At the end, just before Utah, the landscape swallowed itself—bare flesh to bone, silica to blood-iron rock—and plunged, like raw breath, into the Virgin River Canyon, a vertical maze docked with dwarf cedar and bright bands of falling water. Kohlman shivered at the beauty, and in his shiver felt a skeletal realignment . . felt his joints, where the major bones joined the major bones, lubricated.

.   .   .   .   .

In St. George, the two asked where there might be a concert. "A piano concert," Kohlman said.

"So it's, then, like, a *cultural event?*" the blond receptionist at J. B.'s Big Boy asked.

"Something, probably, *like* that," Kohlman said. The Challenger shadowed . . watching, listening, grinning. The receptionist wondered whether it might not be at the college.

"The college," Kohlman repeated.

"Yes," she said.

"Which college is that?" Kohlman asked.

"Dixie," she said. "Dixie College."

Kohlman asked directions to Dixie College and thanked her. Walking out, he noticed a poster, silver with blue lettering—IN CONCERT/ ALYCE BARNETT—taped inside the restaurant window. As they drove the main street heading to the edge of the town and campus, Kohlman saw posters in every shop, store, and restaurant window. The Challenger shook his head and laughed. "Ol' C.E.O. Barnett!" he said.

"You know him?" Kohlman asked.

"We all 'know him,' " the Challenger grinned.

"We *all?*"

"We all . . we all!" the Challenger said. "He deals the steroids. He deals the steroids to all the 'ath-el-etes.' He the Man wi' the Goods. Whatever goods is Goods! We had a breakfast one day. I said: 'You need some steroids yo'sef!'—I do 'black talk' on people sometimes: 'You need some steroids *yo'sef*!' I said. I'll say one thing for the dude, though: he's got an early start!"

They drove under a silver Mylar banner spread across the street: ALYCE BARNETT—IN CONCERT!—ALYCE BARNETT. It was four-thirty in the afternoon.

·   ·   ·   ·   ·

The Challenger told Kohlman he wanted to spend two or three hours in the encircling mountains. "I want to run up a couple of them," he said. "Then sit on the top—an' get my focus." He said he'd find the concert and be there before eight. Kohlman watched him lope off toward a grove, above where the limousine idled, of yellowing aspen.

·   ·   ·   ·   ·

He found the auditorium. Janice ran to and embraced him. "I'm so glad!" she kept saying: "I'm so glad; I'm so glad! I'm so relieved!"

"Mr. Bookwriter!" C.E.O. Barnett said.

Kohlman thought it best to wait to tell his whole story. "I had a problem," he said. "I'm sorry."

"You know anything about sound systems?" Barnett asked. "This system is shit! I can't believe it! I got another one coming in from Nashville on a Learjet. I may have to kill somebody if it doesn't get here."

A young Scandinavian-looking man in a dark suit moved hesitantly to C.E.O. "Mr. Barnett?" he said.

"We got the fucking sound system?!" C.E.O. asked.

"Mr. Barnett—could you please not use those words that you've been using?" the young man said.

C.E.O. Barnett looked at Janice. He looked at Kohlman. His face had a quizzical asymmetrical look.

"C.E.O: these people are religious," Janice urged gently. "These people are Mormon people . . and they've been extremely cooperative. Be considerate of them."

For the first time since Kohlman had met him, C.E.O. Barnett seemed uncertain, even shy. He held his hands up in, if not surrender, truce: "Okay," he said. "Okay. I'll try."

"We'd be most grateful, Mr. Barnett," the young man said and moved away.

C.E.O. rolled his eyes. He took an enormous breath. Kohlman knew the moment, knew the precise cloud inversion in C.E.O.'s head. "Alyce is in a practice room," Barnett told Kohlman. "I've got her on some Xanex. The auditorium holds twelve hundred . . all we've got left's eighty-seven seats. I sent Leonard Bernstein an invitation and a first-class plane ticket. I've been calling his office. Guy doesn't even have the grace to return my calls." He looked at his watch. "Two hours forty-seven minutes . . we're in *history*. All we can do now is hope."

"Did you get my note?" Janice smiled—so soft, so sweetly at Kohlman. "I wrote you a message . . on your screen."

". . I got it," Kohlman said. "Thank you. I did." He felt something like a trace element shuttle just beneath his skin, back and forth, between his shoulders. He wanted to take Janice and move her aside, go somewhere.

"Was it okay?" she asked. "My words?"

"They were fine," Kohlman said. "They were very okay."

"I'm glad." Janice smiled.

"We need to talk," Kohlman said.

"We will," Janice said. She leaned up and kissed him—less a kiss, more like Kohlman's own skin opening.

"I need to ask you some things," Kohlman said, his voice barely recoverable. "There's one, at least, very important thing, which, for me, needs to get asked."

". . 'Which, for me, needs to get asked'?" Janice teased.

"I have to know something," Kohlman said. "Really, just—more than anything else—to have your answer. It's whether . . Did . . ? That night, the night of . . ."

Janice set her finger to his lips.

"I don't think *what* the answer is matters. I just need . . *some-thing* which won't leave me alone."

"You'll have it," Janice said. "You'll have everything. You'll have colors . . even before the light is on them." She touched his lips with her finger again, moved her finger to three different places, pressed softly. "Always," she said, and then, "ever." She had a way of rendering language as though it were entirely private, as though each word were a secret.

". . Did you know the President of the United States is here?" Kohlman said. "I mean, in Las Vegas? To make an MTV video?" He was trying to shift the subject away to where his available oxygen felt less in jeopardy.

"I know." The quiet light kept playing from Janice's eyes to cheekbones to lips; she nodded. "It's my friend, Comus," she said. "The President's working with my friend. Comus is excited. —Oh, and . . !" She looked suddenly puzzled and concerned. "Do you know two people named Shane and Alexander?" she said.

"I . . . Well . . yeah," Kohlman said: "Shane and Alexander? Yeah. Writers. Why?"

"They came to the Nugget," she said. "Last night. They wanted to talk. They say my brother, Philip, has sold them the rights to my story. They offered me money. They said that you had no name and that I shouldn't trust you and that if they needed to their publisher —'Row and Harper'?"

"Close," Kohlman said. "Close enough."

"If they needed, Row and Harper could get a court order stopping publication of whatever book you wrote."

"And what did you say?" Kohlman asked.

"I said that you *did* have a name. That your name was 'Benjamin.' That your name was 'Benjamin Kohlman' and that I loved your name. I said you'd had it for a long time. Since you were born. And I said that I was . . 'committed.' I loved using that word. I used it as many times as I could, because their faces *slipped* and they looked at each other . . whenever I used it. I didn't, of course, say what I've said to you: that we were married. I don't see that as being any of their concern."

"And what did they say?" Kohlman was aware of Barnett— dispensing orders, directing traffic less than ten feet away. "What did they say? When you dealt with them in that way?" he asked.

"They said that what they wanted was: for everything to be agreeable. But that if I didn't agree, they could create a lot of publicity and attention . . that I might not want to have in my life. Now. At this moment."

Kohlman ran his hand through his hair, gripped the top of his scalp as he might palm a basketball. "They won't do anything," he told her. "They won't cause you any problems." And although he knew he hadn't the right to, he added: "I promise."

"I know, Benjamin," Janice said. "I know *you promise*. I've felt your promise. I know it." She left her lips apart, slightly, at her sentence's closing, as if she were waiting for him, perhaps, to kiss her.

Kohlman saw the moment. He felt dissolved and invisible, inside her mouth, within her blood, a spiral lost in her bones. He felt that brutally intimate, yet . . still, in public. Kohlman realized he'd been holding his breath. He touched Janice's hair and it leapt to fire. He turned to Barnett. "Can I do anything?" he asked. He startled himself; he had not really planned his offer.

"Yeah, in fact: Look at this," Barnett said. He handed Kohlman a program. "Check this. You're the writer. Let me know if everything's spelled right."

Kohlman read over the program. He felt his muscles tense at one line. "I think you ought to cut this," he said to Barnett.

"What do you mean?" C.E.O craned his neck to see the spot on the printed program where Kohlman had placed his finger. It was in the "About Alyce Barnett" section. "But it's true!" Barnett said.

"Well . . it may be true, but . . ."

"Which line?" Janice said.

"*Alyce Barnett is the victim of incest*," Barnett quoted. "It's true! Hey, look: *I* didn't invent it! It's verifiable!"

"Possibly," Kohlman said. "Fine. I'm not disputing that. It's more that my point is . . ."

"Right: your 'point.' Big writer! You can write anything you want about Janice . . because it's true. But because I'm not a writer, I can't write true shit about my sister!"

Kohlman hadn't an answer. He thought of saying: *But I'm not going to write the book I'd planned!* He thought of saying: *No: It's the wrong kind of truth! People are too interested in the wrong kind of truth! Don't encourage them!* He thought of saying: *Just because, instead of looking to God, we look at psychopaths . . !*

But before Kohlman could say *any* of those things, Barnett went on: "Look: Incest is big now. Okay? They have shows on *television* about it. 'Child abuse.' Should I change 'incest' to 'child abuse'? I could do that. Except . . ! I took a Writing For Executives course at UNLV. They said, 'Be specific.' This is specific. 'Child abuse' is . . *vague.* 'Incest.' No . . I think not; I think it stays! I've got records. There was a court hearing."

"Okay: You're the boss," Kohlman said.

"I am. Excellent observation. I'm the boss."

"It was only a suggestion."

Another nearly-albino Scandinavian approached C.E.O. "Mr. Barnett?" he said.

"The sound system?" Barnett asked.

"Could I speak with you for just a minute?" The man bowed slightly. Or nodded. His voice modulated with an almost unworldly deference.

"Is it about the sound system?" C.E.O. asked again. "Have we got our sound system finally?"

"It's about the reception, sir," the blond man said.

"Okay—but quick," Barnett said. "I've got to check that my sister's wardrobe person and hair person are doing what they're being paid to do."

"Sir: the wine . . ?"

For all his air of apology, the blond man began to strike Kohlman as absolutely ferocious.

"Cool all the white," C.E.O. said. "Fifty-four, fifty-five, fifty-six degrees. Leave the red out. Begin to open it about nine-thirty."

"No; well . . . We don't allow wine on campus," the man said.

"No: wait: I'm sorry: I beg your pardon?" Barnett turned frontally to the blond man.

"We don't allow alcoholic beverages of any kind on the campus," the blond man said, without a quaver.

"That's seven K *plus* worth of wine," Barnett said.

"I'm just telling you . . ."

"Right. I understand. But that's for your students—that rule? Right? That's for your . . what do you call them—your 'student body'?"

"It's a state regulation," the blond man said. "Besides, no one in this town would want to . . ."

"Well, I don't care! You understand what I'm saying?! Because I'm the guy who's put this together! And I'm the guy who's paying the bills! And *I* want the wine. I want fine wine at the reception following the debut of my sister, Alyce Barnett, concertizing on the piano! Okay?!"

"Yes, sir. But . . in this town and state . . ."

"Well, watch my lips—because I'm gonna say: *fuck* this town! Okay? Does that make its point 'periodically'. . and with a certain style? And I'm gonna say *fuck* this state! I want the wine!"

Janice took C.E.O. quietly but directedly by the arm and led him away. Kohlman could see her eyes; he knew the meaning of their clarity. The scene was a thirty-six-year-old mother 'in conference' with her eighteen-year-old son. Kohlman heard Barnett's voice rumbling, rumbling, then, unable to check itself, rising: ". . *Seven K worth of imported wine!*" The blond man folded his hands and stood impassively. "How are you?" he said to Kohlman and smiled. Kohlman tried to set aside thoughts of Janice and pressures she might have from Shane and Alexander.

"I'm fine," Kohlman said.

"We're just very grateful for the opportunity of this concert," the blond man said. "We're most appreciably grateful for people who share their wonderful creative talents."

"Right," Kohlman said. He wondered how he might keep Shane and Alexander away, wondered what kind of deal they'd struck with Janice's brother. He wondered when he might get the chance to ask the question that he knew he must ask Janice.

Janice led C.E.O. Barnett back. "Mr. Barnett understands," she said to the blond man. Kohlman had never seen Barnett sweat, but he was sweating now. "He wanted me to tell you that, given your regulations—which we of course understand—we will be calling over and switching our reception to the St. George Hilton."

"Certainly," the blond man said. "Of course we can't refund the deposit."

"*Tonio?!*" Barnett boomed to a swarthy man adjusting lights on stage. The man turned. "*Tonio?! See this man?!*" Barnett pointed to the blond.

"*C.E.O.!*" Janice cut into Barnett's command sharply. Kohlman felt jolted by her clear and assured chastisement.

Barnett stopped. He moved away a half dozen paces and beat his head with his fists.

.   .   .   .   .   .

The sound system arrived an hour before concert time. Ten minutes later, a telegram arrived: Leonard Bernstein, apologies. Barnett had given Kohlman a new job: "Trouble-shooter! Circulate!" Kohlman was circulating. The audience began to arrive. They all seemed known to one another, hundreds of men in dark-vested suits, women in print ankle-length dresses. How had Barnett managed to sell all these tickets? The auditorium began to smell like soap. Kohlman thought he could almost hear the programs rattle in unison when the browsers got to the biographical line dealing with incest. Then, suddenly, at seven-forty-five, there was a commotion at the entrance. Kohlman, as "trouble-shooter," moved to check it out.

His friend, the Challenger, stood at the auditorium doors in a fine midnight-blue tuxedo. Couples filed past, looking unsure: men with missionary smiles; women double-checking their necklines. A girl in grape chiffon and a blond man stood with the Challenger: both stiffly overgracious. "Is there a problem?" Kohlman asked.

"No." "Oh, no!" the couple said.

"Benjamin Kohlman!" the Challenger grinned. He introduced Kohlman as his friend. The couple both said they were pleased to meet him. "These people are being *kind*," the Challenger said. "They've let me know how happy they are to have a 'dark brother' here with them tonight. I said I was a '*black* brother.' They said: 'even *better*.' "

Everybody tried to laugh.

"I see," Kohlman said.

"So then: are you . . Mr. *Barnett?*" the blond man said. "We've been hearing a lot about Mr. Barnett."

"I'm . . helping Mr. Barnett," Kohlman said. "I'm . . my name's Mr. . . . I'm Benjamin Kohlman."

The man took Kohlman's hand in his own scrubbed hand. He pressed . . as on a hand grip . . and held tight. "Mr. Kohlman," he said. "Eldon Markham." He thanked Kohlman—for *what* Kohlman couldn't discern. "I'm sure you know about the Church's revelation," he said. He still did not let Kohlman go. "It's been a good feeling: to be enlightened. So this is a very special occasion. About which we're all very pleased."

Kohlman had the impulse to take a felt pen and scribble on the man's white, presuming skin.

He went on: "My wife, LuJennifer, and I"–LuJennifer smiled– ". . were just saying . . just, in fact, telling Mr. . . Challenger . . how much we both admire . . how much we're both . . fans of . . well, to put it mildly . . strength. In contests. Because strength tests–as I'm sure is no secret: *is* it?–preparation and ability. And preparation and ability . . are both very real things: wouldn't you agree?" The man, Markham, smiled. His wife, LuJennifer, replayed her mild agreements.

Something in the couple's stance . . the man's cadence . . set circuit breakers off in Kohlman. All involuntary. Flares. Like those which had lit him out of himself, on gathering occasions, to draw lines: "Don't ridicule . . ." "Don't shoot people!" But the couple had only tried to be embracing. Perhaps his edge came from Janice's news of Shane and Alexander.

Kohlman felt the Challenger touch his shoulder–pressure, gentle, still infusing. Kohlman turned. "You okay?" he asked.

His friend spread his arms and opened his hands. "I be fine," he said. "I be eager for the music!"

Kohlman grinned.

". . We are very honored," the man, Markham, once again, said. And others–eavesdropping and watchful and aware and passing by–responded: "Very honored" . . "Yes" . . "Very honored" . . "Thank you."

The Challenger shook hands then walked, elegantly, down the auditorium aisle.

· · · · ·

The lights dimmed. The audience's soft buzz at the Challenger's entrance trailed to a private hum. Alyce was to play a Chopin Etude, a Mozart Prelude, and George Gershwin's "Rhapsody In Blue." When she walked onto the stage, moving toward the immense Steinway, the audience sucked a collective breath. Janice turned to C.E.O. Barnett, her face white suddenly, her eyes injured. Kohlman heard her say: "C.E.O. –*no*!" C.E.O. looked hurt and petulant; it was not a moment he wished to be upbraided. "This is wrong." Janice's head fluttered with sad, hurt oscillations and looked almost unstable on her neck. "This is wrong," she repeated. Barnett's eyes pooled. "You could've waited to say that," he whispered. "This is supposed to be my big night!" "It wouldn't wait," Janice whispered back. She touched her eyes as if they burned.

Alyce looked like a child whore. She'd not had breasts two nights previous when Kohlman had first met her. But she had them now: rock-solid uplifting mounds that strained the gold satin of her gown. She wore a huge, tangled wig, hair like spun Puerto-Rican rum. Her powder and gloss made her look like a confection. Kohlman felt Janice, beside him, crying. He took her hand. She turned her face into his coat jacket, tight at his shoulder. "Women aren't allowed to live!" she said. "Women aren't allowed to live in this world. They have to die for everybody!" Then, suddenly, she moved her hands to her head in a gesture, for Kohlman, now familiar. The crowd waited for notes; Kohlman waited for blood.

·　·　·　·　·

Alyce's playing, though, was exceptional, and Kohlman found himself, in turn, checking Janice's pain and that she had not begun hemorrhaging . . then leaning forward, attending, framing sometimes very complex musical measures. Alyce was gifted, clearly. She had touch and discipline. She had been given training that made strict demands. And whatever the preliminaries might have indicated, this was an audience that seemed to understand her remarkable feats. They were held, thrilled in certain passages; they applauded forcefully. Then, abruptly, Kohlman could feel Janice turned toward and studying him. He looked to her. Her face looked shattered. "I know . . ." she began; "I know now what your question was." Faint blood, like fissured capillaries, blew lines under her eyes. *What was her guess? What was her knowledge? Did* he, *even, know his question?* "How . . ." she began again, stopping, moving her teeth back and forth against each other and against her mind: "How could you even think . . !" Then she pulled away and rose and vanished into the black auditorium. Kohlman reached for her . . but she was gone. Alyce's hands lifted and swept. Kohlman rose to follow Janice, but Barnett seized his arm. The music powered to its final crescendos. At the concert's end, Alyce was brought back five times onto the stage, each successive encore more enthusiastic. C.E.O. Barnett shouted "Bravo!" and again, "Bravo!" Others joined. A crystal punch bowl with two hundred long-stemmed roses arrived for Alyce on her third encore. "You like that?!" C.E.O. turned to the distracted Kohlman: "Baccarat! You like that touch?! I redeem myself! Right? I'm okay now! Where did Janice go?"

. . . . .

An usher in lemon taffeta told Kohlman she'd seen a woman leave and run in to the sandstone bluffs that backed the campus. "Did she have a white dress? Sort of silky?" the usher asked. Kohlman thanked her and gave chase.

The moon, washed out the previous night, now flooded the scape – ghostly dominion making pale red-rock into glowing bread: fundamental and leavened. Kohlman jogged the patched incline, cupping his hands and calling: "Janice . . ? . . Janice . . ?" Poorwills flew from all the cornices in the rock at his voice. A terror never before felt and unspeakable broke again and again. The words, repeated in the burning alley earlier: "Last chance . . !" swept his mind. Should he heed? Should he leave everything? Just take off? Kohlman felt responsible. For *what*? But he knew: knew, denied, accepted, hated the knowledge, embraced it. He had been a coward too often. He had failed at courage. Let the judgement come! Let the wrong trial for the right crimes move itself on to a verdict!

. . . . .

He saw her where the rock made a chimney. She stood in it, her arms out against either side of its flume, her white dress like milk, the moon pouring against her in her tortured pose like a cool guardian.

Kohlman approached. The blood of "Eve's Disease" flared from her nostrils and from the corners of her mouth where it had run across her shoulders and out, streaking her arms, shining from the backs of her extended hands. "Stay there," she said to Kohlman.

". . Angel," Kohlman said.

. . . . .

"Let me help you," Kohlman implored. Then, "Angel," again. Then, "Please."

"Your question is whether I took Salem Levinworth's life," Janice said. "I'm right, aren't I? That's true. How could you ask that?" Her face looked razored; her eyes, cut away.

Kohlman understood his trespass.

"How could you ask that?" she said again.

．　　．　　．　　．　　．

"Jan . . ?" From behind Kohlman swept the voice of Alyce. She stood with the Challenger. "I be the lady's escort," the Challenger said. He raised a hand quietly to Kohlman. "I have to go," he said, his voice soft now as a ground squirrel. He turned and left.

"I wish you'd come to me," Janice said to Alyce.

"I should have," Alyce said.

"C.E.O. was wrong," Janice said.

"I know," Alyce said. "I know now."

"Benjamin–go," Janice said.

"Let me help," Kohlman said.

"No," Janice said.

"Please," Kohlman said. "Please. Why? Why not?"

"No. Because I have to be here with Alyce. Because we need to be here. Because I need to show her my body and she needs to show me hers. Because we need to talk about being proud and not being ashamed and about being women."

Feeling, thick as mud, rose up in Kohlman's throat. From somewhere, his child-friend, Pamela Arnold, spoke . . saying . . what? . . *some*thing. Crying about . . . And *Kohlman* was crying. And it had to do with . . ?! Something Janice had just said. But . . then it was gone; he couldn't retrieve it. And all he knew was: how much *despair* he felt at being a man.

"Benjamin: there will be times I have to banish you," Janice said. "There will be times–bound though I be, given as I am–that I will have to say: 'Benjamin: be away. Be in another city, or . . be on another hill; I need this night; I need place; I need this time for my prayer; I need this woman.' So . . please . . go. It's over: the pain; *my* pain. You came. Alyce came. My blood is Alyce's blood and she and I need to talk about that. Leave me. I was angry. I felt all the Great House feelings. Small again. Mute enough to be a decorative egg. I wanted the red rocks . . here . . *in* on me . . but then I held them back. Go."

Where Janice had taken her hands from the sandstone chimney, their blood print had remained. Alyce had come to her. Now the two women held each other against the primitive moon. Kohlman was wracked uncontrollably. He turned and left.

. . . . .

About two hundred of the audience came to the Hilton reception. No more than twenty at the reception drank wine. At first, Barnett was anxious . . about the missing Alyce . . and the missing Janice . . and the missing Kohlman. But when, first, Kohlman, and then, an hour later, the two women, arrived, Barnett cheered instantly and circulated, trying to encourage guests. "I'm not gonna tell!" he said to the women. "One drink! One night!" and "I'm gonna feel very bad unless you have some of this! This Cabernet put me out forty-five a bottle!" The mood was becoming festive. And even Alyce, hand in hand with Janice—both with eyes soft and mouths mended—seemed to glide and skip shyly through the assembled crowd, more like an uncomposed child who arrives Halloween night, dressed as a creature beyond its imagination—and not like the possessor of the remarkable musical talent she had displayed.

Barnett warmed to Kohlman. They discovered that *both* were obsessed with baseball. "Who hit a sacrifice fly in the fifth game of the '56 Series . . which ultimately accounted for the winning run?" Barnett asked. Kohlman knew. "How many lifetime triples did Johnny Pesky have?" Kohlman knew. Kohlman asked: "1963 All-Star game: . . who was the relief pitcher who got called for a balk . . and what inning was it?" Barnett knew. They laughed and got buzzed together on C.E.O.'s wine. "This is a great night!" C.E.O. kept saying. "This is the best night of my life!"

. . . . .

Later, Janice and Kohlman shared a room and made love. Kohlman said he was so sorry about any suspicion in his heart. "I know it's wrong," he said; "I know it's wrong. I learned it from too many other people." He told her about his being shot and about the fire in the alley, and she cried: "Benjamin, Benjamin: don't die! Please!" He cried. "Don't be killed!" she said. They were both sobbing into each other, smearing each other's skin. He thought he might suggest that they both go away . . *some*where and both be safe . . but he didn't. He understood it to be both uncourageous and impossible. She told him how her initial visit to Salem Levinworth had become a nearly-weekly ritual. "I thought," she said, "that if I didn't go . . he wouldn't praise me. And if he didn't praise me . . then Kenneth would go away. And, of course, if Kenneth went away . . then my own family would stop seeing me. . . And I would have stopped existing . . and gone back to being a tanager again! Stopped being actual." And then their tears took over their words, and they slid over and within each other's actuality—now, again—until there was no doubt.

They lay joined and proven for a long, sweet, and breathless time—until Janice spoke. "We're invited to see my friend, Comus, tomorrow," she said, excitedly. "First thing! I want you to meet her. I want you to see the new show she's creating."

"She?" Kohlman queried.

"Yes!"

"That's interesting. I thought . . ."

"She's amazing," Janice said. "Then she'll take us with her to see the President . . and to see her making the President's video."

Kohlman promised again that he would not let Shane and Alexander bother her. And again they wrapped each other: Kohlman, slow; she, incredibly wet and muscular . . in all her truth and joining. Kohlman felt his breath go, go again, go repeatedly, return suddenly, rush away. He understood that such must be the way with all things valuable. His brain felt athletic, dancing, giddy, victorious, alive! He would stay where he had a right to stay. He would not wear disguises. He would use his own name. His heart felt like a powerful, unsteady lamp.

– NINE –

In dreams and in waking reveries, Kohlman saw Janice's hands in print, moonwashed on the face of sandstone, blood on rock the color of spawning fish. And he heard his own voice, at first tentative, then unwinding toward her: "Angel . . . Angel." From their first day, some circle of uneludable danger had grown. Now the whole world seemed provisional: a place where acts bore judgement and then, spontaneously, sentence. Yet hadn't that been always? And why had Kohlman forgotten?

Then he would see, as well, mixed with the print on rock of hands: a child, solitary—like the child of his brief Iowa revisit, tall on the black saddle of the still tractor in her Sunday dress—hands outstretched and upraised into the day's modeled light. Once, light in such globed air had talked to *him*. Once, the ripeness of seeds and stalks and black providential earth had spread into *him* and through his brain, and had meant something. And the numinous world had been like so many messages in their season.

. . . . .

All along the return—St. George to Vegas—their landscape lay redefined. *You thought you had seen . . but you hadn't*, it seemed to say, and Kohlman marveled how, in scissored flights, even the birds seemed changed. And the spiky ocotillo stood alert differently. Permanence everywhere . . dependent upon *impermanence*. . . *True?*

"Beautiful day!" C.E.O. boomed.

"Yes," Kohlman said.

Janice stared off, absorbed.

"I want the silicon out," Alyce said to her brother. "I don't like it." No rancor edged her voice. It was her thought only, her statement.

After a silence, C.E.O. said, "Okay. Of course. If you want that."

"I want that," Alyce said, then looked back to where Janice and Kohlman rode. "Sometimes you feel like my mother," Alyce said to Janice. "Sometimes you feel like my sister. Sometimes you feel like my friend."

"Who batted fifth for the Chicago Cubs of 1958?" Barnett shot over his shoulder.

Kohlman knew.

· · · · ·

Entering, through North Las Vegas, Kohlman asked Janice how long the President planned to stay to film his video. She thought: a week. He wondered if she might not call her friend, Comus, and postpone their visit. "If we had three days," he said, "even two . . just that . . we might . . ." His words ended. His thought parked in a cul-de-sac. They might . . *what*? *do* what? *try* what? What joint adventure had he in mind? Win a jackpot and retire? Collaborate on a *different* book? Marry in *fact*? Take a vacation to Manzanillo? Become insulated from the random world?

· · · · ·

He asked that she move into the Maxim. She did. He wanted her to get security, at the Nugget, to keep Shane and Alexander away.

"What about *your* security?" she said. "What about men who throw you into burning alleys?"

Kohlman thought. "I can't be afraid," he said.

"You can be afraid, Benjamin," Janice said. "*I*'m afraid. It's not bad. I think everybody should be more afraid than they generally are."

"I have a secret weapon, anyway," Kohlman said. He smiled. He grabbed the sides of his head, his hair, pulled it straight out like blown wheat.

"What are you doing?" Janice asked.

"I'm not sure," he said. He smiled again, stupidly. He thought of his friend, the Challenger. "Trying to look like a mad genius," he said. He groped in his mind to retrieve the Challenger's volcano, saw it waiting on a rim wreathed in cumulus clouds: it would keep for now; it could stand by inactive. He wondered how the day's fight training had gone. Had his friend gotten back safely across the night desert? And how did the hills south of Mesquite appear in the lunar white?

.   .   .   .   .

In their Maxim suite, Janice thumbed an earlier Shane and Alexander book, now paperback, that they had left with her—the love affair between a famous photographer and a cardiologist.

"Take a week off," again Kohlman suggested.

"Listen to this!" Janice said. She read from the book. "*The snowfall grew. She kissed his neck. She bent and kissed his leg. Lights grew out of the snow every once in a while to pass.* . . Is that good writing?" she asked.

" 'The snowfall grew. She kissed his neck'. . ?"

"Yes."

"Well . . it's straightforward," Kohlman said. "Reader's not going to get lost. I mean, they're professionals. They know what they're doing. . . Strong verbs."

"What are 'strong verbs'?" Janice asked.

"Well, like . . *grew* . . and *kissed*."

"What would be some *other* strong verbs?" she asked.

". . *Struck* . . *broke* . . *ripped* . . *careened*, I guess."

"*Careened*?"

"Yeah—as in . .'the car *careened*'. . you know: like . .'out of control.' "

". . How about *opened*?" Janice asked. "How about *survived*?"

"What about taking a week off?" Kohlman said again. "What about what I just asked?"

"I couldn't," Janice said.

"Why?"

"I'm needed," she said. "I have work. I have an obligation." She turned pages so fast they quaked like aspen leaves.

"Why are you interested in that book?"

"Show me some writing of *yours*," Janice said.

"My writing's changing," Kohlman deferred.

"Show me something, then, with changes."

"I've just, so far, written pieces," Kohlman said.

"I see. Only pieces."

"I haven't done a full project."

"Why?"

Kohlman grabbed her Shane and Alexander book and tossed it. "Don't read that," he said. "It makes me nervous. It makes me insecure."

Janice smiled. "That's good," she said. "*Be* insecure." She came close. She bit a button from his shirt. She offered the button, on her tongue, to Kohlman. He took it and bit a button from her blouse. They undressed each other, filling their mouths with each other's buttons. Kohlman felt at once exquisitely reckless—yet bound to some long-standing and deep-driven axis. He felt startlingly enabled, almost incautiously so! Screw the gravelly "last chance!" warnings! *Let the games begin*! . . whatever the phrase! He would tell them: *A man is not born for intimidation!* "*He that sleepeth in harvest is a son that causeth shame*". . something like that . . from Proverbs, he recalled. Kohlman was placing buttons where he had never placed them before! And he was being buttoned! It was an extraordinary world!

. . . . .

Though Kohlman knew he would never write the book that he had come to write, still he kept hoping Janice might talk of the night she and Salem Levinworth had been together in the fire. And her survival. And his burning.

"When it's right," she said. "When I've told other things."

"You've told a lot," Kohlman said.

"I don't think I . . ." Her eyes clouded; her chest locked momentarily. "I don't think I've told *myself* . . really, entirely," she said.

"You just . . ."

"What?"

"Well, I guess what I'm asking is: You won't tell Shane and Alexander."

"I probably have no strong verbs," she said. "Besides, I'm not *married* to Shane and Alexander."

. . . . .

Janice liked the television on without the audio. It helped her, she said, to concentrate on what their life might be when there were images in the room, when there was light flickering. She pulled the curtains. Neither of them wore clothes. Janice moved endlessly. She insisted Kohlman talk. "*You* tell *me*," she said. "You tell me about Iowa. Iowa's *green*, right? I had a map in my room in Essex, and it was green: I remember. Connecticut's yellow. When the air drew lines in your back yard . . so that they were there, in the morning, in the dirt . . where did the lines go? In which directions? Did you tell me 'Templeton'?"

"Yes."

"That's a lovely name. What did the lines, left by the air . . in 'Templeton'. . trace? What shape? In 'Templeton'? Where did most of the light in Iowa—in 'Templeton'—come from?"

Kohlman reached and groped at some articulation so that he might answer her.

"Don't think!" she urged and urged again: "Don't think."

He tried. He drummed his head against an archway in mock brain-bashing. The thrum made him feel more sure of himself. And more giddy. He spoke almost belligerent nonsense—and believed it! He said: "The light in Iowa came from behind the tractor . . sometimes from one particular tree . . and also from the drugstore. The lines . . left by the air . . traced the shapes of prehistoric birds and fish. And also . . ." He tried to free his mind as much as it would be freed. ". . And also . . it . . made . . the . . the glyphs . . the glyphs—*yeah*—of the language of the mound people!"

$$\cdot \quad \cdot \quad \cdot \quad \cdot \quad \cdot$$

They rode down to the casino, sat in a lounge and drank mineral water. Janice took Kohlman's hands and kissed them. He still had buttons between his fingers. She bit his knuckles, licked the backs of his hands. She started crying and talking and clutching him so that her fingernails dug in: "I hate violence," she said. "I love death. The Assistant Rector, at the Episcopal school I went to in Massachusetts, bled to death on the morning of my Commencement. Everywhere, on the school grounds, there was dogwood. . . Proust was a revolutionary. Death is a memory. Mostly, they say, America has no memory. So perhaps it won't die. Las Vegas isn't America. That's why I came. America is Las Vegas. Look!" She waved her hand into the casino pit. "Mostly it's the sun."

Kohlman nodded, the whole time, as he'd nodded, involuntarily, the night before, to Alyce's Chopin. He understood. It *was* mostly the sun here—absolutely! And there were clear Connecticut connections between blood and dogwood! At one point he laughed aloud at how stupid he'd been—trying to understand her, in their first days. Now, he didn't try . . and he *understood*. Now he simply listened . . and *saw*. He felt attuned; he felt *close*. Were a bullet to . . *careen*, now, at him from some ambush, he would . . *snatch* it . . from midair with a free hand and . . *fling* it defiantly to the lounge parquet. That was what he would do!—Sharon's long invective to his "Does it hurt?" displaced, momentarily, by blind free-falling adventure!

·   ·   ·   ·   ·

Rising again, sometime later, to their room, Janice stopped the elevator. "What?" Kohlman said. He knew and welcomed that it could be anything.

"Imagine we're in this elevator," Janice said.

"We are," Kohlman said. "I am! . . Then what?!"

"Making love," she said.

He smiled. He nodded.

"Okay?" she said.

"Okay!"

"Ready?"

"Ready," Kohlman said.

Janice pressed the *start* button. They rode up. Neither said a thing; the elevator had no language; there was only the sound of breath quickening.

·   ·   ·   ·   ·

"Don't go to work," Kohlman said. "I'm serious. Please."

"Wasn't Alyce wonderful?" Janice said, changing, somehow, the fall of her hair in their mirror. "In her concert?"

"She was," Kohlman said. "It surprised me. I don't know why. She seemed . . 'unlikely' or something. But I'm learning."

"I love her," Janice said. "I love C.E.O. We're citizens together. In the same country."

Kohlman laughed. He wanted citizenship!

·   ·   ·   ·   ·

They talked whatever came into their heads: horses, Jello, toll booths, water skis, the smell of footballs. "I'm happy," Janice said.

"With you. I mean it." Kohlman said it had been less than a day that they'd been together.

"So what's your point?"

"I used to know every point I made," Kohlman said. "Now I don't know *any*. You've corrupted me." He laughed.

Janice leaned into him with the most sexual kiss he had ever known.

. . . . .

They walked downtown. They sat in the Hofbrau at the Golden Gate and ate shrimp cocktail. "Where did C.E.O. learn so much about baseball?" Kohlman asked.

"He asked that about you," Janice said.

Kohlman played dice nearly all Janice's shift. He swung up four hundred dollars. Down three. Up two. Down seven. His racks were empty, almost. His racks were full. It all seemed hypnotic and, like a dream, amusing. He took his Rolex off and put it on "Hard 8." The stickman asked what he was doing. "If a hard eight comes up before a seven I win *nine Rolexes*—right?" Kohlman said. "I'm just trying to see if I understand this game." He felt as if he were being Janice. Did writers sometimes *become* their subjects? There were accounts, he knew, but always, before, they had just seemed *stories*. He saw Shane and Alexander. Shane was tall and lean and had a woman's long straight blond hair. Alexander was short with a head that looked radiated; he wore checks and a gold medallion. They looked like writers . . and like a lightweight tag wrestling team. Every editor or agent or network news-media pro who had ever advised Kohlman, helped him "rise," congealed like old gravy, like clotted cream, in the paired image. They were arguing with two Golden Nugget security officers, and had no idea Kohlman was watching them.

. . . . .

Janice got off at four a.m. They had breakfast at Binnion's—chateaubriand and nova scotia and eggs for $3.95. They walked together across town to North Las Vegas. Janice talked without visible transitions about her former marriage: Kenneth at home, Kenneth in New York when they would be with associates, Kenneth with her family. Kohlman talked about what he felt had happened when he'd gotten to Princeton: what he'd experienced, what he'd felt as change: "Self-consciousness," he said. "Self-consciousness . . and then more self-consciousness. I could hear myself hearing myself hear myself," he said. "And then, of course, there were all the *other* people listening . . who probably weren't, any of them, really. Why do you think those things happened?" he asked.

Janice looked at him. "You want *me* to answer that?" she said.

They went to a female strip joint. It was six in the morning. The place, "The Catery," featured their "Breakfast Amateur Special." They went to a male strip joint. They went to a third strip joint where the strippers had no observable genitalia at all. "I feel comfortable here," Janice said. "Me too," Kohlman said. They had brioche and cappuccino.

.　　.　　.　　.　　.

An hour later, back at the Maxim, they made love. They made love again. Kohlman's brain felt in a meltdown. They slept. When they woke, they talked immediately: both at once. Both spoke and both listened—there was no wasted exchange. There were no gaps, no waits, no leaps to change the subject. They made love again.

Janice ordered salmon souffle, delivered to their room, from the Dome of the Sea at the Dunes, and they drove, in a rented Lynx, together out and into the north desert. The light in the desert sky seemed the densest, most unmitigated light Kohlman had ever seen. The world, even the black-rock and cactus landscape, tumbled and retumbled upon itself, became recombined, extravagantly random. There seemed no time. Only time. How long since their first El Cortez breakfast? What was the day; what date? Where would Kohlman's brother be: on a return flight? How many days were left, now, for the Challenger? They sat on volcanic boulders and peeled oranges and watched small scissor-tailed birds flicker in, flicker out of vision. "What would it be to *name* everything?" Kohlman asked. Then, abruptly, he picked a dry ancient broken root from the desert floor and bashed his skull with it.

"What are you *doing*?!" Janice asked.

"I heard myself hearing myself," Kohlman said. "And the self that *heard* the self then was getting ready to *explain* . . something like: 'I was just being silly.' " God, I *hate* that. "Or . . 'Of course I'm just being whimsical.' "

"But you cut your forehead," Janice said. "You're bleeding."

"Not badly," Kohlman said.

There was silence. Kohlman dabbed his fingertips to his head and checked them. Janice took his hand, tracing one of her own fingers up and down the in-touch of Kohlman's fingers. "What would you name those birds?" Janice said. She had a small and lovely brushfire in her eyes and Kohlman saw it and smiled.

". . *Lentils*," he said. "And then I would rename the *beans*."

"What would you rename the beans?"

"*Burds*." He spelled it. He didn't want her to get confused.

They spread skin cream over one another, then walked, neither talking. They saw lizards, saw a snake, startled jackrabbits. The light shifted its weight. The rocks seemed breathing through volcanic pores.

"I come here at least once a week and read Camus," Janice finally said, then, shifting time, said, "When I was twelve, I tried to organize my sixth-grade class into vigilantes. . . We were all scared. We tried to arm ourselves."

". . Against what?" Kohlman said.

Kohlman jumped in front of her. He waved his hands. "Against what?" he said "Hello? . . Ms. Stewart? Hello? This is your Interviewer speaking."

She still didn't answer; she seemed remembering something; finally she said, "We were ahead of our time." Then she ran into Kohlman and knocked him down. They fell into the sand together and kissed. "I am not always present in my body," Janice said. "Have you noticed that?"

"I've noticed *some*thing," Kohlman said.

"We take separate vacations." She smiled. "My body and I. Actually, that's a line from a former lover: 'You and your body, I think, take separate vacations,' he said."

Kohlman felt jealous.

"What would you name a former lover?" she asked.

"I wouldn't," Kohlman said. "I wouldn't. I've been asked not to."

. . . . .

They talked, all the drive home, about Janice's trial and why she'd chosen silence. "My headaches were getting worse, of course," she said, ". . but that wasn't the reason. It just seemed something that was . . unspeakable." She elaborated. Kohlman listened. He'd

left his Nagra recorder in their room. But he didn't want it, anyway. He didn't need it. If he were going to write, really write, he
should be his *own* Nagra. She talked about attorneys: the shapes of
their faces, their eyes, how they dressed, the ways they formed their
vowels, their voice inflections. "How could I speak when there
were people like that?" she said. "People who pronounced 'reckless'
'*reg*less'? One man . . had so much anger about women. Another,
clearly, had never had close friends. They were like bad dancers.
The attorneys; the judge. It was like an estate auction. I couldn't
enter it. One man began his opening remarks . ." and she quoted:
"*When God gave us His commandments, what He clearly hoped was* . . .
Don't you find that frightening?" she asked. "Lawyers telling us
about God?"

"But it was your *life*," Kohlman said. "It was your *life* and
future."

"I could see!" Janice said.

"So why be silent?"

"No one ever wanted me to talk *before*," she said. "The only
reason they wanted me to talk during the trial was so that they
could *punish* me."

"Janice . . !"

"No: Benjamin: finally you make yourself take on substance!"
she said. Her voice took on a passion that opened Kohlman's spine
like a chrysalis; ephemerids leapt to shivering flight from it.
"Somehow!" she went on, shameless tears running, "Somehow . .
even when your head feels like it's cracking . . and its *cracks* are
cracking . . like dry mud. You have to . . ! Don't make me angry!
I became very real for all those lawyers . . and for my family . .
when I refused to speak. For the first time—I could see it—I scared
them. For the first time . . I could feel their eyes on me . . as
though I were a bomb . . in a public place . . being dismantled . .
by who-they-hoped-were-experts."

Janice's memory of the trial—testimony, cross testimony, objec-
tions, words denied, words sustained—startled Kohlman in its detail
and accuracy. Silence and seeming withdrawal during the whole
six-day event aside—she had been, Kohlman now saw, unyieldingly
present.

．　　．　　．　　．

They had steak tartare, and Janice meditated before going to work. Kohlman drove her downtown; he wore no disguise. "What about sleep?" she asked. "You haven't had much."

"What about you?"

"I'm used to it."

"I'm *getting* used to it."

"Remember," Janice prompted, tracing a soft line on Kohlman's face, "After work—she's expecting us; you'll like her—we're meeting Comus."

. . . . .

Kohlman sat in the keno lounge and watched her. Shane and Alexander were there as well . . being watched by a security guard. The other runners were constantly asking Janice to help: "Angel? Could you get the west bar for me? I'm running late." "Angel? could you get me an assist in the poker room?" Kohlman could see her: lifting the numbered leaves of paper with her hands, veined white on veined white. They would build on her tray. Sometimes she would roll the sheafs together and send them cross-casino in a mail tube.

"They keep that girl busy," Kohlman said to a slot mechanic.

"Angel's the best!" the mechanic said.

Once, when Janice was gliding, like quicksilver, from area to place, Shane stepped forward and took her arm. Kohlman intervened. Two security men were there, as well, immediately. "I'll handle this," Kohlman said. He nodded to Janice. She kissed the knot of his tie and moved on.

"*My* goodness!" Shane spoke in an upper register.

"The youngish Benjamin Kohlman!" Alexander's voice was more bass.

They both laughed.

"Go back to New York," Kohlman said.

"*Go back to New York*," Alexander mimicked.

"*Go back to New York*," Shane mimicked Alexander. This time they laughed *a cappella*.

Kohlman drew a breath. Inside his head, distantly, he could glimpse the shape of a volcano. "I think Ms. Stewart's made herself clear," he said. "And so I'd suggest you leave."

"Perhaps you don't realize . ." Shane began.

"That Ms. Stewart's elder brother, Philip . . ," Alexander picked up their new fugue.

"Was court-appointed legal Conservator."

"And gave us her rights . . exclusively."

"*He* gave you *her* rights?" Kohlman said.

"We have a binding agreement," Alexander said.

"For *her* rights," Kohlman repeated.

"With Harper and Row," Shane said.

"We can stop any book you write," Alexander said.

"We can get her recommitted."

Kohlman felt anger, deep and thermal, begin to move. He closed his eyes against the shuttle of half-thoughts.

"Our plan is . . ."

The two stopped. Their eyebrows rose; they half turned; their faces lit with a concert delight; they laughed—a shrill chord—a D-minor dyad. Their cutoff from the chord was precise. They'd practiced. They'd been partners for a while: Kohlman could tell.

"Our plan is . . ." It was Alexander . . then waiting for Shane to take the phrase, their song . . which Shane did . . with clear baroque echoes.

". . Plan is . . sort of a Raymond Chandler . ."

"*Half* Raymond Chandler . ."

"Good! Half Raymond Carver approach."

"Half Capote . ."

"Half Norman Mailer."

"Half Jim Dickey . ."

"Half Joe McGinnis."

Kohlman's head was spinning. He broke to walk away.

"We'll pay well . ."

"For any information you have," they said, almost in unison.

Kohlman turned back. It was a cheap shot . . but *cheap* appeared to be the *lingua franca*. "I heard one of you had AIDS," he said. "Is that true? Which one?" He moved off.

Shane and Alexander spun on one another.

·   ·   ·   ·   ·

Kohlman called Caesar's to talk with the Challenger, to find out how the last days before the fight were going. He was told his friend was in complete and total seclusion. "No one's seen him," the responding voice said. "No one. His bed hasn't been slept in for two days. But that happens. With him. That's not unusual."

. . . . .

How much truth, how much reality, lay in the threats of Shane and Alexander? What rights *had* they? What piece of paper, signed by who*ever*, backed by what*ever*, might abridge a decent person's rights? No system—did it?—enforced such compliance. Kohlman thought of his parents. Another postcard, from Laughlin, Nevada, on the Arizona border—glass-towered hotels on the Colorado River—had been slipped earlier under his Maxim door. He thought of their farm. *Why?* He remembered the girl on the tractor . . who, it seemed, brought half himself, half Pamela Arnold to him. Which was which? And what had it been of Pamela, burning then vanishing, in the moonlit sandstone, so violently the night before—Janice racked, sobbing, face/hands streaked with blood; Alyce beside her?

Kohlman saw himself—blue shirt, rep tie, shetland coat—leaving for Princeton on a Trailways bus: all his known maps: the stones and ditches and posts and panes of glass, drugstore signs, chimneys, unreadable daily faces . . tailing off to exhaust, shimmers only, a vapor blur. Why had he not understood the magnitude of his leaving? That it had been, for him, so large! It *had* been. Of *course*: his world, every affection, mute and ritual though it may have been, erased—Jesus!—in *dust*?! So: had Pamela seen the bus off? Had she been . . ? Jesus Christ! *What was going on*?! All the night-and-morning-before's manic adventure flew—waxwings from a wire—out and away. He thought: *if Shane and Alexander hurt her in any way, disturb her goodness, then, Jesus Christ, I'll . . !* But then he held his breath and fought the closure. He squeezed the beer in his hand in its dark bottle, fighting, fighting back the closure of the thought he'd begun. Because it was violent. But it came: *then . . I'll kill them!* Well . . ! Whatever—his civilized self and his brainstem fought with each other. . . Of course he didn't mean it. It was a reaction. Not "kill." It was an emotion. Only. A . . "figure," just a . . what were they calling it now? . . "trope". . just a "trope" inside him, that *represented* his . . unsettled self. In language. It was only a signal, really, to himself, more than anything, to say . . that he was serious . . in this caring he felt for her. So that . . *I'll kill them*

. . when all was said and done . . really, was simply a figure of speech standing for: "I feel deep concern."

. . . . . .

He played blackjack and lost. He kept feeling that the cards would be bad, and they were. His choice invariably defeated him. When he wouldn't draw, he needed to. When he drew, he broke. A woman in an elaborately beaded, white knit dress sat down beside him. "Remember me?" she said.

He looked. "Gloria," he said.

"No blond hair," Gloria observed. "No beard."

Kohlman shrugged.

They played two hands together in silence. Gloria won. Kohlman lost. Kohlman felt Gloria's hand on the inside of his thigh; he saw her smiling.

"Where's Walter?" he asked.

"Walter's in surgery," she said. "I have a room upstairs. Why sit here and lose money?"

"What kind of surgery does Walter do?" Kohlman said.

"He's interested mainly in the hypothalamus," Gloria said. "Are you familiar with the hypothalamus?"

"Yeah; I have a pair . . in an aerated forty-gallon tank . . in my home," Kohlman said. He tried to force a smile . . then a laugh.

Gloria laughed and squeezed him. "Come upstairs," she said. "I have some things I need to talk to you about."

Kohlman slid another chip into his 21 square. She reached and pulled it back. She slid her stack of green, $25 chips to him.

"Here. This is much easier," she said. "Take this."

Kohlman slid them away.

"Why haven't you left town?" she asked him. "I'm supposed to ask you that."

Kohlman checked her. The dealer waited, like a shadow, just beyond.

"These are serious people," Gloria said. "You have to know that. People don't do what these people have done . . and will go *on* doing . . and not mean it. Please, this has nothing to do with myself and Walter. Myself and Walter are another thing entirely. The night I met you with Walter, I had no idea who you were. We honestly thought you were another person, a friend: Walter and I tend to play practical jokes on this particular friend. I bet Walter he couldn't hit you. The bet was for, actually . ." – she ran a hand over the fabric at her bodice – ". . this dress . . that I'd seen at Neiman Marcus. But that was not this. Walter and I have our Walter-and-I agenda. This is another agenda I have – totally discrete; totally separate – and in another life. – Why haven't you left?"

"Let me buy you a drink," Kohlman said.

.   .   .   .   .

They sat over Cherry Heerings, and Kohlman tried to explain that he had no interest in the hotel fires: half the hotels in Las Vegas could burn for all he cared; that wasn't his concern. He had come here for another purpose. He had come to write an entirely different book . . connected to an entirely different fire . . which had been set in an entirely different place. "Yes: there was a fire central to that book – but that fire was a fire in *Connecticut* . . totally unrelated to any casino or resort fire. That fire was a *coastal* fire. These are *interior* fires: The two are entirely different! But if your people . . ."

"They're not *my* people," Gloria said. "They're their own people. I just have an arrangement."

"If *these* people," Kohlman went on, "need to kill me for asking about fires I'm *not* asking about . . then they're just going to have to *kill* me – that's all," Kohlman said. "Or *try*."

Gloria listened. She kept dipping her fingers into her Cherry Heering, applying it to her lips like gloss. Then she'd apply it, like breath freshener, to her tongue. She said little during Kohlman's long, repeated, looping explanation. When he was through, she just stared at him, her thin, lightly-contoured chest rising and falling with its breathing.

"So can you tell . . whoever it is you share this particular 'agenda' with . . that they're off base? That they're barking up the wrong whatever? Tree?"

Gloria stared at Kohlman as if he knew why she was staring. "Yes, I could do that," she finally said. "For a consideration."

Kohlman felt like hitting the woman. It wasn't a standard emotion for him, particularly. He had known impatience, *felt* impatience – but this was not the same. This was physical. This was an

emotion charged with *damage*. This was a dismantling and breaking emotion, one that wanted to take her apart. This was porno-
graphic.

"You *do* understand what I'm saying to you—don't you?"
Gloria said. "You've told your tale. I have a room upstairs. You
want something. I have the power to deliver that something. *I*
want something. It all seems very classical. Very geometrical. To
me. At least at this moment." She smiled.

Kohlman drained his cordial.

"Life is a negotiation," Gloria said. "Cost . . and benefit."

Kohlman stood. She stood.

"Have you seen the new lobby?" she asked. "It's really lovely.
White marble. They have antique reproductions of writing desks in
the rooms."

.　　.　　.　　.　　.

Her room was elegant, frontier, Victorian. She extended an
open straight razor, and when he didn't take it, laid it out promi-
nently on the writing desk. "What's that for?" he asked.

"What's anything for?" she said.

"I don't get . . ."

"*Use* it," she said. She crossed her hands over her head and
lifted her dress. Its beads cracked like tinder, like seeds in a gourd,
like the helical drill-bit tail of a small rattler. She wore no under-
clothes, stood before him, shaking her hair out. Her abdomen and
upper thighs were a hatchwork of healed and unhealed scar tissue.

"Holy fuck!" Kohlman said.

"Precisely," she smiled. "How well you speak."

"No!" Kohlman said. "No! No way. I'm sorry."

"It doesn't bother *other* men," she said.

"Well, it does me," Kohlman told her.

"Why? Aren't men *about* cutting into the soft sides of women
. . and leaving no visible scars? I thought . . ."

"Take it up with . . enlist Walter," Kohlman said.

"I have. He has. He's a surgeon, after all—and he's marvelous."

"Well . . not from me!" Kohlman said.

"I thought this was an exchange."

"Not . . !" Kohlman's breathing seemed to snag on some
bone fracture in his chest.

"Sweetie . . ." She fingered her white skin like lace. "Now come: we agreed. This is for consideration. I'm going to save your life. And you're going to . . do something . . with mine."

"No!" Kohlman said. "No . . no!"

"Then I'll have to do it myself," and Gloria picked the straight razor from where she'd set it on the writing desk.

"*No*: Jesus, *no!*" Kohlman said, and he moved toward her.

"Then *you'll* do it?" Gloria said.

"No!" Kohlman said; the recanted word almost more, now, a body sound. He was sweating.

"All right, then," and Gloria began to move the flickering blade to a yet-unmarked block of skin between her visible ribs and navel.

"No! Jesus Christ!" Kohlman said, and he reached, involuntarily really, and grabbed at the razor. She pulled it back; he could feel his left hand—the palm, its nerves—sliced deeply.

"Then you *will* do it?" Gloria said.

Kohlman felt thick blood beat from a blade of pain inside his clenched left hand. "*Why are you doing this?!*" he screamed.

"It's a long story," Gloria said, her drawn face lacquered suddenly with tears. Then she began, again, almost surgically, to move the blade toward an unwritten page on her skin.

"*What are women doing?!*" Kohlman screamed. "*What are they doing to themselves?! What are men doing to them if we've gotten to this?!*" And he snatched now with his right hand, and, again, she pulled back, but this time he clamped determinedly, so that he *had* the razor and, though his other palm sliced sharply, he was, still, able to pull the instrument from her. He stood, more blood in his burning closed fists than he could carry, staring at the woman, his breath coming in tatters. "What is going *on?*" he said—his voice barely even a voice after his shouting. "What is going on here? What is happening? What are we . . ? Why am I . . ?" She was laughing now . . *and* crying . . and looking as if he were the most stupid person she'd ever seen. "Give me back my razor," she said.

"No," Kohlman said. His head felt light. He held his fists over his head: half warrior, half in the pose of surrender . . some crazy notion that he should elevate the bleeding to stop it. Thick blood seeped between his fingers . . down his arms.

"I'll just get another," Gloria said.

"Not from me," Kohlman said, and then he screamed a crazy thing at her, a thing impossible, a thing absurd: he screamed: "*Is this MY fault?! Is this because of ME? Did I do this?!*"

"I have to tell them now to kill you," Gloria said. "You *know* that."

"Did I . . ?!" Kohlman began. "Is it because I never . . ?!" He couldn't find a direction. Then all he could finish—his face washed, his arms and hands dangerously slick with his own life—was to say: "I'm sorry. . . I'm sorry. . . Whatever I had to do . . with this . . I'm sorry." And then, keeping the straightedge, not giving it up, Kohlman fled the room. He ran. He took the *exit* stairs, and vomited on the landing.

Security guards found him inching his route down the fire stairs. "How did you . . ?" Kohlman began, all functions slowed. The guards explained the surveillance cameras in the ceilings everywhere, said their monitor center had reported the emergency. Then, suddenly, he was in a room filled with medical equipment. A man with wire-rim glasses, hung from a thin gold chain, deadened, stitched and bandaged his hands with the speed and off-handedness someone might use to wipe a spilled drink from a table. "Little time . . you should be back in shape," the young medic said. He smiled. The guards opened a door and Kohlman walked out into the main casino, cut glass dancing above a now nearly familiar world.

· · · · ·

He drove back to the Maxim and packed his clothes. He was in trouble. "Angel: Understand . . understand; okay? . . I can't . . take you into whatever all this craziness *is* with me!" He talked as if she were there, as if they were in a knot, bound together, as if she were *that* close. He boxed all his tapes, all his floppy disks, cased his word processor. He talked angrily: yelled, accused, paced, berated himself, cried, argued. Someone in the next room thudded the connecting floor, the wall. Kohlman called McCarran Airport, reserved a dawn flight. He dressed as when he had come—everything, same tie. It was three-thirty. He began to shake.

He felt foolish . . up-ended, idiotic. He walked out onto his balcony and could smell the desert, trapped weakly in the poured industrial stone of resort palaces and boulevards, and felt cut loose.

Faint Dixieland, all the way, he knew, from the Barbary Coast, came like sugared glaze under the engine sounds of the traffic: such a confectionate and crazy music. He thought what it was he should say . . in a message, in a letter to Janice. He wasn't gone yet, and he missed her. He wanted her. *What* would he say? How would he word such communication? What would its language be? He couldn't even imagine. He felt gravity, his own resistance.

He tried to make himself into the self who had arrived two weeks earlier. Not be who he had become! Become? If not *become*, then . . ? He was *dressed* at least—wasn't he?—like that person. If he called Sharon . . *she*'d make him into that person; *she* wouldn't forget! He tried to find that person's brain: working himself up, saying that person's words: "Save your ass, Man!" he tried and then kept repeating, so that it might become practiced, learned, ingrained, authentic: "Save your ass! Come on! Save it: Save your ass! You're dead if you stay! You can't stay here! You can't love her! She's a crazy woman! And she's dying. She has a disease. You can't love a woman like that! Stop fucking yourself over; stop fucking yourself up! Don't run some crazy trip!" He once, fascinated, had watched his mother in Iowa scoop the steamed flesh out of a squash. He felt, now, as if *he* were doing the same thing . . to his own brain. He could *see* it; he could *feel* it: His own wrapped, lacerated hand . . being its own instrument . . hollowing his own substance. He wondered about . . he couldn't voice it any more precisely: ". . about the things we do to ourselves." Why? What are they? Why do we do them? His hands still smelled, at once, like oranges, from their day together in the sun, and like the violent surgery they had just come from. He walked inside and hit his walls. Someone on their far side pounded back. "I'm sorry," Kohlman cried to the unseen fists. "I'm sorry. Please."

He tried, in fact, to leave, but his baggage wanted to mock him. He'd drag it to the door . . then it would be in the middle of the room again or lying open on his bed. He had trouble with his bandaged hands. Still, it was just baggage . . and it kept running away! *All right . . true:* he tended to give too much credence to control, but . . *come on!* One time, when he'd pushed the door open and clumsily picked all his things up to wrestle them past the threshold, the locks on his large Hartman bag exploded and he tripped over the downfold and ended on the paisley carpet, suitcase over him, his legs half wrapped around, one elbow into his shirts and ties and underwear: it was absurd, mocking, childish.

He left *without* his baggage. If it wouldn't cooperate . . ! He flagged a cab, reflexively, the way he might in New York. He was still trying to be the Kohlman who'd first come. "Take me to the station!" he blared. Within ten minutes, the cabby dropped Kohlman outside a casino he'd never seen: the Palace Station. There were full-scale *train engines*, all from another era. Just beyond the grounds and lit trains, the east-west traffic sped by on Interstate 15.

Kohlman didn't even enter. He hiked. He stood by a guard rail on I-15 and considered hitching. But it was the *west*-bound traffic. Did that matter? He crossed to the median. A '62 Chevy pickup, shuddering east and loaded with furniture, sprang some object loose from a box, and the object leapt into the blue and gold arc light above Kohlman and then fell. He caught it, his two hands making a small cloud of gauze. It was a bottle of Grand Marnier, uncracked. He broke the seal, looked off, saw the pickup a quarter mile already past, and took a drink.

· · · · ·

Hiking the less-lit Industrial Road behind the boulevard, he tugged the Grand Marnier and cried, erupting finally: "Let me leave! . . I can't stay!" He spun so that the refracted glow furled neon hoops over his head, and he called out: "*Angel . . !? Angel . . !?*"

· · · · ·

Whatever the compass; wherever within—Kohlman found himself winding familiar light: the Sands, the Nob Hill, the Holiday. Along the wall, by the Imperial Palace, at what seemed his eternal post, sat the quadruple amputee—drinking Miller Lite from a can; his neck, nearly his entire face, coiled around the can like a snake somehow holding it, clamped, allowing the head, tipped back at the right angle, to drink. The image made no sense. It wasn't possible . . a man with neither arms nor legs . . drinking Miller Lite from a can.

Kohlman stood and tried to focus. Janice had told him the man's name . . *Tim? Ken? Ron?* . . she knew him. She'd spoken well, said the man cared and helped people. How was that? Kohlman dropped a twenty into the man's cigar box. "You getting by?" Kohlman asked. They'd never spoken.

"Hand to mouth," the amputee smiled.

"Hit?" Kohlman held the Grand Marnier out. Janice would be happy.

The small man did something with his head so that the Miller can flew up and out and arced back and into a mesh litter container. He extended his chin. Kohlman tucked the dark bottle beneath the chin, and in an interval like a power surge, the man had coiled his face and neck again around the bottle, and had lifted it to drink.

Kohlman retook the bottle when the man was done.

"Thanks," the man said.

"No problem," Kohlman said.

"So: You . . up or down?" the amputee said.

Kohlman looked uncertain.

"This trip: up or down? Ahead or behind?"

"Oh . . ahead," Kohlman said; "I think. Mostly. Pretty much. Yeah; ahead."

"I know what you mean," the amputee said.

Kohlman nodded.

The amputee smiled. "It's a bitch—isn't it?—keeping track?"

Kohlman agreed.

"You make mistakes. You try to keep the books . . it gets away. You know what I'm saying?"

"I do," Kohlman said. He didn't.

"I believe you," the amputee said.

"It's true," Kohlman said.

"It is."

Kohlman liked the beat of their conversation. It felt like jazz.

The amputee paused. He looked pensive . . then sad. He went on: "It happens," he said. "You do surveillance; your eyes are your life; they're everywhere . . but it gets away. You make mistakes: right people lose; wrong people win. Good people with the wrong missions: you find yourself chasing. But, I mean: they enlisted! Right? They chose their missions. You can't rewrite *Leviticus* or, say, *Second Samuel*. A warning's a warning. And all you wanted, any of the time, was—am I right?—Justice? But at least, sometimes, you catch it. You know?"

"I do," Kohlman said. He didn't.

"Every once in a while, if you're vigilant, there's restitution. You try to warn people. You try to read them the telephone book. But, so, anyway: you're getting the goods. Things are moving ahead. If not on schedule . . then at least *ahead*."

Kohlman hesitated. *Should he be paying closer attention?* he wondered.

"I mean: you're more up than down. You're less behind, more ahead. So . . for the most part: you're getting the goods."

"I'm . . ? Sorry: I'm not sure what . . ? I probably am but . . which 'goods'?"

"Essentially . . what I'm getting at is: on the houses. On these places here. Whatever's your mission."

"Was . . ?" Kohlman had a question. "Was it the war?" he tried . . reaching, drifting, nodding into the spaces around the man, the envelope where his arms and legs should have been.

"It was. Pretty much," the man said. "Yeah. The war. Essentially. —Listen: how're your hands? You have opposition? You have sensation in the fingertips? Most of that comes back. That is, unless you lose it *all*." He laughed, curiously: a shrill, infuriated laugh. "You can't send ganglia into thin air—well, you *can*, of course, in a sense . . but that's a different story. But . . yeah: right: it was essentially the war." The man swung back to where he'd begun.

Kohlman felt dizzy. He'd been trying to follow. He'd been trying to make a connection between himself and a man he supposed few people spoke to. The word *war* seemed the ember. He'd asked about the *war*. The subject had been *war* . . and the man had given an answer. "I was too young," Kohlman tried. It felt close. He was warm. "Just barely though . . then."

"It happens," the amputee said.

"Take care," Kohlman said and moved on.

"You too," the man said, his voice fading behind. "You too . . especially."

·   ·   ·   ·   ·

His phone rang just after four. He answered. "Did you go back . . to sleep?" Janice asked.

He couldn't breathe. He couldn't say anything.

"Benjamin . . ?" she said.

He tried. He had intended to be out of there . . away . . gone.

"Benjamin . . ?" she said again, more concern, more urgency, like a wind picking up, he could hear, in her voice.

What was it she had asked? *Did you go back . . to sleep?* "Yes," he said.

"Did you take the car?"

He could hear her reading him, reading something about him—the uncertainty, the caution.

"Benjamin . . ."

His name again. ". . I'm sorry: yes," he said. "The car. I did."

"Are you dressed?"

"I am. Yes. Dressed. Dressed . . I'm dressed."

"I'll be right there."

．　　．　　．　　．　　．

He tried to leave again. He wanted to leave: he *knew* leaving: leaving was leaving; you broke; you freed the other person; you left. He couldn't leave. He called the Frontier and reserved a room, hoping the act of *reserving* some different future might dislodge him—if not get him on a plane and out of town, at least move him *away*, disconnect him. What had begun as work was now, crazily, uncontainably . . a longing. It felt humiliating. It felt . . too *clear*. *Clear* was what happened to children. *Clear* . . you didn't make distinctions. And distinctions were the crux of—hadn't he learned that?!—a thinking mind. But he couldn't even put his hand on his room's door handle. So he unpacked, unboxed, unfiled, disassembled, and waited. His whole face hurt from some kind of sadness—had he felt it before? He had no idea who the person was inside his skin, the person living there *in* him. He hated the person, the way you loathe any intimate invasion, any close intruder or stranger. But he couldn't ask the person to go away.

– TEN –

"**D**o you feel rested?" Janice asked.

Kohlman lay on the bed, facing away into a watermark on the wall. His hands were crossed so that, from where she'd entered, Janice could not see his bandages.

"Excuse me – I've got to pee," she said. She touched a hand to her lips, pressed his cheek, swept past into the bath. He heard the seat drop. "I had a great night," she said. Her voice sounded *inside* him, like a thought he was having – echoed dimly, muffled, resonant, trapped in his brain. "That's better!" she said, appearing. "I had a *great* . . great night!"

"Good." Kohlman nodded.

"Ask me why."

"Okay."

"Ask!"

". . Why?"

"You've never asked me why I do what I do."

"I'm sorry. Why do you do what you do?"

"You've never asked why I chose it, why I love it. I've kept expecting you to."

"I'm sorry. I guess it seemed to me that I must, somewhere in the course of things, have asked . . ."

"It's such a logical question." She danced the room, steps and bends and turns of the obvious lift inside her. "So . . turn the tape on," she said. "Because . . this is 'it.' This is the 'nub.' This is the 'crux.' Are you ready?"

"I don't think we need the tape."

"*I* need the tape."

"But, Angel, I'm not writing . . ." How would she feel if he told her he'd dropped his intentions? "I can remember," he tried. "I can remember everything that's important." He hid his hands under a pillow so that their image, should she see them, wouldn't undo her mood.

"You can remember?" she checked.

"I can remember."

"Everything?"

"Everything."

"The wording?"

"The wording."

"My voice?"

"Especially your voice."

"Okay . . ! Okay!" she grinned. "Here we go then! Good! . . My work . . my choice . . my *raison d'etre* for becoming what it is that I've become: a keno runner in the city of Las Vegas. And tonight was special. Tonight was just amazingly great! Tonight was wonderful! Tonight was perfect! Turn the tape on! Are you *sure* you don't need the tape?" She was seeing herself, checking herself, in the room mirror, like a great actress, preparing, on an opening night.

Kohlman stood from the bed. "All right; just in case," he said. He crossed to the Nagra, fumbled because of his bandages, plugged it in, set up the mike.

Janice was studying herself, studying some numen of herself, freshly escaped from the pleasure of her night. "Are you sure you slept?" she asked.

"Actually I didn't," he said. "I lied."

"You seem very weary."

Kohlman nodded. "I am, somewhat," he said. His back was to her. "Anyway . . ."

"You seem sad, too. Are you sad? Your voice sounds sad. Don't be sad."

Kohlman pressed the *record* button. "Why have you come to Las Vegas and chosen to be a keno runner, Janice?" he asked, trying to make his voice sound as majornetwork as possible.

Janice smiled. She stood tall. She raised her shoulders, her head, began to stride, elegantly. She tossed her words back, like rosewater, in the direction of the microphone. "I bring the numbers," she said. Her face lit. She seemed in a delicious pleasure.

Kohlman watched. He checked the levels on the recorder. Maybe he *could* write the book. Maybe he hadn't thought it through entirely. Maybe he could *lose* the person he'd become . . get back to the person he'd been. Which was which?

"I bring the numbers!" Janice repeated, snapping, with her sure authority, Kohlman's interior loop. "I bring the one-spots and the three-spots. And all the four- and five-way combinations. I carry 63s! And 39s! And 4s! And 16s, 17s and 18s—all in my hand! I carry 52s! I carry 80s! I carry 3s and 2s and 1s! I take them all! Old women in wheelchairs. Truckers. Marketing executives. Mad handkerchief-chewing women in shawls. Junkies. Nuns. Murderers. I find them all! I take them. I move for them. I bring them back. I take the numbers from the numbers to the numbers! And I bring them back! I watch them watching. I watch them watching the board. And I watch. And I feel a great satisfaction! And I feel each light! All numbers. And all the numbers reaching even before number. Before *word*. And those to come. And I am a keno runner in the City of Death—running, moving, moving back. And I love always what I do. And I wouldn't change it!"

Kohlman looked up. In her walking, she had shed all her clothes and stood, highlighted and toned, in the center of the room.

He felt strangely and compellingly chilled. The room was ice. The air conditioner seemed to have gone berserk: Kohlman was shaking. He was trying to control himself in a leather chair, and Janice noticed. She came and knelt, her eyes full from her own pleasure and declaration, and she kissed his knees. "You are very dear," she said. And then she saw his hands: "Benjamin!" she said; "Oh, dear . . oh, God . . my Benjamin! What . . ?"

He told her; he said: "There was a woman . . who I thought might . . hurt herself . . and I tried to stop her."

Janice kissed the gauze. She kissed it again. She licked what, uncovered, would have been his hands. She wiped her tears there. "Was it me?" she asked. "You did this for? Was *I* the woman?"

Kohlman thought of saying: *I was going to leave you.* He thought of saying: *This morning . . in my head . . I dared do anything. But, now . . !* He thought of saying: *You've been hurt too much. I can't involve you.* What had her question been? He took her head between his wrapped hands and pressed it softly to his chest.

"Your hands are beating like hearts," Janice said. "In the wrapping. I can hear them. Two soft ghosts."

Kohlman hadn't a response.

"I feel safe," she said.

Kohlman wondered. He wondered, *from what?*

"Thank you, Benjamin". . and then again: "Did I say 'thank you'?"

"Yes," Kohlman said. "You did." His breath felt thin and had the taste of butane.

"Sometimes I can't remember."

"Well . . ."

"I *feel* words . . then can't think . . ."

"Well . . ."

". . If they got out."

"Well, those did."

"Does that happen?"

What was she asking? "Where?"

"To you?"

"Angel . . ." It felt, to Kohlman, as if Janice were searching for a gas leak, inside his chest cavity, by lighting matches.

She looked up. Her smile was celestial. "I'm excited for you to meet Comus," she said. "Especially now."

•   •   •   •   •

Janice's friend, the light and video genius, Comus, worked nights in a warehouse off Maryland Parkway, creating a new edition of *Hallelujah Hollywood* for Bally's Grand. The stage was set up at the north end of the building, and Comus sat on a scissor lift, arms wrapped around an I-beam, trying to wrestle a fixture, something hybridized from a klieg light and a 64-mm film camera. She was a woman, six-four at least, a centerfold twice a centerfold's size, stunning even in shorts, sneakers without socks, and a "Save/the/Whales" T-shirt. She seemed sculpted: cheekbones, brow, bust, waist, ankles . . a kind of monumental male fantasy daring itself to reach limits. Kohlman could feel his musculature tighten, his breathing grow quick.

"Men don't know how to deal with her," Janice said. "How even to begin. She's so beautiful . . and strong. We're such good friends."

Comus shouted at her shuffling stagehands. "Could you move your cute little butts a little, please, for once?!" The stagehands were directing four other workers, driving forklifts, each at one edge of a construction that looked like the corner of a hotel, the first four stories. Comus dropped a wrench. *"Christ!"* she bellowed, then: "I'm sorry. Would someone bring me up that wrench?!"

None of the workers stirred.

"God: do I love unions!" she bellowed. "Could someone . . ?! . . bring me up that wrench . . ?! . . please?!" she called again.

Janice stepped forward. *"I'll* bring the wrench up!" She waved at her friend. "Hi! How do I get up there?!"

"Hey!" Comus said. "Angel! Wonderful!" Her lips smiled every young sailor's dream. Her mouth seemed limitless.

Janice grinned. "Look! I brought him. I brought Benjamin. I brought my husband!"

A power surge buzzed Kohlman's spine, neck to tailbone.

"Fantastic! Great!" Comus yelled below. Her voice had the same oversized huskiness as the rest of her. "Never mind bringing up the wrench! I'll be right down."

. . . . . .

They listened to the scissor lift moan, watched it drop. Kohlman watched and had strange stirrings like those he'd had once as a teenager when a special "40+" issue of *Gallery* magazine had been delivered accidentally to Mr. Silento's. But then Comus was there, blond and massive, smelling thickly of sweat and Irish soap, beside them.

"You're getting fat," Janice teased and pinched a spot at Comus's waist where Kohlman couldn't see any fat at all.

"Drinking too much, obviously," she said and smiled at Kohlman, extended her hand. "Hey," she said. "Hi, Janice's husband."

"Pleased to meet you," Kohlman said.

"This is Benjamin," Janice said. "Here's your wrench."

Comus cupped her hands and called over to her workers. "You guys see who got this wrench?! A woman!" She laughed. The men milled and groused. "Union goons!" Comus bellowed. She took a Bailey's Irish Cream minibottle from her shorts pocket, cracked the cap, took a tug. "For my complexion," she smiled. She drained the mini and hurled it in the direction of her shuffling workers . . who ducked. "I think you have to have tertiary syphilis and arthritis to get in that union!" she said.

Up close, Comus was even more unsettling, lubricated skin flashing under each turn of muscle, eyes so blue they made their own azure shadows, breasts like breadfruit, like thick ceramic bowls. Kohlman found himself swallowing, wetting his lips, wetting the insides of his cheeks. He wanted eyedrops. His circulatory system felt overcharged. "It takes a bit," Janice said, leaning in; "it's all right." What took a bit? The humiliating male things happening to Kohlman? Was she aware?

"What happened to your hands?" Comus asked Kohlman.

"No big thing," Kohlman said. "It's just . . brief." His eyes signaled Janice that he wished her not to enter in.

Comus walked them around. Her new show had a World War II theme: Pearl Harbor, dogfights, the invasion of Normandy, ending with the bomb drop on Hiroshima. Today was the Hiroshima section. The structure the union men had moved into place *was* a hotel. "When the bomb's dropped," Comus said, "it radiates . . so that that entire building actually *glows* . . structural illusion where it disintegrates into rubble. Some of the stonework *runs*! If you come back, tomorrow night, it should be working. I'll show you. —But now I can show you another part!"

Comus walked them over to one of a number of Day-Glo-green X-marks on the stage. Kohlman felt seedy, an abased freak of his own glands. He was dry and wet in all the places he would never choose to be. "One of you stand there," Comus said. "Ben . . ! Does Angel call you Ben or Benjamin?" Comus asked. Her thick, wonderful lashes beat when she asked the question.

"Whatever." Kohlman thought he understood, for the first time, the pleasures of flagellation.

"Good: so . . if you would stand over there. I can show Angel. Then I'll have her stand there and show you. Angel: back here now with me!" Comus took out another Bailey's mini.

·   ·   ·   ·   ·

Kohlman stood where Comus had instructed. He watched Janice follow to a light panel near the far end of the space. He saw

the lights dim in the warehouse, heard one of the union men call
out: "Hey–do you mind?! We're *working*!"

"A historic moment!" he heard Comus yell.

There was a jolt of light, like an enormous bulb flash; then
Kohlman could see something being projected on his figure. He
heard Janice scream crazily, hysterically, from the dark. "Oh, shit! I
wasn't thinking!" he heard Comus say. "It's not real!" Kohlman
heard Comus reassuring, but Janice was still shrieking in waves.
Whatever it was got turned off. "Angel: come on! It's light! It's an
image; it's a picture; it's not real!" Kohlman touched himself, to
see if he could feel, on his body, what might have happened.
Janice's horror subsided, trailed into small, barely audible moans.
Her sound was like a traumatized animal's. The warehouse lights
moved up. Comus was holding Janice, patting her head, comfort-
ing her. "You're so fucking sensitive," Kohlman heard Comus say.
Janice looked tiny, wrapped by that extraordinary woman. The
tableau was an early painting by Picasso: flesh of a larger woman
holding a child; even the returned light seemed blue. "No . . no . .
no. Don't be so sensitive." Comus's voice was gentle. "Angel,
c'mon." Comus took Janice by the hand.

They walked toward Kohlman. With her free hand, Comus
clamped the new Bailey's mini into her palm with her small finger,
and, with two others, twirled the cap off. She took a tug. "My skin
gets so *dry* doing this," she said.

Kohlman thought he felt a pair of the union men studying
him.

"You okay? You okay now?" Comus was saying to Janice.
Janice nodded. "Can I show your 'beau'?" Janice nodded again. She
held one hand to her chest to steady her own broken breathing.

"Are you okay?" Kohlman asked now. Janice nodded for him.

"Okay, then . . change places," Comus said. She took Kohlman by the elbow, moved him from the X, set Janice on it. Kohlman could feel a static set the fine filament hair on his ears aloft.

"Do you know what happened?" Janice called.

"Just remember: it's an *illusion*," Comus said to Kohlman,
moving him back to her projector. "It's a computer-laser technol-
ogy . . which, within a decade–unless I miss my guess–is going to
fundamentally alter everything visual . . from live theatre to window-
display." She tossed the second dead Bailey's mini off into a warehouse corner. Kohlman could feel her hand guiding him. He tried

to fight—because it made him feel so stupid—the almost cartoon eroticism. "It's just a light illusion . . of our country's history," she said. She set Kohlman where she'd set Janice. "So . . *what* happened to your hands?" she asked.

"I was . . just trying to do something I wasn't . . quite ready to do yet, I guess," Kohlman said.

"Let me see," Comus said. Then she called the length of the warehouse: "Angel! Just a minute! . . All right?" she asked Kohlman, starting to unwind his gauze.

"Sure . . fine," Kohlman said. It occurred to him that what was happening were the feelings men had . . submitting to more experienced women.

Comus unwrapped Kohlman's hands, down to the stitches. "That's pretty ugly," she said; "but it's well sewn. Can you move the fingers?"

Kohlman tried. The try was stiff and kicked a radial pain up to his elbow, but all the nerves seemed there.

Comus nodded. She held both hands and looked into them. Kohlman couldn't help himself, looking down her shirt then feeling, again, unclean, hating his twenty years of male residue. "I've got some cream," Comus said. "Actually . . should be much better than covering them up." And then she pulled up her left shorts leg to where Kohlman glimpsed pubic hair. Christ! He wanted to attack himself—his sweating, his stirring. Did people get to hate their own biologies?! Comus traced a scar of her own now, considerable, though faint. "I dropped my work on me once . . when I wasn't being careful," she said, "and did this. This cream was nearly miraculous." And she reached back into a box behind her projection equipment. "Thirty seconds!" she yelled out for Janice to hear. From a coral-colored jar she took some coral-colored cream and spread it where Kohlman's palms each had been stitched. "See if this helps," she said. "It should. I'd tell you the major ingredient . . but it would embarrass me. Let's just say it's a natural lubricant." She smiled at Kohlman. Her eyebrows rose. She pulled the cloth of her shorts down. Kohlman wondered if he had embraced his new world too soon.

Comus dimmed the warehouse lights, flipped some switches.

Suddenly, with the same strange jolt of light he'd seen before, Kohlman saw Janice, first in what seemed a green gel, then in what, clearly, had triggered her scream: he watched Janice *melt*, skin whiten, split, char, blood and musculature break through the skin surface, ooze, run, burn, radiate until there was just a skeletal structure with the most vague network of nerves and vessels tangled, until, finally, Kohlman could see *through* Janice, *beyond* her. "OhmyGod . . !" he'd started saying as the illusion had traveled. "OhmyGod . . Jesus . . OhmyGod . . ! He felt his body jolt forward as if, as she had done, to run *to* her.

Comus leaned in, close, her warm breath like thick cream, her warm breath like mint. Kohlman had *no* breath; his chest was tight and dry as lumber. "Amazing . . right?" Comus said.

Kohlman couldn't help himself: he wanted to save what he knew to be just an illusion. He had no air or voice, no moisture even to clear his throat.

"It's a three-dimensional, moving, contoured laser image," Comus explained. "Projected directly *on*to the form. The image adjusts. To fit. Automatically. Whatever size and shape! —Hand is quicker than the eye! And light's quicker than both!" She laughed. She switched the projection off, restored the warehouse lighting. "I'm supposed to have this all together and in place by New Year's Eve," she said. "Good luck—right?!"

Kohlman could hear his own pulse amplified in his head. Comus laughed. "And *now* . . on *top* of this: as if *this* weren't enough pressure—and, I mean, how could I say 'no'?!—I'm shooting a *video* for the President! God: Life is interesting!"

.   .   .   .   .

The three left the warehouse and had breakfast at the Peppermill. "*Some*one leaked the President's video," Comus said. "So now they're counterleaking that he's here to see the *fight* tomorrow. It's nuts!"

They drove in Comus's van out to Nellis Air Force Base. "We're meeting the 'Commander in Chief' at nine-thirty," Comus said. When she threw her head back to laugh, Kohlman held his breath at the arc of her neck. Kohlman had asked Janice: "Does she have . . people in her life? You know, relationships?" He had tried to imagine: "like . . I guess I mean . . lovers?" "*I* was her lover . . once . . one time," Janice had said. And it had seemed, curiously, possible . . then threatening, briefly, to Kohlman . . and then only simple and clear.

Comus's van spilled with video equipment. A green Mercedes moved up beside them: two men in the car glancing over, then the car dropping back into the traffic. Kohlman thought, briefly, that the men looked familiar.

Inside Nellis, there were temporary trailers and Secret Service men outside, milling, in ties, holsters, and shirt-sleeves. Comus kept calling the Secret Service "Boys" and laughed: "How you Boys doing today?" "What you Boys hearing on those walkie-talkies? Any Willie Nelson?" She talked to a colonel, introduced Janice and Kohlman as her "assistants." The wind, off the desert, came in strong southerly gusts. "Your pilots going to have any trouble with this?" Comus asked the colonel. "My pilots can brush dust off a contact lens!" the colonel said.

The President arrived. There was a rustle like peacock feathers.

"Mr. President!" Comus said.

The President shook Comus's hand, smiled. Comus introduced Kohlman and Janice. "I understand she's a genius," the President said, nodding at Comus. The President wore an outfit specially tailored: half, a pair of bib overalls and denim shirt; half, a dark business suit, white shirt and tie. The illusion, the division up the center, was perfect, no visible seam. "Man of business! Man of the People!" Comus said.

Kohlman felt a shame.

"I may get twenty of these," the President joked.

It took shape like weather.

"So where's your hat?" Comus asked.

The shame was distant. It rolled in like sickness.

The word "hat" flew like a cliff swallow and echoed through the crowd. Suddenly a blue, visored ranking officer's hat appeared and was placed on the President. "The Cat in The Hat," the President joked.

"Officer–Executive–Common Man!" Comus said.

Kohlman turned away and walked apart until he was at the crowd's edge staring out. He heard his father: *We have no common language . . you'll excuse my silence.* His shame broke. *No common language? Hey . . no . . Dad! . . wait! Here; look; my closet! Check out the bib overalls!* The rock and coarse sand and creosote brush turned, in Kohlman's mind, to fields; the fields, back to chafed landscape. *Of the people! What people?* The lung-thick choke of dense alfalfa, falling to an imagined combine, swept through Kohlman's brain, burned his lungs. He saw his father, his father like Iowa stone, unmoving, inexhaustible, riding . . riding . . riding green machinery through a gold field. *Man of the people . . Common Man . . !* It was a joke only. That was all. It was a moment of low mockery at an Air Force base.

"Okay . . !" Behind, Kohlman could hear Comus's commands. "Okay: we're ready! We're in business!" Kohlman looked away at the Interstate. An Airstream moved west. Were his parents in it? Again, at his back, Kohlman heard Comus, this time saying: "It's for my complexion." And then the shouted command: "Dancers?! Billie?! Where's my choreographer?! Three minutes?! Planes ready?". . the last question to the colonel.

"Planes ready," the colonel's voice said.

Far north . . another Airstream passed . . another. Were all the small farms of America mobile now? All sleek and compact? After their final battles? Sons gone off to Amherst and Princeton? Then were all these restless, circling, impermanent silver wagons Kohlman's people? His town? . . his neighbors?

". . Thirty seconds," he heard now behind him. Then: "Planes up!"

An eagle circled high, north, somewhere above the Moapa River Indian Reservation and Valley of Fire.

Kohlman turned back to watch. His hands, open now in the desert air and even with cream, felt contracted, tokens, hands in miniature. Kohlman moved in against restraint, closer, to watch Comus's scenario: The colonel switching on his walkie-talkie: "Planes up . . twenty-seven seconds, . . signing off."

"Dancers?!" Comus called again. "Billie?! Could we have your people?!"

Kohlman watched a chorus of men and women in Air Force uniforms file from trailers. A tall Jamaican, in a tank top and cut-off levis, herded and began placing them.

"Can I help?" Janice asked.

". . Small-talk the President," Comus suggested.

Kohlman wondered how.

He saw Janice's smile. He saw the President smile back. He heard Janice say to Comus: "He looks really lonely–this close," then she moved to talk. Secret Service men edged in. "When will your video be shown?" Janice asked the President.

"Early November," the President said, smiling. "We're hoping to sell our programs . . Party . . best we can. If anybody can help . . all reports . . this woman is a genius."

"Except I worry she works too much," Janice said.

"Well . . everybody does *some*thing too much," the President said and smiled. "I try to make history too much. But that's . . being President!"

"*Planes up and ready!*" Kohlman heard the colonel announce.

"Okay!" he heard Comus say. And then: "—Mr. President?!"

"Excuse me," the President said to Janice then moved, with his Secret Service, over to Comus. "Where should I be?" he asked.

"Could we have the hammer, please?!" Comus called.

Someone handed the President a sledgehammer. Comus had eight cameras. She began running from one to the next: sighting, checking. Intro music started for "He's Got the Whole World . . ."

"Hold the music please . . ?!" Comus called off.

Kohlman looked at Janice, who held one hand above her head to keep her hair from the wind.

"Mr. President . . ? . . on the runway, please?" Comus shouted. Two assistants moved the President to the runway.

"Okay: twenty seconds!" Comus called. Her command echoed: . . twenty seconds . . twenty seconds. "Okay: Mr. President: Like we rehearsed—hands up? Palms flat? Good!" Someone placed the hammer behind the President's neck, so that it was held in place, threaded in and out of his raised arms. "Terrific!" Comus said. "Wonderful! Perfect!"

"Which one's his head?" Kohlman heard one of the crew say.

"Sensational!" Comus chimed. "Now, when I say, '*Go,*' you move . . forward, mouth the third and fourth verses of the song. We'll lip-sync the music and your voice later! Okay . . four—three—two—one: Go: *Rolling*!"

"You still seem blue," Janice said to Kohlman, close beside him. "You've seemed blue all day. Are you all right?"

"I'm . . I've just been . . going over some things," Kohlman said.

Kohlman and Janice watched the President stride forward down the runway—smiling, mouthing words. The uniformed chorus danced on either side in perfect choreography. There was a growing, violently loud sound. Two fighter planes swooped down, one on either side of the President, flew over his upheld hands, his extended palms. For an instant it appeared as if the President *carried* the two fighter planes, held them, with their jet trails, aloft. "*Perfect!!*" Kohlman heard Comus shout. "One take! Brilliant! Wrap! Pool at Caesar's at two!"

. . . . .

They went to the Tropicana for lunch. Comus drank two double Bailey's, poured another over her chicken and pineapple salad, explaining that what they'd shot—cut, edited, superimposed— would comprise six seconds, seen at three different points, in the video. Kohlman thought the veins in Janice's forehead looked like calligraphy.

"You can do *anything* with images!" Comus said. She picked up her salad plate and drank from it: "That desert wind!" she said, Bailey's and mayonnaise running together, and then: "Forget the bomb . . go after the optic nerve!" She laughed.

Kohlman saw two men eating three tables away who looked like the men, that morning, who'd pulled beside them in the green Mercedes. When he looked back, they were gone.

. . . . .

Caesar's, when they arrived to set up at poolside for the final video sequence, was a mob. The Primavera terrace spilled with blacks in $300 Fila running suits. Kohlman left Janice with Comus; he needed to find the Challenger. But the Challenger's grandstands were bare. The Peterbilt cab sat alone. Just beyond, crews erected the next night's fight arena. Kohlman asked whether anyone had seen his friend.

"Everybody knows he's here . . but nobody knows where," one of the roustabouts said.

. . . . .

Inside Caesar's Olympic casino area, where Kohlman searched next, it was all the Champion! He joked with players; crowds followed him, he signed autographs, looking the whole while like a film star on a weight program and a diet of steroids. "Who wants to be the first woman here to give head to the Champion after he wins tomorrow night?" he called into the crowd. Shrieks. Thirty hands went up. "Why wait?" the Champion said. He thrust his pelvis forward. "I'm ready!" He winked at a nearby circle of men: "Whaddaya say, guys? I'll give you the overflow!" He was dressed in American-flag sweats with an Olympic gold medal centered back and front; he had perfect teeth.

"How much should I bet on you, Champ?" someone in the crowd called.

"Bet it *all*," the Champion said. He grabbed the dice at a table that were being handed back to a shooter and rolled them.

"*Natural*!" the stickman called out.

The Champion raised his hands over his head in a victory tableau.

At one point, the Champion moved his followers to the marble Joe Louis statue in the foyer between the tower elevators.

"How ya doin', Joe!" the Champion mocked; "What's hap'nin', Bro?" The crowd laughed. The Champion crouched and crossed a slow-motion right to Joe Louis's abdomen: "Good thing you not about these days!" he warned; "Ole Brown Bomber! 'Cause we got *new* Bombers now! Bigger Bombers! Better Bombers! More belligerent Bombers!" The crowd roared. Suddenly the Champion stood up as if taken aback: mock shock; mock offense. "Say what?" he said. "Say what, Brother Joe? . . You say you bigger? You say you better? You say you the biggest and best of All Time?" And then the Champion jerked his shoulder back as though the statue had pushed him. "Hey!" he said, and then: "Watch it!" He pushed the statue back. Then the Champion jumped back as if pushed even harder. "I said *watch* it, my man!" he said and then leapt forward and gave the statue a brutal push, which set it wavering, the crowd clearing, wavering, crowd separating; "I warned you!" the Champion said and gave a final push to the off-balance statue, sending it to the marble lobby floor, white gloved arms breaking from its shoulders, marble fragments breaking from its tight-curled skull. Again, the Champion raised his arms over his head, the crowd unsure now about the moment: "The Champ of All Time!" the Champion shouted. Kohlman felt sick. The weighted world was falling as entertainment. It did not bode well.

Kohlman called the Challenger's room. He got the Challenger's voice: "Hi. This is the Challenger," the message said. "I'm not in right now; 'cause I'm in seclusion. But if you would like to wish me well—or to leave any other message, please feel free to do so after the beep . . which is coming right up. Thank you."

Kohlman waited. The beep came. He felt hesitant; he felt uncertain, needful, hopeful, small, but he began. ". . Hi . . yeah; right. This is . . Benjamin. Benjamin Kohlman. Are you . . ? . . I assume everything's okay . . true? So . . . Thanks again for driving me over to . . I think it's getting serious . . I mean, with the hotel-fire-people. But . . yesterday, I had this feeling . . anything was possible; I could deal with . . whatever. And I guess today, I'm a little less . . sanguine, or whatever the right word might . . . Don't worry, though. I mean, whatever happens . . obviously, happens. So . . I just don't want Janice to be . . I need to figure if I can keep her safe from . . . I'm sorry; I'm rambling . . to a recording. So . . . Good luck tomorrow night. I'm rooting. I'm sorry about the Joe Louis statue, what the Champion did, but I guess there's really nothing, at this point, that anyone can . . ." The circuit opened, and its hum came on. Kohlman set the phone back. How had he thought his friend might help him? The two . . three minutes he'd talked had felt . . like something he'd felt, once, as a boy. Kohlman remembered being fourteen and being alone outside and in the corn and talking, or . . doing something . . basically talking. To . . ? A person? Someone listening. Or someone he *hoped* might be listening. Who, actually, *did* feel, then, to be listening. Someone away . . out . . beyond him . . somewhere. It was a thing he'd called . . *prayer*. Someone he'd called . . he'd said: *Father*. He remembered. Talking. Having a conversation. Expressing . . . Wondering . . . Exchanging . . something . . with someone . . not exactly there but somewhere. . . . And believing it.

·   ·   ·   ·   ·

At the pool, just before two o'clock, there was tremendous excitement. The pool area itself had been cordoned—Las Vegas Police and Secret Service stationed the entire perimeter. Something was being constructed down the middle of the pool, and, on either side, a corps of water-ballet swimmers rehearsed designs. Above the pool suspended by invisible wires was a Steinway grand and piano bench. Barnett had obviously gotten to Comus. In fact; yes; there he was, poolside. With Alyce—now planed, no silicon pushing at her new designer gown. Kohlman, back from his phone call, stood at the rope cordons, waving. The President hadn't arrived. Janice saw Kohlman and spoke to Comus, who sent word to let Kohlman through.

As Kohlman stepped over the ropes, though, a sudden commotion flared up behind him. Shots cracked the dry air. Secret Service men melded into a knot and Kohlman turned. He saw one of the men from the Mercedes drop in a bed of larkspur, blood across his shirt front. The man carried a gun. Kohlman heard the word *"Assassination!"* hissed and mumbled like a tremor through the moving crowd. He felt his own chest constrict. He moved forward, breath fluttering, to where Comus and Janice stood. "I got it on film," Comus said. "I always leave the cameras running." She cracked yet another Bailey's and spread it on her hands and cheeks like lotion. Kohlman put an arm around Janice, drew her in. What was the gesture? Inclusion? Protection? Or was he taking her hostage? She was shaking. Had she had his sense? That the man's target had *not* been the President? He looked down. In the confused light and shadow, her skin looked like flaked pastry.

"You know that guy?" he asked.

"What guy?" she said.

"In the chair?" he said. "By the Imperial Palace?"

"REM?" she said.

"Say his name again?"

"REM."

"*REM,*" he said. "I couldn't remember it. We had a talk last night. Sort of a talk. He makes strange transitions."

"He makes *what*?"

"He makes strange transitions," Kohlman said.

"Is that like *strong verbs*?" Janice asked.

·   ·   ·   ·   ·

The President arrived. The milling strides of the Secret Service bore rekindled briskness. At the pool's perimeter, at every compass degree, lingered men dressed and trying to look like casual bathers and recreationists, but whose jaws looked forged in bronze and whose carotid arteries all pulsed.

The cameras started their hum. Comus orchestrated. They shot the segment. A clear Lucite ramp had been constructed down the center of the pool, just below the surface. In the segment, the President strode toward the pool—as he had down the Nellis runway—singing. He made no hesitation—stepped into the water and walked the length of its surface, while swimmers backstroked and made huge morning glory designs to either side, and while Alyce

Barnett played the following-and-tracking Steinway eight feet above, like some instrument of Annunciation, some arpeggio-filled cloud. Comus did four takes. Kohlman noticed Janice's hands moving frequently, it seemed clutchingly, to her head. He asked if she were all right. She said she was fine. The shoot took an hour and a half. The President invited Comus and her friends to his suite afterwards for "something to munch," and a drink. When they left the pool, Kohlman watched three Secret Service men trying to remove bloodstains from all the flower petals.

· · · · ·

The President's suite was smaller than the Challenger's but nice. There was a four-foot entertainment-center television with several smaller monitors. Comus drifted with a steadi-cam strapped to her turquoise jumpsuit, filming everything. She looked renewed, considerable, her lips deep with gloss, her eyes in a dusk, her exposed body carrying the outside day like a pulse. Janice stood with Barnett. He looked proud and fraternal; she kept pinching something from her eyelashes and looked tired. Kohlman began drinking too much. He felt mute and graceless. He manhandled the hors d'oeuvres: squeezed the stuffed snow peas too hard, brutalized the phyllo triangles. In his presence, all puff pastry seemed to be at risk. Alyce wandered over. "Hi," she said.

"Hi," Kohlman said. "Hi. How're you holding up?"

"Not that much to hold up today," Alyce said. Her child part seemed, for the evening, to have surfaced. She touched her bodice and worked a shy smile.

Kohlman smiled back. "It's better," he said. "You look more . . appropriate or . . right . . or something." Then he added: "I'm sorry. I don't have the best words. I left my best words somewhere else tonight. I've been drinking."

"I'm glad Janice gave you her life," Alyce said.

Kohlman filled his mouth with ice cubes; he pushed three fingers stiffly against his neck. "Yeah," he said. The word circled back: "Yeah."

"It's good for her."

He moved the ice cubes against his teeth. Something in the night's innocence of Alyce . . and in her candor . . loosed his mind: she was *like* . . a person, another person; her words, *like* . . whoever that other person had been.

"She tried to tell me . . last night, alone . . what it felt like inside . . when you . . any of us . . women . . became . . she used the word . . 'rare.' "

Kohlman swallowed the cubes. They dropped like smooth, cool pebbles in a stream bed.

"Because," Alyce went on; "because . . did you read the program? About me? In the program? And about what happened once? When I couldn't stop things? Before here and before Janice? Did you read . . last night?"

Kohlman took one of the breaths he'd been famous for. "I did," he said. He remembered whose words Alyce's came to him as. Pamela Arnold. They'd been . . just her age . . eleven, twelve . . had been at the river. Walked there. The sun at . . oh . . five, six and heading down. It had been the summer before junior high. They'd lain on their backs, looked up . . just at clouds. And there'd been hawks . . but not disturbing . . not unsettling the universe in any way . . just moving . . stitching clouds with sky. And Pamela's hand had found Kohlman's . . the way one finds one's own infant hand . . or finds a small robin in tall grass. And taken it. He'd taken hers. And she'd started crying. Or perhaps he. But it wasn't sad . . no. It felt more nice. And Pamela had said: *I can hear all our bodies starting to change. Can you hear?* And they'd squeezed hands hard . . but not hurting. And had cried more. And now Kohlman was crying again . . no spasms . . just fat tears balling involuntarily in the close corners of his eyes . . his tongue sliding to the side, working the lip there, catching the tears. His mouth bore the taste of earth, like that he'd scooped and eaten, weeks before, on his return. And in the lightweight summer weave of his sports jacket clung the smell of one of his father's old woolen coats. "I'm sorry," Kohlman said to Alyce, who, for all he knew, had made no judgement. He plucked yet another old-fashioned from a passing tray. "You . . play . . like . . someone . . twice your age," he said. And then he pinched his face strangely, pushed it up against his cheekbones. "I'm sorry. I'm not sure, even, what I'm crying about," he said.

"Would you tell me something?" Alyce asked.

"No," Kohlman said . . and then he said, "Of course. Yes. What?"

"A story?"

Now Kohlman's mouth felt dry. "I'm worried about Janice," he said.

"Do you have any with children?" Alyce asked. "Stories? I never really . . there was no person who could read me or tell me stories. I always wanted that. But when I asked C.E.O., he just laughed and said: 'Go to the library.' " . . So I was thinking: since you *do* that . . that's what you *are* . . then you could . . maybe . . something with an animal? And a place? Outside? And . . night? And . . magic? Those things? And then . . something . . I don't know . . that feels . . "–she smiled–". . you know . . 'rare' when it's over? Please . . ?" Alyce stood very quietly and looked at Kohlman with the most constant eyes. "I wish they had pizza here," she said. "Don't you? No one ever has pizza."

"I think she's getting her headaches." Kohlman said, keeping his own subject. "I'm concerned."

"I loved riding on the piano today," Alyce said. "It was like a blue pony!"

The President moved, unannounced, between them, put an arm around Alyce. "How's my girl?" he said. "How's my accompanist?"

"I'm okay," Alyce said.

"Well, what would you say," the President said, "if you knew I'd just booked you at the White House?"

"That would be okay," Alyce said. "Would you have pizza?"

The President laughed and brought a hand out from behind him. It held a doll. "For you," he said, and Alyce took it, studying it, looking back and forth between the President and the doll. "You're right," the President said. "It's me. I had it made. It's a Cabbage-patch President." He grinned.

Kohlman moved away. He tried to compose a first line in his slack brain . . to a story about a blue pony: *When the Blue Pony pranced the dark fields of Pendleton . . .* Bad! Silly! Where was Pendleton? He looked across the room, where Janice stood in a small group of guests, there but marginal, trying to keep the smallest flutter smile on her face, not entering but listening. She held a washcloth and dabbed her temples and back of her neck periodically.

He couldn't be responsible! He couldn't feel responsible if she . . !

He strolled directionless. *At night, the Blue Pony always left the barn and ran. And when his horseshoes hit stone, they would kick stars up into the night.* Not exactly memorable. But better. What had been the parts? What had been Alyce's requirements? . . *animal* . . *night* . . *place* . . *magic* . . . animal, night, place, magic . . . animalnightplacemagic . . . *'rare'*! . . Angel's word! So . . what was the opening, he'd just thought of? *At night* . . *when the Blue Pony* . . . Shit! He shouldn't be drinking like this!

He wandered over to the bank of small monitors. They were closed circuit, focused on certain live casino games. One of the games, a dice game, played as well on the large screen. Kohlman realized that people at the party, some, were calling bets in over the telephone. He watched dice twenty times their size roll on the screen, heard people shout, and felt unsteady. *Always at night, Black Pony* . . . *Always at night in Templeton, Black Pony* . . . Kohlman wove a path to Janice.

"I should get out of your life," Kohlman leaned in, kissed her, and whispered. "You're getting headaches again."

"No," Janice said. "Really. No."

"That's not what I'm seeing."

"It's just, more . . ."

"What happened last night? What was that?" Kohlman asked.

"Last night was . . fine," she said. "Last night was okay. It was all right. I got through it."

"But, I mean, if I hadn't . . . The truth is: if I'd never . . ."

"Benjamin: if something happens, then it happens to *me*. All right?" she said. "You can't . . ."

"You look tired." Kohlman traced one of her cheekbones.

"How much have you had to drink?"

"Your eyes—you keep touching something somewhere behind them. I get worried that . . ."

"That's not the headaches!"

"What is it then?"

"It's just . . ."

"What?"

"Signals! Of . . some kind. Different sorts of . . overlapping . . signals!"

"From . . ?"

Suddenly a crowd buzzed around the big screen. "Okay," the President's voice rose from its center: "Okay . . I'm ready. I'm game for this. Go ahead: Call it in!"

"That guy outside was trying to shoot *me*," Kohlman said. "Not him. Not the President."

"I know," Janice said. "I know. I understand. C.E.O. told me. What are you saying?"

The President laughed. "Put the National Endowment for the Arts Budget on the 'Don't Come' line!" he said.

Janice took Kohlman's face in her hands, opened her mouth, kissed him. "I'm fine," she said. "All right? I'll *be* fine. I'm *getting* fine. Don't be impatient with me."

"I'm not impatient with you."

"Don't be impatient with yourself."

Kohlman swayed. Something in his chest and behind his eyes chilled then hurt. He stooped; he hugged her; two last dancers in a marathon. She seemed too . . *some*thing. For him. For *any*one. Too spectral, brave, honest, frail, present. He imagined that in the most dark room he would always know her . . because her bones would be spirit tubes of light; her eyes, like music boxes. He lifted her hair then let it fall from his numb fingertips. He lifted it again, kissed it, set it in his mouth. His eyes closed and opened, opened and closed, lubricated. "I think I'm crazy," Kohlman said.

"You're not crazy," Janice said. "It's just that to be good, sometimes, *feels* crazy."

"I'll think about that," Kohlman said. "If I can . . I promise . . I will." And then he kissed the top of her head and wandered away.

"Should we go home soon?" he heard Janice ask, behind. "Should we be thinking about tomorrow, Benjamin? We've been going a long time."

Kohlman crossed to Barnett. "How many doubles . . did Ted Williams have . . in the month of August . . 1948?" Barnett told him. Barnett asked: "How many of those doubles . . did he cross home plate on?" Kohlman answered and was off by one. Barnett crowed. Kohlman's eyes filled unexpectedly. He nodded at Janice. "Can you . . ?" He started to cry . . dumb, sloppy.

"Hey!" Barnett boomed, even in his low tones, "Hey . . none of that shit here, Benjamin! This is the Government!"

"Listen . . I'm sorry," Kohlman said. He pressed his teeth into his upper lip in an exchange of pain. "I'm sorry . . but listen:

I need . . you have to get Angel to the specialist again, okay?" he said. "She's getting the headaches."

"Don't leave—okay?" Barnett's voice, even *sotto voce*, buzzed and the visible buzz broke up the surface tension of Kohlman's drink, like light wind riffling a lake. "Okay?" Barnett repeated.

"Okay," Kohlman said. He laughed for no reason. "Okay . . sure . . okay."

"Okay, then. Then stick around," Barnett instructed.

"I will," Kohlman said without energy.

"This is important stuff," Barnett said.

"Important stuff," Kohlman repeated.

"We'll talk."

"We will."

"Oh—and don't worry about those writers."

Proust? . . Dostoevsky? Kohlman wondered.

"Whatztheirfaces! Alexander." That guy! "And the other one. They're out! They're gone! They're away! They got some instructions!" Barnett laughed. "But, anyway: listen: I just have one person I have to catch before he leaves. Don't go anywhere. I don't want this business with Angel to drop."

"No. Of course not," Kohlman said.

Barnett made a line for a man, silver-haired in a tan lightweight cotton suit. Kohlman stood talking to his absence: "Absolutely . . !" he said. "Right on! Check . . double check . . Mr. Advisor, sir. *It was just . . it was only in the dusk of . . something . . of tall stalks! . . and grains! . . that Blue Pony turned gold!* Getting there! . . Kohlman thought. Slowly! Maybe I'll get a *children*'s book out of this! He laughed. He staggered off.

"Hey, I mean that, Benjamin!" Barnett called over to corral him: "You don't go anywhere. You stay!"

Kohlman moved toward the door. His focus felt random and arbitrary. He passed huge silver bowls of prawns and cocktail sauce sitting by ice sculpture. His anatomy felt soft. He looked across and saw Janice where she held a glass of rosé and stood by the room's high cathedral window, looking out at Caesar's pink and blue and gold lit fountains spraying up and into the night. Kohlman's rib cage felt broken apart . . like spring ice. Or the toppled Joe Louis statue. Comus stood some distance from Janice, alone, looking into a bloody mary, moving its celery stalk around and around the rim of its glass, eyes so deep, so liquid and blue they seemed

twin seas . . solitary, melancholy. Alyce passed and said "Hi again."
"It was only Blue Pony who knew God lived in his hooves," Kohlman
said, mumbled. He would keep it, keep that opening . . if it would
stay. He turned. He found a door.

"Benjamin . . !?" Barnett's voice boomed.

He went through the door. The President's party made its
noise behind . . sounds . . like being in the lobby of a triplex with
three films, off somewhere, rolling . . or standing outside a zoo . .
sounds . . continuous . . shrieked . . barked. Riotous, mournful,
threatening. All noise. Just and only. Noise. Traffic. No people.

He took the elevator down.

– ELEVEN –

It was late afternoon. The outside city held so curiously still that Kohlman wondered about his hearing. He worked the bony flaps of his ears against their canals to experiment. Perhaps the gunshots or the din at the President's party had occluded something. But he seemed fine. It was just the hour . . perhaps the contrast. He'd stepped out into a pause – whatever moment comes in cities before change. A limousine slipped by like a yacht. There was the sense that, somewhere, rain had tried to fall but had evaporated and jellied the air. Kohlman could taste the boulevard's dry heat drying, see it give phantoms up to the traffic.

He went to the Maxim, threw what was visibly his together. It wasn't right; Janice was not some experiment in adventure; he had to stop. Yes: All right: he was on an unimagined map with her; he was in a country without borders. She swept across his brain in updrafts and as sweet as candlewood. She inflamed him like a sirocco. She was the moon in a sky he had never seen, names of all the towns in Iowa he had always forgotten. She was some gift out of a month of stones and water and spiced resinous air. She was a moment on a street corner . . two people turning to one another . . glad, laughing, claiming a thing that they called, for the lack of other language, "friendship". . but a thing that they knew to be more. But . . ! No . . no . . come on! Leave it be! It was wrong. No more! Because she'd been those things . . because she'd loosed him, spun his heart . . been who she was and helped him see he could be unafraid . . still . . still, he could not then *use* those things, use the prompt of her to then go somewhere else, to travel

some *new* map, and be *more* unafraid, *more* convinced about whatever it was he was growing daily more convinced of. This was *not*,
Jesus Christ! some laboratory: this life we had . . with ourselves
and with other people. Not some bloody University center! Cows
tethered to polyurethane hearts! Toucans wired for additional long-
term memory! He had to stop trying . . to hook himself up to her
. . or herself up to him . . for an answer . . or ride . . or *some*thing
. . God! some result. *Angel. Angel, Angel! I can't! I'm sorry, I
can't! I love this! I love what's begun, but* . . ! She was a person
whose head could crack! She had almost died. Once. He had seen
pain come again to her eyes—like stress on glass, filament lines on
fine glaze. Enough! Enough! Leave her alone! Stop it!

He called the Sands. He called the Dunes. He called the
Tropicana. He should have called the airport, but couldn't. He
called the Desert Inn. Everywhere was booked. He called Sharon at
her studio in New York. "Benjamin: we had this conversation.
Remember?" she said and hung up. He called the Las Vegas Visitor's
Bureau: "Not too far from where I am," he said. "Please." They
got him a room at a place called the Found Motel, between the
Sands and the Riviera and across from the Fashion Mall. When he
arrived, the room was low, in what they called their "Fortune Unit"
at the rear of the property. It smelled like wet blighted applewood
trying to burn in winter.

It was wrong: he ought to have stayed concealed; that had
been the object. But if he couldn't be *with* her, he could, at least,
be in her city.

He *did* try to sleep, but the spackle on the room's bowed ceiling kept him awake . . like sleeping under broken glass, sleeping
outdoors under a sky with too many stars. *Look: don't do it,* Kohlman told himself. *Stay in. Don't go out.* Still . . because people
sometimes wander in the neighborhoods of old lovers . . the attrac-
tive danger or because it hurts so sweetly—Kohlman left. And went
outside. And crossed the street to avoid passing REM at his constant vigil in his motorchair. Yet . . REM, more diminished, more
thin, more unshaven, more with deficit and inhumanly burning
eyes, had changed his post. He was there! He materialized by the
chain-link bordering the debris once the Castaways. Kohlman
dropped another twenty. "New command post," he said.

"You're still here," REM said; his voice with no discernible
play.

"Still here: yeah," Kohlman said. He tried to smile: "Barely. Still doing battle."

"It's getting difficult," REM said; all flatness. The night before, his words had tumbled more like ashes or confetti–falling everywhere; no visible weave.

"*More* difficult?" Kohlman tried.

"Casualties," REM said.

Casualties. Kohlman wondered if REM had flashbacks. "See you," Kohlman said. He started off.

"We try to keep the books accurately," REM announced.

Kohlman stopped, confused.

"We try to keep everything balanced. We're still working on what's right!"

Kohlman took a breath. The man made no sense. His words flew like brood in a crowded coop–feathers dropping, wings colliding, making other wings impossible. He could feel the man, feel his eyes, waiting for a response behind him. *We're still working on what's right . . ?* What could he answer? What did he know about such things?

.   .   .   .   .

He tried Comus's trick: loading his pockets with minibottles– his, tequila–drinking them as he wandered, with no focused direction, the Fashion Mall. A floor manager in Men's Clothing at Neiman Marcus told him: "When we first opened . . I asked people like yourself to leave. Now . . I'm used to it. It's everywhere. Private shame in public."

Kohlman grinned. *Private shame in public. Go for it!* he thought. Better than *public shame in private.* He was drunk. "I'll take a dozen of those ties," he said.

Kohlman put all twelve ties on and rode up and down the escalator. "I'm the Tie Man!" He bowed to all the ascending people as he rode down. "I'm the Tie Man!" He swept an imagined hat, his stitched hand parting the conditioned air like a thing separate. Shoppers averted their eyes and checked their watches. He went into a store called the Artjoue Emporium where they had a restored Wurlitzer lit in greens and deep wine colors. It played the Everly Brothers and Patti Page and Glenn Miller and Frank Sinatra. "How much for this?" Kohlman asked. It was beautiful; its music came from some escaped time. "I'm serious. How much?"

"Eighty-four hundred dollars," the man said.

"Eighty-four hundred dollars," Kohlman repeated.

"Eighty-four hundred dollars," the man said again.

Kohlman dug into his jacket. He opened his billfold, squinted, fumbled inside. "What'f I give you . . fifty . . seven?" he asked. "Hundred."

"Eighty-four hundred dollars."

"Eighty-four hundred dollars. . . What'f I give you sixty-two?"

"The price is fixed," the man said. "I don't barter."

"Good. I respect that. I don't barter either. . . What'f I give you sixty-three?"

The man walked away.

"How late're you open?!" Kohlman called.

"Eight!" the man said. He feather-dusted an antique slot machine.

"You deliver?"

"Sure. Someone gives us money—we deliver," the man said.

•　　•　　•　　•

Kohlman took off his ties, found his way to the Riviera. The stillness, the preternatural sense of waiting, held its sway. He had less than an hour. He hoped he could find his man, the pit boss, Jerry Lessac. Or at least Lonnie, the dealer. If he could be "Mr. B" for them again, then they would give him two thousand in chips. Two winning hands—he could parlay the two thousand into enough to buy the Wurlitzer. He had two of his tequila left and popped one down. He couldn't find a familiar face in the casino.

He walked up to a blackjack table. The dealer had a name tag: "Charles." "Charles," Kohlman said, nodding to him.

Charles nodded back.

"How's it going?" Kohlman said.

"How are *you*?" Charles said.

"You recognize me?" Kohlman said.

"I'm sorry; I don't. No, sir," Charles said. "Should I?"

Kohlman tried two other dealers—"Elaine" from Shreveport and "Matthew" from Buena Vista. Not even an ember of recognition. "I'm Mr. B," Kohlman said to Matthew.

"Pleased to meet you," Matthew said.

Kohlman sat at Matthew's table, took out a thousand dollars.

"Black?" Matthew asked.

"Black," Kohlman said.

Matthew slipped him ten black chips. Kohlman left the two stacks of five chips in his box. Matthew hesitated to see whether Kohlman might not withdraw some. When he didn't, Matthew called, "Black plays—a thousand!" back over his shoulder into the pit and dealt the cards. Kohlman hit a fourteen with a four; Matthew hit a fifteen with a seven. He paid Kohlman and checked his watch. Kohlman let the two thousand ride and lost. He took another thousand, played it all, won the hand, let it ride, won again, let it ride, and lost. He was down two thousand, had a little less than five thousand left in his billfold. "Enjoyed playing with you," Kohlman said to Matthew, rose unsteadily and, again, wandered the casino.

He wanted the Wurlitzer. If he couldn't have Janice, then he wanted something beautiful. Like the Wurlitzer. He had never really admitted to wanting anything beautiful before: shouldn't he be able to have at least one beautiful thing?

He sat down with a Japanese dealer, "Teiko from Kyoto." "You ever seen me before?" Kohlman asked. She shook her head and said she was sorry. He called Teiko's pit boss over: "You ever seen me before?" The man's name was Fantasia, and he asked Kohlman to refresh his memory. "Mr. B," Kohlman said. "Right! Of course!" Fantasia said and shook Kohlman's hand. "Mr. B! Good to see you!" Kohlman nodded and smiled. Fantasia checked his watch. Kohlman smiled at Teiko. "Good luck, Mr. B," Fantasia said and walked away. "I'd like two thousand," Kohlman said to Teiko. Teiko's eyes glazed with fear; she called Fantasia over, asked about two thousand for Kohlman. Kohlman tried to smile. He was having trouble seeing a focused image. Fantasia asked whether he had any other outstanding markers and when Kohlman said *no*, got on a pit phone and made a call. Fantasia told Teiko to start Kohlman with two and watched. Kohlman played the chips, a thousand a hand, and lost both. "You want to pay that marker off now, Mr. B?" Fantasia asked. Kohlman fumbled his billfold, took the money out. Fantasia tore up his paper. Kohlman had lost four thousand dollars in less than twelve minutes.

He had a Margarita at the bar. "Mr. B!" the bartender recognized him: "What happened to your Johnny Walker Red?" It was seven-fifteen. Kohlman really wanted the Wurlitzer. He counted his money. He walked out into the casino, got another two thousand, played it all, won. He was sweating; he could feel his shirt slick against his back. His hands shook. He could feel the sea of his body burning at his retinas. "Give me a minute," he said to the dealer; "Give me just a minute; I have to put together a strategy."

What was he now? Even? No: two thousand behind. If he played the four and won, where would he be? Then . . if he played the four twice? He nodded for the dealer to start. "Got your strategy now?" the dealer, "Biff from Toledo," asked. "Yeah – win," Kohlman said. He laughed. Biff laughed. They played. Kohlman won. He motioned Biff to hold again. Biff held and studied the second hand of his watch. "Almost time for the test," Biff said. Kohlman, as far as he was concerned, was *in* his test; he had no idea what Biff was talking about. He asked Biff how much he had. Simple addition seemed complex. Kohlman wondered if the President's party were still in progress. Where the Federal Arts budget stood? Whether Janice missed him. "What's the limit?" he asked. "Five," Biff said. Kohlman bet it. Lost. He bet his remaining three. Won. Bet the limit again.

Suddenly his spine vibrated, the top of his head buzzed. Chips at all the tables leapt from their racks, dealers' quick arms, like reflexive scythes, gathering them in, voices throughout rising in a throaty rumble. The light quaked in a sudden shimmer, the color of a photoflash seen underwater. Something dropped into Kohlman's lap and he found it, closing his senseless hand around the edged milling of three chips. "Big one this time," Biff said.

"Big . . ?" Kohlman started to ask.

"Test," Biff said. ". . Test."

Kohlman squinted: not quite tracking, not connecting.

"Underground nuclear test . . at four-thirty-eight . . in the desert," Biff said.

"Oh . . ." Kohlman nodded. "Right." He took a moment. Something had been released . . or established . . or restored; any one or all, because, now, the casino's normal buzz, its soft commercial gold light, its set exchange of life, returned. There was more laughter.

Kohlman pointed to the box where his five black chips sat. Biff dealt. Kohlman won. "How much do I have now?" Kohlman asked.

"Eleven. With a mark for two," Biff said. Eleven . . minus two . . ." Kohlman paid back his paper. What had landed in his lap were three pink chips, each a thousand, and so he cashed those in, a total of twelve, took a cab to the Artjoue Emporium and asked to have his Wurlitzer delivered. "I'll ride in the delivery van," he said. "Room 1207. At the Found."

.   .   .   .   .

He sat in the dark at the Found watching liquid light twine again and again upward in color, listening to the Everly Brothers. ". . Bye-bye love. . . Bye-bye, happiness . . ." He felt sixteen. Had he *been* sixteen? Ever? What had happened at sixteen? Not much. Not enough. Not enough at home. Or at school. Not enough when he'd prayed, shaking in the cornfields, to his God. He could barely remember. He'd been determined, certainly—whatever *that* was, whatever that meant. He'd been determined with grades. He'd been determined when he'd run cross country. But . . what had he been determined *for?* . . or *to?* Once he had struck down two bullies, on the town street, who had Adam backed against a building wall and were pricking him with long needles and laughing. Kohlman had seen it from work at Mr. Silento's, across the street, and had rushed out like a crazed person: *You don't do that to my brother!* he had screamed and taken both of the larger, older boys down. And Adam had been furious: *"What did you think you were doing? I was fine! I don't need you! Now everybody in town thinks I need you! What do you think you are, my Big Savior?!* Jesus! Right! That's where that came from!

Had he listened to music? None that he could place, really. His parents had listened to gospel and the farm report. Adam had turned the radio off whenever he could do it unnoticed. So . . ? . . Okay . . ! . . What about them? What about those people? From then. Called . . what? "Neighbors"? Called "parents"? The people who sent him postcards now. And never called. And always moved. And never wrote. Who were they really? They embarrassed Adam . . Adam said . . . Did they embarrass him? Had he embarrassed them? And was that right? Was it embarrassment? Kohlman had admired one girl. Mary Ryan. Lust? Perhaps, partly. She'd looked shy. And kind. Like the possessor of remarkable secrets, which, were someone to become close, she might tell. She'd been the one person who'd made him feel uneasy and excited. Like Janice. And protective. And admiring. And curiously un-self-conscious. Free. Why had he left the party? Why had he walked away? What didn't he want? What did he want? Jesus . . that was the question, wasn't it? *What didn't he want?* Sacrifice? Self-pity? Which was which: "want" . . "didn't want"? Was he being noble? Was he being afraid? Were there issues of worth? His? Janice's? The worth of what they both might . . ? Kohlman shook his head. Don Everly sang, "Can't get the car—my marks ain't been that good," and Kohlman cried. He was pissed at being confused. He was pissed at crying. He was pissed at being pissed. He was crying all the time now . . lately. It had been gone . . it had been lost to him, a lost art; he hadn't really cried like this . . not since he'd been small and seen his father's hand caught in a baler, seen his father's face stiffen but never give. Now, it seemed to Kohlman, he was like one of those freeway pile-ups—emotionally. He'd be fine; he'd be back in control, but then he'd rear-end himself, come at himself blindly out of a fog or snow swirl or whatever. How did a person who had been determined and who had stopped, for the most part, losing control start just *doing* that, losing it again?

Glenn Miller played "Tuxedo Junction," and Kohlman couldn't tell whether he were still drunk. Bubbles of light played on the flocked hotel wallpaper. He was a lobster . . in a restaurant tank . . claws pegged . . pathetic and stone-stupid . . no more idea of who he was or where his future lay than a crustacean.

He gathered up his interview tapes, a hundred hours. He stacked them. Restacked them. He read their labels: "J./ Essex/ 1st memories," "J./ bro. Philip," "headaches: #1," "headaches: #2," three tapes in which she talked about Salem Levinworth. Kohlman put on the second headache tape. On it she talked about her father sending her, at the age of seventeen, for a year to Cuba: "*He said, 'maybe a different climate will cure you.' But I think he just wanted affliction out of the house. It was a business friend's plantation. My father said the man owed him a favor. Hiding me was his favor. I lived in a room that smelled of cilantro—it was over the kitchen—cilantro and rubber. And I tutored the young children. Reading. Simple arithmetic. I had only a half dozen headaches in the thirteen months I was there in Cuba. It was a dear time. I felt very different than I ever had in Essex. I never saw my father's friend. I only saw his wife. She began to talk to me—more and more. She said her husband was a cruel man. And she cried. Almost every time she talked to me, after a certain point, she cried. And then she belittled herself for crying. And then she belittled herself for belittling herself. And then she thanked me for being there. She said: 'You're so good for the children!' Her name was Leona. Isn't that beautiful? I think, if my name weren't Angel, I would change it to 'Leona.' . . My father thought my headaches were cured, and he brought me back, but they began on the boat returning. —No doctor has ever said this . . but I think my headaches are my head yelling that I'm a person and am alive. Like a good deal of the rest of my body might forget, but my head says: 'No. No way! You're here!' Benjamin: because you love me . . because we have a binding understanding . . I don't have any more headaches. I don't need my head to remind me that I am a person in the world and am alive."*

Kohlman shut off the cassette. Frank Sinatra sang, ". . not like a small room, a hallroom . . ." Now *Kohlman* had a headache.

He tried to imagine what it would be like if he brought the tapes to Janice. Gave them to her. Gave them up. They had become *his* life. Could he give *his* life to *her*? Had Barnett told him, at the President's party, that Shane and Alexander were out of the picture, not to worry? "I guarantee it—out of here!" Was that true? Was he remembering right? Kohlman tried to see himself spilling his tapes (*her* tapes?) into Janice's lap, giving, offering, bringing her back, sitting with her by the amber Wurlitzer in the dark and listening to Patti Page sing "Wheel of Fortune." Perhaps he would just mail them to the Nugget. She would understand. He ejected the second headache tape, took it, studied it. He pinched the slick chromium-dioxide ribbon, then, suddenly, pulled it from its cassette and wound it angrily, crazily, around his fist. He began to pull and tear, snapping the tape in pieces, wrapping sections of it around his head, his neck, pulling tight until the tape snapped. He had no idea why he did what he did or what his actions meant. He left his room, walked. He felt like hurting another person. He was here now. He was not the person who had left New York. He was not the person Sharon thought she had said "never again" to. He had found things. He was finding things. What had he found? Why wasn't he finding *all* of the things? Did he even know what they were or if they'd been lost? Where were his parents?

He stopped in a liquor store to buy more tequila. When he stepped out, he heard his name called. A cab idled near the curb, his brother, Adam, craning out the back window. "Ben!" his brother said. "Ben—hey!"

Kohlman moved to him.

"Hey! Hey . . this is a miracle. I didn't think we'd see each other again." His brother smiled.

"Hi," Kohlman said.

"You become a secret drinker?" Adam asked, nodding at the liquor store.

"How'd your paper go?" Kohlman asked.

"Ride with me—to the airport," his brother said. "I'm leaving." He swung his door open, slid to the far side, motioned Kohlman in. "I'm serious," Adam said. "I mean it. Come on. Ride with me. Please."

Kohlman got in.

"Thank you," Adam said. He nodded for the cabby to move on. The cabby did. Adam was nodding at Kohlman, trying to smile. "I was at the Desert Inn," Adam began. "Just now. With my group. My . . well, they're an 'association,' I suppose, more accurately. And everybody was getting cabs with other people." He paused. He moved his mouth, but no words came out. His eyes clouded. Finally, he began again: ". . Everybody was . . you know, asking somebody else—you know what I'm saying?—to share a cab . . ride to the airport with them. And I . . ." Adam moved his jaw again, as if to test whether it might not be broken. "And I kept thinking . . if somebody asks me . . well, *I* have no use for *them*; I'll say *no*. Why do *I* need . . ? But, of course, nobody did. I mean, they . . they all admire me. I know that. They're my colleagues. I know they all admire me . . in that sense. But . . the point is . . no one asked me to . . you know, share a cab." He moved his teeth forward and bit his upper lip.

Kohlman nodded. He felt brutalized. He put his arm around his brother, and Adam stiffened but let the gesture hold.

"So I'm glad I saw you." Adam smiled again, uneasily. He began to nod himself.

Kohlman nodded back.

"Where did we get this nodding thing?" Adam asked.

"We're the Nod Brothers, I guess," Kohlman laughed. "I also . . take in big breaths of air. I think Father . . ."

Adam cut him off. "Me too! My students sometimes, when they think I'm not looking, mock my doing it. The real clowns nod and suck breath at the same time."

Kohlman laughed. It was a sweet, free laugh. "Father sort of . . bobs his head forward," he said. He imitated. ". . when he's concentrating. It isn't nodding exactly. It's more . . rhythmic . . you know? It's instead of talking."

Adam nodded. They both laughed. Kohlman pulled his fifth of Jose Quervo from its brown bag, undid the cap, offered some to his brother. Adam smiled more freely, took it, tipped his head back, drank. He returned the bottle; Kohlman drank. They both smiled and nodded.

"Goddamn, fucking Determinism," Adam said, and they laughed again. "What happened to your hands?" he asked.

"A thing," Kohlman said. "A thing that happened."

. . . . .

At the flight gate, just before Adam entered the connector, he hugged Kohlman. Kohlman froze, loosened, then returned the hug. "I don't know why I did that," Adam said. "You did it in the cab, sort of. So . . ."

"I talked to Beth," Kohlman said.

"She told me," Adam said. "Thank you. It's a mess now. It's really a terrible mess. I need help."

"Stay over," Kohlman said. "Take a day. That guy who grabbed you at Caesar's? He's my friend. He's fighting tonight for the heavyweight championship of the world. I'll take you. I won't throw food. Stay. Really. I would like you to. I'm sort of . . well, lonely myself. We could talk."

Adam shook his head. "I . . . I'm sorry," he said. "But I can't."

. . . . .

It was one in the morning. The boarding area had emptied. Kohlman had a drink in the Sky-bar and watched Adam's flight lift. The air traffic seemed only occasional. Arbitrary. The tinted dark bore the colors of a bruise. Kohlman felt cut off from specific people. He felt very measurable distance. And he felt measured, in turn, by it. Drawn by its cabled lines. Its horizons and longitudes. Distance seemed, in a final truth, his doing: tripod, transit, all his singular tachymetry.

. . . . .

Kohlman had imagined Janice – given his departure – as relieved. But he'd been wrong. What he hadn't considered were her eyes, the abandoned tunnels they seemed, in the Maxim lobby, to make in her skull. What he hadn't imagined was the change in her face, coloring, the blood at her nostrils, streaming. Both Barnett and one of the Maxim's guards moved immediately to get her off her feet, help, stanch what was happening. But she'd shrieked, something C.E.O. had never seen her do: "No! No: I'm fine! Leave me!" And, when they'd persisted: "No, C.E.O! I said, *no*! – Women bleed! I know how to take care of it! Leave me!" Kohlman hadn't considered any such scene.

. . . . .

What if, Kohlman thought, he stayed in Angel's city, but never saw her, just took pleasure in being near where she might be? He took a cab downtown. *Find a notorious, mysterious wild woman and capture her!* What a notion! "*Where*, downtown?" the cabby asked: "Where do you want to be . . let out?"

Did it matter? "Here's fine," Kohlman said. They were at Eighth and Ogden.

He paid. He stood on the sidewalk: no agenda, no program. Was he in danger? Were there people? Was he being watched? Did they still think *her* fires, Angel's fires, were *their* fires? Jesus! Christ! Let them gun him down if they needed to make that mistake! *It was only Blue Pony who knew a Power that lived in his hooves.* Was that the line? Close. The opening? Close but apart. Close but apart: that would work as a strategy. Then maybe he could watch over Janice, or try, the way the Challenger had seemed to watch over him. Insure her well-being; insure her safety. So then . . ? Where, now that he was downtown, should he go? What would be best to do? What ought the larger plan to be?

Kohlman saw the sign for the Ogden House. It was at least a bearing, and he moved toward it . . a place, a temporary destination.

From outside the Ogden House, he tried to feel his way, some rightness, and crossed to the El Cortez. He remembered his and Janice's first breakfast: how aloof he'd felt, how disdainful, annoyed at her candor. He went into the Cafe Cortez, recreated their breakfast, looked for her, the image of cups and saucers moving under lazy coffee steam. But it was just beyond two-thirty, and she would be at work. She would be . . *carrying the numbers from the numbers to the numbers*. Right? How her words, how her voice were still so in his mind! He wanted to see her. None of what mattered made any sense. She loved him. She loved him: that was what wouldn't go away. But hadn't other women . . said things like that, those words? *Benjamin I love you*? They had; of course. He wasn't a pariah. So . . what then was this thing? this time? Who was *she*? How did *her* saying *Benjamin I love you* not allow the words to go away? Why was there a *hole* in him? A wide hole, and echoing. And what made it feel so . . *without*, so void? He'd loved Sharon, hadn't he? During their . . ? Hadn't *they* gotten to this point? *You never quite passed the test*, Sharon had said. So . . what? . . then had he *passed* the test with Janice? She with him? And what was the test? And how did you pass it? What were the questions? Was the test over?

He couldn't eat. He walked down Ogden and stood in front of the alley into which he'd been shoved, thinking he could still smell the carbon. His hands tightened and felt shrunken, small. He walked into the alley, touched a brick wall, checked his fingertips. The lampblack was still there; his hand came away marked by it. He took two fingers and wrote Janice's name in the smoke. Further down the alley, he became aware of a prone curled body. It seemed natural though, now, expected now, commonplace. Someone discarded, dead . . a drunk. Or was he thinking of . . was that Manhattan? He walked back to the street, moved down to a casino called the Lucky Strike, and entered it.

He played some dice. He'd never really played any. He lost two hundred dollars. A cocktail waitress told him he looked sad. He shrugged; he tried to smile and gave her a tip. What would he do with their tapes? *Would* he send them? Destroy them? *No!* God, *no!* Never! And so, then . . what would he do with the Wurlitzer? When would he go back, if ever, to New York? The boxman at the dice table told him he'd just won a bet and asked whether he wanted to pick his money up.

He went to Fitzgerald's and to the Four Queens, just wandered, watching keno runners. He watched them move. He looked closely, wondering. Were these all women he would misjudge, unless he knew them, as well? Would he fall in love? He sat in keno lounges and watched the boards light with numbers, darken, light again. At the Four Queens, he saw a man sitting, playing keno, who looked like Woody Allen. He wore no glasses; his hair was slicked, parted down the middle; he wore different style clothes . . but Kohlman felt sure about the face and the bone structure. He studied the man for twenty minutes, then approached. "Mr. Allen?" he asked.

The man said nothing. He looked at Kohlman with visible irritation.

Kohlman nodded. "I thought it was you," he said. He smiled and nodded again.

The irritation on the man's face became, almost, contempt.

"Benjamin Kohlman," Kohlman said. "We met at a party . . in New York . . about a year ago, year and a half . . a lot of *New York Times* people; I was *there* then . . at the magazine. Your films . . are wonderful; they . . mean a lot to me; I don't say that lightly; I love them. I didn't think . . that is, the 'word' I suppose is, you never leave New York . . except perhaps for filming. So . . . This is a very different city. It's . . the . . *antithesis* in many ways. Of New York. So I suppose that's why I'm surprised to . . ."

When the man moved to stand, Kohlman stepped back, afraid the man might strike him. Instead he simply brushed past Kohlman and walked away.

Kohlman felt ashamed, then angry, then ashamed again.

He went to the Nugget. One of Sharon's favorite lines, during their time, had been: *Kohlman—you want it both ways.* And he'd understood. But this, going into the Nugget now with her working, was different. He'd only *approach* her; he'd keep the distance; he'd maintain the break; he wouldn't try to have and not have her at the same time; he just wanted to see her face, know that she was all right, have some picture, at a distance. But not . . *join* . . not join her any more . . ever.

She moved in the lanes she always traveled, threading aisles between the poker room and lounge, sweeping in and out of the small cocktail bars: ". . Keno?" Kohlman hid behind a bank of slot machines. When she'd cross his vision, certain of his bone structure—along his jaw and across his shoulders—felt drained and marrowless. She looked worn. She looked different, something in her teeth, her upper lip. She wore more eye shadow. She'd pinned her hair differently. What he couldn't see was that she'd stuffed her nose with absorbent cotton.

Kohlman knew; he understood; he had it clear—*a break was a break; gone was gone*; Sharon had instructed: *You can't hang on, Benjamin. Something's going to get fucked. You can't say "no" and then say "yes" in some other way.* So . . he should leave, Kohlman knew, but he didn't. He cashed a hundred into silver and dropped coins, spiritlessly, into a remote corner machine. He would play three, win two; play twelve, win five. Whatever the gain, he would not take it; he would give it back, an emptying pattern: fixed, humiliating, programmed. He felt so mournful. He felt so bruised. He felt so unentitled. Yet no reason. He was playing to lose. It made no sense. He watched himself, bound to the pattern. What locked a person in? What drove against contrary power? Kohlman stopped. He started to retrieve and gather coins. Okay . . . Okay . . . Okay, then, he *wouldn't* leave. Okay? He wouldn't say "no"; he'd say "*yes.*" He'd not disenfranchise himself. He'd learn. He'd stop. Stop what? What was the issue here? Well, come on, Man: the issue was: he could say *yes*—all right?—to something. He could go to Janice. He could say as much as he understood. He could confess. He could admit. All right? *All* of those things. He could reach toward, allow, protect, own, absorb, risk, try, hope, worry, attempt! Were those strong enough verbs?

Apparently not. Because then Kohlman felt someone move behind him and felt pain as vividly as it could be felt. He was still a marked man. He had not yet made the truth heard with enough force, and his mouth was pried soundlessly open. His eyes watered abruptly at their rims. He felt a very precise line of vertical heat open on his back. He felt the line spill, spread. He reached behind, under his jacket, touched his sticky shirt, drew his hand away covered with yet new blood.

Then, as if called, two security guards arrived beside him. Kohlman looked at his hand, the blood; he looked at them. "I've been cut," he said. "Someone's cut me."

"We see," one of the security guards said.

"Someone came up behind!" Kohlman said. His voice rose. He felt his stability wash and loosen.

"This way," the same guard said. The second guard was larger and said nothing. Both guards took Kohlman, by his upper arms and elbows, and moved him, directed him, down the aisle of slots, past the long cashier's cage, through a door printed RESTRICTED PERSONNEL, down a set of stairs and into a small office—fabric chairs, a glass coffee table, a bare desk. The guard who talked pointed the other guard to a cabinet. The other guard opened the cabinet and took out a drop cloth and spread it over one of the chairs. "I think if you sit down . . ." the talking guard said. Kohlman sat. "I'll be right back," the talking guard said and left.

The silent guard stood by the door. Kohlman tried to focus on him. Fixed images broke into atoms then recombined. The materiality of the world seemed to come and go. "People . . can't . . just . . take *off* from . . where this might happen," Kohlman said. "Can they? . . I mean, you can't just let . . ." The guard who had said nothing gave no indication of having heard a word of Kohlman's question. "Is it *bad* . . do you think?" Kohlman asked. "My back? The cut? What happened?" The guard opened the room's door a crack, peered out, shut the door again. "I think I'm . . losing . . a fair amount of blood," Kohlman said. "Last time . . there was a doctor . . or medic—were you the ones last time?— medic . . who . . ."

The guard who talked returned with an emergency medical kit. "Stand up a minute," he said. Kohlman stood. His anatomy felt plastic. The talking guard nodded for the other to transfer the drop cloth to the top of the desk. ". . If you'd remove your clothes, please," the talking guard said.

"You mean my shirt?" Kohlman said.

"I mean . . your *clothes*, please," the talking guard said.

"I don't . . ?" It made no sense to argue. The line Kohlman could feel on his back felt fueled with increasing heat. His ability to hold an image shimmered, beautiful in its way, unsteady as a reflection. The guard who said nothing supported him so that he might remove his clothes. He did. Both guards helped. Kohlman caught a brief image of the talking guard riffling his pockets, removing his room key, nodding at the silent guard. The two guards moved Kohlman to the desk, lifting him, stretching him on it.

"We're going to have to put you out," the talking guard said.

"Put me . . where?" Kohlman said.

"While we fix this. Out. Don't worry. It's just necessary. Because there's going to be some pain."

"Pain," Kohlman said, and then he repeated the word: *Of course*, he thought; *of course . . "pain". . what else?*

"Don't move," the talking guard said, and Kohlman could feel the grip the guard who didn't talk had on him tighten. A hypodermic stung his buttocks; there was the throb of its being emptied. And then nothing.

.   .   .   .   .

What Kohlman first grew aware of in regaining himself was his skin. It felt bristled. He imagined it humming. There was a sense of his body being braille.

He was stretched out on the drop cloth, across the two fabric chairs drawn together. Neither guard attended; his clothes were folded nearby and he studied them. The shoulder wound, where he had been shot ten days before, ached. The scarred palms of his hands felt dull and fibrous and wooden. His back felt badly tailored, pulled together too tightly and stitched with industrial thread on a bad machine. He reached behind to where he had been cut and found tape. Still—he was alive. Not bleeding. He dressed. He looked in his billfold; the count he had on his money, roughly thirty-four hundred, seemed accurate, seemed to match what was there. He sat in the room for five, ten minutes. No one came. He tried the door. It was open. He walked out, up the stairs, opened the fire door into the casino. Everything in the vaulted and furnished world, as he entered it, was again, as he had left it, light and noise.

– TWELVE –

They had hit his room: whoever, the experts . . come . . hit him . . taken his tapes! All! *"Bastards!"* Kohlman screamed. He felt crazy. "This is *me!*" he yelled. This is me and *her*, you pricks! This is *us*. This is all we . . !!" Kohlman kicked the bed and wrenched his foot. *Fuckers! Bastards! Don't we get to keep our words at least . . you shits?!* his mind tore on. *Don't we at least—goddamnyou!—get to keep our voices?!*

But they had taken them all! And his Compaq. And his Nagra. Experts: making it then look, after they'd done their damage, as though maids had been by to tidy up: the bedspread flawless, tight on the bed and clean; shaving gear lined with precision on the chipped wash-area formica. Loose change stacked neatly in a Found Motel ashtray. There was even a new postcard propped on his pillows, the image on it totally black, broken only by white script: "Inside the Lehman Caves–Baker, Nevada."

Kohlman pounded the wall. "Bring her back!" he yelled. "I want us back!" His fist went through, and he saw into the next room . . filled with stuffed circus animals. Kohlman tried to pull the sheetrock and lapsed plaster in to cover his hole. He dropped quarters in the Wurlitzer. Buddy Holly played "An Empty Cup– And a Broken Date," and Kohlman tried to sing, but his notes came out growled, lost, violated.

He threw his change at the wall and it sprayed angry music. His back still felt tight and stitched. His hands felt raw; his shoulder ached. He wanted her, wanted Janice: *"Angel! Angel . . ?!"* He hated that she'd been taken! *She hasn't been "taken," Jerko. Come on!* some miniature Princeton of his mind argued. Okay: he *understood* that! He understood it might be useless thinking—still, clinging to an absurd idea which infuriated him felt *good* and filled a dead space.

He left his room, locked it, laughed at the precaution: Why lock?! Nothing was private! *Public shame in private! Private shame in public!* It was late afternoon, an hour and a half, only, before the Challenger's fight. Kohlman still had his ticket. He would walk. He would move and think. He would work off the fury somehow then go to the fight.

He crossed to the Sands, tried to watch games but couldn't stand still, hated the fixed amber quality of all he saw. The dealers looked worn, indentured, like old waiters. Had they aged in a day? Had the blast traveled underground, traced some fault, seeped up bubbling radon from the carpet and decanted their white cells? Kohlman thought of playing. He reached for his billfold. "Did you want to play?" a dealer asked. He couldn't answer. It seemed too complex a question.

. . . . .

He walked outside. How did the sun glare so consistently here? Janice had talked always about the light. *I love, here, the light always shocking*, she had said, *never even . . no equanimity. In New England, it's all equanimity. With no radiance.* He wished for dark polarized glasses, stood feeling the sun, glad suddenly for it: it was her; it was Janice; she was in it and around him. He set off across the Sands lot, feeling stronger, toward the Holiday.

But a man moved from obscurity behind a Lincoln and blocked Kohlman. The man wore a ski mask. He held an immense handgun with a silencer. "Oh, Jesus!" Kohlman said. "Not again. Not today. I'm sorry."

"Quietly . . ." the man said, muffled through wool.

"You're asking for trouble," Kohlman said.

"Quietly . . slowly," the man said.

"I'm beyond obedience," Kohlman said. "You need to know. I'm past the pale. I'm over the border."

"Quietly . . slowly . . give me your money," the man said.

But Kohlman laughed.

"C'mon. No big deal. Easily. Quietly. Like you were checking your watch for the time."

"It isn't the money," Kohlman said.

"All your money. Then, just turn . . ."

"It's . . the principle." Kohlman laughed.

"Turn . . walk away . . wherever you were going . . slowly."

"Do you hear me? Do you understand what I'm saying? The fact is: it's the principle. You're making a wrong choice."

"Otherwise—straight shit, Man—I'll blow your fucking head off."

There was an instant. A moment. A flash of something . . *radiant* . . *shocking* . . *unequanimous*.

"C'mon, Man. —Quietly. Slowly," the man said.

Kohlman saw what he thought he might—a crater, a firecone, a volcano. His arms shot out, knifed. The pistol fired—a sound like distant expectoration . . on a quiet night. There was something like pain which Kohlman wasn't even sure touched him. There had been so many moments *like* pain, *around* pain, the entire day.

So now Kohlman had the masked man, just below the shoulders.

Now he held him by pinned arms.

Now Kohlman's *own* arms swung, pressing.

And now swung up.

And now jettisoned the man out and into space.

. . . . .

The man rose into the air above the parking lot and above the glittering roofs of the unending parked cars.

Kohlman could hear him screaming, ejected.

Kohlman watched him trace an arc.

The thing like pain at the side of Kohlman's head came back, then went.

And now the thief was falling.

And now he came down.

And now he fell.

Now he hit a Chevy Caprice, caromed across the roof of an El Dorado, thudded, falling between the El Dorado and a Cordoba.

"You shouldn't have done it," Kohlman said in a voice simple as its statement.

Kohlman's next moment's awareness was of holding the thief out, like dry-cleaned laundry, presenting him at the Sands casino entrance to Security. The man's pistol was still jammed in his broken fist. "He tried to rob me," Kohlman said. "Take him somewhere. Tell him: 'think next time.' "

"You're bleeding badly," the security guard said. "Your head."

"It's nothing new!" Kohlman said and left.

. . . . .

The beggar, REM, held the sidewalk, this time outside the Frontier. He looked more than ever like a soiled cocoon. "You're changing tactics," Kohlman said.

"There may be an error," REM said.

"Used to be, one could count on you . . now you're *everywhere*."

"I bear the responsibility," REM said.

"Our very *maps* betray us!" Kohlman said. "What's a traveler to do?" He felt crazy, open, reckless. He dropped a hundred into REM's cigarbox. The amputee shrank into his own eyes: a look of shame, a gloss of rue. "I don't know your needs," Kohlman said. "But whatever . . Godspeed."

"My needs are to take pictures," the amputee said; ". . then develop them."

"One-man studio," Kohlman said. "You know . . I had that sense."

"I'm severe," the amputee said. "You *have* to be."

"I agree," Kohlman said.

"*Truth* is severe."

"Absolutely."

"It doesn't cheat."

"Though it tries."

"You spoke of my needs."

"I did . . yes . . but I was only . . ."

"I never hope to be *cruel*."

"No. Good," Kohlman said. "Good position."

"You're bleeding," REM said.

"People point that out."

"But not us."

"But not us. Right. What do you mean?"

"But not us. Your head isn't us."

"No; no; my head isn't you—that's true. No."

"It's a *lot*," the amputee said.

There was something vaguely hypnotic again about their talk . . even though it made no sense. It was conversation, Kohlman felt, one could nod his head or tap his feet to . . and feel a license, feel unassaulted.

.   .   .   .   .

However, there *was* blood – people were right – on Kohlman's head, and in profusion. Still, it was more blood than damage. The shot had carved a deep line on the right-hand side of his skull, a groove about a half centimeter deep. His face was streaked; his hair, matted. In his room at the Found, he washed and cleaned the wound. The bleeding lessened. He held a hand towel to his head. He could hear the fight crowd, gathering, outside, two blocks away at Caesar's, through the walls of his unit. The rumble made a sound like waves. Or chanting. Kohlman kept the towel pressed, clamped it, with his right hand, to his scalp, and left again for the fight.

.   .   .   .   .

The temporary arena was enormous. The computer billboard on the boulevard, as he approached, had flashed: THE FIGHT! . . . THE FIGHT! The crowd was thick and agitated and rocked and swayed and shifted weight like an unsettled animal. Kohlman's seat was in the thirty-second row on the north side. A squarish woman to his right asked whether he'd been in a fight of his own. "Possibly," Kohlman said. She laughed. "I love fights!" she said.

The preliminary bout was being announced. An Italian and a Hispanic. The Italian was a stalker. The Hispanic had the quicker jabs and was a dancer. It was all the Hispanic for the first three rounds. Kohlman kept checking his towel for blood. The bleeding seemed to have slowed. Kohlman lowered the towel to his lap.

In the fourth round, the Italian, from what looked at best to be confusion, crossed to the Hispanic's right cheekbone with a powerful left. The Hispanic staggered, moved back, flat-footed, into the ropes. The Italian plodded in, following with two hard, connecting body blows, then a partly blocked shot to the side of the head. The Hispanic shook himself, like a creature shaking off water, and danced away. He found his form again and controlled the rest of the fourth round.

Kohlman scanned the crowd. He looked for Janice, hoping he might just *see* her. He was looking for C.E.O. Barnett and Alyce.

Would Comus be there? Where was the President? Would the President sit, exposed, in a crowd like this? Or would he have some "bubble"? How many *were* there? Thirty . . forty thousand? What would the Challenger be feeling? What were the odds? He would have to tell the Challenger about having the volcano come—without request, without call—into his head for the thief.

The Italian threw the first punch of the fifth round, a hook to the Hispanic's ribs that doubled him. Then the Italian missed a brutal shot to the Hispanic's head. The Hispanic peppered in response with jabs. The crowd began catcalling the Italian for his inability to field the Hispanic's quickness.

"The old story," the squarish woman said, out of the side of her mouth, to Kohlman.

"What's that?" Kohlman said.

"Quickness—Power."

"Quickness—Power," Kohlman repeated.

"Quickness—Power."

Kohlman nodded.

"Which do you bet with?" the woman asked.

"I'm not sure," Kohlman said.

The Italian scored a straight blow on the Hispanic's nose, knocking him off his feet and to the canvas. The Hispanic scrambled up. The referee held him, checked him, held the Italian at arm's length. Then, the referee broke from between the two fighters, let them resume. The Hispanic began picking at a spot below the Italian's left eye. He worked and reworked it with jabs. The spot opened. The cut began to flow. The Italian took another wild blind shot and knocked the Hispanic to the canvas again. The Hispanic scrambled up. The fifth round ended.

"I love contests!" the squarish woman said.

Kohlman couldn't see anyone, no one he knew—but the crowd was endless and immense.

The sixth round, until the TKO, was cruel. Close-up, the round was the image of a cut opening, a face breaking open at its seam. The end was ugly, inevitable. The Italian's face looked like slashed upholstery. The crowd went with the Hispanic. "Yes . . ! . . yes . . !" the squarish woman beside Kohlman kept barking; "It's quickness!"

Kohlman wondered if the Italian felt any pride. In the Italian's mind, had he understood anything, seen anything, endured? Or had he just lost the fight? Kohlman could see flocks of swallows, bursting like black sparks out of the fronds of palms on Caesar's grounds, then returning to cover. He could see cars strung out, parked along the eastbound shoulder of I-15 above the arena.

Amplified music ground itself against the night air. Fans started a chant: "The Fight! . . the Fight! . . the Fight! . . the Fight!" Kohlman could feel a personal tension for the Challenger. Anticipation. Anxiety. Fear. His friend had been so good to him—so generous and kind. Kohlman hated the thought of his black friend having to suffer any assault, any wave of ill-sympathy.

The time seemed to drift lazily in hiatus. Then a rumble started undiscernibly, somewhere, pointing its own direction: a new attention. Something was happening, and the Arena, in its own involuntary way, began to signal. A collective nervereflexed. A system woke. A sense began: *now . . now*! Kohlman looked to see.

Something titan and white, veined lightly gold and grey, was being carried along the long aisle from a back door of the Palace by four fight handlers in silk *Caesar's* jackets. Over their heads, the gold *Omnimax* dome shone. All the rough-and-tumble hushed. Necks craned. Heads turned. It was Joe Louis! It was the restored, eight-foot figure of Joe Louis, flawless and without fracture, even under the power of the overhead floods. But who had done that? How had that happened? Kohlman recalled the Challenger and his anointed hands: "Arise and walk!" Weren't those the words? Isn't that what Kohlman remembered from his time in the corn, from back then, from Templeton: "Arise and walk!" He almost expected it.

Then the crowd took its life again, slowly. The figure of Joe Louis—despite referees' and judges' denials—was placed in the center of the ring. The Challenger's manager and handler appeared in a harvest of flashcubes and gospel thresh of voices and began to walk in ceremony down the aisle cleared for the fighter's entrance. They wore jackets imprinted CHALLENGER. That seemed in line. That all seemed standard. But what wasn't standard were their masks. Each, manager and handler, wore an enormous, carved African mask. And with them was an almost emaciated shirtless black carrying a crude small set of drums. The crowd's murmur seemed questioning, unsure. "Whaddo they think this is—Big-time Wrestling?" the squarish woman said to Kohlman. "I love it! . . *Bullshit!*" she yelled . . then, downshifting: "Go for it! Do it to me! Don't stop!"

Kohlman watched as each in the small retinue took his place. He sensed the pause; it had happened earlier; it was like being in the beat *before* music. Then the new rumble. The new blooms of light. The new turn and shift: the new attention. And the Challenger—as Kohlman knew he must and would and was timed to—appeared and moved and made his slow, elegant entrance. There were no others from his camp around him. No ring to keep the crowd away. The crowd leaned in . . but only so far. There seemed some sort of force field, shaping a fluid-clear chrysalis of space around the Challenger. He wore a simple black silk robe simply imprinted; moved with slow ritual stride. The murmur built, then hushed, then tried to build again but couldn't. Something about the presence kept the crowd reined in. The emaciated and shirtless black in the Challenger's corner began a beat, nearly a very beat of silence at first, on his drums; then, behind the rising and falling soft beat, he began to chant. The Challenger never broke his stride: slow and deliberate, he moved down the arena aisle toward the ring, toward his corner. And when he reached the ropes, he stood motionless for perhaps thirty seconds then pulled himself up, ducked, moved into his corner, stood perhaps another twenty seconds, and then crouched. Kohlman felt a certain kind of glory in his friend's entrance.

Then the Champion arrived, and it was all script: the crowd uncoiled, the hoopla, the bravado, the triumphant gestures, hands high always above his head, the theatrical menace. He was all gold and silver. Fireworks went off above the arena in the night sky. Martial music played. The American flag dropped from somewhere—huge, impressive—so that it draped wide above the ring. Men with microphones and wearing tuxedos milled preparatorily in all the angled and converging shafts of theatrical light. Then, just before the Champion stepped between his parted ropes, the Challenger's handlers converged to lift the restored Joe Louis and set him on a pediment behind the Challenger's bench.

The Champion, in his corner, stripped now of his robe, muscular, played directly to the crowd, made his ritual threats across the ring. The Challenger—still, meditative—seemed sculpted. Nothing, not even his breath, stirred in him. The drums thrummed on. The Challenger's manager and handler stood as guards. Their tribal masks stared in, pinning the Champion. The Champion moved to the center of the ring, and talked to one of the officials in a tuxedo. He started to gesture. They seemed to argue.

"The Champion has demanded . . that all masks be removed!" a voice announced over the public address. ". . And that the drumming . . stop!" The crowd took sides: *"Yeah—stop this shit!" "Get on with the fight!"* A widening patch in the crowd started to chant: *"Third World! . . Third World! . . Third World . . !"*

The public address crackled on again: "The fight's referee . . Mr. Vincent Consatino . . has ruled that . . as long as the masks do not enter the ring . . they may be worn!"

Approval and disapproval from the crowd.

"The drumming . . will be allowed . . between rounds. But it must not continue . . within any given round!"

More shouts and jeers, catcalls and eruptions from the crowd.

Kohlman felt frozen. He felt the whole night sky beyond its visible and electronic skein, in his chest. And he felt ashamed. And humbled. And thrilled. And insignificant. And extraordinary. He remembered praying. He remembered what that had felt like as a boy . . when prayer . . outside, in the field, at that age . . had seemed so *physical*, almost . . so possible. He felt overpowered by something far beyond himself. He felt an immense magic in his life. He felt awe.

". . Refusal to comply to these rulings . . may result in forfeiture . . on the part of . . any of those . . so refusing!"

Again: the swelled communal response.

Kohlman watched the Challenger. He did not move. He seemed so fixed. Not until the p.a.'s "Ladies and Gentlemen . . our National Anthem!" did he stand, with the others, stare straight overhead at the draped flag, clasp his hands behind him.

Where was Janice? Was she here? Was she in this? Was she where these feelings were?! This place?! This light and world?! This power?! Kohlman hoped for her! He hoped! Hehopedforher, hehopedforher, hehopedforher! Let her be here! Let her see this!

The introductions came. The Challenger found a subdued, reverent response, some booing. The Champion set off a round like mortar fire. The two were called to the center of the ring. Kohlman's chest felt strapped in metal. Something was of *that* force. Something was *that* powerful!

The Champion danced in. The Challenger walked slowly. The Champion was still agitated about the masks. He kept pointing into the Challenger's corner with his glove and raising his voice. A mike, overhead, snapped on. The referee gave instructions. The Challenger bowed to the Champion rather than slapping glove to glove. Kohlman found that he had begun to hold his breath. How long had he held it? Sharon had told him once: that the word for "breath" in certain languages . . was the same as the word for "soul." So: was he holding his . . *soul*? Then for what? And what would a held soul . . how would a held soul . . help? Was the habit one from his father? What was he trying to speculate about anyway? What was his thinking? "Who do you want to win?" he said to the squarish woman.

"This guy's a fraud," she said.

"Which guy?"

"The whoozits—the Boogie Man there—the Challenger."

Kohlman nodded. Then he shook his head.

"He's all front!" the woman said.

"Well . . ." Kohlman said.

"You think he's got it?"

"I just . . ."

"What?!"

". . Think he's aware," Kohlman said.

"Right . . and he's gonna get all that 'aware' shit beat right outta him!"

The drums throbbed to a halt. Both fighters held their respective corners. The Challenger crouched one last time. The first-round bell sounded.

The Champion broke from his corner like a bull. The Challenger rose, moved with exquisite, gentlemanly grace, in. His hands stayed by his sides. He did not raise them, take any posture of defense or any fight stance. The Champion studied him, momentarily uncertain, then began a volley of hits, scoring hard and hard again on the Challenger's head. Kohlman's *own* head thudded and snapped back, blow, nearly, for blow. The Challenger made no move to escape, even flinch. He stared directly at the Champion while the Champion pummeled him. The Champion struck, and Kohlman—flesh feeling palpably assaulted—watched as the Challenger's skin flowered, then enflamed, then bled. Kohlman could barely breathe. The referee stepped between the two fighters. He addressed the Challenger. Kohlman imagined him saying: "You have to fight. You have to defend yourself. That's the way this is done. You can't just stand there."

The Challenger gave no nod of acknowledgment. The drums sounded lightly under the interval. The Champion barked something at the Challenger through his mouthpiece. The Champion's handlers all yelled instructions from his corner. The referee seemed to be trying a second time to get the Challenger to understand. Considerable pockets in the crowd began to boo. Kohlman looked down. The stitches on his right-hand wound had burst and some blood was flowing. He clenched his hand to a fist.

The referee said a final word to both fighters, then stepped away. The Challenger changed none of what he had been doing. He simply stared hard at the Champion, arms lowered and by his sides. The Champion came in on him again, like a piece of machinery. He drove to his face. Kohlman's scalp wound opened. The Champion drove now to the Challenger's body, opening up his skin, exposing flesh at will. Kohlman could feel the slice opening along his back. Blood seemed to flow like water. The bell, ending the round, rang.

"This is goddamn crazy!" the squarish woman said to Kohlman, then saw Kohlman bleeding from his mouth and scalp. "Jesus!" she said. "You take this *seriously*."

At first Kohlman said nothing.

"You're right *in* there," the woman said.

"Possibly," Kohlman said. His chest felt caved; his stomach felt pummeled and knotted. He could manage little breath—and when he tried drawing it, it caught and tore, like fabric on barbed wire. He knew his friend. His friend did nothing without the idea of it first. Harsh as it might have been, Kohlman sensed that what the crowd was seeing had its reason. He watched one of the Challenger's men hand in a large carved wooden bowl of water, watched the Challenger dip his beaten face, ceremoniously, into the bowl. Kohlman held his hands, the one open and bloodied, cupped out to the squarish woman. "Might I have some of your beer?" he said.

She studied him. "You're in trouble," she said. But then she poured Miller Lite into his hands, and Kohlman thanked her and dipped his face as he had watched the Challenger do. *Lavation*. He remembered the word from . . somewhere . . an earlier time. *Lavation*. It made a sound. It made the sound, nearly, of its own washing. The drums intoned beyond, hollow, echoing. The Challenger crouched. And waited.

The second round gave more of the same: the Champion ripping open the Challenger's flesh, splitting apart his face, his body; the Challenger holding ground, not defending, unresponsive, unfellable. Again, Kohlman's own wounds broke apart. He felt torn open. How was this happening? New wounds split; blood poured from his nose. He fell forward from his stadium chair and onto his knees; he made no attempt to stanch what was happening. Again, the referee stopped them. He seemed angry. The Champion seemed angry. The crowd seethed with boos. The woman beside Kohlman yelled, "Call the morgue!" and then seeing Kohlman said, "You're not going to last—getting into this fight like this. Get back in your chair. Sit back. Take it easy." Kohlman could see the referee gesturing to the Challenger. He could see the Challenger's lips move. He could see the Challenger shake his head, expand his chest, throw his head back proudly, as if to say: "What's the problem? I'm fine." Kohlman tried it. He found some breath in the night sky; he stood, then doubled over and was again on his knees. He asked the woman for more beer. She poured it but wouldn't look at him. He washed his face.

"But you have to fight!" the referee shouted. His words boomed through the entire arena. Through all the torn flesh, the bloodied and swollen lips, Kohlman was sure he saw the Challenger smile. *He* smiled; he felt curiously sure; he felt curiously happy. He looked up above the smoke in the night, far far above the near density, and could see the stars were like crystal. The Champion was pacing, jumping, flailing the air in his corner. The Joe Louis statue, on its pediment, seemed to take on its own internal light. The drums were working, steadily, low. The referee signaled for the fight to go on. The Champion coiled himself, cocked his right glove back, a pile-driver. He smashed it into the precise center of the Challenger's face. The Challenger's nose seemed to burst like ripe fruit. *Kohlman's* nose burst open. "Jesus Christ!" the squarish lady screamed; "You just sprayed my pantsuit!" and then, "Get this guy outta here!" The Challenger was unmoved. A second-round bell froze the fight in its moment.

Again, between rounds, the Challenger moved through the ritual of bowing his carved face into the curved bowl of water. Kohlman bought a beer from a vendor and imitated his friend. The drums built their rhythm. The Challenger crouched, seemed to be wrapping himself *in* himself, tightly, precisely. Kohlman crouched at his seat. The terrible damage of his flesh seemed an insignificant envelope. The referee came into both corners, talked to both managers. He was unhappy. The Champion was unhappy. He was pacing in his own corner.

When the bell rang for the third round, the Champion sprang violently from his corner, let loose a rhythm of combinations that had even the most hardened of fight fans turning heads away, closing eyes. Kohlman tried not to flinch—though both his own eyes swelled nearly shut, though his rib cage felt squeezed almost entirely of breath. He gasped; he focused; he fought for air.

.   .   .   .   .

Then, in a moment no one in the arena saw the precise priming of, the Challenger opened. On the clock, *no* time elapsed. Within the event, time informed circles. Sound stopped. All reflex held. Something . . the *start* of something, began. Emanation. Radiance. The air rippling. The mute night resinous. The collective spine thrummed with a low and boreal shudder. Changed alphabets of light. Incense of shadow. Breath cut to half and then quarter notes. The place diminished. The place fine in its modulation. The still moment a hum. The hum a chord. The chord deep chromatic. Somehow the entire night grew concentric . . from a point deep within the Challenger's pride. And from that point . . and moving out . . and then out . . the Challenger, from stillness first, then from repose, then containment . . breathed . . reached, became centrifugal. He lifted up . . lifted a right. It struck the Champion's jaw, raising the Champion four feet, sending him back in flight against the ropes . . which he hit, sprawling, in a lash and tangle, before collapsing into the mat.

Then the moment was over. The night seemed folded, temporal again and restored. The Challenger walked to his corner. The referee counted the Champion out. The Champion made no move; he was unconscious. Kohlman breathed himself; his own bleeding eased, his bones again felt live and elastic; possessed, malleable, and free. The fight was over.

. . . . .

Perhaps Kohlman had gone deaf: there was no sound in the arena. The squarish woman rose, silent and staring into the ring, brushing Kohlman's blood from her denim. She stood immobile, studied Kohlman—his slashed hands, slashed face, clothes stained. "Stay away from fights," she told him; "You're a menace." Then she left, her dissolve part of the arena's larger pattern.

There was little of mingling, of milling or round-by-round fight talk. The crowd spread . . like rumination. Whatever tribal adrenalin had been there dispersed and softened in the lamplight like fine mist. It was curious. People had no language. Kohlman felt it on his own tongue . . which was fat and sore. A tongue with weight, knowing the ache of itself, but without words. In Kohlman's brain impulse lived. Urge. And pictures. But however he might rotate his jaw and slip his tongue in the way and think the feelings and insert the pictures . . however: no language came. So, too, the crowd. They had no conversation for what they'd seen. They stood and tried to imagine. They tried to see something, fumbled, made weak undirected sound, felt inadequate, shuffled, left. Perhaps only the Joe Louis marble, holding its aura, saw, observed—short moments later, when the referee declared the Challenger the new Champion over the mike and public address—that half the stadium had emptied.

. . . . .

So now Kohlman stood. He felt very tired. He felt very relieved and tested and at some edge. He felt sweet . . and good. He felt something deep inside had withstood a promise and now might, if he were careful, be redeemed. He looked across the arena. Hundreds filed silently out and down aisles and back toward Las Vegas Boulevard and its casinos. He saw Janice. And she was seeing him. And C.E.O. and Alyce and Comus—all were there . . close, together: relieved, pleased. C.E.O. had his thumb high for Kohlman to see.

So Kohlman waved. Janice waved back. Kohlman's teeth drove hard against one another, his lower jaw leapt against his upper to keep the epicenter of himself, the quake he felt, from unloosing. He waved again. He was crying. She waved. The Challenger stood in the center of the ring—the drums soft as rain under and behind. His hands shone, high over his ravaged head. It was glorious. It was fine. Kohlman could feel it through his wrecked yet durable body: it was a fine and glorious night.

– THIRTEEN –

When Janice saw Kohlman's ragged wounds and blood, she felt ashamed. She felt proud and angry and sad and impatient with herself: she understood he'd not simply left. She understood the cost. She told him: "When you were gone, I thought . . *Benjamin has broken something because he didn't know it could be* not *broken*. And I was angry. And I was hurt. And I wanted *you* hurt. You to feel *left*, badly, by another person. I thought: *Benjamin has pulled away because the word 'with' was too hard . . and he couldn't say it*. But 'with' is 'away,'—isn't it?—and 'away' is 'with' and you found that . . and now you're fine," she said; "I can *see*."

At first, Kohlman could find *no* reply, no language of "with" *or* "away." No words. He couldn't speak. He couldn't *say*. Anything. There were words . . *some*where he knew: in stores, in airports, in tall glass buildings or cafes. They were left jammed in telephone wires. They choked all the dark television sets at news time. But none for him. None *in* him. Now. None joined. *And now you're fine*, she'd said. Was he supposed to . . ? Was there an appropriate . . ? So . . what, if he couldn't *say*, if he'd lost *words*, their use . . what would mark his place . . in whatever this was: Sound? Back and forth sound? Could he make that? Could he do that? . . make the sound of *with?* Make the sounds of . . *away* . . *with* . . ? Were those words or sound? *And now you're fine*, she'd said.

I believe I can be. That's what, had he words, he would have answered.

And now you're fine. I believe I can be.

– 234 –

And *that* would have been all right. *Those* would have made a sound that was okay.

"Benjamin can't talk," Alyce said. "He was making me a story—*Blue Pony*—but now maybe he won't . . ."

Blue Pony . . if Blue Pony . . when Blue Pony . . .

"Benjamin Kohlman!" the Challenger said. "Been in some *rounds*!" He grinned and drove an affection jab to Kohlman's ribs.

"Who batted clean-up for the National League in the '58 All-Star game?!" C.E.O. asked.

Kohlman opened his mouth. He could see players. He could see a man in a striped grey uniform . . with the number seventeen . . a man with a small nose . . growth of stubble . . large hands . . small thumbs . . a high inside curve. But . . his name was . . the word . . . Kohlman's mouth chewed the air . . shut . . open.

"Wrong!" Barnett crowed. "I know who you're thinking . . and you're wrong! Because he was *younger*!"

Comus, half-lit, hair lifted by invisible dark, surely desert currents, stood apart, concerned, her light, backless summer dress nearly without weight, looking at once full and transparent—like a screen image, like a goddess, in film, larger and less substantial. She looked struck by Kohlman, by the sight of his broken skin and lost language, as if the image forced some new thought or reconsideration, some new way she might invent and conjure light.

.   .   .   .   .

In the dressing room, soon afterward and side by side, a stripped Kohlman and stripped Challenger had their bodies cleaned and tinctured and oiled while their friends drank champagne. Kohlman had begun to shape at least, "I . . ." unable to get further, move past bodied and animal sounds, beyond them. "I . . ."

"Don't hurry, Benjamin," Janice comforted.

"So what you think, Benjamin Kohlman," the Challenger teased and spread a wide hand around Kohlman's skull. "You like this? This fight game for you?"

"Ben's gonna fight all the other writers!" Barnett joked.

"So . . whose body would you rather have—if you could have another body— Benjamin's or Turner's?" Alyce had started calling the Challenger "Turner," his true Christian name. They'd grown that close.

"So now . . do we call Turner 'the Champion'?" Barnett asked.

"Don't you dare!" the Challenger said.

"And don't you dare call the Champion 'Turner'!" Alyce said. "He said: only me."

"Only you . . !" the Challenger crooned.

"Use some of this cream," Comus offered to the handlers working over Kohlman; "It helps."

.   .   .   .   .

By the time the six friends broke into pairs at Caesar's rotunda— Alyce and the Challenger, Comus and Barnett, Janice and Kohl- man—Kohlman had perfected "Hi" and "See you" and "I don't get it." The seven syllables had made discrete shapes and the shapes, sounds in Kohlman's brain, so that he could utter them. And of course the group had quickly made it their language, formed it into a kind of round, sounding even Kohlman's own peculiar inflec- tions, so that when they made their partings, it all sounded some- thing like:

"Hi."

"See you."

"See you."

"I don't get it."

"See you."

"Hi."

"I don't get it."

"I don't get it."

"Hi."

"See you!"

And the music all made Kohlman joyous, the syllables, their nonsense or no-nonsense echoing above the traffic, seeming not to stop, not to disjoin, yet taking leave of one another clearly, draw- ing quieter. And then, even with Janice close and the night jammed with primrose, the joyousness fled, briefly; something else edged in: Kohlman hearing himself . . his own stupidity, the dumb shuffle of his thick words . . and then the others . . and not in dance as it had first seemed, not in play. So . . were they mocking? In their calls and recalls of his few syllables? Were they not his friends? Were his words foolish? It was a moment again, though clearly brief, when Kohlman looked everywhere for his lost breath. Then he heard: "Call us!" Barnett's bark. And . . .

"We will!" Janice beside him.

"In case he gets out of hand!" Barnett with a laugh.

"C.E.O: Benjamin's fine! He loves her!" Alyce now . . in the other direction.

"Be fine!" the Challenger. "Thas' fine! Be who you are! No shame!"

"See you!" Kohlman managed, in a strong, carrying voice. He waved, joyous again, north . . south: "See you! . . Hi! . . I don't get it!"

· · · · ·

They made love twice, stretching themselves, making their bodies long so they might be with one another. They wanted so, both, to be entire, more, longer than themselves, to have their room filled with all their breath. They felt each others' chests fill, touching, then quiet. "I feel like the needle on a compass," Janice said.

Kohlman began finding speech . . though it did not always match hers. "I thought . ." he began, ". . the man . . ."

"Yes," Janice said; "I know."

"Because . . ." Kohlman said.

"I need to tell you what I haven't," Janice said finally.

Kohlman shook his head.

"Benjamin . . I need."

"No need," Kohlman said.

"About the fire."

Kohlman made a gesture, drawing Janice's fingertips across his own throat.

"But you've wanted me."

"Yes," Kohlman said, and then he placed some of his hair, short and thin as it was, in Janice's mouth.

· · · · ·

Janice loved the Wurlitzer. "It's like being under water," she said; "In the ocean. I mean . . on my skin." She cried. It played Frankie Valli. Kohlman cried. She laid the soft membrane of her ear against his wounds: the crease at his head, the taped slice down his back, the small crater at his shoulder, the palms of his hands.

"What are you hearing?" he asked.

"What hurts," she said.

Neither had been able to touch enough, take hold. They were the pressure in each other's hands, the weight each had on the other's skin. The music in the room, the bubble lights, compassed them.

Janice shifted her body and sat up.

"What?" Kohlman asked.

"Something," Janice said.

"New?" Kohlman said.

"I don't think so," Janice said.

"But . . might be?"

"Anything 'might be,' Benjamin," she said, scanning and hyperalert to any distance.

Kohlman pulled her down, rolled up, over. He kissed her nose. He kissed her neck. He kissed a breast. He kissed the flat of her stomach.

"Don't rule anything out," she said.

"Is your head okay?" Kohlman asked, kissing it, inhaling hair in hazy strands. "I'm a vacuum."

"My head's like . . consomme; it's like wonderful consomme!" she said.

. . . . .

A sudden rap fractured their slow lift of reunion and broke at their door. "What . . ." Kohlman said. "Who . . ?" asked Janice.

"Yeah . . ?" Kohlman called.

"Mr. Kohlman?"

"Yeah?"

"Mr. Kohlman?"

"Yeah?"

"Can we talk?"

Kohlman wondered.

"Can we talk?"

"I don't . . ."

"Just a few words."

"How . . ?"

"Mr. Kohlman?"

"How many?" Kohlman asked.

Janice stayed close and ready, a sailor.

". . Mr. Kohlman?"

"I'm . . busy now," Kohlman said, proud of his sentence.

Nothing came. No attack. His sentence had stopped them! Quiet. No sound. Only strategy. Kohlman left their bed. Janice stayed. He moved across the musical, gold-and-cranberry-braided dark . . past the closet, past the bath . . to the Wurlitzer.

"Mr. Kohlman?" The voice started again.

"Yeah?"

"We're peaceful," the voice said.

"You'll be fine," Janice prompted.

"Just a bit of your time, sir, please."

"I thought . . just words . . you only wanted . . ."

"Well . . a few words . . a little time," the voice said.

Kohlman pressed Patsy Cline's "I Fall To Pieces" on the juke.

"No major issue," the voice said. "We understand you're busy . . we appreciate that." The voice paused. ". . But the point is . . we've caused some trouble. . . Physical. . . Other. Discomfort. We had a wrong notion. We had a wrong idea. And—are you there, sir? Are you listening?"

"Right," Kohlman said.

"Good. So . . in the process, of course, we haven't made your stay in what-we-regard-to-be-our-city . . entirely pleasurable—true? We've gotten in the way of your work, and . . feel we owe you some . . well . . let's say 'exchange'? We owe you some 'exchange'. . and some courtesy. Okay? . . It was a mistake. We thought you were . . another person. We need to . . remedy that."

"So, then . . ?"

"I think it's okay," Janice said. "I think I know. I think they're . . people."

"Mr. Kohlman?"

"So then . . ?" Kohlman spoke each word and discovered he had no feel for sequence. "So then . . I want to . . should we . . ?"

"Our employer, especially, feels extremely apologetic," the voice said.

Janice sat, legs drawn up and into herself suddenly on the bed. She began touching relieved bones as if recalling them. She fixed on and began to shape, end to end, her clavicles. Kohlman watched.

"So . . Mr. Kohlman?"

"Yes? Yeah?"

"So . . did you hear what I was saying? . . about . . ? . . we're coming in?"

"No," Kohlman said.

"It's okay," Janice said. "I just . . ."

"Yes?" the voice said.

"This will be the last station," Janice said.

"But . . ." Kohlman said.

"No, really," Janice said.

"We've done some unkind things," the voice said; "and now we're under strict instructions to be kind."

"But . . ." Kohlman said. Now Janice was touching her cheekbones, reading them.

"And if we're not kind—the point is: our asses will be most very definitely on the line. So . . ."

"Wait," Kohlman said.

"No," the voice said. "We're coming in. Don't stand close."

"I . . ." Kohlman began.

"We're under strict orders," the voice said.

". . Dressed?" Kohlman said to Janice.

Janice smiled. She hugged herself and seemed confident. "It's good. It's the last station, Benjamin," she said.

"Angel . . ?" Kohlman said.

The door ripped open, tearing bolts and hinges. It fell forward, flat and onto their floor.

"I asked myself and I answered," Janice said. "I heard."

"From . . ?"

The two security guards from the Golden Nugget, the one who talked and the one who didn't, stood in the exposed doorframe.

"So . . I know you were probably having an intimate moment, but . . this just, obviously, happens to be the timing: it's very important that we be kind, so . . could you, please, get dressed?"

"Hi, Luke," Janice said.

"Angel," the guard who talked answered.

"You know . . ?" Kohlman asked.

"Hi, Lee," Janice acknowledged the other. "They work with me," she told Kohlman.

"So . . get dressed now?" Luke said.

"They're Luke and Lee," Janice said. "We all work graveyard."

Now Kohlman worked *his* fingertips into the loose skin at the flat of his brow.

The silent guard, Lee, brought their clothes.

"Okay?" Luke said.

"Benjamin . . ?" Janice said.

"Because, frankly, we've got other things . . and we need to get this kindness shit over as soon as possible."

"I think . . ." Kohlman began.

"Mr. Kohlman?"

"Are you . . ? Do we eat . . dinner now? Is that . . ?"

"Sir?"

"I think . . I've *done* this," Kohlman said. "I think . . this . . happened."

"Not in this way," Luke said. "Definitely – I would very much doubt . . in this manner. So . . put your pants on, please, sir."

Janice started to dress.

"But . . we didn't . . ." Each word now in Kohlman struggled . . until it had a next and they'd found a sentence. "But . . we . . don't . . have . . to . . do something . . just because . . you . . say," he said.

"Benjamin: they know that. Of course," Janice said; "It's all right. They're friends."

Luke and Lee stood silently, one on either side of the split-out door frame.

Janice fastened her bra and looked double-jointed. She punched in Patsy Cline's "Crazy."

"These guys took . ." Kohlman began; "I mean . . what I . . they stole . . ."

"Okay; true; right!" Luke said. "For the record: We stole your tapes! We sliced your back! We threw you into a fire! We fucked you over! No argument! But the point, though, is: it was a *mistake*. Okay? We understand now . . and we want to repair it."

"I *have* . . done this," Kohlman said. He watched Janice buttoning her blouse. She hummed Patsy Cline's *I'm crazy for tryin'. . and crazy for cryin'* . . and seemed unafraid. "So . . how're you guys doin'?" she asked.

"We're overworked," Luke said; "and underloved. But, basically, okay, Angel. How 'bout you?"

"I'm in love with Benjamin," Janice said. She hummed a bar. ". . So I'm wonderful."

"More power!" Luke said. Lee nodded. "And . . so . . how's your back, Cowboy?" Luke nodded to Kohlman. "We stitch it up to your satisfaction?"

Kohlman didn't answer. He slipped his pants on, picked up his socks. "I don't get it," he said, aside, to Janice.

"Everything comes," Janice said. "Everything comes . . finally."

. . . . .

Luke told them they would have to be blindfolded. Janice said *fine*; Kohlman didn't resist. The two guards moved them out of the room and into a car. Janice leaned into Kohlman in the back seat: "This is sort of exciting," she said. She felt for his cheek with her blind lips, kissed him.

. . . . .

They were in the sounds of traffic wound with the sounds of music and radio patter from the Union Plaza. Luke and Lee didn't talk. Janice kept moving into Kohlman's ear and whispering: things that made him feel afloat and fevered. "You're still *in* me," she said, and asked: "Can you feel?" And when he edged away gently, she moved back: "No. Don't!" she said. "I like you there. Stay . . !"

"Please . . ." Kohlman said, his breath crazy and without decision.

"Yes . . ! Like that!" she said. "Now! Left . . yes! . . See? I told you."

Kohlman's throat went dry. "Janice . . ." he tried. He bumped her lightly away with his elbow.

"You're mean," she said.

Kohlman felt her pull from him and felt bad. But then she was against him again, hard, tickling. "Hello," she said. "Hello. I'm back. You'll learn."

. . . . .

The car lurched in two abrupt turns then broke to a stop. Both front doors unlocked—that was their sound—then swung open. Outside, something large and mechanical frothed the night air, and drove the taste of a metallic dust. Sudden gusts pulled at both their blindfolds. "What's going on?!" Kohlman yelled to the windy engine of *whatever* fueled a new adrenalin; the adrenalin, new words. "So—What *is* this?! What's going on now?!" he said. But Luke and Lee weren't in the car to answer.

"Helicopter!" Janice yelled, her voice, discovering, gleeful, yelling over the sound: "Helicopter!"

"Think . . ?!" Kohlman shouted.

Their back doors opened and each was led from the car. "Just walk where we go." Kohlman assumed the voice to be Luke's, though it was hard, in the windy flap, to tell.

"Janice!?" Kohlman called–to see whether she was with him.

"Hello . . !? . . Benjamin?!" Janice called. "I'm here!"

"Okay!"

"You here?!"

"I'm . . yeah; just checking!" Kohlman called.

"This feels like an adventure!" Janice called.

"It *is* an adventure," Luke shouted.

"It *is* an adventure!" Janice called. "Luke *says*! He shouted it. That's why!"

Kohlman said nothing.

"Benjamin . . !? *Let* it be an adventure?! Okay?!"

"But if . . ? What if . . ?!"

"Okay?!"

"Okay."

"Because I feel we're totally married now! Forever and more! Don't you?! No turning back!? Benjamin?!

"I do!" Kohlman said. And he *thought* the words, held them, didn't release them, and was moved. Even so far from speech, the *I* and *do* seemed to take a kind of local dominion.

"So now . . what*ever*! . . right?!" Janice said.

". . Whatever!" Kohlman said and smiled.

"And we don't *expect*!"

"What're you guys *talking* about?" Luke asked.

"And we don't expect!" Kohlman promised.

"And we expect *every*thing!" Janice said.

"*Every*thing . . sure!" Kohlman laughed. He could feel the full wind and the tremor–down from the blades and copter's rotor–traveling through him.

· · · · ·

Soon, they were beside each other again, inside the machine bubble . . and they lifted off. The bubble doors shut, and the flog of the rotor seemed more muted. Someone had turned on a tape: the Statler Brothers. Kohlman felt what he presumed to be Janice's hand gripping his leg. She leaned in. "I'm excited," she said. "Are you going to kill us, Luke?" Janice asked. She laughed. And Kohlman saw, even blindfolded, her smile. "Is this an assassination?" she said.

"Not this time, Angel," Luke said.

"This time 'kindness'—right?" Janice said.

"This time kindness, Angel," Luke said. "Our orders exactly! 'Do kindness!' Well put! Absolutely!"

Absolutely, Kohlman thought. And the word rolled down some mountain; its din, terrible and merciless, a thunder, an old code or wrath tearing blackly, a sudden scourge; and Kohlman imagined himself meeting Luke's and Lee's employer, lifting the man by his shirt front, slamming him against a wall: *Don't burn people! Don't ever hurt this woman!* the enraged version of himself demanded.

"Benjamin . . ?" Janice said.

Kohlman wondered if he would do that. If he would *need* to do that. Who would their employer be? Had they met? Were there *true* crimes of passion?

"Benjamin . . ?" Janice said again.

But then the copter swung like its own belly through the sky, so that the two could feel it . . turn, rise, drop, drop again, drop ever so slowly.

Then, inside, encased, the available air seemed to grow more liquid and more chill. New sound.

"Water!" Janice called.

"What do you mean?" Kohlman said.

"The sound. *Water*."

Luke and Lee laughed.

"But . . ? We're in . . *air*," Kohlman said. "Water? We're in a helicopter."

"Hold your fire," they heard Luke say, ". . just a minute, you'll see! What you're hearing!"

They heard the bubble doors roll open, and on every side, all *around*, came turbulence—booming, thunderous. It was like the sound the word *absolute*, made stone, had made, rolling down Kohlman's mind, and they felt in*side* it, whatever it was, wherever they were.

"*Can you guess now?!*" Luke said; "*without seeing?! Can you feel and guess?!*" He was bellowing at them.

"*Some kind of water!*" Janice spoke in a voice louder than Kohlman had ever heard her use.

"*Okay . . here! . . Then try this!*" Luke shouted.

There was a strange lapse—no words. The copter felt its way down—inches . . inches . . then inches again. A wind and rotary churn from outside whipped the copter cabin and froze it, wet as rain.

"*NOW?!*" Someone—it had to be Luke—was asking them something, which they couldn't determine. And then both, Janice and Kohlman, found their arms being taken, hands guided. "*CARE-FUL!*" That word from whoever spoke—Luke, unless Lee had begun—and the next "*SLOW!*" And Kohlman felt a force of water nearly rip his hand off. He heard Janice scream. He jolted, saw the hot fire cone, the volcano in his brain. His hands flew to his temples; his head felt like a mass of old, weak seams. But then he heard Janice laugh, shriek, erupt with pleasure! "*Oh, my God!*" she said, screaming, hallooing over the thudding whirl and boom of water: "*Oh, my God! I can't believe! I believe! This is wonderful!*" The volcano faded, and Kohlman felt his blindfold being snapped off. Janice was saying: "*Is it?!*" and then "*It is!*" and then "*Is it really?!*" again. And at last Kohlman could see that the copter had set down nearly on a roaring black charge of water—wide, thunderous, thick. And he could see walls, all high and moonish stone walls, a canyon rising wherever he might turn his head.

"*Amazing: right?!*" he saw Luke beside him, heard Luke ask. "*Amazing: right?!*" Luke repeated.

Kohlman couldn't find his words again.

"*It's the Grand Canyon, Benjamin!*" Janice shouted.

"*I . . !*"

"It's the Grand Canyon!!"

"*Yes, I . . !*"

"What?!"

" . . *I figured,*" Kohlman said.

"*It's the Grand Canyon!*" Janice repeated, and then, "*Oh, my God: We were touching the water moving in the middle of the Grand Canyon! We were inside the air inside the water moving in the Grand Canyon . . with our hands!*"

Luke was smiling. Lee was smiling. They had done their work!

"*Benjamin: It's the Grand Canyon!*" Janice said finally.

"*I . .* " Kohlman said. ". . *know. Right . . I saw.*" His voice slipped, folded, wasn't fully audible. "*I saw,*" he said. "*It is. . . True.*"

"*Our employer said this was a must!*" Luke cupped his hands and shouted; "*He said this was definitely . . the way we should start!*"

"*Thank you, Luke!*" Janice said.

"*Yeah . . thanks,*" Kohlman said.

The helicopter began, slowly, to lift. Luke grinned. "*Our employer said . . he said: 'First of all . . what I want is . . Comp them to the Grand Canyon!'*"

.　.　.　.　.

In the air, the two were, again, blindfolded.

"So . . not over?" Kohlman asked.

"If we were having dinner . . it would just be the first drink!" Luke said; "the first taste of the first drink!" He laughed.

Again came the sounds of the night air. Then the sounds of their landing, doors opening, the scape itself, somewhere where the low brush, its skin, smelled like petroleum, not an Iowa smell in any way, not a New York smell ever, a place probably high, remote. Some kind of animal barked. Then there were sounds of car doors and of the car itself: engine, motion, its interior, a hum, a rasp, breathy almost, amplified dimly, vaguely hollow. Then came the grate of tires on dirt grade, then pavement. The sounds and criss-crossing vibrations of general traffic. Now they dropped some-where, a place more hollow, underground now, a ramped place, the cavity of some parking garage. The car slowed. It stopped and idled. The back doors unlocked and opened. And Janice and Kohl-man, again, were guided out.

"This is like my life," Janice said to Kohlman.

They all moved into what felt to be a small elevator, its door clattering—trashed metal, not the sounds of glide and air compres-sion, rubber and steel quietly meshing that were, in Las Vegas, almost everywhere. The lift shuddered and tossed; the doors col-lapsed open. Kohlman and Janice felt the guards' hands: "We go left here," Luke guided. "Now right. . . . Right again." Wherever they were gave off the smells of junk: food oil, old sour paper, burnt-out appliances. Kohlman felt himself being let go; his blind-fold slid silently from his head.

.　.　.　.　.

They were in a rat-trap office: tube kitchen chairs with slashed naugahyde, a scarred and dusty oak desk, an ancient water cooler and classic bare overhead bulb. The single window had one pane broken; the others were streaked. Outside, sounds of traffic and construction machinery droned; carnival lights splayed and inflated the night edging on to morning. It seemed they were on a side street; Kohlman made out the backside of some hotel tower, the Grand or Hilton, perhaps the Desert Inn. Off to one angle, and not far below, was some palace's lit and gemlike pool. From behind the desk, in his motorized chair, the mendicant amputee, REM, sat, his face forever serious, and addressed them.

"How was the canyon?" he asked.

"It was wonderful!" Janice said.

"I'm glad," REM said. "For you as well?" he asked Kohlman.

"It was . . good," Kohlman said. "Yeah. It was . . . Are you . . ?"

"It was being *birds*!" Janice said. "It was like being *fish*!"

Kohlman was amazed: *He*'d thought that.

"Good," REM said.

Kohlman looked at the man, trying to understand. Did he use all of his cigarbox money to rent this office? Its sadness, certainly, and brokenness were *like* him. But Luke and Lee, or *Luke*, at least, had said, "our employer." That didn't make . . ? How . . ? Kohlman looked for a connection: a man with no arms or legs . . the calls, the warnings, the assaults, the breaking and entering, the confiscating of his tapes. Was REM—that would be possible—an observer? Just a person *aware*? So, then . . ? Okay: if he'd taken it, or most of it, all in, if he'd *seen*, then . . ? But then, what . . ? . . how? So what was the tie to their flight into the Grand Canyon?

"I'm sorry about the confusion," REM said.

Kohlman made a gesture he hoped might spark a word . . so that *that* word might bring another. But his mind wouldn't float properly. It wouldn't drift on the full current of his body. It could with Angel. It had at the fight. It had with his friends, for the most part. But it couldn't float yet on every alien logic. And this held off. No language came.

"We try to be careful," REM said; "about our own needs. And our own interests. And sometimes that means being *too* careful. We've talked about this," he said straight at Kohlman: "mistakes occur."

Kohlman tried to conjure something brute and appropriate were REM, in fact, Luke's and Lee's "employer." Because he'd endured pain. On whoever's orders: Luke and Lee had threatened and set fire and violated; they'd opened Kohlman's skin. He sought an answering: images: snatching up the amputee and slamming him to the wall; making demands: *Don't ever . . !!* But no outrage came. No wrath. Only curious attention. Who was REM? Some smoky trace in Kohlman pressed to reject the man's meek and unlikely flesh. But more compelled him in claim. The room filled with a fine cadmium dust that bore almost its own light. Who was REM? From whatever, *for* whatever, the man had caused Kohlman to struggle. He'd been harsh. Unyielding. Where was Kohlman's volcano? Why no destruction when it might be called? Instead, Kohlman stood simply to be instructed. Where were any of his gains?

"We're almost there," he heard Janice say. "Benjamin: . . soon . . almost."

"I . . ." Kohlman tried.

"Say what's on your mind," REM invited.

"I don't get it," Kohlman said.

"Well," REM said . . and he started to zigzag like a man pacing and launched solely by impulse, through the small room. His motor whined—approaching, fading—like a mosquito.

Was this to be another riff? Kohlman wondered, another drum solo of non-sequiturs?

"You were in the war," Janice interposed; "weren't you?"

REM held his flight like a hummingbird. His blood rushed to some center . . then out. It colored him. He seemed dangerously electric, a fuse. "The war?" he said. He paused. His teeth made sounds against one another. "Yeah," he said. "Yeah. Myself. A lot of people. Myself and a lot of people." He brought his motor chair head-on to the window, stopped there, stared out, began again. "And a lot of us . . ." The moment was painful; it grew. Both Luke and Lee stood waiting and felt the pain. Luke put a hand to the top of his own head and pressed it; Lee pushed a fist against his chest. REM lifted a bony shoulder and cleared his eyes; Kohlman could hear swallowing and a terrible congestion and a readying of himself to try again. "I'm not angry," he began. "I'm not angry. That's not what I want to say. I don't want to be angry. There isn't . . ." He turned from the window to Janice. "You've been in a war," he said.

Janice made small half-movements with her lips and fingers. Kohlman had never seen her self-conscious.

"You're going to write her . . into a *book*?" REM asked Kohlman.

Kohlman shook his head.

"I played your tapes," REM said. "Your tapes seem all about making her into a book . . so that she can be another national freak. And you can be on the Today Show. And the Tonight Show. And the Tomorrow Show. And the Early Morning Show and the Late Night with Whoever-That-Asshole-Is Show. And then you can make her into a See-the-Freak-in-Action television miniseries. That *isn't* what all these tapes are about?" He nodded toward a small cardboard box in one of the corners.

"No," Kohlman said. His throat went dry; but he had words and knew them: "No. Once, maybe. But . . not now."

"I've given Benjamin my life," Janice said, "and he's given me his."

"I'm sorry that I'd tagged you with the wrong fires," REM said to Kohlman.

Kohlman shrugged. It was still a mystery: the events . . where they fit with REM.

"We're a small group," REM said. "Very. I mean . . ." He laughed crazily. "Look at this office. But we've gotten some small leverage. People know we're *out* there; people know we exist. Not who we *are* but . . that has its benefits. I . . try to keep the organization together. I work the streets. I keep my eyes open: they're the reach I have, and I try to use them. I see what's happening. Who's doing it. Where. To whom. I saw you. I see. Most times I'm right. Most times. And sometimes . . when it's at that point . . I ask friends . . to help. To act. When the casualties reach into the streets. And the people are scared. And no one has courage. Then . . well, we try to have courage. Maybe *for* them. And do something. We take . . oh, you know: take out a private airplane. Or airstrip. Light a fire. Discourage the . . "bullies" I guess . . however we can. *She* knows about that kind of stuff," REM nodded again at Janice. "*She's* done it—not for us directly . . but she knows."

There was a break. Like a silent prayer. Like a directed thought in private. Then REM began again . . jaw moving, tongue wetting and rewetting his lips: "You know I lost . . ." And now he drove himself back to the window and stared out, took his time. ". . I lost a lot of myself . . in 'the war'. . being taken apart by others . . and for the wrong people. But I never lost . . . I never . . . What I never lost . . was what I saw . . what others had seen . . before. That . . . Those . . *pictures*, I guess. I dream a lot. I dream all the time. Terrible burning dreams, of course. But others. Others too. Others that were there way before I had them. And so I decided . . and I mean it when I say: I don't want to be angry; I don't want to intrude on other people's freedom to . . I don't want to make petty value judgments. But I decided to try to . . establish a kind of network . . whereby . . a small group of us might, neverthe-less . . . *Fuck*!" He wiped his eyes with his shoulder again, took several moments to restore his breathing, turned back in. "I'm sorry," he said. "I can't . . . You get the general picture, though."

Janice crossed to REM, knelt, bent, kissed the small pink-grey nubs, the joints where, once, there had been a whole anatomy. "If I were the light," she said; "Oh, sweet Jesus: if I were all the light, then I would fill you."

REM's scarred, stubbled face, an area nearly a third of his cleft body, wrenched and contorted. "I know. I know you would," he said. "I know you would. I heard. I heard your story."

Kohlman felt shamed, felt jealous.

Janice set her head in REM's lap.

"But the point is," REM's voice strengthened: "The point is: for *now* at least . . we've committed some errors as far as you people are concerned. And it's our intent not to have that go un . . well . . *corrected*. And so . . for the next forty-eight hours . ." REM took an enormous breath; Kohlman thought about himself. ". . I've sent the word out . . onto the street—the word is out—for the next forty-eight . . nothing in our city . . will be refused. We made a mistake. We acted prematurely. Against the wrong person. Good faith needs, if possible, to be recovered. So . . nothing will be refused. It's your city. You own it. It can be extraordinary. Enjoy."

Then REM motored behind his desk and began paperwork, scanning documents, lifting them with his teeth, slipping them in color-coded file folders. "Lot of shit to be dealt with here," he said, his mouth full. "It doesn't stop. It keeps coming. You get up in the morning. You go to bed at night. That's all you can do. Honor the planet. Pray."

Kohlman realized, then, what had struck and stopped him before: full-bodied and in other clothes, REM could have been his father.

．　　．　　．　　．　　．

They were blindfolded again, dropped by the rickety elevator to a parking garage. When the blindfolds were taken off, valets were opening their car doors. It was the hotel entrance to the Aladdin.

"Just remember," Luke said from the driver's seat, as they slid out: "Forty-eight hours. We ask . . maybe I should say *require* . . that you not say anything to anyone about what has happened tonight. But, for forty-eight hours . . you own it all!"

FOURTEEN

"**M**r. Kohlman!" everyone said. And: "Mr. Kohlman! . . Sir: Mr. Kohlman: how *are* you!" And: "Mr. Kohlman! . . what do you need!" It was unsettling; it made Kohlman uneasy. Bell captains! Staffs at front desks! Pitbosses! Everybody, startlingly, recognized . . well, *both* of them, yes, certainly; but it was Janice's city; she'd *lived* here; she had a certain notoriety . . so that the *Good evening, Ms. Stewart!*s made a kind of sense. But . . "Yes, Mr. Kohlman!". . ? . . No. Kohlman felt off-balance. And "We have your room!" And: "Did you want it, sir!?" What was that!? What was he supposed to say? Who was this person carrying a shoebox filled with Memorex tapes whom people recognized? When he had come from New York, Jesus, *no* one had known him; people had *mistaken* him . . constantly. He'd been, in fact, cloudy about himself. But now! "Mr. Kohlman!" "Good evening!" "This way, sir!" It was hard.

"Relax," Janice said.

Into what? Kohlman thought.

They walked into the Aladdin. They walked into the Dunes. They walked into Bally's Grand and the Flamingo and Caesar's. In each, hosts offered amenities. Janice smiled: "It's running!" she said.

"I'm not accustomed," Kohlman told her. His whole back felt tight.

"It can happen," she said. "You hit runs. You step in . . they take you!" She seemed high. "They go. My friend calls them *shifts*. But they're *runs*!"

Kohlman closed his eyes. He'd as soon enjoy it. He'd as soon go along. If they'd said, *Mr B!* Or: *Evening, Mr. Napoleon!* But . . "Mr. Kohlman!" That was *him*. It was like . . where? . . not New York. Like Templeton. You couldn't go anywhere. People had your name. And when they had your name, they had . . true? . . expectations. It was all right if a *few* people knew you, if a *few* people saw and recognized. That, in fact, was nice. He loved that with Janice! And, now, with C.E.O. and Comus, the Challenger and Alyce. That felt like . . *home* or something; they felt like family. But . . .

"Mr. Kohlman, sir! Good evening! What would you like?"
Kohlman pivoted; he left the Bally Grand lobby.
Janice chased: "Benjamin," she laughed. "Come back. Have fun. It won't last. It's just a run!"

Everything was permission. Was that real? It seemed dangerous. Every aisle was safe conduct. Every need, an invitation or generosity. As someone you *weren't*, you could, perhaps, *claim* such things. But as *yourself* . . ?!

"Benjamin . . ! Come back! Really! Slow down!" She laughed. "People want to be good to you! It's a run! Don't be grumpy!"
"It's not real."
"Of course."
"People know who I am."
"That's fine."
"I don't know."
"It's just temporary. They'll know and then they'll *not* know. They'll forget. You'll be in the run . . and then you'll get thrown out. Everyone does. I see it all the time. Every day. With numbers."
What did she mean?
"It's just like . . or maybe it *is* . . the numbers. Sometimes people get, say, in the *thirties* or in the *teens* . . and it's *all* thirties and teens . . for maybe three hours! And then it's over. But when it's running, it can be nice. It's no big thing. It ends. It's nice. It's just a taste of something. It goes away."
What had REM said? What was their clock? Forty-eight hours?
"I'll try," Kohlman said.
"Take my hand."
He did.
"Now walk. *Amble*—I love that word—back into the hotel."
"Okay."

They did. They ambled. Entered. Stood. The lights seemed softer. The glass on the chandeliers made less clatter and more chime. It sent slow waves of phantom rippling. And the lobby played all the songs Kohlman could remember. He tried to relax so that he might feel Janice's *whatever* . . her drift, the turn, her *runs* . . being known, hospitality, comfort.

But, then . . were there shifts in him? Had *he* run? With her? Ever? And had that . . ?! Had they run together? He'd run in Iowa. But that wasn't . . not her sense, but . . he had. Long distance. Cross country. Flat pinched roads, rising and falling, curving less than the earth. Had any of that been . . ? Kohlman swayed; he felt giddy, eyes tight. He smiled. "What are you doing?" Janice asked. "I'm running," he said. He grinned.

They laughed.

"Can you feel?" Janice said. "Can you feel it?"

"I think so," Kohlman said.

"Is anyone close?"

"I think so."

"Who?"

"You."

"How close?"

"I'm not . . . *In*."

"In?"

"Yes. Yes: *in*."

"I *am*," she said.

"You *are*. You're in the run," Kohlman said. He was getting it, catching the wave. "There! In! You stepped in."

"I did," Janice said. "Good. Yes."

"Yeah."

"But *you* stepped in."

"Me?"

"Yes."

"When?"

"Before."

"Oh. . . That's true. That's true; I did."

"That's what happened."

"It is."

"Am I right?"

"You're right. I'm with you."

"You stepped in."

"I did."

"I was there."

"You were there . . definitely."

"I was already running."

He smiled. "I'm sure."

They were in the lobby. Kohlman was smiling, smiling and rocking on the balls of his feet, teetering like a fan palm or a eucalyptus in a light sirocco.

"So . . are you willing to do this?" Janice asked.

"I'll try," Kohlman said.

"Just try?"

"It seems very tentative," Kohlman said: still smiling, swaying.

"It *is* tentative," Janice said. "That's what it is — *tentative*. That's what I said. Somehow you step it. It ends: you get thrown out. That's the world. That's *running*."

A voice broke: "Mr. Kohlman: Try our health club? . . in the new tower? . . on the seventeenth floor?" It was a bell captain.

Kohlman surfaced. He saw the hotel. He saw the man talking . . waiting for what Kohlman might request, might initiate. Kohlman felt lighter, less tracked by gravity. His skin felt sure: protective yet soft. The night felt possible. He began to nod. "It ends," he said to Janice, checking.

"Benjamin . . it always ends."

"Whenever."

"Whenever," Janice said, confirming.

Kohlman paused. The bell captain waited. "So: how does this hotel *feel?*" he said to Janice.

"It feels too large," Janice said.

"Thank you," Kohlman said to the bell captain. "We're just browsing."

"Well, I'm here if you need anything," the bell captain said.

They moved on. They crossed a street. They moved through lights, past fountains.

.   .   .   .   .

"So: how does *this* hotel feel?" Kohlman asked in the next lobby.

"I think . . too small," Janice said.

"And . ." at the next one: ". . this?"

She turned in place, floated, danced, tested the space. "It feels . . ."

". . Just right?" he asked.

". . Quite nice," she said.

"Then—should we stay?" He was getting into it finally.

·   ·   ·   ·   ·

The Flamingo host wore a dark suit with a rose. "It's a lovely suite!" he said. "You'll be pleased."

"Count on us," Kohlman said. "Write us in."

"Very good, Mr. Kohlman!" the host said.

"Do we need anything? To sign anything?" Kohlman questioned.

"No, sir," the host said. "It's all handled."

"It's handled," Kohlman told Janice.

"Good," Janice said.

"Should we look?" Kohlman asked. "Make sure? Check?"

"I just think it feels right," Janice said.

"I agree," Kohlman said. "We're fine," he told the host; "We're happy."

"Do you have luggage?" the host asked; "Anything . . you'd like . . brought up?"

"Just the key," Janice said.

"Just the key," Kohlman repeated.

"We may not even stay," Janice said.

"But if we had the key . . ." Kohlman said.

"Then we'd have . . ."

"I understand," the host said.

"He's good," Janice said. "Don't you think?"

"I do," Kohlman said. "The thing is: he anticipates. I think he's been in the business."

The host gave them the key. "Enjoy your stay," he said. "Did you want . . dinner? breakfast? Something to drink? Can we bring anything *in*?"

"Very kind," Kohlman said.

"Thank you," Janice said.

"What's the temperature?" Kohlman said.

"Here?"

"Outside."

"I'm not . . sure."

"Do you need a coat?" Kohlman asked Janice.

"We have a lovely fur shop—in our arcade," the host said.

·　·　·　·　·

They gave Janice a red fox cape. She and Kohlman went out-side, stood in the late wind.

"Did you want a fur too?" Janice said.

"I never thought of it," Kohlman said.

"How about a shoulder bag—for your tapes?"

·　·　·　·　·

They crossed back to the Dunes, took rooms there as well, rode an outside elevator, up. The rooms were high and glass and rose two stories. Kohlman removed Janice's fur. He removed her dress. She removed everything he had and took his chin between her teeth and balanced his jawbone on her tongue. She released it and smiled: "You were your own word in my mouth," she said; "and delicious." They sat in their jacuzzi and drank Bern Kastle Doctor, and Janice began her last chapter.

"On the night of the fire," she began, and abruptly Kohlman felt the real and *tentative* world that bound him return and rush in with a brute force. A cool froth swept from the jacuzzi aerator, then dimmed. His frame shifted, their play momentarily dissolved. *On the night of the fire*, he had heard and his ribs had tightened.

"Perhaps *later* would be a better time to . . ." he began.

"No; now," she said.

Again the tentative world pulsed. REM had said forty-eight hours. At most they'd had three.

"I told you at REM's," Janice said. "I told you: 'we're nearly there.' "

"Let me raise the temp in this jacuzzi just a little," Kohlman said.

She said, "No." She began again. Kohlman tried to hear. He closed his eyes. Her words moved in humid breaths between them: wanting entry, saying *Benjamin, Benjamin: here! Here we are! What you came for!* He felt the ache of his body from the Challenger's fight. He had come to see. He had come to be there and had felt every blow. He had opened, bled, fallen to his knees. He had cried.

He'd rejoiced. He'd reclaimed the woman he loved, embraced his friends. Shouldn't that have been plenty? Weren't they in the *run* now? . . and supposed to have it a little longer?

But there he was, naked, in the water. With her. With himself and her. And her words. And her story.

He felt thirteen. And remembered. Late afternoon. Iowa. Templeton. By the riverbank. He was in some structure of poplar staves crossed with lightning, wanting . . words, wanting speech, but . . fearing too, hungry yet appalled. *I want to be like him. I want to be like Father*, he had said in shaking words in those woods. *But we're not . . . He doesn't talk. He doesn't say. Just work. How can I . . ?*

"On the night of the fire . . ."

Say! Don't say! Please say! Don't say! his brain yelled. The water felt too cold. *Say!* Don't *say!*

He remembered. He remembered, thinking . . frightened: *But when someone says . . then they've told. Then you've heard. Then you know . . but if you don't know . . . Speak/Don't speak! Give/No; don't!*

Like mountain talus—skull, piecemeal; eyes, tumbled—Kohlman lay at some foot of his own upheaval, small desert animal feet, only, alive on his parts.

Janice took his hand. "On the night of the fire . . ." she said. "Benjamin, listen: On the night of the fire . . ."

Janice . . ?

"I . . ."

Don't . . ? Please . . ? Yes . . ?

"I had sent . . ."

And if she finishes . . ? And if she gives me her words . . then . . ?!

"I had sent Salem Levinworth's letter . . ."

The choice bolted. The choice flew past. Angel spoke, inevitably, all the heat of the water bubbling back. And Kohlman heard and, listening, started to carry her narrative *in* . . like a final tape: words in the jacuzzi that would last, that would leave, that would stand . . and dry their skins, and put on at times outrageous clothes . . and walk the night . . from lamp to lamp . . cafe to lounge, hotel room to milling street corner . . words he wanted . . words she needed to have out . . words in the jacuzzi: hers, from her, her mouth, the image of her face, Angel's face, its skin, its kind patina and the sense of moisture all around and, all around, the warm scented life . . life like blue verbena and like fruit . . everything of their days . . and weeks . . and all that ahead to travel with them through their unwinding night: words in a jacuzzi . . everywhere, ready to leave, ready to descend elevators, part gliding doors, stride the running night . . like breath, their breaths, like soap embedded in their skins.

We're almost there, Janice had said.

They would have drinks at the Barbary Coast and listen to an Irish band. And their drinks would be the color of nectarine and of flesh.

We're almost there.

They would hold hands and drink kier royales. Kohlman would brush the back of his hand against her cheek repeatedly. And her words would play and play, out and out again, *in* him and *through*.

It was crazy to think he might stop her. So: "Say," he said; "Say. Please say. Don't stop. I never meant *don't*. I'm sorry."

On the night of the fire . . .

She squeezed his hand tightly. "We stepped in together," she said.

"I know," Kohlman said. "I know. We did. Say."

*On the night of the fire . . I had sent Salem Levinworth a letter several days earlier. Because I could no longer . . . I had decided . . . Our strange relationship had gone on, you see, after Kenneth's and my marriage. I had gotten it . . into my head . . or wherever such things get . . that whatever I had been given by the world—a husband, some small embodiment, a name, a recognition—*the word "recognition" jarred Kohlman. He hadn't realized how perhaps even happily unprotected he had become—*had gotten it in my head*—she went on—*that even the little that had been given me . . might all be instantly withdrawn were I to break the curious pact I had with my husband's father. He had seemed so powerful. In his way. Able, even more than my own family, to award or withdraw. But I had reached a point. I suppose that's the best way I can say it: I had reached a point. And in my letter, I had . . .*

Kohlman had imagined but not imagined. He had guessed . . but not, and the impoverishment of his reaching, of his attempting to trespass into her life, even carefully, only astounded him.

He wept. He raged. He had few words. He pulled her close . . and would continue to, all night, in places where they both would be . . lounges, jostled and bunched aisles, in the slip of other perfumed and aerated baths . . again, again, this word or that, the shape of her mouth, the lift of her tongue, her eyes: such things would trigger . . and all he wanted to do was: merge, protect, hold—in whatever place, on the street, wherever.

I never imagined, he said . . and then would say, again: *I had my own thoughts . . but I never imagined*. Emotions came, battled, collided. His heart felt mismatched. He wanted to correct things. He wanted to change all of Angel's history. He felt ashamed, demeaned, proud, angry. He felt profoundly sad. He felt incensed to live in a world so inconstant, so shortsighted, so provisional, so tentative. Emotions came in pairs, impossible: protection and rage, preservation and cruelty, recklessness and love. He would pass himself in casino glass and be unnerved by the new and thicker tension in his neck, the changed carriage of his shoulders. He looked unkind. He looked uncompromising and, like some dark witness, too austere. He looked too focused.

．　．　．　．　．

At one point, in the middle of their night, they strolled Las Vegas Boulevard south, and a well-dressed, desperate man stopped and tried to sell them a fat ruby/diamond ring. "I'm empty!" he said. "I paid thirty-six hundred. You can have it for five. I'm empty. I need a plane ticket. I need a flight."

Kohlman measured the man, measured the moment. He felt that he could hurt or help: that he had the choice. Janice watched. Kohlman declined. Without missing a beat, the man stopped the next car exiting the Travelodge: "Check this ring," he began: "Five hundred. I'm empty. I need a flight."

I need a flight, Kohlman thought: *I need a flight. Jesus!*

．　．　．　．　．

Soon after, Kohlman thought he saw his parents getting off a bus. The sight rocked him. *Was* it? Had they been trying to find him? He looked different, *felt* different. So: would they know and recognize? Say: *Good evening, Mr. Kohlman!* Or just . . *Benjamin*! How would he introduce Janice? The couple looked old. It wasn't them. All the bones in Kohlman's body seemed suddenly ragtag . . like a car made of other cars; himself, made from some grab bag:

bones from different times: infant fingers, mid-age shoulders, a strong young man's spine.

He told Janice: "I thought I saw my parents. I thought, with that couple, right there, I was seeing them."

"It's not wrong," she said; "It's not wrong to see that."

They followed the couple into a small casino called the Nob Hill. The couple wore identical golf shirts and levis. They held hands. "Is it them?" Janice asked. "Are you sure? It could still be. Are you sure it's *not*?" Kohlman leaned against a bank of quarter slots, hyperventilating. "Is it, Benjamin? Are you happy to see them? Are you sad?" Kohlman couldn't answer. "They've sat down," Janice said. "At the bar. They've ordered something that has Galliano in it. They're playing video poker." Kohlman shook his head. He steadied his breath. Janice took his arm and stroked it; she kissed the back of his hands. "People make mistakes," she said. "People do that. —So you made a mistake . . about who your parents were." Kohlman nodded. He blew hot air into the knuckles of his fist.

·　·　·　·　·

She took his hand and led him out into the night past the mistaken couple, Kohlman's briefly imagined parents, who were laughing. "It's nice to see a couple enjoy life together, though," Janice said. She put her arm around him; he put his arm around her; they strolled. "One time," she said, "in the keno lounge—there was this wonderful man who, all weekend, played the same two cards. One was *his* card, he said. And one was the card—the numbers—his *wife* had always played. 'I lost her . . last November,' he told me. 'And I miss her. So much.' I asked him how he'd been doing, playing, over the weekend. And he said: 'Oh, I've lost a little. But my wife's done well!' "

". . I wonder what ever happened to the tiger," Kohlman said.

Janice asked what tiger.

He described, weeks earlier, the "Beyond Belief" tiger. "It went outside," he said. "It went out the front doors. At the Frontier. I heard police sirens. I forgot to check the paper the next day."

Janice started crying. Her face riffled, disordered light and small muscles. Words came back. From before. From earlier. From the bath. Her story.

On the night of the fire . . .

Kohlman remembered the section, its pain: he could hear. He felt inside it again: *Because it had gone on, Benjamin . . because it had gone on . . and I had allowed it . . .* She'd been trying– in addition to telling *him*–in the speaking, in the *say*ing, in the *resay*-ing, to *close* her pain. It had been so hard . . the words: *I discovered that I had . . that I had to . . that I had to not. . .* She'd broken, snarled, growled, angry at the cage of herself, gathered, focused, set her teeth, found her breath, started again . . determined: *Because it had gone on, Benjamin . . and I had allowed it . . I discovered that I had to . . stop. And not allow it . . any more. Because I had reached a point where I just couldn't . . I wouldn't . . accept . . or allow my being . . ! I just couldn't . . take . . what he . . what Salem . . what my father-in-law had been . . doing to me . . using me for. And so I sent him this letter . . .*

Kohlman asked of her tears *now*, on the street, here, outside this small, funny place, this casino, this Nob Hill: what were the tears for? Relief? Memory? Pain? Gratitude? Was she happy now? Was she sad?

"I was just thinking about the cat," she said.

"Oh," Kohlman said. "True."

"I was just thinking about the cat," she repeated. "And my . . . The fire. That night. Disappearing and appearing . . and disappear-ing again . . as a person . . forever. And going crazy with all of that."

Kohlman again felt surges: fury . . caring . . resolution . . the new, dark sense of his own musculature and weight. He thought about how she'd been, beside him, opening, *say*ing, crying, before: soft, her words . . like the silk on wheat, moving.

He seemed so powerful, she'd said. *So from time to time, I would go back. I didn't want to. I hated myself. But . . .*

Now Kohlman wanted to speak. Insert. Undo. He didn't want his story about the tiger to have reminded her. He wanted to say something, something that put a large black-and-red magician's cape over the tiger and made it disappear. But all that came was the first syllable of her name: "Jan." Still, it seemed all right, not a broken word.

"*Do* you know how that feels?" she asked, in front of him, facing him now, backing the boulevard like a dancer, eyes searching to make sure he understood. "Benjamin? . . What it feels like?

. . That sense? There . . and then not there–then there again . . for an audience?"

Suddenly, the night sky lit–like a power flare-up, some central terminal struck by lightning. "What . . ?" Kohlman asked. The light shrank then stayed; Janice, like a delicate creature, alert: face scanning; tongue moving to taste the change. "What!" Kohlman asked again, but could then sense. Something. Something radical. An event. A change: as abrupt as the bursting into the world of the Beyond Belief tiger. Fine hair on Kohlman's neck went out, curled in, electrical. "Jan: what?!" He imagined a new burning casino. He considered yet another underground test. But neither were . . . He looked, remembering, for all the tabloid boxes to be lit like luminaires . . because there was smoke now, roiling in a broth of used industrial carpet and cheap cinder block. The smell was somehow familiar.

Then . . .

"REM," Janice said: eyes wide, sensing, panicking slightly, seeing.

"REM?" Kohlman repeated.

"REM!" Janice said. She was turning. She was tasting her own mouth with her tongue; she'd placed the smoke. "His building!" she said. She was like a trapped bird in a house, looking for an open window.

"But we had blindfolds!" Kohlman said. "How can you . . ?!" Still, he knew better. He'd heard her story.

She was wheeling, churning, spinning, yelling "*REM!* . . *REM!*" trying to sense the man's, the fire's direction. Then: "*Benjamin*," she yelled: "*Benjamin!*" Her voice coiled with charged, grainy weight.

"I'm here," he said. "I'm here." He touched her. "Here. I'm just trying to . . ." His attempt was, *with* her, to somehow breathe the place, somehow, breathe the direction.

"*Benjamin! REM!*" Every word came like ash, like inferno: lit cruelly, burst open, aflame. Her eyes tore open all the free space.

"Just . . !"

"*REM!*" Now her face was marked; her face was fissured and streamed with blood.

"Oh, Jesus!" Kohlman said. "No! Jesus!" He understood! It was *there*. It was *in* her. She was *with* him. REM. All her memories! All her story! Her reliving! was there. She was there, *now*, inside the fire . . *with* REM! Wherever that was! Kohlman turned on Las Vegas Boulevard. He spun. He tried again, now desperately, to sense the fire's direction.

"*REM!*" again Janice's cried. "*REM!* . . Benjamin: they've . . ! Someone's . . !"

"Angel . . !"

"Benjamin: I have to . . ! I've got to . . !" she began to wail. She moved north; she moved south. Kohlman tried to hold her. She sent words . . *out*, into the predawn, like flares. Screamed. Called. Nothing Kohlman could do contained her: she was inside a history: inside a night; inside the flames. She was in the flames of *her* flames somewhere; and she was the only savior of her own future.

"Jan . . ." he tried again; "Easy. Angel . . !"

But then some greater sight within connected; some probe, some sounding, some sense for the endangered; some glint, some taste of rising ash. "*Now!*" she shrieked. "Now! Follow! Follow! Benjamin!"

And Kohlman followed. With everything. With everything he had. He followed, equal. Equal, with her . . following. Left when she veered or angled left; right when right: they raced together the small lanes behind the Flamingo; together, raced all the shortcut alleys. "*I can't let . . !*" Janice kept shouting. "*I can't have . . I can't allow . . !*"

The flowered air grew granular with smoke. They closed. They neared.

"*I can't allow . . !*" Janice said again. And Kohlman could almost see the tropical sky eddy in pools not natural, backwash, then still.

How do you know where . . ?! he wanted to yell. But he trusted. He knew. Of course she did! Of course! And she kept being the small bird in the closed room, sensing the sky, sensing the opening: past back-street topless lounges, the discount liquor stores and pawn jewelry, the sad Prince Albert Motel.

Then Kohlman saw: a cheap, blackened, three-story place with grids for windows, the broil of light inside its frame. "That . . ?!" Kohlman barked, "That?!" But he needn't, of course, have asked the question. He was asking the obvious.

"That!" Janice said. "That! Yes! Go!"

Immediately, they were in it, then: fighting smoke, feet clang-
ing on a thin, corrugated staircase . . up . . one flight . . up a second. And, somewhere, there was a full voice, clear and hopeful, in
the furnace, somewhere, near . . nearer, asking . . "Please . . !"

"REM?!"

"Hello . . ?!"

"REM?!"

"Can you . . ?!"

"Yes!" Janice promised, her voice a light. "Yes!" and "Almost
there!"

And then . . fire on fire or whatever . . Kohlman set his bare
hands on REM's motorized chair. And Janice hers. And the chair
was up, somehow, and they were carrying it . . through dense
fulminant and oily waves. Had Kohlman summoned his volcano?
Had he called the Challenger's firecone? Was it all adrenalin: intent
and focus? Steelworkers told tales about the spill of liquid ingots
down their forearms—"I told that sucker *ice*, Man . . and that hot
metal *beaded!*" So . . was that what . . ? And Angel? What about . . ?
Had she, as well, learned . . ? Was she marked by it? . . Unmarked?

· · · · ·

But then they were on the street: all three safe; REM's chair
set down, Janice and Kohlman by it: a crowd, gathered. "Thanks
. . thanks," REM was saying almost shyly; "Good work." There
was almost a smile on his usually wan and harrowed face, and his
eyes seemed lunar in his half-self, wonderfully huge and lighted in
his lampblack face: "Fire zone!" he said. It was almost a joke.

Janice swept and sailed, all energy, in tight, proud, exalted
circles. "Yes!" she kept saying: "Yes!" and "Yes!" She seemed so
filled and brimming! Like a one-woman locker room after the winning game of the World Series: "Yes! . . Yes!". . throwing her fist
up, slapping hands with Kohlman: rights together and then lefts:
"Yes!" Someone in the crowd threw a cold bottle of Korbell in, and
she sliced the covering foil off with a single lance, spun the wire
basket, popped the cork. In an instant, REM and Kohlman and
Janice were in a champagne shower, laughing, the two of them,
with her, saying: "Yes! . . Yes!"

"We survived!" REM's voice battled emotion. He was all,
even in miniature, dignity. "We survived, Man." And Janice laughed

again and leaned down and kissed his meek lampblackened face. "We *did*! We *did*," she said . . and then, to Kohlman, "We *did* . . didn't we, Benjamin."

Sirens first, then cornering wheels, then snakes of water had slashed the night and arrived and uncoiled up and onto the roof and through the windows of the small building. The crowd, watching, grew. It was an event. Some watched the flames lapping air through the tiny windows. Some watched the tight and embracing circle of Janice, Kohlman, and REM. It was a choice.

Then, in the midst, another sound, the sound of something being unstopped, a flash, went off. It broke in. It pushed aside. It intruded. It seemed a light from nowhere. A *wrong* light. It seemed untrue, unreal.

Kohlman turned and saw a man in a blue-logoed blazer and a camera: a frontal stance, facing their circle: facing their joy, facing their victory, facing their celebration. "Don't," Kohlman said. His word was simple.

A second violating flash fixed him almost in the saying of his simple word.

"I said: Don't," Kohlman said.

Again the imposing camera caught him: mouth open, mid-request.

A final "Don't!" lit the close and immediate air. But this time, Kohlman, in what looked like a perfect power-backhand, reached, gripped, drew back, hurled. The camera ripped from the journalist's fingers and flashed a fourth time . . but only as it became metal fragments against the burning building's wall.

"I'm sorry . . but I said *don't*," Kohlman said.

Behind him, Janice held a singed REM high in her arms and the two were hallooing.

"*You pay for that!*" the journalist shouted at Kohlman.

"Take a break," Kohlman advised and turned in to his friends.

. . . . .

But then another *larger* camera—parting spectators, barging forward—rolled in, this one getting *life and near-tragedy at the very moment it was unfolding* . . *ALL OF THIS LIVE!* . . down on half-inch videotape.

And Kohlman saw. "Fuck!" he said, under his breath . . and then, "*No*," to the local affiliate's television-news-team man. "No! Come on! You saw . . !"

But the steadi-cam rolled. It wouldn't hear. It wouldn't heed. Its newsman hunched over its lenspiece, bug-eyed, like a mantis or a cicada, and the steadi-cam wouldn't stop.

"Okay!" Kohlman said: "Okay!"

Behind him, REM was asking: "Does he need help?" And Janice was saying: "No: Benjamin's fine. Benjamin's wonderful! Benjamin's running—he's fine!"

But then . . .

"You're a hero!" Someone shoved a mike nearly up Kohlman's nose. The man pressed. He moved in with a Nagra like Kohlman's Nagra. He was local and of the local *team*, wearing an identical affiliate blazer. He tried to bolster Kohlman. "You're a hero!" he said: "You're a headline! You're this Tuesday's news!" He moved in, if, in the space, *in* was still possible . . grey foam cutting the ambient sound on his directional mike. Then the other man, the man Kohlman had just said "Okay . . !" to, crowded the brutal space even more, winding foot after foot into the feed of his camera.

Kohlman pushed the two men away.

"He's fine," he could hear Janice say, behind him.

"Hey . . !" first one then the other of the two news-team men said.

"I said, *No*," Kohlman said, his syllable stripped of all ambiguity. "I said: *No* and *Don't*."

But nothing, of course, stopped: nothing in the world: because it didn't do that . . even on plain and dignified request. Because it never felt it had to. Because it felt entitled. And glibly, unexaminedly privileged with *rights* and *guarantees* and full birthrighted *protections*.

Kohlman understood.

Because, after all, this was the world . . from which Kohlman had come . . had left Templeton for. This was the world the awestruck child on the tractor seat, arms out, reverent, to the sky, had rolled away toward on a Trailways bus. This was the world of strong verbs and personal violations, and of lead sentences like: *Blood. Everything was blood!*

And so Kohlman—very simply, very cleanly—snapped waist-bands, tore shoulder straps, ripped the Nagra recorder, broke the steadi-cam loose from technicians . . and hurled the lot, cases and wires, microchips, battery packs, cassettes against the near building's hot and fiery stone in a strike of dark and focused sound, sending spent and feeble electrical arcs into the coarse air; in one strike, unleashing alloy scraps and dust.

A team production chief stepped up. "Hey!" he said: "I need your name!"

"No," Kohlman said.

"What do you mean?" the production chief said: "What do you mean: *No?*"

Behind Kohlman, Janice and REM waited, REM with his eyes as large as Pole stars.

"I mean: *no*. You can't have it," Kohlman said.

Go for it! someone in the crowd yelled. Then someone else called in: *I heard there was no such thing as EyeWitness News!*

It was theatre! It was a comedy. It was a farce. Everyone but the media team was amused. The *team* enlisted two uniformed officers, one short, one tall, both of whom, from their glances, seeming to be friends of REM.

"Look! He destroyed our equipment!" the production chief said.

The two officers looked over to the heap of wires and alloy and trashed energy packs. They shook their heads. "Satellites fall out of the sky. There's junk everywhere!" the taller one said.

Apart and head thrown back in delight, REM grinned. Singed and meager as he was, he could have been a crescent moon: his face, *pressed* almost against the unfolding dawn.

Kohlman left the media behind him, moved to join REM and to be with Janice. The three wove themselves away . . through the congestion, through the crowd. Their "gift" time, after all, had hardly begun. Freed to think about it, they realized: It was still the first morning.

．　　．　　．　　．　　．

From time to time, I would go back. Because, I suppose, I would begin to worry that . . unless I did . . . . I wasn't sure. I felt some-thing would happen. Some . . thing, some occurrence. Or, sometimes, he would just call. Salem. "Come." And I would come. And we would drink excellent scotch. And he would burn me. Hands. Neck. Back. Breasts sometimes. And then treat . . he would treat any of the burns—so that they were only visible faintly. It seemed crazy—you know—but reasonable. Like everything else. Everything around. Crazy but reasonable.

·   ·   ·   ·   ·

They ran again!
"Good morning, Mr. Kohlman!"
"How're you doing?"
"Good morning, Miss Stewart!"
"Hello!"
"Can we *do* anything for you this morning?!"

·   ·   ·   ·   ·

It was nice to have their fun, much of its dance and words, again.

·   ·   ·   ·   ·

They tried the Tropicana. They tried the Hacienda. They took the penthouse at the Taj Mahal, a room with its own waterfall and fruit trees and live Rousseauesque birds. They renamed everything. The queen-sized bed . . they called a *phlage*. The jacuzzi . . they called a *lavaclava*. The large-screen television . . got called the *kakastadt*, and they let it run without its audio: "Picture-spill," Janice said, pointing; and Kohlman said, "Meldatainment!"

They loved, shifting weight, randomly, *into* one another. "Will I have to return the cape?" Janice asked.

"I don't think," Kohlman said and kissed her neck. Again. "REM seemed to suggest . . ."

"I will anyway," Janice said; then she asked: "Do they use the *tongues* at all . . the fox *tongues* . . when they make a cape like this?"

Kohlman didn't know.

Janice bit his cheek. She sniffed where she had bitten. The heat from her bite . . the phrases her sniffing made . . formed a language, which made him want to write the *Blue Pony* for Alyce. And brought back Janice's sad, pure, necessary voice, in the bath, earlier . . its: *The letter I sent to Salem said: "This is wrong." It said:*

"I won't do this. Any more. It's crazy. You can't force me. . . He had gotten the letter that afternoon. Apparently . . he'd read it. I say "apparently" since . . .

. . . . .

They left the Taj Mahal for the Landmark and took a much shabbier room. But her words from much earlier traveled with them and traveled in elegance: *When I got to Salem's house, something, I knew, was wrong . . .*

"This used to be remarkable," Janice said. "This place. At first—actually for a number of years—everybody knew the Landmark."

"I just want to be with you," Kohlman said. "I just want to think . . wher*ever* . . *I'm with her.*"

Janice kissed him—her mouth, like her story: so true he could hardly bear it. He heard her words again, he heard her *say*ing . . her final words from the bath.

When I got to the house, Salem's house, something, I knew, was wrong. I could feel it approaching. The drive was along a small road, trees on either side. Touching—the trees—over the road, above: beech and leaf maple and honey locust. "Canapé": somebody . . I heard that word—but I think it was more accurately . . "tunnel." The leaves . . . It was windy. Dark. Leaves were slapping. The moon . . clouds were going by the moon . . like rags . . thrown. It was violent. Everything was violent. The world was violent. I'd said, "I can't do this. I won't. It's wrong," and the world had become violent. "You will have to learn a thing or two about this world, little lady"—my father several times had said that. And I could feel the world saying . . warning . . "Don't refuse." "That is not something that you get to do." And though there wasn't smoke where I was, approaching, still, I could taste. There. My window was rolled down—even though the night was angry and even though I was being "taught a thing or two, young lady," or would soon, and the night, outside, tasted like thick slippery salt. It was smoke as well. Even without the smoke, yet. It was smoke and fire. Do you know what I'm saying?

. . . . .

Her *say*ing and the courage of her saying kept resounding in Kohlman: *Do you know? Do you know what I'm saying?* she had asked. And Kohlman had said *Yes.*

. . . . .

They lay on the hooded, circular bed. Janice set an eye to the
crater in Kohlman's shoulder, where he had been shot. "I can see
your auricle," she said.

Kohlman's face spilled.

"It's beating," she said; "your auricle". . and she climbed *onto*
him. She laughed and sat still—thoughtful. Her lips made small
movements. "After the night I fell," she said, ". . and hit my
head . . ." She touched each word carefully, like a stone. ". . And
they began calling me 'Angel'. . I cried for months." She cupped
her hands at the tiny crater in Kohlman's shoulder. "Hello," she
called in. . . Her words never stopped.

*And so the world was violent, she had said and said now again,
said . . somewhere . . in him . . And I could feel it . . in my driving,
as I drew . . near, close, approached. And there were gypsy moths. The
whole road was like a puppet show of gypsy moths and they hit my Tercel
windshield like . . an infection. The house was shadow. It wasn't . .
"house," I mean; it wasn't house; it was shadow. Salem's. No light.
It had no actual light inside. Except being there, in front of the sea
wall, only because there was light somewhere else and because—however
such things are arranged—the shape of a real house had been placed
between the actual light and the shadow of what I drove up to in that
world. —Do you understand what I'm saying, Benjamin? I'm saying:
The shadow-house scared me . . because it had stood; it had lasted. But
it seemed very sick and cruel and without light and dry.*

. . . . .

And she'd shaken: Like a thing . . *any* thing, any of us *as* a
thing, from our nucleus, coming apart: *bone* shuddering, brain-and-
heart shuddering. And then she'd touched her chest . . with her
hands, both hands, like a *Pieta* . . healing, pressing . . going on—
telling . . telling!

I drove in, she'd said.

. . . . .

*I drove in. My Tercel drove to where the shape of the house beat
my eyes without actual light. The house hated itself. The house hated
all its floors—I could tell—its beams and windows. It was setting its
teeth into something like I sometimes did when the headaches came and*

I didn't want blood—"Eve's disease!"—and I would set my whole wrist in my mouth . . teeth, bone, my life; my teeth could feel my heart . . beat . . I'd bite . . to where I thought it would all stop. The house hated . . all that it couldn't imagine itself to be. Salem's house. No more. If it could stop itself, it would . . sickness, the fine scotch whiskey on the burns of women . . who couldn't see themselves except in that . . in fire, in pain, in being only wives . . of people they never knew, only sisters to the men their husbands, like a foreign language, found plea-sure in. And Salem was there. He was inside, holding, somehow, onto it all, onto the house's hating itself and hiding there . . .

.　.　.　.　.

And then she'd told . . and now told, again . . *in* him, *with* him . . of the night . . the fire . . the Truth . . *her* Truth . . *her* Story: why he'd come, even without knowing . . what he'd come for, to this city. And the truth was: *Benjamin . . ! Do you know? . . Had you guessed?*

Benjamin . . ! Do you know? Had you guessed? . . He was in there. In there, Benjamin. In the house, the shadow house . . burning. He had set himself on fire. He had gotten my letter. My words saying: "No." Saying: "No; I won't any more. I won't." And he had lit him-self, then. And was burning. And the house . . shadows . . all . . was burning. And I could see . . the Truth. And the Truth . . that I never told . . at my ordeal, at my trial, was . . that I . . .

Something choked from her lungs, something clawed and ragged. And she stopped, one hand to her chest, fingers working the bone there, trying to push cartilage back in place. Her breath was all without rhythm, all swept and patchy, lost then found again. *The truth . . was . . that I . . .* Small, almost etched blood-lines penciled out at her nostrils. *Truth was . . that I . . went . . .*

. . Truth . . I . . went in . . I went in, Benjamin . . and tried to save him. I went in, where the man had only tried to hurt me . . and I tried . . so hard! . . to save him from what he'd done! But he wouldn't . . he refused me . . !

.　.　.　.　.

They left the Landmark for the Stardust.

It was a sense, a feeling, a thought: that just the two of them, there, alone, in the Landmark . . even touching . . even naming the furniture—that just the two of them weren't enough.

And so—since REM had said the city was theirs—they chose. They kissed and dressed and walked together to the Stardust . . where Comus and the Challenger and the Barnetts all sat, waiting in the Lounge, somehow expecting their arrival.

"It's about time!" C.E.O. said.

Comus laughed. The Challenger, mock-military, saluted them.

"Hi, Benjamin! Hi, Angel!" Alyce said.

"We've been having a celebration!" C.E.O. boomed.

Alyce blew a kiss to Janice.

"We're all getting married!" Comus said.

"So celebrate!" C.E.O. roared.

The top of their table sat arranged with magnums of expensive wine.

"Sit!" C.E.O. demanded, loosening some glitter from the Stardust ceiling with the roll of his voice. "Stop all your private goddamn huglamugala! And join the real people!"

"Who caught . . for the Atlanta Braves in 1956?" Kohlman asked. He beamed and clenched his jaw in full anticipation of a victory.

Barnett squinted. He bared his teeth. "Okay: No wine for the writer!" he said. "No wine for the writer! The writer's trying to trick me!"

"You're too shrewd!" Kohlman said. He grabbed an open bottle of Richelbourg and drank.

". . Gross!" Alyce said. "Gross, Benjamin! Please: no! Gross! Use a glass! You'll get drunk . . you won't finish my book."

"I'll finish your book," Kohlman said. "I'll finish your book. And you'll be glad!"

"Did you hear about the fire?" Comus asked.

Janice stopped searching for a brush in her purse. Kohlman stopped talking.

"We got their attention," Barnett said.

"What fire?" Kohlman asked.

" 'What fire?' " C.E.O. Barnett boomed and grinned at Comus.

"It was on television," Comus smiled.

"It was . . ?" Kohlman looked at Janice.

". . Nearly," Comus said, white perfect teeth coy on her lower lip and looking almost legendary.

The group exploded.

"Definitely got the writer's attention!" Barnett roared. "Younger people are ironic, Benjamin!" he cawed. "Younger people–you'll see this!–tend to mix humor in to their–you're gonna love this word: definitely–'discourse.' Hang around more . . you'll see it more. It's . . happening." For a third time, Barnett roared. One of the magnum bottles uncoiled its wound cage of wire and popped its cork.

"C.E.O.–See . . he be just makin' all this fire shit *up*!" The Challenger flaunted his wickedest dialect: "Don't you fret, Chile!"

"This is a rough crowd!" Comus said and threw her head back, hair rising like spray in an image, in the Stardust Lounge light, that took Kohlman's breath.

"See: the point is," the Challenger said, "It be a fiction, Mr. Benjamin Kohlman . . dig? With no basis in . . ." He turned to Comus for help: ". . no basis in *what*?" he said.

"No basis in Daily Life as We Live It," Comus said. "No basis in the Bright Lights and Big City of Our Working World." And the whole table tumbled its ongoing medley of raw pleasure: they'd been at it; they were having fun.

The Challenger winked at Janice. He enunciated, lips snake-like: "Angel . . ? . . *Fic-tion*."

The whole table picked it up: "Fic-tion . . ! . . Fic-tion . . !"

"Maybe we should stop doing this," Alyce said. "And just celebrate." The table paused; Barnett cleared his throat. "I mean, like . . you know: Because . . maybe this isn't the kindest thing we could do. Benjamin?" she asked: "Do you understand we're just kidding?" The table smiled, felt a gentle shame. Kohlman took Alyce's hand and kissed it.

"Whatchoo doin't'that chile?!" the Challenger rumbled.

"Are you still going to marry me?" Alyce asked the Challenger.

"Snow White," the Challenger said. "Snow White . . Snow White!" And he smiled.

"Who do I have to threaten to get some dim sum at this table?!" Barnett suddenly shouted.

Two floor managers, a cocktail waitress, and a white-jacketed oriental materialized.

"Dim sum! Dim sum!" Barnett demanded.

"Dim sum," both the floor managers said.

"Dim sum," the oriental bowed . . and greeted: " 'Evening, Mr. Kohlman, sir! 'Evening, Miss Stewart Angel!"

"For everyone!" Barnett said.

"And more wine?" one of the floor managers asked.

"*Always* more wine!" Barnett commanded. "I mean . . come on: This isn't Utah!"

Janice looked renewed. She glowed, in relief and dear exhaustion, ran a hand through Kohlman's still smoky hair and down his face: "Benjamin . . Benjamin . . !" she said to him.

"And oysters!" Barnett added.

"Hello, Benjamin," Janice said—looking straight on, not allowing his glance away, and something essential was in her eyes: something let-go in the most natural gesture, in the freest light. She was herself. That simply. With Kohlman. And with some family, here, of her own choice and construction. Herself. And though she seemed, at one time, curiously soluble in whatever her mix and shy, she seemed whole and irreducible. "Hello, Benjamin," she repeated. "Are you there? Are you with me? Do we know each other?"

". . I am. We do," Kohlman said, all considerations, other, dissolving.

"Okay: You heard it!" Barnett shouted. "You heard it! Double-ring ceremony! . . All right! Here we go! Excellent!"

Janice moved her face to Kohlman softly. It trembled.

"*Dim sum and oysters!*" Barnett bellowed so that the entire contained Stardust world heard: "*Dim sum and oysters! We want a youth-nouvelle-newage menu here! We got a double ring ceremony!*"

Hundreds of gamblers applauded, glad for fortune *any*where.

The Challenger giggled. No one had ever heard him giggle. Comus and Alyce took one another's hands.

"People need to think about what they do," Alyce said. "That's why I love Shostakovich."

Kohlman was nodding; his face, reflecting and rippling in on itself again. He tried to form it, hands on either side, like bread.

"Okay! Jesus! Can we get this show on the road now possibly?" Barnett bellowed. "A baby Steinway! My sister needs to play Shostakovich! We got a celebration going here!"

A baby Steinway arrived! Three plates of dim sum and oysters—the oysters on a mountain of ice!

"Okay! Cheers!" Barnett crowed. "To all the brides and grooms!" And they all raised glasses.

"To all the brides and grooms," everyone echoed.

They all drank. Alyce played frenzied Shostakovich. The Challenger did a wonderful moment of Tai Chi. Comus climbed up on a table and reset the lights over the Lounge so that everything looked under water.

They all laughed. They all touched each other. In twenty minutes they would all be at the Graceland Wedding Chapel . . in gowns and cutaways, taking vows, listening to the binding words of a man who was a dead ringer for Elvis Presley. And they would all be kissing each other again. And standing proudly, happily in the background, silent, yes, but in significant witness, would be Kohlman's parents, who had finally arrived.

.   .   .   .   .

Kohlman shook. He had never been in such a world. He had never known one. Still, he was there. And in it! Cut loose. Bound and unbound. Wild. More alive than he'd been since he'd been a child. He could *feel* it–himself, his own blood coursing through him! And he was grateful. And determined. And a part of others. And sure. And terrified.